CHRISTOPHER WALLACE

The Pirate

Flamingo
An Imprint of HarperCollins*Publishers*

Flamingo
An Imprint of HarperCollins*Publishers*
77–85 Fulham Palace Road,
Hammersmith, London W6 8JB

www.**fire**and**water**.com

Flamingo is a registered trade mark of
HarperCollins*Publishers* Limited.

First published in Great Britain by Flamingo 2001

1 3 5 7 9 8 6 4 2

Copyright © Christopher Wallace 2001

A catalogue record for this book
is available from the British Library

This novel is entirely a work of fiction.
The names, characters and incidents portrayed in it
are the work of the author's imagination.
Any resemblance to actual persons, living or dead,
events or localities, is entirely coincidental.

ISBN 0 00 225858 7

Set in Bembo and Hiroshige by
Rowland Phototypesetting Ltd,
Bury St Edmunds, Suffolk

Printed and bound in Great Britain by
Clays Ltd, St Ives plc

For Ann, For Fiona
With thanks for the friendship
of the McLeish family

I asked for a price, Jesus Christ, I actually asked for a price.

There have been many low moments for sure but this one stands the test as one of the worst imaginable. Not that I thought this at the time; no, it all seemed reasonable, another transaction. The scary thing was that when I heard my voice making the enquiry it didn't shock me, not at all, I listened to what I was saying and ploughed on regardless. *Go down deeper.* I was cool with it, cool with everything. Days later when I was a little less high and remembered what I had been asking for it made me feel sick enough to need to run to the bathroom. And when I got there I stared at myself in the mirror, wondering who was on the other side of the glass. I looked for a long long time. Half an hour, one hour? I tried and tried but didn't have the time to find him.

Miguel and Torres 'Tony' Carcera didn't look particularly shocked to hear it either, that's when I realized they were the real thing. The only issue for them was how much, there was never going to be a set fee for this kind of deal, no; pitches like mine must have come along so rarely that every case had to be treated as a one-off.

Big Tony toyed with his drink, sticking a fat cigar-shaped finger into his glass to mop up the dregs of the froth left on its sides. The finger of a thug, filthy, oil-stained, the real thing, nail chewed to a stump that gave up less than halfway on its struggle to the tip. He stuck it into his mouth and sucked, blinking slowly at his brother, long eyelashes, dark and effeminate yet perfectly suited to the macho pout that rested so easily on his lips. The pout of a psychopath. *I don't know,* it seemed to say, *you work something out for me, brother, how much would it be for us to kill someone?*

Miguel gave all the signs he was thinking it over. It was as simple a matter as just quoting a price and terms of payment; he was pondering the wider picture.

'So this guy, it's you or him, yeah?'

That was how he saw it, and I had to agree.

'Well, we can help, but we need to know what happens when he's gone, yeah?'

Miguel liked to know you were following him, that you were on the same level of understanding, that you were listening intently to the guttural drawl of his Catalan voice, following every word of wisdom that came out of him. He was a weedy-looking guy with thinning jet-black hair tied tight into a ponytail. You could tell that somewhere along the line Miguel had had it rough, maybe his childhood in the cockroach palace high-rises of the mainland, maybe prison in Barcelona, maybe a lifetime keeping the lid on his younger brother's wilder enthusiasms. In years gone by he would have made a perfect extra in one of those spaghetti westerns, a pistol-toting desperado blown away by Clint Eastwood in the first reel. Miguel wanted a starring role though, one that meant he was around to stay.

'What do you mean? Are you asking if anyone is going to come looking for you?'

A wave of his hand throws the question off. A different hand from his brother, more gold rings, cleaner, more delicate; a hand that found it easy to turn to brutal chores all the same.

'No, I mean here, the bar, Puerto Puals marina, yeah? Who inherits?'

'*Who inherits?* It's my fucking bar, I get to have it back, I own it anyway.'

'The other places?'

'I guess they go to whoever Herman has left them to, the organization, whoever. What does it matter?'

'It matters because we want to help you, Martin, not just with this problem but anything else to follow. You come to us for help, and we are looking for opportunities here in Mallorca. We know bars, me and

2

Tony, we run them, in Barcelona. Nightclubs, discotheques . . . We got ideas, haven't we Tony, yeah?'

Tony licked his finger by way of reply. Miguel moved his chair closer to mine, warming to his theme, speaking faster, forcefully. I could feel his breath on my eyes.

'Us and you, Martin, yeah? You think about it. What a team, you, me and Tony. Nobody fucks with us.'

I didn't like the way this was going, I only wanted them to murder someone, why couldn't they just agree and name the price?

'I'll think about it. And you guys think about how much you want to charge me. Listen, I got to go, things to see to tonight. Can you excuse me?'

'Sure, yeah.' Miguel smiled. Neither brother moved an inch though, they were already sizing the place up, already acting like the new fucking owners, did they expect me to leave them here?

'You got a girl coming round?'

To my surprise it was Tony doing the asking now; maybe he was trying to reach out to his prospective business partner.

'You bet. A shy girl, should be a good lay. I don't want you two handsome guys distracting her, so I'm afraid I've got to ask you . . .'

The two boys smiled, perhaps not fully appreciating the irony I had intended.

'Hey Miguel, maybe we should hang around to see Martin's new girl, maybe she'd like a threesome?'

'Hey, me first, yeah?'

'No, fuck you, you guys can wait, me first this time.'

'Hey, what do you mean, if she likes me, she has me, she won't need use of either of you when I've finished, yeah?'

'Hey, fuck you.'

The general tone of the debate now established, it proceeded, the two of them arguing about the order in which they would take their pleasure from a girl who did not exist. The strange thing was, I suspect that somehow they knew there wasn't any girl about to call, but that they enjoyed sparring with each other anyway, as if it was a rehearsal for the kind of argument they would have if they became partners in the Arena Bar. All they had to do to make that happen was to do what I had asked them, kill someone. The real thing. The shit I find myself in.

I was born in Greenock. Just like Captain Kidd. I could tell you about Greenock but you wouldn't thank me for it. Not that it would take too long – in fact, the opposite; it's more that it has no particular relevance to what I am about to tell you about the rest of my life and the shit I find myself in. And you will probably need all your strength and powers of concentration and whatever compassion you might have at the outset to deal with that. So the only thing you really need to know about Greenock is that it is what I left behind, like Captain Kidd three hundred years earlier, and that anyway the decision to leave wasn't taken there but in another place, on the shore of a foreign land many hundreds of miles away, and that when I decided to leave I left *everything* behind, there would never really be any road back. Not that I knew this at the time, it's just the way these things go. When you choose to become a pirate it is a strictly one-way ticket, you are on a ship that can never turn round.

The shit I find myself in. I will amaze and appal you with it, none of which you can ever have imagined. The shit in my head. Too much goes on inside my head, things I never share. For all I have achieved, for all I've been able to do and say, and for all the tenacity and spirit I have surprised even myself with, there has been a price to pay. And part of that price has been the way I have had to dig so deep to make my way along the bastard path I have chosen; the way I've had to dig so deep inside, the way I've had to do these things alone. I didn't know it at the time but all this came at personal cost, not just isolation, detachment or separation. It's the way I have lived as a stranger, removed from everyone and everything, a stranger to myself. There will be men right now serving time in solitary confinement who have more companionship than me. At least they would know for what they stand, who they stand for and how that relates to anyone else.

I will try to explain but perhaps you will never understand. Maybe you can be a dispassionate bystander to these events in the same way

4

that I was, even when I was at the heart of them. Something changed in me along the way so that I forgot how to judge, or how to *empathize* . . . how to feel angry about things, the *right* things other than just when losing money or graft. So you can watch and let me try to explain how it is and even how it might have been in a different life and in a different time, like three hundred years ago. I will show you another life, one that has grown with me from childhood, one that I chose to ignore until almost too late, one I never shared. You see, I was a normal boy, in a normal town going to a normal school. And I would read normal books full of exciting tales and adventures of piracy and duels on the high seas. But even then, when the villainous Blackbeard or his dastardly men fought their enemies, I knew whose side I was on. The shit I find myself in goes all the way back to then because I grew up with all these battles in my mind and eventually tried to live as a pirate, just like Captain Kidd. Like him I became a hunted man; somewhere along the way the whole world turned against me without explanation. Understand, if you can, that in this life there's only so much they will let you get away with, and it's not always the criminal stuff they object to. No, if you really want to confront the system you'll have to attempt something much more subversive than that.

I will tell you what it is of course, and how I found that I had been declared an enemy without anyone ever telling me why, just like my heroes before me. Let us study the past, to see if we can find where it was I crossed the line of acceptability, and let us study the old maps, the antiques of a bygone age; perhaps X still marks the spot. Let us find where the stinking treasure is buried.

Great moments in my life. Gatwick Airport 1989, the unwelcoming, strange and tiny country lying between freedom and tyranny that is the Goods to Declare zone. I walk in, struggling manfully with rucksack, holdall, oxygen tanks, mask, mouthpiece and flippers. I would need at least another three pairs of hands to keep this lot together, and then maybe I could appear more serene, like a scuba-diving Vishnu. The sound is of a thump and things spilling as I make it to the only occupied desk. I have to snatch to keep the pile together and stop the rogue elements crashing to the floor, swearing under my breath in frustration.

5

'What have we got here, sir?'

The officer on duty is a little startled and taken aback by my obvious ill-humour though he tries not to show it. He looks a kindly type, even under his prison guard garb of white nylon shirt and black tie. His skin strikes me as being very pink, the freckled bald scalp to layers of double chin one big ball of its different shades with only a grey moustache to break the colour code. He's maybe four or five years from retirement and ten minutes from lunch. The sort of guy my father would play bowls with.

'Diving gear . . . bought it in Spain. Some of it brand-new, most of it about a year old. The breathing apparatus is the expensive stuff, it's specialist equipment so that you can go down deeper, not your normal scuba bits. The belt in the lining of the suit is the BCD . . . sorry, buoyancy control . . . see? Yeah, special. Anyway I've kept the receipts because I knew I would be bringing it back sometime, but I didn't know what kind of import duty I would be liable for, or whether I'd have to pay on all of it or just the new stuff. Must be worth about eight hundred pounds all told. What do you reckon the score on tax is?'

Go down deeper. I've thrown myself at his mercy and he's not going to thank me for it. I hand him the receipts and he's almost reluctant to take them. The gentle wind-down towards lunch that he must have promised himself is looking in distinct jeopardy. I watch him peer at the crumpled pieces of paper in his hand, they are all in Spanish and won't mean a thing to him. Not that he's about to admit that to the much younger man opposite him, the ridiculously tanned and footloose hombre with his tousled hair, faded jeans and hippyish air who has obviously spent the last couple of years in his carefree life having a whale of a time diving, sunbathing and fornicating with all kinds of exotic types you sometimes see in Nothing To Declare. No sir, the dedicated customs man will not admit to any kind of inadequacy to someone like that.

'Hold on sir, if you would.'

And now the test, the biggest test of nerve I'd ever had up to then, as I'm left to stare at the gear whilst he vanishes behind a panel door to consult with his colleagues and superiors. There are security cameras above me capturing all this for posterity, and I begin to concentrate on my performance. It would be better if I could look frustrated rather than aggrieved, agitated rather than nervous. The trick is to look normal, whatever that is, I guess the trick is not to appear extreme. I'm Martin Law and I'm normal, I tell myself. I used to live in Spain and now I'm coming home. I take in a breath and let out a little sigh. The air in here is stale, there's no ventilation, no windows, just the cameras and fluorescent lights above, white Formica tabletops, plastic chairs and lino floor below, these being the only props for one of the key scenes in my life. These and the gear in front of me of course, and maybe the dust that has settled on every available horizontal surface in sight. I stare at the door behind which my fellow performer has disappeared and catch a dull reflection of myself staring in. Is there a problem? My hair, is it too extreme? It had been bleached in Spain, streaks of blonde to join the other strands that had turned yellow under the sun. Hair to go with the times. Maybe not. Anyway, I'd been concerned that I might look too much the beach-bum and dyed it dark just before this trip. Very dark, jet-black in fact. I hadn't meant to at the time, but that's the way it goes with hair dye, and now I was left like an impersonation of Elvis during the Vegas years. I studied the impossible mop on the top of my head; it definitely had a sixties showbiz look, a third-rate night-club crooner or a sleight-of-hand magician . . . A magician, yes, let me tell you about magic, that would be relevant.

How does a magician make something disappear? Easy. He doesn't, he just hides it. He will invite you to look for it in all the obvious places – up his sleeves, under the hat, inside the box. He challenges you to search in all the usual kinds of places, but when you do it is on *his* terms. So *he* turns his palms one way and then another, *he* waves the sleeve under your eyes, *he* lifts the lid on the box; and when you look you assume, because of the confidence he shows whilst doing all of this, that there really is nothing there, the answer must be elsewhere, somewhere else he is not showing you. This is not magic at all then, merely a trick, a confidence trick based on his confidence your thoughts will be elsewhere when he is actually showing you the only places where the item could be concealed.

7

The relevance of this? Well, it's like someone having the confidence to walk up to a customs inspector in Goods to Declare and have the nerve to explain to him how a BCD works – or would work if it didn't have three kilos of cocaine stuffed inside – and giving that man the headache of having to work out the import tax that is liable on the rest of the mess that's been brought in when all he really wants to do is have a good rummage through everything and then piss off for lunch.

Go down deeper. My reflection is shunted out of view as the door re-opens and my fellow performer returns. He is perplexed, like an audience stooge who has to admit defeat to the delight of the rest of the crowd. Well I just don't know, his shaking head seems to say, go on then, show me, where have you put it? But of course I'll do nothing of the kind. A grim sort of smile emerges under his moustache. He's fumbling for some sort of way out that doesn't leave him open to ridicule.

'Sir . . . You said most of this stuff was over a year old?'

I sense there must be a mountain of forms that he doesn't want to fill in. Lunch is calling him.

'About eighteen months . . . the purchase receipts are dated –'

He puts up a hand to stop me talking, he has no desire to hear the detail, he's already made up his mind.

'I guess we can let you through on this occasion, given the relative age of the goods in question. Is there anything else you wish to declare, sir?'

I'm beginning to like this guy but there is nothing else I feel inclined to tell him. He nods and with a wave of his hand I'm gathering up the gear again and walking out of customs. Abracadabra. I'm twenty-three years old and I've just earned more than he will ever make in his lifetime. I went deep down inside and was able to hold my composure. I've passed the test.

Originally I had studied to be an engineer, like James Watt. Engineering has a fleeting relevance to the events I'm about to describe so perhaps it is worth lingering on this subject and my studenthood in general for a moment.

So what can I say about it? I suppose engineering in itself was never something I had a particular fondness or aptitude for, aside from a bit of tinkering with bikes and boats – of which more later – but it was what I found myself immersed in during my very last teenage months and most of my twentieth year. Quite why is still difficult to fathom. In those days you finished school and you went to college or university in Glasgow and studied. The only way out was by being too thick for the process or such a genius that you by-passed any Scottish stop and went straight to Oxbridge. I fell into neither category. I fell into engineering after a two-minute interview with my careers teacher at the end of sixth year. An interview, I might add, with all the depth and interaction that you have with your average dentist whilst he's giving you root canal treatment, and only slightly less pleasure. So it came to be agreed that I would enrol at The University of Strathclyde and in the autumn of 1984 I was to be found living in a tiny room, six feet by twelve feet, on the thirteenth floor of the art-deco splendour at the Baird hall of residence, downtown Sauchiehall Street. Glasgow might not have an awful lot going for it as a hedonistic metropolis but after nineteen years in Greenock it was like New York, believe me. Even my little cell with its white walls, single bed, wash-basin and desk seemed like a Manhattan penthouse suite looking down on the throbbing alleyways of decadence below when compared to the dormitory set-up back home. Far away now, though the memories of having to share everything – walls, air and light – with my older brother are still close enough, and all with the glorious sound of my father next-door snoring loud enough to warn the ships to keep from the shore of the Clyde. Yes, my student days were carefree days by comparison, even if they only amounted to barely three hundred. I didn't know it at the time, it was just the way things were going to work out. A few hundred days of getting drunk as cheaply as you could, trying to get stoned as frequently as possible, and toiling to get laid. Just a hundred-odd shots at this bohemian debauchery before it was over. Sometimes myself and other like-minded souls even stayed up all night.

What would I have been like then, I wonder? Well, young I suppose, youthful and youthful-looking, no doubt in a wholesome and earnest way. The look I craved was that of an amphetamine-washed Iggy Pop, or a Satisfaction-era Keith Richards. Sadly, the face that confronted me in my bed-sit mirror would have had more in common with a tubby farmer's lad reared on generous portions of Aberdeen Angus, rhubarb crumble and custard. A shy lad at that, boyishly shy, guiltily holding a tenuous notion of what it was he wanted – libidinous sex, a life of excess, high times – and an even more tenuous notion of how he might actually get it. A normal boy brought up in a normal west of Scotland household wanting the normal things. There were many others like me of course, and we sought each other out at the normal places; the student bars, alternative clubs and Cure concerts. We could tell each other by our spiky hair with long fringes, our grey raincoats, and our curious way of dancing, twitching our shoulders whilst gazing vacantly at our shoes like heavily sedated battery hens let loose on an electrified floor. Laughable now but normal then, ordinary boys expressing their individuality by dressing and acting the same. Where I differed I suppose was that I was more willing to push it a little further than the rest, always hungering for anything a little more intense on the basis of the timeless equation that more insane plus less legal equals more fun, a formula which must have marked me down at those times as mad, bad and interesting to know. For a while I wasted energy trying to take people with me before realizing that the most interesting journeys are those where you travel alone. Back then these were the first signs of the way my life was to go, back then this would have been one of the first opportunities to draw the line, to settle for what those around me wanted – the four years of harmless frolics as a Glasgow undergraduate, a decent degree, future wife and job at the end of it. I didn't know I was rejecting it at the time, I only wanted to experiment for a while before taking it all up again at some point in the future. A naive assumption to go with the times. I would later come to learn that there is no such return option. Once a pirate always a pirate. Like Captain Kidd.

Then there is the other story, the one I read. The story I rewrite so many times in my head so that in the end I star in this one too. An adventure story. I will be thirty-five soon. You would have thought that I would have grown out of these things rather than into them but I suppose that's the way it is with me, everything over and over if I'm ever going to learn any lessons. Anyway, I'll share this tale as well, why not, I enjoy playing it through, rehearsing the cast. It's meant to be over three hundred years old, and truth be told it is authentic to the period. I have read all there is to read so that you can be sure of that. So it is spring 1698, although what will happen is just as resonant to the here and now, just as relevant. It is how things maybe could have been.

It begins with a man walking on to a ship, one he knows will never reach its stated destination. He boards anyway. Why? It's impossible to tell at first, maybe he doesn't even know, except that he's some kind of fugitive, a man on the run, a misfit born outwith his time.

The ship lies at harbour and is being prepared for a long voyage when he arrives. He travelled far to be here, from the north, another port – Greenock, in Scotland – although he has journeyed across land to this part of the southern Devon coast. A trip that has taken him from one country to another, across mountains, plains and rivers, a multitude of dialects passing like languages as he progressed by coach, horse and on foot. Yet this distance is as nothing compared to that he is assigned to undertake once he steps on to the *Anne*'s deck.

As he approaches the vessel for the first time he pauses briefly to study the activity all around him at the quayside; the loading of cargo into the timber holds – bales of linen, cases of carbines, brass pans and carpets, barrels of spirit, firkins of gunpowder, spare sails and rope, lots of rope. Nothing moves without the application of strenuous labour by men on and off the ship. Nothing seems to move without being noted by the men with pens and notebooks. There is a strange sourness in his mouth for a moment as he realizes that those who do not sweat are undoubtedly the ones who are making the money here. Who were they? The officiators, the clerks, all the king's men; the supercargoes – agents of the merchants who had funded the voyage – the tax inspectors, the captain's mate. He noticed that they managed somehow to maintain composure and concentration amidst the distractions all around; the screeching and bawling of the traders pitching their goods to the departing ship's crew, the barking of stray dogs sniffing excitedly at the tubs of lard and tallow about to be loaded. All ignored, eyes fixed instead on the glimmer of silver that the boat represents.

He let his own gaze linger on the freight still on land. Which goods would be traded with the savages on the Guinea coast, he wondered, and which would make it all the way to the table of some rich colonist's plantation mansion in Jamaica? This was only a passing concern to him though, something to occupy his mind other than the growing disquiet he felt when studying the vessel itself, all creaking timbers and spindly masts. So this was the craft that would take them to the edge of the world? She seemed barely able to hold water amongst the gentle lapping tide at Plymouth dock; what chance would she stand in the wilderness of the oceans, how would she cope with the malevolent mountains of waves that lay waiting for her there? He had once persuaded himself that he was happy to let fate decide his path for him – looking at the worm-ridden hull of the *Anne* he wondered if he was giving it the chance to make his path lead him anywhere other than the bottom of the sea.

As he moved nearer the gangplank the cacophony around grew ever more shrill in its urgency. Here the agents and tariff men counted aloud and traded insults as well as the goods they sought to barter. Here the merchants yelled their demands for payment. Small children, hands and faces blackened by exposure to the hot tar being painted on the ship's bow, darted in between the departing crates, pilfering fingers eager for any spillage that might fetch a coin at the paupers' market. Incessant noise, incessant demands, incessant questions, unrelenting squalor. Yes, the sea might make for a desperate gamble but it could also mean freedom, the one escape left open for men like him. Even a craft as unkempt and graceless as the *Anne* could be a transport of beauty capable of taking him to a heaven away from this hell. Only a few more steps to endure as he picked his way through the last casual traps of trip-ropes, splintered wood and excrement that marked the very end of England's shore. He gripped the varnished rail of the *Anne*'s deck and hauled himself aboard. He did not look back, even though the premonition that he would never live to see it again grew all the heavier as he cleared the land in that final stride.

It was the captain who came to see him, announcing his presence outside the cabin with a hearty cough and gurgling of phlegm. A hand knocked loudly on the door.

'Are you there, sir?'

'Here, aye.'

The door opened and an almost ashen, pock-marked face confronted him. He put his book down to the floor and swung his legs free from the hammock.

'Martin Law, sir, it is a pleasure to make your acquaintance. Thank you for accepting me aboard.'

'*Doctor* Law, yes?'

The uncertain smile which greeted the remark verged upon the bashful. 'Aye . . . and you are Captain Henry?'

'Correct.'

A silence then hung between them. Evidently the captain expected the new arrival to lead in conversational matters, perhaps at this stage offering some presentation of credentials as to his suitability for the voyage. The younger man declined to do so, for surely his initial letters and the acceptance he had received in return correspondence had completed such formalities beforehand.

'How long until we set sail?'

The captain took off his hat and scratched at his shaven head, black fingernails clawing at the silvery stubble as if being filed upon a piece of flint.

'Some time after even tide. There is much still to be loaded and properly stored below deck. It may be that we cast off before the latter is complete and we bind the cargo down once we are under way. We might make back some time, aye, if the sea is calm . . . Still, we cannot leave of course until the damned tariff-keepers have had their fill.'

There was another quiet as the captain contemplated the blight of inspectors that assailed his ship, leaving the other to study his complexion. How old had he been when the smallpox struck? To leave scars like that it must have been severe, life-threatening. Did it ever recur? The medical journals spoke of fevers that would erupt amongst some men in the heat of the Africas; were these new diseases or old ones rekindled from deep inside? He would have to seek out what the books had to report. The captain moved to bring his mind back to practical matters.

'I take it you have arrangements in place to bring your personal cargo aboard?'

'I have no cargo as such, sir, only a few volumes of writing to assist in my work. These should be at the quayside shortly.'

'No cargo? No personal venture? As ship's surgeon an allowance has been made for you in the stern hold. I would rather you kept this cabin clear of possessions, there will be seven or so using it once we are under sail. Please have your books directed to the holds.'

He knew that the captain's bafflement was understandable. The wages for voyages like this were pitifully poor, the only worthwhile consolation for those privileged enough to receive it was the opportunity to speculate on their own efforts to trade during the course of the trip. Senior crew-members such as the captain could expect to multiply their earnings tenfold by such means and the tonnage allowances permitted to each were eagerly sought and guarded.

He watched the captain move to the door before halting.

'So . . . Doctor . . . If you are not taking up your due I take it you would have no objection to others doing so?'

'On my behalf?'

Another silence, another scratch of the scalp. 'On the ship's behalf, sir.'

'Of course.'

The captain smiled. His first smile. It lasted but an instant. 'Then I should bid good day to you, Doctor. I have work to do.'

14

From Glasgow to the south of France, summer of 1985. My first summer after starting university, four of us – myself, Paul, Ian and Maurice, all Strathclyde first years – living in two tents at a campsite a mile or so inland from St Raphaël, the heart of the Côte d'Azur. The excursion and its location was my idea, as was the stop-off en route in Paris to visit the grave of Jim Morrison. Not that we thought the stiff Lizard King would appreciate our visit, it just seemed appropriate to pay tribute to someone whom we, laughably, thought to be a kindred spirit. Jim Morrison had lived and died the full rock-and-roll trip, for him there was nothing that was forbidden, nothing that he denied himself. He had tested the parameters of the possible to glorious destruction. We four gathered around his tomb in silent salute and then made our way to the train that would take us south, our group preferring not to hitch its way there because it was deemed too risky by our parents. Welcome to the home of the existentialist French, where you live for the moment, once you've checked out it's OK with mum and dad. Yes, things would have to change, for me at least; soon it would be time to cut loose.

France was liberating though, almost immediately. After a little more than a week's stretching on the sun-baked sands I changed colour and became a different person. The heat also killed any appetite I might have had, it would have been from that time on that I took on the thin shape I have now, losing any normal appetite at least. And the rest of the boys? Well, I had taken them there, not that I had set myself up as expedition leader or chief fucking scoutmaster, but as the only one with any idea and any kind of will to see it through I became the travel coordinator, navigator and complaints department rolled into one. That would also soon change – I hadn't sought this sudden elevation and I wasn't cut out to be a consensus leader. Camping wasn't really my bag either, truth be told, it was the lack of money and alternative options that had forced us under canvas. The site itself – Les Acacias – had been recommended by two Australian girls I'd befriended at Gare du Nord. They described it as the hang-out and rendezvous for the Riviera's dispossessed, by which I took them to mean poor, but which just about described everyone when compared to the Cartier-garbed *hommes* and *femmes* hanging out in the yachts and restaurants of St Raph and the glitzy brand-new marina at Port-Fréjus. Millionaires, all of them, so it seemed. I'd never seen wealth like that before, the jewellery, sunglasses, white linen suits and limousines. Wealth worn and flaunted, to my open-mouthed wonder, though studiously ignored by the rest of the have-nots for whom the word 'insouciant' could have been especially devised. No, it was far, far away from the drab and rain-soaked quays at Greenock and Port Glasgow. It was hard to believe that the water that lapped these harbours of my youth was part of the same worldwide ocean. There was something that drew me to the sea in these places, even though I always felt as if on the outside of the people and activity that gathered around them; at home it had been almost by choice, here I wanted in, I wanted to belong to the crowd who had it all.

The Aussie girls had told me of the enlightened policy regarding campsite rents at Les Acacias, in that very few people actually paid them. You were meant to of course, the total due was added to on a daily basis, but most of the patrons tended to prefer a midnight exit through a hole in the hedge when their time was up. Strictly speaking then, it was those particular customers who were the enlightened ones, and with budgets being tight I intended to join them. Knowing this in advance, I had Paul give his passport number when we checked in. I wonder if he has ever had any comeback from our eventual abrupt departure? Perhaps, maybe many years later, he was arrested on arrival at EuroDisney with wife, in-laws and screaming kids because of this shameless plant. I hope he can forgive me for setting him up. The shit he found himself in.

Anyway, at the height of the season there would be over a hundred tents rigged up on the hissing summer lawns, one giant lattice weave of wires and ropes, zips and poles, all intolerable sweat-holes under the morning and afternoon sun, damp with cold condensation at night. I remember queuing for the toilet every morning behind some farting Belgian, and the smell of gas and cooking bacon bringing out a curious sensation of nausea and hunger at the same time. Everyone would congregate at the wash-houses to shower and shave, then you would wait in line for fresh rolls and croissant at the site shop, the same place you would buy your cheap white wine at the end of the day. All of this was achieved with a degree of harmony the United Nations would have been proud of; there was a huge cast of nationalities managing to get by, despite their different languages, colour of skin, and reasons for being there. I remember it as almost like being in a Benetton ad. After a day or so of witnessing the clear-out that would occur after breakfast, when an assortment of beat-up cars, creaking trucks and rusty buses would arrive to pick up the same people we had been behind in one queue or another, I realized that whilst there were some holidaymakers on site, they were in the minority, everyone else was working.

One of the pick-ups was a yellow Volkswagen dormobile, showing up every day, audible before it was visible, its bleating, rasping engine shivering and shuddering as it coughed its phlegm of exhaust into the fresh morning air. The driver was a stringy guy in a vest, cut-off jeans and sandals. Usually the same vest, cut-off jeans and sandals, but that's the French way I suppose. He had dark eyes and heavy eyebrows, again the French way, like Charles Aznavour. I guessed he might have been in his late thirties, although he seemed cool about this, in fact, cool about everything. It came to pass that one fateful day he caught me looking at him; I would have been getting up to meet the guys for breakfast some way into our second week. When he saw me he motioned for me to hop in and join his crew in whatever it was they were leaving to do. A simple gesture was all he needed to convey what he needed to convey; a shrug and a dropping of the chin, cheeks puckered, a stabbing sweep of his arm towards the back of the van. Blink and you would have missed it, blink and the door to a new way of life remains shut. I didn't miss it, nor what was meant by it, and in an instant we understood each other in a way that would have been impossible to communicate by him in his fractured English or me in the 'plume de ma tante' French that had recently been drilled into me at school but had proved – surprisingly – to be less than fucking useless when tried out on natives who didn't behave in the beret-and-onions way the textbooks would have had us expect.

So what did the rapid fire mime mean? Well, firstly that there was some kind of scam going on, one that I was invited to join, probably at a low or lightweight level, and that this venture wasn't likely to be one currently under investigation by Interpol – I wouldn't be joining in an armed robbery or sophisticated international fraud. In fact, it would be simple enough to pick it up as I went along, as indeed the others who were packing into his Tardis-like vehicle had done before. Most importantly though, the gesture indicated he was reaching out to me, trusting me to come and try, and not to squeal or rip him off if I didn't like it; I'm cool with you, the motion said, can you be cool with me? I took a look at the state of those clambering in – there didn't seem to be much room left amongst the German chicks in bikinis, Parisian hipsters with their stubble and crew-cut hair, half-caste reggae-boys in Bermuda shorts. I turned to seek out Ian and Maurice who had been behind me at the check-out in the camp shop; they were outside juggling rolls, fruit and wallets as they counted out their change. I knew where I belonged and where I wanted to be. The rattling door was closing over as the rusty machine revved up. I smiled through the window and they held it long enough for me to squeeze in. The tin rocket took off. I was a passenger looking out on its convulsive spurt of fumes, wondering where it would take me.

It was dark when the *Anne* finally cast off, Captain Henry quarrelling with the customs men to the last over a set of barrels which he insisted were to be loaded empty. The tariff-keepers seemed dubious and threatened to stay and observe the procedure until it was completed. Martin would hear later that the captain had told them this would happen at daybreak and had thus persuaded them to depart from the scene. Sure enough, no sooner had they done so than another set of traders appeared, men who made quick work of filling the casks with French brandy. The anchor was raised the very moment they were done and the booty on board. Below deck in his quarters Martin listened to the grumblings over the captain's apparent greed and his willingness to employ such deceit and subterfuge simply to avoid the ten per cent duty which should rightfully have been due on the outgoing goods. There were other complaints too; that the late loading had left the stacked cargo now out of balance, heaviest highest in the hold and not properly bound in the evening darkness below deck. What might this do to affect the ship's stability in the open sea? These arguments would be aired over and over as the voyage progressed, and initially Martin would remain indifferent to them. In fact, he was almost reassured. Captain Henry had proved that he was an experienced mariner; his actions, although dishonest, were hardly those of a novice.

They did mean however that by the time the vessel began to move it was loaded to the full, every possible inch carrying provisions of one type or another. Martin found no space where the captain had directed him to lodge his books and duly stacked the volumes in the cabin, disobeying the earlier instruction. Here they would be safe from the water that would wash through the decks when the waves were high, here they would be close to hand if needed. Martin was not dissatisfied with this outcome, his only concern being whether the colleagues who would share this space would be offended by his presumption. In time he would learn that they, like himself, had their attentions focused on other matters.

Forty-four hands in total, that was the roll call when the *Anne* made off for the Guinea coast. Martin was surprised at the number, having witnessed earlier in his youth the ships leaving Greenock with a fraction of such a crew. He surmised that this quantity of men was indeed required and would have been taken only if strictly necessary, given the efforts of Captain Henry to cut the costs of the voyage on every other front. In the full light of day it was the state of the sails which had shocked the most; a patchwork of discarded rags, hastily sewed seams struggling to cope with the scarcely bracing winds of the Channel. Still, the almost admirable philosophy of the trip seemed to be to mend and make anew in these early, gentle days, rather than have the ship tied at anchor whilst the same work was carried out in presumably more expensive surroundings. Consequently Martin was to spend his initial weeks observing the industry of the crew on the decks as the carpenters, coopers and even blacksmiths went about their business. Sailing men on sailors' wages, earning less than their fellow craftsmen back on land – this had to be another ruse of the parsimonious captain. All the while Martin would try to ignore the creaking sound of the hull under strain as the *Anne* sat deep in the water and the sight of a hundred rusty nails growing ever more prominent by the day, like green shoots appearing through the earth in spring. Perhaps it is as well that there are so many of us, he thought, there is ample enough work to do.

Yet he knew that the fact that there were over forty hands manning a three-hundred-ton vessel owed more to the demands of the cargo that they planned to load off the African shore than it did to prudent maintenance. High numbers of men would be required to guard and subdue the holds filled with savages once they were on board, and perhaps to ensure that there were enough of them left once the malarial and yellow fevers had taken their toll on the outgoing crew. Back on shore the bars and taverns of the coastal towns were rife with tales of trading ships arriving back carrying nothing but ghosts once the illnesses that lurked in the jungle had taken their grip. Some said it was the lands themselves that were cursed, damning any civilized man foolish enough to visit. Others blamed the savages and their magic, and their attempts to poison the soul of the white man. Whilst Martin found no reference to either theory in his medical volumes he knew that it stood to reason that at least a quarter of the men he watched would die of such affliction. Yet they, like he himself, had boarded regardless. Indeed, to his knowledge, there was never a shortage of those willing to enlist and bed down in the vermin-ridden corners of the merchant fleet. This curiosity, he thought, watching the toils of the crew against the shifting backdrop of the restless sea, had to be worthy of debate and investigation, and he made a note to question the captain on his views later in the voyage, once he was sure he had gained his confidence.

But such a day seemed far off as the *Anne* followed her early course towards Cape Verde, blown by the favourable wind. Captain Henry kept himself remote, locked in his cabin with his papers, issuing instructions through his bosun and mates. It was only the purser he had time for, and the two would be in conference from dawn to daybreak poring over the balance sheet, if quarterdeck gossip was to be believed. And so it was that Martin found himself becoming fascinated with his more accessible new shipmates: some old like the master craftsmen on board, riggers and carpenters bearing the scars of a lifetime spent at sea, all bent bones and rotten teeth, with sallow skins that were testimony to endless scurvy-plagued voyages; others younger, boys hardly in their teens but already marked by the poverty and brutality of their childhoods ashore. Martin would watch them and wonder if their adoption of the sailor's life was a noble defiance of the hand that fate had dealt them or a surrender to the inevitable. Were they like him, chancing a final throw of the dice in the hope of a different kind of life on the seas or merely succumbing to a different kind of servitude from the one they could expect on land? Irrational though he knew it was, he felt more of an affinity with the men climbing the masts and rigging than he did with his cabin-mates on the quarterdeck. That he who was educated, like them, and born into the relative middle-class privilege of officer life should somehow feel *removed* from them and more at one with the common crew was a cause of an unsettling disquiet. Was this not the trip that was going to cure him of such conceits, were these maritime endeavours not the ones that would so occupy his thoughts as to leave no room for such subversive and ungodly meanderings in his mind?

That was the problem at this stage of the journey, the paucity of stimuli to exercise his faculties. For all that he chose to observe the men of the ship at work and amuse himself with the formulation of theses as to each one's past and future prospects, he knew that these were not his charges and represented neither reason nor purpose to his presence on the *Anne*. No, he would have to wait for his work to begin, once they were moored off the African shore. Then the trading would start and his scant medical knowledge would be put to the test. Which of the negroes on offer would make the best slaves, which would be most likely to survive the trip to the Americas, which hid the fever they were already surrendering to? *Ship's Surgeon*. A gloriously impotent title, he reflected bitterly. Who amongst the crew would seek his advice for their ailments? None. They would be better served following their own instincts, given the inadequacy of his expertise. Somehow the tawdry nature of his qualifications seemed ever more transparent now his maiden voyage was underway. Conversations with his fellow officers had been strangled, stunted affairs as he struggled to conceal what he felt were ruinous shortcomings. *Ship's Surgeon*. By what right did he answer to this preposterous title? By virtue of the handful of lectures he had attended, by virtue of the boxful of dusty volumes he had brought aboard to saddle the *Anne* with even more dead weight? Yes, these, and a curiosity which did not always serve him well when dealing with figures of authority, and the ten guineas which had secured him his practitioner's certificate. No, the privilege he had been born with had brought him to the title, his space in the quarterdeck cabin and his exemption from onerous duties on deck. Was this the reason for the vague sense of guilt which ate at him with a growing relentlessness, the same sense of guilt which he had taken to the sea to escape? Perhaps, he thought without pleasure or emotion, perhaps. For this identification was worthy of no respite, it was a diagnosis without cure. All he could do was wait for Africa, wait to busy himself amongst the savages; at least they were unlikely to be inquisitive about his past.

The stringy guy in the vest and cut-off jeans turned out to be called Henri. Once you were up close to Henri you could appreciate why he didn't tend to talk much. Not that I hadn't seen worse teeth, just that they usually belonged to horses or ancient shrunken heads. Once you were up close you could study his skin colour and still be none the wiser as to whether this was a tan or ingrained dirt. For all this, my first impressions of the man were accurate, he was cool about most things; cool with you if you were cool with him. I'm about to describe how I, on the face of it, ripped him off after he'd trusted me enough to give me my start in the apple donut trade, although I can't say I meant to rip him off from the start, it was just the way things worked out. Anyway, in advance of going through how this came to be, let me also point out that for every franc, centime and pastry that I took from him I would estimate that I repaid him twice or threefold in increased revenue from my efforts and those of the recruits that I brought to him. I'm sure he knew this and would be cool if I were to see him right now. And how I would like to see him now, a friendly face; could he take me back to those times?

Henri's van took us to the beach where we would meet with the car of Henri's pal. Henri's pal's name is not relevant, he was just the supplies man, he had made the journey to the bakery whilst Henri had been gathering his itinerant workers from the campsite and a host of other equally prestigious Riviera addresses. We, the contents of the van, were then introduced to the contents of the car, the donuts. Our mission was then explained to us in tones of exhortation. That mission was simple and straightforward: sell the bastards, lots of them. At least, that was how it was explained to me on that very first day, in a mixture of Henri's, and giggling German chicks', pidgin English. They knew I would have a hard time that day, they must have been pissing themselves at the look of bewilderment on my face as I was kitted out like a cinema ice-cream girl – minus torch – with my tray of donuts, bag of change and patch of land to patrol. I was shown the rendezvous point where the van would come to collect me and my leftovers at the end of the day's toil. The money I would be paid was dependent on my own success in selling; this was made very clear, together with the final, crucial, part of the briefing.

I never figured out whether this was Henri's own personal scam or whether he was part of a higher chain. Quite who had decided that what the droves of horizontal French crammed up beside each other under an eighty-degree-plus heat like a giant herd of poisoned wilde-beest at the side of the waterhole really wanted, and wanted with a perverse craving that defied all logic, was apple donuts ripened under the sun by being walked up and down the beach all day was never made clear. The chances are that if I'd have met that person on that first day, the encounter would have resulted in extreme violence. I trudged my way through the few narrow corridors of sand left uncovered and unclaimed by beachtowels for over three hours without selling a single crumb. Occasionally I would pass a fellow hawker from the morning crew and would be dismayed to see their inventory now significantly depleted. Mine seemed to be breeding in the tray – I'd started with around thirty and must have had over forty by lunchtime. It did strike me of course, that I was at a disadvantage in not being able to shout my pitch in French. Somehow I'd forgotten to ask how this might be done, maybe I'd just assumed that English was the recognized tongue of seaside cake selling. Around midday I sat down, defeated, ready to rest my burning feet. Suddenly, an ambush. A pack of predatory old crones waddling along the beach perimeter by the road fell victim to a strange hunger. Seven donuts later, they left. I had my first sale.

To understand the point of it all is to understand that I had let them come to me. Unwittingly, sure, but I had toiled and toiled and not sold a single thing until I had stopped and stayed still and thought of something else. It seemed obvious later that nobody was ever going to buy from a stressed-out malcontent with a bead of sweat dropping from his nose. No, they were only going to be tempted by someone at ease with himself, someone confident in the power of his goods to attract purchasers by their own merits. Forgive me for lingering on the details and understand that there were lessons I learned on that beach, that summer, with that tray of donuts – universal lessons that formed the foundation of everything I became. At the end of the season my friends made their way back to Scotland, back to university and the coming term. I didn't need to, I had received my education.

The main lesson? That there are signals we give off, signals that tell the world how we would like to be accepted. That how we are accepted is in our control. That sometimes when we are freed from the expectations of others who know us from our past we can surprise ourselves with the energy and eagerness with which we reinvent ourselves, how we reinvent how we would like to be *received*. And some of the signals are easy to change – the way we dress, or wear our hair, the language we speak – all external signs, all easy. The ways we think and confront the world, these all come from inside, these are harder. The way you gesture for someone to get into the back of your van. An example? I'm trying to sell fucking donuts. I want to be approachable, warm,

24

uncomplicated, purposeful; someone with integrity handling quality goods. What I don't want to be is withdrawn, burdened, arrogant; someone with whom the transaction, however brief, is going to be unpleasant. I need to be a success, not a victim of the tray hooked on to my shoulders. The signals I give will dictate whether the market sees me as one or the other.

I sold another three items on that first day, and ate two myself in lieu of lunch. My total day's commission was fourteen francs, just over a pound in real money. It was still more than Henri had expected, being used as he was to the negligible impact of new starts. They all had to go through this learning curve before they decided to give up or get very good. I wasn't going to give up, although the hardest part of the day was trying to persuade the lads back at the campsite that my efforts had been worth such a derisory wage. How they laughed. Within the week though, things were different, I was carting round my own ice-box and selling my own range of drinks bought from the super-market and suitably marked up to reward my investment, as well as my original tray of sugared delicacies. I could clear a hundred and fifty francs, more than ten times what I had made at the very start. Hard work, sure – not so much I let it look that way; the signals I gave were the opposite. So much so that my initially dubious companions soon joined me in the endeavour. And when they did we sold to a plan, my plan.

My plan involved the occasional lifting of the daily wage to even higher levels. This involved exploiting the weak point in Henri's oper-ation, and I'd known what that was from the very first briefing he'd ever given me, in fact I'd known it from the moment he'd gestured for me to climb into his wagon. Henri's operation was illegal. You weren't allowed to sell anything on the beach without the appropriate licence, let alone organize whole squads of hawkers to cover every grain of sand. The CRS – the municipal guard – were out there on the same ground determined to maintain public order. Henri had mentioned them in what he probably thought was a casual way right at the start. If you see them, he'd said, drop the tray and keep your money, run like fuck. According to him they would detain us if we were caught but he'd already given the game away. The CRS were never likely to imprison us, not for more than a couple of hours anyway. What they were likely to do was to confiscate our goods and sales proceeds, that's what scared Henri. Hold on to the money he'd said, hold on to it so you can give it to me. Sensible advice? Perhaps not. Perhaps, occasionally, you just can't run fast enough and they take all your merchandise and your revenue and your change. Perhaps no one else sees this and Henri just has to take your word for it. Perhaps it happens to everyone once in a while, perhaps it's inevitable that way. In my plan, such an occurrence would take place to each one of us every three weeks. We just happened to have repeated bad luck that way. Henri cursed it as much as we did, muttering in his curious way as he drew his breath in, so that the words all came out as one, almost backwards in the anguished tongue of the possessed; mer-mer-*merde*!

We would look the other way whilst he came to terms with his grief. There never were any arrests, the CRS and *gendarmerie* didn't seem that interested in us. Just as well – I was soon carrying goods which were more dangerous than apple donuts.

Great moments in my life. Sometime last year, sometime in the morning. Sometime when what I had to do was clear enough. I've closed the bar maybe ten minutes ago, at which point I felt as if I would fall asleep in mid-conversation with the two remaining customers who were busy telling me what a great place I had, what a great guy I was and how they envied me my lifestyle here on the island – the sunshine, the spot here at the marina, the holiday atmosphere. So sincere, so drunk, so very keen that I understood *exactly* what a great guy I was. Were they Danish, or Dutch? Doesn't fucking matter, they all speak in the same, confident English with American a's and r's. MTV has a lot to answer for. They tap their feet to the latest bland anthem going out to Europe on all the screens like mine, talking to me as they groove along. My bar is a happening place thanks to the satellite pap my guests steal their accents from. 'Martin . . . up . . . *Marrt-in*, could you turn the volume up?' And so I do, and then shout above it to ask the usual stuff, had you heard of Puerto Puals, of the Arena Bar, will you be back?

These are not the questions at the front of my mind though, those are to do with the money. Do you know how much you have spent here, how much you owe me, how much I have taken in total tonight? No, neither do I but I'm dying for you to go so that I can see, so that I can clean this place up and get it ready for tomorrow morning when we open for breakfast and start this whole thing up again like we do all summer. Go on, fuck off. I pour a couple of whisky shots. The third glass, my glass, already has its liquor in it, flat ginger beer, not that these two will notice. An old trick, if you want someone to leave, ply them with cheap whisky. If they drink it as fast as they should, once they have seen me down mine in my impressive manly gulps, the dizziness and nausea will carry them out the door before I can shout time. Yes, goodnight, thank you gentlemen, that last one was on the house.

When they leave I count the takings. A so-so night, every table outside taken in one way or another. Some Germans who laughed loudly and bought a lot of beer. Some middle-aged British who sat quietly, probably intimidated by the whole ambience of the bar and the glam parade it's part of, here by mistake at the club of the beautiful people. They drank even more beer and the best part of three bottles of Irish Cream, we nearly ran out of ice trying to stop the stuff from curdling in the heat. And some girls, Scandinavian girls. Young, early twenties, four of them, all blonde, all Identikit minis, cream lace crop-tops, blue eyes and brown limbs. I gave one of them the treatment for a while, I thought she was going for it but then they were gone, all off to a club to dance under the ultra-violet so that their white bits can at last sparkle. A realization from my early years in Spain: girls like this don't sunbathe to get brown, they do it so that everything can be bright against them – their flashing eyes, their perfect teeth, the whiteness of their underwear, your dick.

I take twenty thousand pesetas for my immediate needs and put the rest of the cash inside the safe-bag for banking tomorrow. The chairs outside are already chained with the parasols tied down and locked, these being the last instructions given to my crack new staff before I sent them home. The glasses can be done in the morning, I just stack them by the dishwasher. My mind is slowing right down as tiredness takes over once more. How many hours' sleep will I get before I'm back in here – three, four?

Not really sleep at all, more a fucking cigarette break; I try not to think about it. What time does the cleaner come, is she coming at all, do I have to do the fucking toilets? The last is not really a question, I know I do. The shit in my toilets, I mean, you would be amazed and appalled by the shit in my toilets, stuff you can never imagine. The men's and the women's. Both as bad. Shit on the floor, on the walls, everywhere but the lavatory pan. Dregs of cheap cocaine on the cistern, on the washbasin, on top of the paper dispenser, everywhere but up the nose of whoever was snorting the shit. Sometimes there might be syringes in the waste baskets, spent and used, like the tampons in beside them, and the condoms chucked in the corner of the floor. The shit in my toilets, God knows what will be in there tonight, but experience has taught me that whatever there is it is better faced now than in the morning when I come back. Seeing it now, it will irritate me, something else to be sorted before I can hit my bed; tomorrow, in the cold light of day, it would break my heart. All this energy, investment, hope, to be landlord to a cast of animals, is that what it was all about? No, I'll deal with it now, my cleaner can do the easy stuff if and when she shows – the tables outside, the windows, the walkway. Easy yet still part of the show, the never-ending show I find myself starring in.

I go into the cupboard to retrieve the heavy-duty gear, the scrubbing brush and disinfectant, the pine-scented detergent that burns off the surface stone from the ceramics and five layers of skin from my hands. There are some rubber gloves in there somewhere but I'm too tired to go hunting, I want this over and done with even if I go to sleep with my fingers stinking of this stuff enough to poison a room. At least it might scare off the mosquitoes. Tooled up, I enter the gents. It's not so bad, I can do this on autopilot, bucket and mop to wash the piss from the floor, wipe for the basin and bottom of the walls, attack of the brush for the crap clinging to the rim of the bowl. For a fleeting second, I watch myself doing this in the mirror, I want to stop and banter with my reflection – you should see yourself pal, you look fucked. Darkness around my eyes, hair lank and greasy, skinny as shit, the friendly face of a psychotic is smiling grimly back at me, you looking for trouble? We both get the joke. Definitely the sexiest lavatory attendant in town tonight. So much for cool travails.

I stop. I thought I heard something. Could have been outside, could have been those two guys coming back after throwing up, maybe they saw the lights still on. Shit. I hear it again, it's closer than that, it's inside. This is worse, I can feel my heart begin to race to a faster beat, I'm suddenly wide awake, am I being robbed? I put down the brush and slowly lift the mop handle; if there's someone there they are going to feel this, I work too fucking hard for anyone to come in and help themselves to what's mine, I don't care if it's the biggest guy in the fucking world who's about to beat me to a fucking pulp, I swear he'll know about me and this wooden pole first. OK Martin, cool it, I tell myself, the adrenaline has got to be controlled, go deep inside, compose yourself and think, then you can take anyone. I hold still – the sound is coming from the women's toilet, someone is in there. I wonder whether to kick down the door and surprise them. Maybe not, maybe it's just a drunk who went in and fell asleep, it's happened before.

'*Hola?* Come out for Christ's sake, everybody's gone home.' The shouting is loud, I'm sending a signal, I'm not scared you cunt, you're not in control of this now. I try to turn the handle. It doesn't shift, the lock is on.

'Come on!' I'm banging hard, maybe it's a junkie, out of it and about to expire, how can I get in there without breaking my own door?

'Martin?'

A voice, a female voice, small and fragile. I calm down.

'Yeah?'

I hear the lock being turned. The door slowly opens.

'Do you want to fuck me?'

It's one of the Scandinavian quartet who were in earlier on. She's standing stark naked in front of me looking kind of alarmed at the mop that's pointed at her face. I hadn't realized she'd sneaked back in, I hadn't realized she was so keen or was even falling for the treatment.

I take in the view. Five-foot-six, maybe seven, small by Swedish standards. Small-to-medium tits pointing east and west, tanned skin with
tiny white hairs in a line from her navel to the chestnut pubes; wide
hips, about ninety-seven per cent beautiful. She has a confidence that
comes from being at one with her own sexuality, either that or she's
just wired on something, maybe just plain nuts. Anyway, it's her that
wants to cool the scene down, trying to fix me in the eye. *Don't be
scared, Martin*. I like that. I'm tired and I stink of bleach and I'm still
annoyed that she scared me pulling this stunt but I know that I will
fuck her, like I promised myself I would fuck someone for every shit
night that I was stuck behind the bar, or for every hour spent talking
to boring Danish sailors, or for cleaning the shitty toilets when I'm
tired enough for a coma. Sure baby, I'll fuck you, I have to, it's my
destiny. Sex is a talent. And I have it.

Another moment, the next one that comes in the sequence, or does
it? In my mind it happened next but the truth will be that it was a few
days later, for various reasons. The first was the sex; it was good,
surprisingly good. The Swedish girl turned out to be German, I can't
remember her name, and it's not really relevant. I remember her talking,
until I placed a finger on her lips to show there was no need. I led her
from the back through to the main bar area. She waited as I switched
off the lights and lit the candles at the front tables. She was naked but
comfortable with it, I liked that. I turned the CD player and amplifier
back on, the disc I wanted – Roberta Flack, *First Take* – was already
on, I had been playing this music more and more to wind me down
last thing. Once it started to play I was ready to give my guest the
attention she deserved, advancing on her to place a kiss on her silent
mouth, gently forcing her backwards until she could retreat no further
and her white cheeks touched the plaster walls. I tried to kiss with
delicacy, no tongues, kissing only with lips, kissing lightly, briefly;
kissing to set the pace, a tender pace, not rushed. I kissed her like this
until the feeling was there that we were synchronized, that we were
in tune, and then I began to explore the touch of her skin, a soft skin,
perfumed with the moisturizer she must have used after her days in the

30

sun. I felt her with the backs of my hands, brushing lightly down her sides, the tops of her arms, then massaging the tightness from her collarbone to shoulder. I turn my hands outside and then run them gently down again, this time the touch lingers and there is more contact, I let my wrists and forearms warm and rub against her, moving inwards towards her breasts, closing in to gently grip her nipples between fingers. My palms are still turned backwards so that when I slowly clench my fists they gently push each breast upwards, cupping them in reverse, softly squeezing each nipple. I kiss them with an open mouth, my tongue coating their tips and sides in saliva. The song on the music system has changed, Roberta is starting to sing 'The First Time Ever I Saw Your Face', my hands release their light grip on cue and I bring them up to run my fingers through her hair. And then they go down again, down to her hips then circling in with the lightest of touch from my fingertips across the tops of her thighs. She shifts her stance slightly, kissing me with more urgency, parting her legs so that I can touch the insides of her thighs but again I concentrate on the lightness of my fingers, brushing the skin almost teasingly, dabbing the lips of her vulva with restraint, and then breaking off from her kiss to place one of my own behind her ear as my fingers make their way towards her clitoris. Her arms are around my neck, hugging me close so that I can hear her quickening breaths. I can sense her whole body tensing as the circle my hand is drawing centres more and more on her velvet lips and the moistness around them. She pushes her legs further apart and tilts her hips towards me. She lets out a sigh and then begins to sink, sliding down against the wall, down to her knees.

She unzips me and draws my cock out, she strokes me and kisses its sides. Then her mouth is open and I'm in then out of it, in then out. This is not unpleasant, but it leaves me with nothing to do. I turn my head to one side and see our silhouettes reflected in the bar window. A man is having a blow job, he's still fully clothed. I feel remote somehow, even though that man is me. I pull off my shirt, throw it across to a chair; my aim is good, a thought that seems to demand my concentration more than it should at this moment. I bend to put my hands under her arms to lift her up. She looks puzzled – did I not enjoy what she was doing, was there something wrong with it? I look at her; no, nothing wrong, just me going mad, my mind wandering off for some insane reason. Occupy me, please, involve me somehow.

With one hand I separate her legs and with the other I guide myself into her, pushing hard, full penetration in one thrust. After the tenderness, the rough selfishness, my preferred combination. Show them a tender side, and a tough side, it works every time. I've seen women leave a gentle man for a rough one, and vice-versa. The trick is to offer both, to explore both. I think of good sex, the best sex, and I always think of Jim Morrison singing with the Doors, how his voice could be soft and gentle, but what gave his performance its edge was the knowing that at any moment it would break into something more base and brutal and that he was almost struggling to keep that element within him under control. That's what makes it compelling, particularly for women who have their own take on this, that it's their destiny to accommodate both in a passionate man.

So.

That was why we were now doing it standing up, then doing it sitting down with her astride, doing it both of us on the bar I'd only recently wiped down. I liked to look at her against the marble, her delicate tanned skin against the stone; I put my weight on her, pinning her down by the shoulders, pushing and grinding so hard into her pelvis. A real work-out, and if there was a down-side to it at the time it was only in the way she kept stopping me and then grabbing my scalp to pull my face right up to hers – not to kiss, but so that our eyes were an inch apart. This was the signal she wanted to give to me; that this was intense, special, a one-off connection of soul-mates on an astral plane rather than a holiday screw with a horny bar-owner. Pulling me away from kissing her nipples so that she could head-butt me again with her passion and our special togetherness in that moment. So it's this staring, staring, staring. What the fuck was she looking for, what did she want to tell herself she'd found?

I came the once and then we shared a couple of lines that she'd brought along – good stuff, actually – so that I was ready for round two which lasted longer, almost too long, so that by the end I was

32

squeezing and pulling and pumping everything so I could just shoot and get back to cleaning up the bar. We finished when I finished, right that very second. I knew it was selfish but I was looking to lock up and get out of the bar sharp. This must have upset her; I think she was hoping for us to go off somewhere together at that point, perhaps to watch the fucking sun rise, and for her to ask more of her questions – *when did you know that we had . . . you know . . . clicked, when did you first notice me; Martin, how did you know we'd be lovers? My English*, she says pleadingly, *my English not good enough to tell you how I feel.* Thank fuck for that, I don't want to hear it. I put a finger to her lips again; silence please, we had our moment, don't spoil it now.

So by then time was running out for me to make it home, as in 'home' home, and I knew I was heading for another couple of hours in the flat I'd been loaned round at the side of the complex by one of Herman's colleagues. I'd taken the key never intending to use the place but by now had spent most of the week there with one thing and another. When I let myself in and looked at the bed lying unmade from the night before I felt a wave come over me, maybe a feeling of regret that here I was again, or a sense of resignation or whatever. A completely bare flat with nothing in it but that bed; yes, something stirred when I saw that. Home, I told myself, make it there tomorrow, slip off for a few hours in the afternoon, it's overdue. And then I sat down to think about this some more. I woke up three hours later, mouth dry and every other inch of me sticky and clammy. Cocaine always gives me night-sweats and I'd fallen asleep with my clothes on.

Time to get moving again, it must be around seven. Time to pull myself together for another day only I'm staggering from room to room in exhaustion, a ghost let loose in the blinding daylight. I peel off my clothes as I wander towards the shower. And when I make it into the cubicle and slouch against the tiles and watch the water that has flowed from my head to toes disappear down the drain I start to dream, the same dream that haunts me in moments like these when the day ahead is still to happen, the dream about water.

There are six of us in a boat far out in the ocean, floating in a calm in the middle of an endless expanse. Five of them surround me, sitting silently, waiting for me to make a move: for whilst I am the one in control of the situation, it is me they all want dead. I know this with a heavy certainty that could drown me even before I hit the waves lapping the sides around us. The sound of the water becomes a call, an invitation to step over the side out into the deep, to walk the plank into the only means of escape. The water will one day take me, always waiting to take me down.

And this is the thought always haunts me in my waking moments, when I'm moving too slow to distract myself with the shit that makes up my life. It casts its grip on me, almost impossible to shake off, even without the drug-induced paranoia that I'm trying to rinse out of my head after the night before. Today, there is help from outside; a blast from a car horn and a squealing of tyres on the bone-dry coastal highway outside is enough to snap me out of the morbid premonition and return me to the present. The noises serve as an abrupt reminder that out there Mallorca is waking, outside the traffic is already building and jousting in the macho Spanish way. Outside, the island is kicking and screaming its way into the day, tetchy and irritable, like a newborn baby left hungry and hot under the stifling heat. I turn the shower to cold and raise my face to take the shock.

Once I dry off I face my next immediate problem, clothes, or lack of clean clothes. I'll go without underwear until I make it home and I'm lucky to find a black T-shirt that I had left behind at the flat a couple of days before. Doesn't smell that great, but better than the one I slept in. The trousers are a matter of real concern though. My fawn linen pair look creased and lined enough to pass for a pair of pyjama bottoms, which in a way they were, and that's nowhere near the worst of it. Somehow, although I don't quite remember the particular detail, I must have started with the girl last night when I still had them on. She herself, lousy bitch, presumably in the heat of the moment, or in the middle of squeezing my hand and locking on her full eye-contact number, had forgotten to warn me that she was having her period, or having it all over my fucking trousers. The shit I find myself in, desperately scrubbing the crotch of my priceless designer gear with shampoo so that a blatant red stain can become a fairly obvious maroon one. No wonder she was so fucking horny, she'd found a man who cared enough to want to connect despite all that. Or one who failed to notice. Until now. How am I going to pass this off and serve breakfasts without looking a complete dick?

This, truth be told, is the final spur to me going home that morning, going home to throw on an unsoiled pair of jeans and consign the present pair to history. That is what made me do it, to walk over to the bar with my hands covering my stained soggy crotch, open it up, wait for the cleaner, give her a note to give to Sarah telling her to do everything the best she can until lunchtime when I was planning to be back, and to ignore Herman's note that had been waiting for me in the door like a fucking German's beachtowel claiming the space and to just head for the jeep and then head off, away from the marina and inland, up the side of the mountain towards the villa at Paguera.

An enjoyable drive, almost an hour I recall, enjoyable up to a point, that point being when I arrived. I had never made the trip at this hour; the road was curiously quiet and slow, it was the hordes of cyclists who were responsible for the latter, middle-aged Swiss pumping their way up the incline in their Lycra shorts and gaudy jerseys. A surreal vision, bankers and credit managers acting out their fantasies of being tour professionals. I smiled for them and turned the car's music system off. The windows were down and the air blowing in seemed to be making a better job of clearing my head than the cold water had earlier. I tried to take in the colours and impressions of the island as the bikers would have been seeing them if they had not been so intent on exhausting themselves; the sweeping verdant hills and narrow valleys filled with wild olive, pine and dwarf palms; up in the higher, drier stretches the scatterings of carob trees standing defiantly and incongruously green under the Balearic sun's strongest rays, a hazel carpet of carob pods covering everything at ground level, insulating the earth from the heat. I passed auburn-coloured hamlets and cottages in amongst the growth as the winding route led on to Camp de Mar and Andraitx. If I stare and stare I am reminded of why it was I came to live on this island, or rather why it was I came to stay.

I turned off and headed sharp left, a new road taking the jeep uphill towards another plateau and another scattering, this time of villas, built within the last five years, built for privacy, to accommodate new wealth. The last of the three, with its iron gates and driveway pointing to the heavy wooden porch doors is the one I draw up outside. There is no other car here, I can change clothes in privacy. Then I notice the gates are unlocked and I'm annoyed, they shouldn't have been left like this; if the house alarm has not been set I'll be seriously pissed off. On the doorstep itself I'm relieved to see that it has; I punch in the code, find and use the key and I'm inside, walking into the cool air and on to the tiles of the open-plan hallway and lounge. Right away, I notice that something is missing, not in the sense of stolen missing that would reduce me to a panic, but missing as in not there, the things that would give this home its normal atmosphere. Yes, it's the atmosphere that's not here – the mess of child's toys on the floor, the pictures above the fireplace, gone. Into the kitchen and there is no food, no fruit in the bowl or bread lying out on the carving board. Walking slower now, into the bedroom, I open the wardrobe, no clothes hanging, other than mine. I sit down on the bed and contemplate the weight of the evidence, it's back to the dream about water and the heavy certainty of knowing events are closing in, the heaviness that could drown me then and there in this room on a mountainside. My wife has left me. My wife and child are gone.

The storm woke him from his sleep in the dead of night. Not that this had come as a sudden shock. If anything the swerving climb and pitch of the bow had imparted an almost agreeable rocking motion to the cabin and his hammock, one that comforted him in his slumbers, worming its way into his dreams and the fleeting visions of a childhood spent in churches, idling away the moments during prayer meetings. So deep was his surrender to fatigue and the serenity of his reveries that when the roar from outside finally erupted into his consciousness and brought him so sharply back into the present it took almost a minute for him to gather his wits and realize where he was. He woke alone. To be fair, there were more than a few disconcerting factors which stood in the way of a ready understanding. The first was the dark, the pitch-black which greeted his eyes. Second were the noises that he found impossible to identify: the strange sound the wind made as it toyed with *Anne* upon the waves, a shrill howl recognizable only to those sailors who had heard it before. To this was added the percussion of the men vomiting on the deck, retching as if in arranged sequence, bells being rung in a tower. Then, more ominously, the stirrings of the cargo in the holds, groaning like anguished souls, then thudding like the anarchic drums of a marching military band.

Martin moved to seek his breeches in the gloom, something telling him that he should be on deck alongside the officers though he knew there was little he would be capable of or expected to do.

They were three days from Tenerife, or so they had told him, progress had been swift, the tempestuous regions of the Arab waters successfully behind them. He cursed himself for believing such assertions as he fed his legs through the seat of his pants. The ship suddenly lurched to starboard, sending him falling into a collision with his books now stacked in a growing sprawl on that side of the cabin. He let go of the waistband as he steeled himself in an instant for impact with the wall and floor but his legs were trapped, as securely fastened at the ankles as if in a pair of leg-irons. He hit the floor with a whiplash force, tasting blood in his mouth immediately, before the force of the ship correcting itself sent him rolling back to the middle of the floor. To his astonishment he could now taste salt on his lips, sea-water salt – the waves had reached high inside the *Anne*. Everything was awash. Another curiosity. Should he live it had to be worth questioning the captain on this too.

He did not wear a hat, though it did not stop him instinctively reaching for it as the full force of the gale hit him once he emerged from the cocoon of the cabin in the quarterdeck. He smiled momentarily, realizing that to an observer it must have appeared as if he were trying to secure his very head against the might of the elements. A preposterous notion, it was as well they were all preoccupied with more pressing matters, huddled against railings, posts and the helm. Nobody stood erect, everyone crouching to present a smaller target to the angry blusters that would have them over the side.

He wanted to join them, to find out what it was they were doing, to offer his help. For weeks he had felt the outsider, the interloper with no legitimate place on board. Suddenly, with the white spray of the water lashing every inch of him he felt an exhilaration that verged upon delirium, as if the ship had been thrown into a realm of opposites where he belonged and they did not. He was calm, invisible, and comfortable in his mind for some reason that the vessel would not sink, that the waves had no quarrel nor place for her. He felt an urge to seek out the captain, to offer his services for whatever the emergency demanded. He wanted to show that he felt no fear, not of the storm, nor the captain himself, or any physical challenge that might have to be met before the night was out. As the ship fell deep into the chasms that yawned open between the rolling waters he felt the gravity keeping his boots on the timbers of the deck grow lighter, so much so that he might be left behind whilst everything else plummeted downward. Again he suppressed a laugh at the oddity of it all, wondering also in that moment if his amusement was that of a madman, for whilst he could not see the expressions on his shipmates' faces, he could be sure that mirth would not be shared amongst them. Had he finally gone insane?

Another thunderous wave smashed into the boat on the starboard side, punching in like a left hook from a vicious opponent who had already set the target up for the hit with a delicate series of jabs to prime it into position for the final blow to strike with full force. It felt as if the *Anne* might topple over, might give up the fight and fully immerse her deck and masts in a desperate bid for inverted stability. Martin looked up and saw the sea above his head, the floor that was once the deck now vertical, like a wall. One more inch and she might have been tempted to revolve the full way but no, the stubborn and spirited nature of the craft suddenly asserted itself as she swung back to reverse herself with an urgency that spoke of an anger at the indignity she had suffered by baring her belly to the air. Martin slid back the full width of the bow, the momentum of the shift lifting him back on to his feet as he came to a halt. He landed right in front of a cowering nest of crew-men clinging to a rail, appearing before them like an apparition that had materialized out of nowhere. There were six of them: Wells, the first mate, Fotheringham the purser, and four deckhands in their sodden rags. They looked as one up to his figure, standing tall, unblinking, traces of a smile lurking somewhere about his eyes.

'Good evening gentlemen,' he said, in a voice they would recall as sounding as if he were making their acquaintance in a rowdy tavern, '. . . I think this will be a night we will all remember for some time.'

It was his second premonition. It would prove to be as accurate as the first, though it was not the night itself that they would remember, but his part within its events. This night would almost come to be regarded as the night the voyage started, for prior to it, Martin's presence had been noticed by only the few who had shared his acquaintance in the confines of officer quarters. This was now his first moment, his real arrival. Later, during the battles that would be fought, there would be those who sought him out in the midst of the action, eager to share his space. There were those who thought him to be untouchable, blessed, impervious to any bullet or blade. This was the night that it all began, when the first of them saw a reason to follow him.

The men were gathered outside, bracing themselves against the excesses of the storm for a reason. They were under orders to check the movements stirring in the holds below. Occasionally, the ship would shudder as if she was being assailed from the deep, her bow scraped along a reef or even shaken by the tentacled grip of an aquatic monster hiding under the waves. For the captain and his crew however, the truth was all the more disturbing; the threat came from within, the precious goods that gave purpose to the entire venture had broken loose and were in danger of destroying both themselves and the ship. Captain Henry had ordered that the movement be halted and this group had gathered around the hatch that would give entry down into the after hold. None however showed any inclination to pass inside, instead they crouched with an ear to the opening as if waiting for a signal from below.

'Is there anyone down in there?'

Martin had to shout just to hear himself in the rain-soaked gale. His question drew only a shaking of heads by way of reply.

'What is the problem?'

Again, no one rushed to reply. Martin had the feeling he was breaking some kind of silent truce between the men. He had had enough though of being treated as an interloper.

'I will go inside.'

He placed one leg on the iron hinge that held the hatch door open and prepared to climb down. An arm appeared to halt his progress and pull him back towards the deck. It was Fotheringham, who appeared excitable and spoke between taking in gulps of air.

'There is no problem here, Doctor, we have been listening out for stray cargo for the last hour. Everything in this hold is properly stacked and bound, I will swear by it.'

'Then why won't you let me go in and check?'

Fotheringham shook his head in a display of exasperation. 'Because you have no business down in the holds, sir. It is dark inside, there is nothing to see, and if harm should come to you when down below I have no intention of being held accountable for it.'

The look on Martin's face made Fotheringham draw the young surgeon closer; he spoke more quietly, pressing his mouth close to Martin's ear. 'It is dangerous, sir . . . a man could be crushed . . . there is no point in courting danger. We must only enter if strictly necessary and that will be if we hear something that makes us feel that is an appropriate action. Then it will be one of the hands, sir; them that were responsible for stowing the cargo should also be charged with securing it when it breaks loose, that's what the captain says.'

'Where is he?'

'The captain? Up on the forward hatch. That's where it sounds as if something is happening, they will have the Devil's job to fix that. I wouldn't go bothering him now, and I wouldn't go volunteering to go inside either . . . Unless you want to be judged a fool, or just plain impertinent, sir. Understand?'

Martin paused; he didn't understand, but the debate hardly seemed worth entering. *A fool or impertinent*. Whose opinion was this meant to be, the

40

captain's, or his supine lackey's? How could it be that the ship – and all aboard – were in danger, yet the situation could only be saved by those who were expendable rather than those charged with command?

The *Anne* rose up on another menacing swell, the surging motion passing through from side to side leaving them all clutching at the rails and each other for safety. All except Martin, who rode it in his boots, hands staying still by his side as he eyed the purser with an expression approaching distaste.

'As long as he doesn't take me for a coward I shall be well satisfied.'

He turned and moved forward, striding against the full force of the wind as he made his way along to join the second group of men on deck. This was much larger, over twenty gathered around the opening to the largest of the holds. As the bows were lifted by successive waves, the *Anne*'s prow was left high in the air, making Martin's journey an uphill hike. He gradually edged higher, closer to the advance party clinging on near the summit. He could hear the captain's voice as his bellowed instructions were blown down towards him.

'No lamps . . . Let your damn eyes do their work!'

The tone was harsh; Captain Henry meant his men to obey. Martin saw immediately that this group had the more demanding of the deck assignments, foremost and most exposed to the elements, entrusted with the largest hold, the one that was making the most noise. Even to a novice sailor like himself, the difference between the echoes emanating from this space and the one he had just visited was distinct. Here also, the men were set about their business; desperately tying down the sails to the yards to stop them being inflated by the blasts of wind, sweeping the water from the deck that the waves sought to deposit every time they launched an assault over the bow, feeding the lengths of rope into the deep, dark, dangerous pit that was the hold where their colleagues were now surveying.

'Captain Henry?'

The captain's head jerked around swiftly. His mouth was drawn tight.

'What?' He looked at Martin with immediate distrust, as if he did not recognize him. His expression barely changed when the stranger's identity finally registered. What use a surgeon in a crisis like this? '. . . What is it, man!'

'I am here to let you know my services are available, sir.'

41

The offer seemed to leave the skipper wrongfooted.

'Aye . . . Of course. We have . . . no need. No injuries.'

'I will do whatever is required, please be assured of that, sir.'

The captain waved a hand, the motion almost dismissing Martin and the rain as one and the same irritant.

'How many are down there?'

The captain ignored the question. It was left to the second mate, Gardiner, to furnish an answer. He tugged Martin to one side, perhaps fearful of being overheard by his superior.

'Jim and Peter . . . the lads. It was them who was meant to have it all secured when we left port, so them 'as to sort it out, Captain says. He's not best pleased, no, sir . . . Can you smell the scent of alcohol?'

Martin pushed his head directly over the hatch; a sweet odour met his nostrils, mixed in amongst the damp wood and salt spray. He nodded. Gardiner stepped closer and spoke with the voice of a man in mourning.

'Spillage, for sure, aye. Captain Henry is not best pleased,' he said solemnly.

The captain's displeasure was obviously the prime concern of the ship's senior crew, a matter more pressing than the danger of the loose cargo itself. Martin wondered how it could be that one man could impose his will so absolutely over others. Was this a hindrance or a help in this current predicament, did their fear of him lessen their fear of the storm, was that the intention of this grim leadership? Or was he a simply a latter-day Canute, trying to command the waves through the hold he had over the crew?

The *Anne* was gaining height suddenly, pushed upwards by a rapidly forming crest so that for a moment she was perched atop a peak within the ocean, gazing down on the waves below. Martin instinctively broke free of Gardiner's conspiratorial embrace to survey the scene. He felt his heartbeat quicken as he scanned across the horizon towards the nearest summit. Here was another mountain, a mountain on the move towards them, built on a roaring wall of water at least forty feet high. He struggled to find the words for what seemed an eternity, eventually hearing himself screaming with all his might towards the captain.

'Another one on the way, sir . . . starboard side. Haul the lads free! Get them to safety, sir!'

In reply, a flash of angry eyes, a glare to warn of future reproach. Captain Henry addressed his comments to the darkness of the chamber below.

'Get our cargo fixed, hear me? Make it fast, damn you!'

Martin pushed Gardiner aside to gain access to the rope attached to the men in the hold. The ship was plummeting downward as he did so.

'Pull them out!'

His hands were wrapped tight around the cord when the wave struck, his intention having been to drag the pair free singlehanded if necessary. Instead, the rope instantly became his means of staying aboard as the full might of the sea raged over and across the tossing deck. He held tight as the ship turned on its side whilst the breaking wave flooded the open hold and swept three hands over into the frothing deep. In that instant he could have been forgiven for believing that the *Anne* had become submerged, such was the force and volume of water that poured over her bows. Yet somehow she remained afloat, righting herself anew although rocking the stern deck free of another two crewmen in the process. No one saw them go, it was only their final cries for help that lingered.

The stinging of the sea-water acting on his raw hands brought Martin back to his senses. He felt a surge of despair as he looked into the hold, now filled to its very brim with the water that lapped at the hatch.

'Bail! Bail out the hold!'

The shouts of the captain and ship's mate had the rest scurrying for buckets and pails, the first of which began to dip into the watery space and relieve it of its unwelcome liquid cargo. Progress was chaotic and slow, the ship continuing to bob and pitch with such violence and unpredictability that seldom would a full bucketload leaving the hold contain more than half of that by the time it was raised clear, the rest spilling back to whence it came. Martin tugged vainly on the rope. Surely what he was watching was a demonstration of the wrong priority being exercised? He looked once more over the bow of the ship. It was now almost a minute since the giant wave had struck. In the moonlight he could see no sign of any other approaching. He would have to take his chance, and take it now. The penalty would be a lifetime of never forgiving himself for not doing otherwise.

The others, to a man, were all studying the entrance in glum silence as he stripped off his jacket. He tried to slow his breathing down, inhaling longer, fuller lungfuls as he lifted his leg on to the side of the hatch. His foot in place, a spring off the deck with the other had him skipping up and over the side and plunging into the uncertain waters of the hold. They greeted him with an icy shock. Reaching for the rope as a guide, he pulled against it to go down deeper, tentatively feeling for the top of the original cargo with his legs. He tried to open his eyes, but they were useless, blinded and stung by the sea salt. All he could do was fight his way down, groping for any kind of familiar shape in the numbing cold. He touched what he imagined to be wooden crates, barrel rims, other ropes and rigging as his discomfort and the lack of air began to bite. The darkness under the water he could have expected, the silence he did not, nor the relative peace this granted from the cacophony of storm and bellowed orders above. Of its own, aside from the cramps and giddiness he was beginning to feel, this was almost worth staying under for.

He had kicked to return to the surface when his left hand ran through what he thought was a mop. Instinctively, he stayed to explore the immediate area surrounding it, in case what he had touched was a scalp. He was floating horizontally and his by now frozen fingers met the texture of more wood, more canvas, more ragged splinters that had once been proud veneers; then shockingly, something less rigid – a substance, a shoulder, an arm, a hand that he squeezed with his. Martin tore blindly at the wall that seemed to have pinned down the components of the torso he had discovered. Was it his imagination or had the other hand sought his, had it pressed his palm in a feeble attempt to signal that Martin's help was needed? He pulled on the rope with urgent vigour, hoping that those above would themselves take its fluctuating tension as a sign that they too should join the effort to free those trapped below. He was running out of air and knew he had to return to the surface, trailing his arm in the darkness a final time in order to deliver a departing handshake, a simple physical gesture that could perhaps impart a more complicated hope; *I have found you, I won't forget you, I will get you out.* He kicked again for the surface.

As soon as his head was above water, the sound of pandemonium returned. Martin tried to shout as he regained his short breath. He had returned to the same scene as before, men vainly trying to empty the hold one pail at a time. The difference in the waterline was negligible and it was beyond belief that only one man held the rope that could be another man's saviour.

'He's alive . . . For Christ's sake pull him free, all of you, we cannot let them die like drowned dogs!'

'Steady with the bailing, men . . . Master Bosun, can you feel any response to the pulls on the rope?'

The bosun looked blankly at the captain. Martin would later wonder if he had actually heard the question above the rain and wind. The lack of a ready answer seemed good enough for Captain Henry.

'No response. You have found nobody with your antics, Doctor. The men will bail out the hold as ordered. You will join us on the deck now, sir, at once if you please.'

'There are two men down there. I have touched one, he is still alive . . . I beg you, Captain, give the order to haul them out, all hands at once!'

Something in the way he had said it, rather than what he had said, made the men halt their labours. His voice had been that of reason, bereft of anger, fear or even any hint of consternation; it had simply said what had needed to be said. This was the first time Martin would learn that men will listen to a calm voice rather than an imploring one.

'On deck . . . now, sir!'

All except the captain would have heeded his call. Martin gave the slightest of nods to the skipper. *I have heard you.* He raised his knees and ducked his head under the water again, kicking and pushing, diving down with his arms in one fluid movement.

Captain Henry confined Martin to quarters once he finally climbed out of the hold and returned to the deck. He went back to the hammock where he had been sleeping only hours before. The same hammock, the same cabin, the same ship. Yet everything had changed.

The bodies of the two young deckhands originally sent down – Jim O'Rourke and Peter McGill – were recovered just after daybreak. By then the storm had subsided and some of the water in the hold had seeped out of the ship of its own accord. Once the *Anne* began to sit higher in the water this process moved it faster than any army of buckets could ever have hoped to. In hindsight, the crew realized that the sudden flood had stabilized the loose cargo better than poor Jim and Pete would have managed, however heroic their efforts. May they rest in peace. Their bodies had looked battered and beaten when eventually retrieved, limbs had been broken and twisted in the struggle that must have ensued in the chaos of the dark below.

The two men were wrapped in coarse calico cloth and dispatched back to the waves that had killed them the evening before, the skipper obviously deciding that the longer they stayed aboard, the more their presence might adversely affect crew morale.

In accord with the tradition that dictated all men be present when the captain conducted the funeral rites, Martin's curfew was briefly withdrawn to allow him on deck.

'. . . *Harrison, Jones, Kennedy, Cooper, Smith, O'Rourke, McGill . . .*'

Captain Henry's voice as he read out the list of the dead was steady, strong and authoritative. As if, thought Martin, the presence of the Bible in his hand granted him the right to speak on behalf of God. The God whose will it was that the men be lost so tragically in the night to the storm. The same God who was to be thanked that he had spared the *Anne*.

'. . . *Praise be to God. Amen.*'

The weather was kind that morning; calm, a gentle breeze working its warm air through the ship's sodden timbers, effortlessly blowing the wet sails dry. A blue sky arched above the gathering of men on the dot on the sea like a cathedral roof. Somewhere, at some point between the madness of night and the tranquillity of the dawn, the boat had been slipped into Paradise.

So it was that the captain read out the names to a sun-filled morning, those names being uttered together in the ceremony and thus united for eternity; as crew, comrades, and victims of the tempest. Martin listened and knew that this was the history as Captain Henry would record it in his log for posterity. He would write how, under his stewardship, the steady progress of the *Anne* had come to an abrupt and unfortunate end when confronted by a rage of unimaginable power. How, under his command, the men had held their resolve despite daunting odds, had remained steadfast, protecting cargo and vessel, a testament to the discipline captain and crew displayed when faced with the most severe of tests. And with his own hand, pondered Martin, Captain Henry would exonerate himself from any blame attached to the deaths of the men under his command. O'Rourke, McGill. *Drowned aboard ship*. A strange history. Left to die in order that the cargo be protected, so that their bodies could become buffers for the more precious goods being transported, the ones Captain Henry had ordered be stacked in such haste at the outset of the voyage. They had died so that the captain's authority could be maintained in the face of impertinence from the lower ranks. Harrison, Jones, Kennedy, Cooper, Smith. Ordered to remain on deck so as to defy the waves that might claim them whereas lesser captains would have had them serve no immediate purpose and stay in quarters. O'Rourke, McGill. Drowned aboard ship. Bodies as cargo. Never again, thought Martin. Everything had changed.

Now let me introduce a great influence on my life, someone who has floated in and floated out, probably without ever realizing the effect he was having. Someone of whom I thought warmly, until recently, very recently; although when I reflect in any kind of detail on the past, I realize he is consistently linked to the very worst decisions I have ever made. Someone of whom now, when I'm trying to remember from whatever memories I have of him, I realize I know nothing at all. I mean, I can tell you what he looked like, how he looks now, the few things he said when I first met him, and the way he finds it impossible to say anything without employing a drop of his languid shoulders to add whatever nuance of irony or malice is required for his pronouncements. All this I can tell you, but what strikes me in doing so is that every attitude, belief or opinion I thought he had is exactly that – those that I *thought* he had. Because Jérome never gave anything away, at least willingly, and maybe that's what drew me to him in the first place. This would be back in the heady days of my donut-selling spree at Camp Les Acacias. I had never met anyone like him before, anyone so aloof, so distant, and yet so in tune and central to the mood of the moment. His was a presence that rock stars spend years perfecting;

of the people but *removed* from them. At least, that's the way he struck me. The doubts came later, too late, that my adulation could be misplaced. You see, I had been raised in a world of certainties, knowing my place in a cheerless family living a cheerless life in a damp and cheerless corner of a cold and cheerless country. Still, the future was there for us to grasp, if we were ready with the grim application required for success, so there was no reason not to be happy, no excuse at all.

Then here, in the south of France in the summer of '85, I meet someone who really doesn't give a shit about anything. I really mean *anything*. Nothing touched him, nothing stuck. So when I try to describe his character perhaps the most relevant thing to say about Jérome is that he had no *character*, only *characteristics*. He could have stepped right off the page of an airport novel, one with a cover of a girl in a bikini holding a gun, or maybe an open suitcase full of cash. As shallow as that in that regard, paper-thin I guess, albeit in an endearing sort of way. Nothing ever exciting or angering him, the only thing that ever mattered being whatever it was he wanted to do at that precise instant. Tomorrow? The shoulders droop comically, like a withered flower in a cartoon; *irrelevant. Les autres*; other people, *what other people?* The shoulders shoot up, raised in query. He looks at me in a blank stare; Martin, *rien*, there is no point, nothing matters. So careers, duty, decency, ambitions – all of the anchors that had held me in place in my life to date were suddenly loosened, cast aside for the others who might use them. This is why I idolized him, the way he made those ties irrelevant, obsolete. And I must have wanted to be as transparent and enigmatic as I thought he was. So the question is, was he the beguiling hero with his own unique take on life that rendered all my cosy presumptions redundant, or was he simply a blank page, a rootless uneducated waster? Yet what I now understand, is that the answer, the *truth*, does not matter. All that matters is my reaction to him, my reading of his signals. It won't surprise you then, that I, an impressionable twenty-year-old took him to be the former rather than the latter, the first mistake I made with Jérome, maybe the only mistake, the one I went on to make over and over. He shows up in Spain fifteen years later and I greet him like a long-lost brother – welcome to my world, my home, Jérome, it's all yours. I do have a brother, a real one in Scotland, I haven't seen him for years, I struggle to see how he could fit into my life and how he might be *relevant*. He has never harmed me though, like my association with Jérome has, so why the difference, why the accommodation for one and not the other, Jesus, Martin, what the fuck is wrong with you?

Anyway.

You would have thought that Scotland had enough like him, that there must have been others equally dissolute and maybe there were. It was just that I hadn't met them, or found them as charismatic, or romantic, whatever. The simple fact was that then and there I was ready to listen to someone like him, for some reason I wanted him as my friend. The things that made him different? I don't know. He was black, or brown, whatever. A mixed-race product of uncertain pedigree, what half was mixed with what was impossible to tell. I remember early on asking him where he was from, meaning to get to the bottom of this. *Marseille*, came the reply, and I was none the wiser, except to know the question was immaterial. There could have been Arab blood in him, African or even Indian, perhaps further afield and more exotic like Mauritius, New Caledonia. Then there was the white bit, the European element that gave his hair its lank rather than Afro quality. I sometimes thought of his mother as one of those cats in heat that becomes impregnated by several randy toms at one session so that when she gives birth it's a mixed crop of kittens with every colour and fur represented. Jérome was the personification of that litter; there was a riot going on in his genes, his collection of limbs and features every bit as anarchic – arms loping down beyond his gleaming thighs, swaying with the rhythm of his walk like a Harlem Globetrotter robbed of the basketball but not unduly worried about the fact – the legs of a ballerina carrying him along, taut and lean, walking on points as if to let his heels touch the ground would be too inelegant, too uncool to allow. I think his face is where nature played its cruellest trick; it was here he managed to combine the worst aspects of his inheritance, round broad features with the paler sickly skin tone of a white man. One flip of the DNA coin and it all might have been so different, perhaps the best of both worlds. But then he wouldn't have been Jérome, *the man*, the man we knew. It might have been revealing to ask him what his childhood was like, growing up in the backstreets of the pressure pot of southern France, with no idea of where you came from, different by virtue of your skin colour. Was he isolated, victimized, lost? It would have been good to explore that with him but of course I was a twenty-year-old dickhead from Greenock more concerned with other important matters – getting laid, getting high, wondering if the girls would think I was cool for hanging out with a black. So the discussion was never initiated – it was all too new for me and I wouldn't admit it. We didn't have black men in Greenock, not like Jérome anyway.

By my own estimate he was ninety-five per cent ugly, there was no avoiding the fact that the mixture in him just did not work. That left only five per cent to be beautiful, and, thankfully, that was enough. What that was, this five per cent, was his emptiness, his melancholy nonchalance. Jérome was indifference cast into a human form. Indifference to what? It didn't matter. The less he said, the less he cared, the more people were drawn to him. He was a star, with a star's mystique, only the fame was missing, but then perhaps fame wouldn't have been good for business.

Five weeks into my stay there, we are sitting round a camp fire at Les Acacias. Some Irish guy is strangling the life out of a guitar and in between gulps of cheap white wine it is possible to hear the strains of 'The House of the Rising Sun' breaking through, like an intermittent broadcast from a far away pirate radio station. Jérome arrived, unannounced and unheralded. He sat down by me and offered his hand.

'*Je suis Jérome.*'

I offer mine back. 'Martin.'

'*Anglais?*'

'*Écossais.*'

Even this briefest of exchanges had taken time; Jérome was a slow, staccato conversationalist. At this point I remember feeling flattered somehow – here is an unusual guy and it is fitting that he has sought me out amongst all the others for this attention. He threw his hands lazily in a kind of rolling motion. What do you do, the gesture asked.

I told him, as best I could in my fractured French, that I was in league with Henri, that I worked the beaches by day. He nodded thoughtfully, an air of sadness and disappointment to him.

'Coool *travail*,' he says, and I recognize the verdict. *Coool* as in uncool, *travail* as in toil or chore. He looks away, judgement has been passed. This kind of work was below him, he thought it might have been below me. I might have wanted to excuse myself, to explain that my French had been too poor for any other kind of work, or that back home I was the grooviest fucker in the university dorm. I didn't though, silence seemed more appropriate, the cool silence Jérome carried around with him. Eventually he stood up, eyes closed, head slowly nodding in agreement with whatever secret thought was occupying his mind.

'*Martin*,' he said, softly but emphatically, absorbing my name as if it were a piece of news in its own right.

'*Oui.*'

A leisurely deep breath before running a hand through his dreadlocked mane, a final acknowledgement that he had made a new acquaintance. I felt as if I had been baptized. The association had begun.

I was doing my rounds, my cool travails, on the beach when the man himself reappeared. I heard him calling, although it was impossible to tell where the shout was coming from. This was the mid-point in the scorching summer of '87, back in the days before the sun gave you skin cancer, back in the days when the Riviera was as chic and precious as you could get in search of a tan, before the *nouveaux* resorts of the Caribbean, Seychelles and the rest had been discovered. No matter that the bodies on Fréjus *plage* were crammed closer than a seal colony in the breeding season, no matter that a trip to the water meant a meandering waltz on the hot coals that passed for sand and required a rugby international's side-step to avoid the spread of towels and pink limbs, no matter that the sea itself if you got there was a soup, a people soup with its own greasy skin lapping around the thousand thighs of the seaside throng. King Canute himself would have loved the scene, for here the waves were defeated, repelled by human force, a mass of democracy scaring away the tide. No sun cream? Just dip yourself in the water sir, it's factor five and a half, just don't dry off when you

51

come out. A swim? In that watery butter? The grease destroys the surface tension, it cannot support your weight, it can't even make you wet. Still, no matter, no matter at all, this was the place to be and I'd already rehearsed my tales for the return to the new autumn term when I would be relaunched as the French parleying playboy of the sands, the beachcomber extraordinaire. It wouldn't turn out that way, not that I knew it at the time. Things just changed, like when he called my name.

It was surprising that I heard him, not that he wasn't loud enough, just that his voice was so heavily accented. *Marre-tain! Yo, Marre-tain!* I look around, back towards the road, and there he is, Jérome *the man*, shaking his head, enjoying the vision of me with my tray, my drinks cooler case, my skip-cap on back to front. I carry it all to him and park myself by his side. *Ça va,* Jérome? He didn't answer, preferring to lift my case to test its weight. Another smile and shake of the head, too heavy, too much effort, an uncool travail.

Of course I know how ridiculous I must seem, and looking at this gangly spiderman's broad smile I can't help but crack up myself. Only Jérome could laugh at you and make you share the joke.

'*Cinq minutes?*' he asked, a hand loosely signposting the path he wanted me to follow, had I a spare five minutes to join him? I can't leave the tray or the ice-box, so I offer the latter to him, I'll come if you carry that. He was less than eager to do so but found himself lugging it anyway, right along to the far east side of the beach and past its end, right along to the marina. We walked in silence, Jérome occasionally breaking into a breathless snigger whenever anything vaguely amusing caught his eye en route; a small dog crapping into the sand, a pink middle-aged man with enormous white tennis shorts and white socks on under his sandals, the sight of me whenever he looked sideways.

Once we were at the marina Jérome halted, dropping the box so that he could slip under the rope that closed off the entrance to the pontoon quays. He lifted it for me to follow. A row of yachts bobbed on either side of the walkway, none of them occupied. This was early afternoon, their owners would still be at lunch. I'd seen before how the boats would come to life when the light faded, when the decks

52

would become the open palaces of the rich. Come and watch us watch you, the plebs of the shore. Watch us sip our cocktails before we hit the clubs and casinos of your land, conquering all with our superior cash. Jérome moved forward purposefully enough, as if his body language refused to acknowledge that he, or I, didn't belong here. He stopped at the last boat on the spur, a sixty-foot monster of gleaming white fibre-glass and varnished wood. I saw it flew the *tricolore*. I looked for its name on the bow; *Anneka*.

'*Ici* . . . *voilà* You like?'

I didn't dislike it, but I couldn't understand why I had been brought along to this berth. A fine boat, sure, but there were other fine boats. Anyway, what had boats got to do with us?

Jérome had put the ice-box down again to hop on to *Anneka*'s deck. I wondered what kind of trouble he could get into for trespassing like this though I tried not to let any concern show, that kind of fretting didn't seem part of the deal. Next he waved me on board as well. I unhooked my tray and joined him, skipping over the ropes and ties that festooned the forward deck. Jérome came towards me and put an arm around my shoulder. 'Welcome,' he said in English, following it up with another English word as he swept the other arm around all we surveyed, 'Home.' And then he laughed, laughed heartily in a way that suggested he knew I would be bemused. *Home*, what did he mean?

Why would he hang around Les Acacias if he could call this place home? He led me inside to explain, down below deck, down past the bridge with its radar and engine control, down to the lounge area off the galley, the plush shag-pile-carpeted living area with its twin sofas and inactive television. Jérome faced me whilst he explained. This could be home, he said in his drawling French plus rapid gestures, home if we wanted it. I listened carefully to his words, thankfully they were slow, as always. Although my French had improved exponentially in the weeks since I had arrived I could still be left behind when the language was fired at me in one long salvo. Jérome took his time, and the point of what he wanted to say was clear enough. Right now, he said, this yacht was empty, the crew and the owners were away, away in the care of the CRS. It was something to do with drugs. The *Anneka* was impounded whilst an investigation went on into those who had been using it. In the meantime anyone could stay here, there was nothing to stop them, the police couldn't give a shit, they would have already searched it and weren't going to bother themselves protecting a smuggler's property, and the real criminals would stay away whilst they thought it was under surveillance. This could be our home for the rest of the summer. What did I say?

Here was a test of nerve, an opportunity for a new experience – would I walk away? I quickly tried to think through the worst possible outcomes, what could happen to me if I agreed, what would anyone do, throw me off the boat one day in disgrace? Jérome smiled at me and I smiled back.

'*Anneka bonne*,' I replied, impressing myself with my balls and all-round cool. 'A good home, *oui*.' I ran my fingers through the silky fabric that covered my sofa and gazed at the painting hanging on the side wall by the bar, an orange and scarlet flash of energy amongst the cream-coloured opulence that surrounded it. It was hard to think this luxury could be mine for any longer than five seconds yet I was willing to gatecrash it all for as long as it lasted. Another tale to bank for the new term, if only.

'You wanted to see me, sir?'

Captain Henry conjured a look of mild surprise. Had he? Yes, of course, *that* matter. His expression grew more stern, a sweep of his arm dismissing the purser and bosun from his cabin. The revised inventory could wait, it made for depressing bookkeeping. A silence grew whilst the men disengaged themselves from the charts and lists strewn across the skipper's desk. Eventually they were gone. Martin faced the captain in the stuffy quiet of his room.

'I am at your service.'

Captain Henry nodded slowly, sagely; a judge sizing up a condemned man before passing sentence.

'Your conduct sir . . . Your conduct during the storm.'

He fixed Martin anew and continued to nod, albeit more slowly. Martin returned the gaze; was there more to this, was he expected to respond?

'My conduct?'

'Precisely, sir. I do not take kindly to panic, not aboard my ship, not amongst my senior crew. I know that what occurred last night could have been *frightening* to an inexperienced mariner, yet I would have expected more . . . expected more . . . *resolve* from you. Yes?'

'It was never my intention either to create or be victim to panic. Two men were trapped –'

The captain was swift to interrupt. History had already been cast, anything that did not tie in with the record was to be instantly dismissed.

'And you *are* a novice seaman, I am a fair man, I appreciate that. What is done is done. We have suffered loss, we must move on. What I require from you, sir, is an apology . . . A momentary lapse of reason. I am a fair man. It could have happened to anyone unfamiliar with the sea, anyone unsettled by her wicked capability. Oh yes, she can be a harsh mistress, the men know that . . . Yes, your apology to the captain and crew. A written apology. To be filed with the ship's log. Once this is done to my satisfaction you may resume your duties.'

'Will that be all, sir?'

'Aye, Doctor . . .', said the captain, returning to the damage reports on the *Anne*'s cargo. '. . . a harsh mistress indeed.'

I had been living on the *Anneka* for three weeks. It was the time of my life. Luxury. Luxury any time, but after six weeks in a tent this was particularly luxurious. Jérome had hooked the boat back into the power supply. I chose not to ask how he had done this or who was paying for the electricity we used, but concentrated on enjoying the thumping bass of the sound system, the coldness of our drinks in the fridge, the flickering images of porn that the video machine fed the television. We had water too, a hot shower and flushing toilet. I bought some bed linen from the supermarket, plus a set for Jérome; some coffee, and started a daily order of bread, milk and bacon. Add the never-ending supply of apple donuts and we were quite the domesticated couple. There was never a word of complaint from our neighbours, mainly because we were an unobtrusive pair. We never entertained in large numbers; the lads refused to join me in my new life at sea, not that I made particularly strenuous efforts to persuade them to come aboard, and having decided that to live this way was dishonest had out of principle – i.e. out of jealousy – refused to come and admire or endorse the new set-up. Jérome himself had few friends, or few that he brought to the *Anneka*. These included a sulking Moroccan who smoked end-lessly without ever offering a cigarette to either of us. He left after a few days once he had exhausted all our food. *Emir*, Jérome called him, meaning Prince, though that could have been a joke, not that there were many laughs going down when he was around. I was glad when he went, as I was with the others, thankfully none of them ever staying more than a night. Why thankfully? Why indeed. Because, I suppose, hypocritically or not, I resented tidying up after these people, resented paying for their meat and drink even if I myself was staying there rent-free. I resented them staying at *my* place, my place because Jérome and I had had the balls to make it our own. And because some of these *arrivistes* scared me with their ways, stubbing out their fags in the carpet, scratching their boots on the varnished oak tabletop, throwing their empty coffee cups into the galley basin from outside of the room. Who the fuck did they think was going to deal with the broken pieces? Part of me was also worried about the price to be paid for all of this lack of respect; Jérome and I were likely to be judged by the standards of these squatters if it ever came to be that we were brought before the boat's real owners. Again I tried to ignore such uncool concerns; Jérome didn't seem unduly possessed by them, so why should I?

The time of my life. I had met a girl on the beach, an English girl named Sue, from Bristol. She was into me, I could tell. I had clocked her on my rounds, her and her friends, first-year art students, English roses ripening under the sun. And this was around the time when I began to feel so comfortable with what I had become, when I saw them looking at me, the deeply tanned, taciturn, donut-selling Scotsman who flattered them with his attention when surely it was him that was the more interesting. Hadn't he addressed them in near-fluent French, didn't he say he lived on a yacht? Yes, I could tell Sue was into me, there were little give-aways like the way she dug her nails deep into my buttocks when she was about to come, the photographs she took of me staring vacantly into her lens, her own loopy take on oral sex, taking my balls in her mouth and going *uhmmm*. Sue got off on me, or what she thought I was, what she took me to be because of the signals I gave; a Celtic renegade, a bit of Scottish rough against which her delicate middle-class womanhood could martyr itself for the summer, a closet intellectual on the run from the profundity of his own philosophy, perhaps living in exile to escape some dark family secret. And don't forget that this guy was also cool enough to have a black Frenchman as his bosom pal and *confidant*. What *did* those two say to each other? Well, Sue, let me explain our mysterious chat now, all these years later. Jérome would ask me, *Elle était bonne? Elle était cochonne? Elle suçait bien?* Was it a good fuck, were you dirty, was your pussy tight and did you hold your breath when I went deep? And we would laugh that we could discuss this in front of you without you understanding any of it, enjoying your friendly smile as the conversation sailed past you. And we would laugh when I told him you were going to write to me once you got back home, write to me care of the *Anneka*, the boat you thought we owned. The dark family secret? There was one, a hideous one. Two secrets. My father was an assistant bank manager and I was going to be an engineer. I am from Greenock, not Glasgow. Three secrets.

Sue, if you read this, I'm sorry. At least the donuts were real.

The delegation came to see me on the beach. I could see they were uneasy by the way they kept catching each other's eye as they glanced around for support. Paul opened up the proceedings and when I made it difficult for him Maurice stepped forward with a let's-be-reasonable-about-this take on the matter. I made it difficult for him as well and that was enough to keep Ian quiet the whole time. I was probably unreasonable, I know that now, and knew it then as well perhaps. What I was doing was conducting my own experiment in group dynamics and enjoying the fact that they were scared of me. Their gripe? They wanted to go home, they had had enough, ten weeks or more to be precise. Selling donuts had never gripped them the way it did me, and they had eventually given up, trade had been hard. So they chose to come to me and do their best to obstruct mine whilst they explained this. I didn't stand in their way as far as returning to Scotland was concerned, or so it seemed to me. They however, unanimously, saw it differently. They wanted money, my share of the campsite rent from when I stayed with them under canvas. It was funny how things had changed. We had set out as four lads, equals, before evolving into a group with me as its leader, though not by choice, and now this final stage, mutiny. I had two problems with their demand for cash. The first was that even if I had still been living with them I would have been reluctant to pay rent as it was always the plan to abscond in a moonlit flit, hadn't that been why we had chosen Les Acacias? This question made for another exchange of furtive looks whilst they silently debated who would answer it. The point is, said Paul, a lawyer now if you hadn't guessed, the point is we are not happy with that kind of dishonesty, they have been good to us at that site and we don't want to repay them that way. He said *we* in a way that managed to convey that I wasn't included. Now here was a problem within a problem for me, because while I can applaud someone's desire to live by a high set of morals I'm fucked if I'm going to be the one that actually pays for them to do so. I said a few words to this effect and also opened up an additional line of enquiry by asking after what I perceived to be their collective loss of nerve on all things outrageous. Wasn't that what the holiday was going to be about, were we really going to end it with a squabble about thirty quids' rent? By taking this line I was hoping to raise the debate to a higher level, a sky-high level where the entire thing might just drift off and evaporate. I was hoping to throw them off the scent of my second problem with their whining for cash, the rather more pressing one, the fact that I didn't have any. Sure I had been living free on the *Anneka* and making more than a fair crack on the very sands we stood on, trade had been good and I had done well. Nevertheless, right then I didn't have a spare centime, a situation purely down to cash-flow. The day before I had paid Jérome two and a half thousand francs – over two hundred pounds – for a sizeable lump of quality Moroccan hash. I hadn't exactly meant to but there it was, I had made my investment, I didn't have any more money and no amount of talking was going to change that until I could get working again. This information was something I chose not to share with the boys even if the price of that was to let them think I was a bastard. I told them I would think about it and lifted my tray and ice-box to wade right back into the throng on the beach. They were smart enough to know that this was a fob-off, smart yet impotent. I haven't spoken to Ian or Maurice since, their loss I tell myself. Paul would come back once more, weeks later, trying in his own way to be a true friend. I would punish him for that.

So.

How do you buy a sizeable stash of drugs by mistake? In my case it was all down to language, Jérome's language. *Du grass?* he had asked. This was one night on the *Anneka*. In the early weeks, in our honey-moon period when we were still getting to know and understand each other, Jérome spoke to me in a mixture of French and English, choosing words individually to suit the level of cool he wanted in the sentence. These components, the words and sentences, would then be thrown into the mix with a full array of gestures, some telling, others not. Some might simply have been nervous twitches joining in by mistake. And the net result was that whilst you could just about follow what he was saying you were never particularly sure of what he actually meant. You could never split the sincere from the sarcastic, the arch and knowing from the naive. *Du grass?* for instance, could mean do you want some grass if taken as literal French, in the same way *du café?* asks if you would like a coffee. It could also mean have you ever heard of grass, do you know of it, have you experienced it. If you took it as a typically pidgin-English expression Jérome might use, it becomes *do grass*, as in *let's do some grass!*, a proposal or exhortation. Jérome didn't talk so much as to communicate, it was more to open up avenues of confusion. That, I suppose, is how it could come to be that he would speak (unusually) animatedly about hash, and how Moroccan hash was the best, how it comes packed and pressed tight together and how the colour of it and its taste are the keys to its quality, and then how he had an enormous lump of the stuff that he was particularly excited about. And it came to be that as he said all this I nodded along enthusiastically, warmed by his good spirits, unaware that I was actually agreeing to buy the whole fucking lot from him. Actually that realization didn't come until two days later when he woke me up one morning to ask if I had that money we had talked about, and that he hoped that I had because there were two guys waiting on the deck who were going to be pissed off if I didn't. I remember sneaking a glance up the stairway and seeing Jérome wasn't kidding; two thick-set swarthy Arabs in bomber jackets looking sore and tetchy fiddling with the rigging. This was when they weren't pissed off and they were scary enough. So the realization had been sudden, with the total time from being asleep to being told I was part of a deal to the tune of two thousand-odd francs to confirming that violence would ensue if the deal was reneged upon to actually handing over the money – my summer savings – being about forty-five seconds. Jérome hadn't even said good morning. The other realizations – that a new career was opening up for me, or would have to if I wanted to see my money again or even wanted enough back for a ticket home – would come later. In the meantime Jérome unwrapped my precious new possession and held it under my nose, a quarter-brick of dry dusty earth with a sharp scent. He laughed gleefully and rubbed its sides with his ebony fingers so that loose flakes and particles began to rain down from it on to the newspaper on the table. I watched him gather these together, folding up the paper so that the hash gathered in the centrefold gutter, and begin to craft a joint, patching one long reefer together from six different cigarette papers. He worked in silence and was kind enough to offer me the first draw once his creation was complete and lit. I was never a big fan of dope, I tended to associate it with hippies and heavy-metal fans back home. However, now that I was an investor, I felt I should make the effort, even if it was still only eight a.m. or some other ridiculous early hour. Besides, I needed something to help me cope with the rapid turn of events. More importantly, and more ludicrously, I wanted to show Jérome I was still cool, cool about everything; staying on the yacht, giving up all my money, smoking dope first thing in the morning. In a way, it was all for show, all just to shock myself. I looked to Jérome and smiled, put the reefer to my lips and drew in, one long draw. The smoke hitting my lungs was hotter than the air off the sands at midday. I had to struggle to maintain composure and not surrender to a coughing fit. What the fuck was this about, I asked myself in that instant, was this meant to be pleasurable? Then it was as if someone had painted a smile on my face, or planted it, a smile so wide I felt my lips were parting to my ears. Everything was turning mellow. I wanted to speak but couldn't think of the French words. Or the English. What did I want to say? I wanted to say Hey, Jér . . . Whatever else you said you were right about this, it's the best. The very best, a cool travail.

An Apology to Captain Henry and the crew of the Anne *by Martin Law. On this the tenth day of April, sixteen hundred and ninety eight.*

I hereby register my profoundest regret at the actions and events of the evening of the eighth of April in the year of our Lord 1698. I do this with particular regard to my own actions and wilful disregard of Captain Henry's orders concerning the momentary flood which affected the starboard hold during the severe storm which assailed our good ship on this night.

I cannot deny that when I saw the extent of that flood and realized the predicament of the two men, O'Rourke and McGill, who had been previously sent down into the hold space to maintain the stability of the cargo during the violent actions the storm induced within the ship, normal sense deserted me.

In short, I became unduly concerned with the fate of these men, unaware that all crew owe their first concern to their captain and ship. It was not my choice to make as to how the men should be retrieved from below the water, it was the captain's alone.

I realize that for ship's discipline to be maintained all crew must await instruction from their captain. I realize that the two men trapped below would also have known this and would have been waiting for instruction to reach them before leaving their posts. My actions could have impeded the slow deliberations Captain Henry was making with regard to the best course of action for his crew.

In the future I will strive to give Captain Henry and his decisions the respect he should expect from me.
(signed) Martin Law

Two days in port at Garachico on the island of Tenerife was all that was required to put right the damage inflicted by the storm. The ship's carpenters toiled in the heat for barely an afternoon as timbers and fractured splints were repaired, Canarian woods replacing the materials of the previous patching exercise. The main work was to do with the restoration of cargo to its original state, the hot sun scorching off the last vestiges of water which had soaked through the flooded holds. Indeed the stopover saw the harbour used as little more than a drying yard for this express purpose. To Captain Henry and his purser, time was money, but so also was the cargo, and with more than half of this being made up of one form of cloth or another it made sense to have this in its best possible condition in order to maximize its trading value. Thus Martin and the crew would become briefly familiar once more with the feel of solid earth beneath their feet as the display of calico, muslin, fustian, West Country plains and Cape cloths dazzled under a bright sky, blossoming briefly under the sun like some giant exotic flower at the quayside before being folded and packed away anew.

The second day saw the end of the process and the final preparations for the next leg of the voyage. A quantity of ropes and lines were brought aboard, together with, at Martin's insistence, several cases of limes. Three new crew-members also joined, Spanish and Portuguese hands replacing some of those lost earlier, hired by the captain after a cursory inspection of their talents on the rigging. Men who barely spoke English but presumably understood the universal laws of the sea, willing to throw in their lot with a cast of strangers from another land. Another throw of the dice. At eleven o'clock on the nine-teenth of April the *Anne* set sail. She was headed for Africa.

Hello girls, how you all doing? Like it here, bit crowded isn't it? Rumour has it that there is some sea out there once the sand ends, never seen it myself mind . . . You're students? I knew a girl from there, studied criminology and archaeology, a joint degree . . . Really! Well that's what she told me anyway . . . Where are you staying? Cheaper at Les Acacias . . . About three miles inland, where we started out . . . No, not any longer, on a yacht, you should come round some time, for a cup of tea, English tea, you miss that? Glasgow . . . Yeah, second-year . . . Art . . . School of art, design and shit, you know? Anyway, you guys got money or are you going to end up a destitute donut seller like me? Don't knock it, want to try one? Fucking delicious . . . One between you then . . . Get your lips round that, wonderful, non? Listen – what did you say your names were? Right, I never forget a name, not a beautiful name . . . I really hope you all like it here, it's a cool place, been here three months and I feel more French than Scottish, honestly . . . Understand it or speak it? Both, can't help it if you mix with them every day, the other guy on the yacht, you know, you just pick it up naturally. Anyway, better be on my way, got to get on with it, these fucking things don't sell themselves, you know . . . See you around, if you ever need anything I'm here on the beach every day, be happy to help you out . . . Yeah, Martin . . . Say, girls – fancy getting a little high?

Did I find it easy? I suppose so, but only because of what I had already learned, how to judge your market, how to see who was likely to be up for it, the signals to give. The trick was to flatter your audience, give the assumption that they were as cool as you and then concentrate on giving the coolest fucking signals this side of the north pole. Been high recently? Want to be high? A subtle approach, not really a question, not really an offer, but if they agree you can hook them into a trans-action, the way Jérome had with me. That's something that struck me in those early days of dealing, that he had known exactly what he was doing when he mesmerized me with his talk. And all that hand jiving that went on with it, the gestures and shapes he would throw, all deliberate, all brilliantly conceived to offer an escape route if things went wrong. All a defence, all designed to unsettle. Maybe that was the legacy of a black childhood in a white city, maybe that's just how they all talk in Marseille. Speaking one moment as a friend, the next as a salesman; drawing you close one minute, then putting up a barrier the next, one that you choose to overcome. To overcome by buying, buying whatever.

On the beach I would put these lessons into practice, parading up and down my patch, giving off the signs that I was having a great time, sizing up the opportunities, the English students in search of the same things I had been only weeks earlier. Girls? The easiest; talk to them and look them in the eye, ignore their bare breasts being exposed to the sun for the first-ever time, they love you for that. Talk to them all like you want to be their friend, that you *expect* to be their friend. When you speak you watch carefully to try and make out who is going for it, who is reaching out to you in return. Then you offer them the chance to prove that they are as cool as you, to prove that they aren't square at all, at least not for these two weeks on the Med. *Want to get a little high?*

I sold that first stash with ease, shocking ease. It was fucking harder to shift donuts. Welcome to the world of repeat customers and recom-mended clientele. There were risks involved I suppose, but I doubled my money on that first trade, and it could and should have been much more than that. Then again, I was hardly in a position to know what the market rate for goods such as mine was, I was more concerned with what I thought my beach punters would pay. There were other things, like where to hide the drugs themselves. I wanted my stash off the *Anneka* if only to keep Jérome's greedy fingers from rubbing any profit margin away into nothing but his own reefer masterpieces. No, it made more sense to take it away from the yacht, away from temptation, away from the CRS who may still have had the craft under surveillance for all we knew. Take it away, but where? I did think about returning to Les Acacias to bury the hatchet with the lads, and bury the gear whilst I was at it. That was the plan until an even better one occurred to me one morning whilst rendezvousing with the rest of the beach patrol: Henri's van. We would clamber in to retrieve our trays at the start of each day and stuffing my wrapped package into the wall cladding was not hard; from then it was just a matter of being inconspicuous whilst recovering it and cutting off an amount to meet the day's sales projection. In the midst of the regular morning mêlée this could be done without drawing too much attention, the real sweat was leaving the rest of it behind for another twenty-four hours, never knowing if you had just said goodbye to it for the last time. It had to be this way though; self-taught as I was, the golden rule of my new game seemed obvious – don't get caught with the full goods. Assuming the worst and you were arrested at some stage, the amount you had on you would make the difference between being treated as a bona-fide dealer or a naive kid trying to help out his mates. I always worked with the latter in mind, thinking of the signals I would have to give from the first moments I felt suspicious eyes upon me.

For all the heaviness of these travails, I have to say, as I have said, that this was the time of my life. If I only doubled my money on the first deal, I tripled it on the next, and so on for the rest of the summer. The money was easy and becoming easier. My French became fluent, and I loved to hear myself speak it, a reminder of how far I had travelled since arriving. I was surprising myself every day with the extent of the transformation that had occurred over the course of the summer – thinner, darker, more assured, wealthier. And girls? In the space of months they had changed too, no longer unobtainable icons to be worshipped from afar, now an endless conveyor belt of ready-plucked fruits, each to be enjoyed for its own unique taste. Yet this was another change that was down to me, or Jérome to be precise. It was his language I had learned here, his knack of seeming bold and direct, but all the while being impossible to pin down in terms of intent. Language and gestures, choice of words. You meet some shy girl from Bristol, or Bavaria or wherever, and you offer your interest. Are you being friendly or forward? When it's the latter are you offering a relationship that might continue for the summer or beyond, or even just tonight? The right word, the right smile, squeeze of a hand or pat on the backside and you can offer them all, you can leave it to her to decide what the score is, that way there is no one else to blame. Ambiguity as a strength, the posting of a challenge. That's what I learned and that summer I could have screwed for Scotland – if only there were international caps for performance at the highest level I would have been up there with the other greats – Baxter, Dalglish, the other Law, all of them. Lessons learned on the sands of the beach, my real education.

The guys left sometime mid-September. Jérome said they had been up to the *Anneka* one Sunday evening, I couldn't figure if it would have been to say goodbye or to harp on about money. Jérome didn't ask me what my plans were, true to form, he didn't really give a shit other than to know when I would buy the next load of hash. I had sussed by then of course that he was making his living from the cut he made in the deals as middleman for his Arab connection. How far down the line they themselves were was irrelevant, as was the question of whether my customers themselves were the end consumers or traders like me. None of it mattered, but sometimes I would find myself staring at the crowds on the sands, wondering how many were linked in our little chain of events, how many were making money from it, and how many were paying out. That's one of the worst problems about being a hustler, and I had it right then, although I was still too young to recognize it as a dangerous symptom. You see everything as part of a deal, everyone as someone to be taken or someone looking to take you, and everywhere the grasping hands hungry for their chance to cheat the system. You judge everyone by yourself.

Anyway.

The guys had gone and I didn't stop to wonder what I thought about that. I didn't stop to think about my own journey home now that the new term was drawing so close. The beach grew more quiet, and trade with it. By the last week in September it had died completely and Henri closed down his operation for the year. I had to find new hiding places for my gear – a locker at St Raphaël train station, the base of my ice-box which would be left overnight with various unsuspecting girls, and, eventually, on the *Anneka*. Crazy risks for the money involved but still part of my education. As for my other education, I hadn't actually realized term had started until Paul showed up one day at the marina. It was a surprise to see him, and even more of a shock to discover that he was back here on a mission, the mission to bring me home.

Of course, years later I begin to understand the sacrifice he would have made in making the journey – he was missing the start of term to come and persuade me to get back on the right path. I also found out that it was thanks to him my father did not travel out instead; no, it was Paul who persuaded him that he on his own would have greater success, Paul who promised he would not return alone. The poor bastard even had to endure yet another night under canvas, somewhere other than Les Acacias obviously, and this time in the cold of late October, as part of the mission. And then there was what I told him, none of which would have been any use in terms of explaining it all back in Scotland. *Well Mr Law, your son says you are a cunt, and that since Mrs Law passed away courtesy of the bowel cancer that had left her resembling not so much a person as a bag of bones hooked into a drip machine there has been a bit of the old joy about family life missing from the Law household, particularly since you seem to have reacted to this by being increasingly cunty to your sons and especially Martin. Now he's not sure if there was a purpose to his mother's death but does feel that if there was it was not so that he might get an engineering degree which he perceives is your take on this. And whilst he appreciates it must have been hard on you it was also hard on the boys who, in hindsight, could have done with more support in any fucking way other than encouragement to dedicate themselves to study in order to ease their mother's passage into heaven. So what has happened is that, just like you, they have closed down, so to speak, or not to speak in that no one has anything left to say to each other and Martin sees little point in returning to Greenock, Glasgow, or any fucking place to be honest.*

We had a kind of awkward chat on the deck of the boat, then an awkward meal together and an awkward couple of drinks until late evening. I couldn't tell him how I'd been making my money or why it was I had stayed on so long. The tales I *could* tell – about the endless female conquests – began to sound like misplaced bragging when Paul spoke of his new girlfriend in Scotland. So I finished the conversation by promising to think about it all, by saying that naturally I would be going back some time only it might be a week or so later. Yes, I would think about it all and tell him when I was definitely leaving so that we could go together if I brought the departure forward like he wanted. This time I didn't mean to fob him off, I really meant to do what I had promised. But I didn't get a chance to think, or even to speak to him again. I might have meant to, it just didn't turn out that way.

You get used to noises if you live on a boat. You would never sleep otherwise. The wind blowing in the rigging, sails and pennants flapping, the groaning of the rudder and belly as they wrestle with the waves; they can all sound like someone talking, or shouting, or plodding about on deck. You get used to it, get used to ignoring it. You wouldn't sleep otherwise. I was deep in the Land of Nod when I realized we had company. Miles away. I was sleeping in the forward berth with an Irish girl called Jane, from Belfast, or somewhere around there, it's not really relevant. Anyway, I'd been with her for about three days and this was our second night together. Jane hadn't got used to the noises at all and had swiftly developed a habit of poking me in the fucking ribs every time there was a squeak in the bow, or if Jérome snored loudly or if a squid farted in the Mediterranean underneath us. She developed this habit and I developed the habit of ignoring it, turning my back on her so she would have to prod my cold shoulder every time she wanted reassurance that we were OK. I wouldn't sleep otherwise. Second night, 15 October 1987, the night Paul and I had been for our man-to-man about my future and she prodded and prodded as if there was no fucking tomorrow. She thought someone had come aboard, thought she could hear voices and told me so, leaning up to tell it right into my ear. I lifted the pillow and buried my head under it, not at my most accommodating when on sleeping duty, why couldn't she chill out, crazy bitch, why was she so paranoid? Then the whole bed was trembling and this pissed me off even more; how was I ever going to kip with this and her freaking out for no reason? Then I was suddenly wide awake and scared shitless as I realized that the trembling meant someone had started up the engine.

By the time we were both up and standing Jérome had run through in his underpants and there we were exchanging frantic glances whilst we tried to work out what the fuck was going on. Jane and I were naked, desperately hunting in the dark for our underwear with Jérome gesticulating unusually fast. There wasn't a lot of dignity in the moment, nor understanding or poise, nor taking in of what each other might be trying to convey. The wires in my brain were wrapping themselves around each other and tying themselves in knots in a desperate effort to close off any redundant thought. That was how it could be so easy to ignore Jane's hysterical whispering, to look upon Jérome with only token interest and to concentrate all energies on finding your knickers. Bragging apart, I've been in more scrapes than most, and I've got out of more scrapes than most, and I'm sure it's down to some kind of ability to focus right down on to the most pressing issue of the moment Staying cool is all about not being overwhelmed by the number of decisions that have to be taken but working through them one at a time. That's what all the great commanders had, this ability to do just that, and they were either born with it or learned the technique so that they could just fire through the issues in a logical sequence, from the first to the next then another, faster and faster. Think of Nelson at Trafalgar, immersed in layer after layer of choices, in charge of his ship, then in charge of the fleet, then the whole British Navy. The guns going off all around but he kept his focus, kept thinking in a sequence of single decisions, refusing to rush into all of them. Mind you of course, he was shot dead at the end of it so keeping himself under cover was probably way down his list. Anyway, you go through it one by one; where are my pants, do we introduce ourselves or wait to be discovered, do we arm ourselves, do we pass ourselves off as *Anneka's* owners and try to bluff our way out or do we volunteer that our stay is now over and wish the new guests all the best? Who leads our delegation, what do I tell Jane who thinks this is our yacht and wants to call the police? And last in my sequence, but by no means least important, if we do leave the boat right here and now, how do I retrieve the kilo of Moroccan hash that I've hidden in with the first-aid kit on the bridge? The answer to the last dictates the answer to all the others as a plan forms in my mind. I need time to retrieve my stash, it's too precious to jeopardize, representing, as it does, both a seven-thousand-franc investment and my whole summer's travails on the beach. Therefore I will introduce ourselves and take the lead in any negotiation. I will offer to leave immediately and with no fuss, if, that is, the people up on deck are serious and not kids larking about. There would have to be another set of choices if that is the case, including just how hard we want to fight to stay on the *Anneka*, and is it worth fighting back-to-back with Jérome, and what would we be fighting for?

It makes more sense to surrender. I speak to Jérome first, in French. I'm going up to sort it out, any ideas who it will be? He drops his shoulders. I guess not, or he's choosing not to tell me. Then to Jane; I'll see what's going on, you stay here and gather up your stuff, we'll probably have to leave right away. She looks confused, *why?* Her question sails past; unanswered, irrelevant. She can work it out for herself later. I'm on to the next decision, walking up the steps to greet the intruders. What should I say?

'*Excusez moi, bonsoir?*'

I said this to no one in particular, before my head reached the level of the floor of the bridge. I wanted to show I was not scared and to give a signal that I expected to control this situation, that it would be talked through. In the event, my announcement was heard by only one man and he couldn't have been less impressed. A stocky, bearded man in sweatshirt and jeans running some kind of check on the bridge control panels. He turned around to stare quizzically at me as I emerged; early forties, vaguely hostile, he remained silent. I would later learn that conversation wasn't really his thing. This was Michel, another discovery I would have to wait for – he didn't introduce himself. Why use one word when none will do?

Then I said something else, I can't really remember, something inane, some attempt to say the same thing with different words, as if that would make a difference, some attempt to fill the silence which was becoming heavier with every second Michel's scowl of a stare was fixed on me. I would have started to get into how there were another two of us in the berths below, maybe trying to ask if he was planning on taking the boat somewhere immediately or if he was just carrying out a periodic examination. And all my flustered attempts to communicate were greeted with more of Michel's very own brand of silence. I began to wonder if he were deaf, some kind of mute. Then I turned to follow his gaze which had lifted so that his eyes were fixed on something over my shoulder. I had an audience, two other forty-ish men, sweating, taking a breath, the boxes they had been loading at their feet. Luc and Jean, they didn't look like sailors, more like stuntmen from a film, extras with a vague resemblance to the star, but never as convincing.

I begin again, this time facing them instead of their cheery colleague. *Bonsoir. Nous sommes très . . ..* That was about as far as I got; this pair were even less talkative than their shipmate, one turning his back on me completely to reach inside a crate, the other closing his eyes and raising a hand as if directing traffic, or, to be more precise, halting traffic. Stop.

'*Allez-vous faire, cinq minutes.*'

A gruff voice, speaking in southern slang, not Riviera slang, but earthy Provence slang. I'd heard the expression just once before, a friend of Henri's arguing with him about the van. *Allez-vous faire.* The speaker had been from Toulon, Henri said they were all animals there. This was Henri, with his never-changing wardrobe and abstinence from any form of hygiene, dental or body. I knew things had to be bad in Toulon though I wouldn't make reference to this fact when I was to learn that this merry threesome, the new *Anneka* crew, were all natives of the city. *Allez-vous faire.* Translated literally it means go make yourself, interpreted a little more politely it could mean go sort yourself out. Inherent in the phrase but not stated in either explanation is the expression of whatever it is that you, the intended receiver, are saying or doing is of no interest or relevance to *me*, the speaker. In that regard perhaps the best English translation might be something like 'you can go and fuck yourself for all I care'. Then again the degree of offence that is intended to go along with the saying depends on the way it is delivered, which in turn depends on the non-verbal communication going on alongside. It also depends, to an extent, on the degree of offence the receiver chooses to take. This multi-scaled tower of meanings was to make the phrase a favourite of mine. I didn't know it right then when I was hearing it for the second time in my life and imagining that the very lowest form of insult was being aimed at me, but it would work out that way. I wasn't to know for instance that years later, in my bar, I would always be showing off with it, whispering in French to easily impressed English girls eager to hear the language of love. *Allez-vous faire*, I would murmur to some enraptured slapper, *allez-vous faire, mon amour*. I told them it meant you make my love complete, as if that in itself made any sense. It didn't, of course, and I doubt whether the truth would have had them pissing themselves like it did me. Still, it's not what you say but the passion with which you say it, and I was always sincere when I was telling them to go fuck themselves.

Sincere.

We had five minutes to get off. I went back down to tell the others.

Unbeknownst to Martin, the ship had been holding a pronounced westerly course, Captain Henry taking great care to avoid being blown into the Bay of Biscay which, with its contrary winds, could have taken weeks to clear, bankrupting the venture before it had begun in earnest. It was this policy that had taken the vessel into the danger of the mid-Atlantic storms, he would later learn. Yet, amongst the crew who would secretly criticize him for leading them into such waters, there was a grudging respect for the skipper's navigational skills; once the almost catastrophic tempest had been cleared and the *Anne* steered in a south-easterly course, progress had been astonishingly fast. Sailing out of Tenerife this procedure was repeated, four days of patient tacking against the wind making dogged headway west followed by a turn to the south to employ a prevailing wind which had the ship hurtling toward the Guinea coast on a strong southern Atlantic swell. Martin noticed that spirits tended to be high when the ship moved rapidly; the crew sang their shanties as they worked, blessing their luck with the weather, whilst the captain allowed himself a discreet smile, although probably more with pride in his own seamanship than at his crew's ringing harmonies, Martin suspected.

These were the halcyon days of the voyage, the ones to be treasured. Such was the strength of the breeze that the *Anne*, which had been using barely half of her sail capacity, was soon employing less than a quarter, taking down the topgallant, mizzen and main course sails to leave only the foremost to pull her along from the front. For an overloaded, overcrewed merchantman she would have made an impressive sight; the captain ordering the larboard watch to slacken off the foremost so that the wind would catch underneath the canvas, lifting her bow clear of the foaming waters that would otherwise threaten to bury her nose. The ship was now clearing more than fifty leagues a day with such effortless sailing. Perhaps, thought Martin, Mr Henry has a right to be proud, for the passage certainly has a momentum.

Halcyon days. They did not know it, but once they reached Africa progress would slow, day by day, watch by watch, hour by hour. Until, in fact, they were making none at all.

Telling moments in my life. I stripped the bed of the sheets and laid them on the floor. I threw my clothes, books, extra shoes, assorted mementos, a cup or two, travel clock, toiletries and all the rest into the middle and gathered up the ends so that I had a makeshift bag of swag over my shoulder. The girl, Jane, was still asking questions, still scared, still waiting for some kind of justice to be served so that we could have my yacht back. Jérome was just sullen, he hadn't gathered much together, maybe he didn't have that much to gather. They followed me up the stairs, albeit warily. When we made it on to the deck we could see that one of the men was untying the ropes that fastened the *Anneka* to the quayside. At the rear deck I could see that we had been detached from the marina's ground line, the hull was already beginning to drift. Departure was imminent. I made to help Jane off and on to the dock. A voice told me to stop whilst one of the men went below deck, presumably to check we weren't making off with the ship's interior fittings. So another wait, another exchange of looks, shrugs and whispers between us three being evicted whilst this went on. I ignored them all as best I could, keeping an eye on Jane all the same, just in case she chose to get hysterical. I didn't know how the new crew would take it if she did, I could only imagine it would be badly. I looked to the bridge. In the panel above the radar screen the white first-aid box remained. And inside that box, as well as first-aid materials, my stash. The question was, how could I get to it? Everything now came down to this, this and how much did I want it.

The bearded man emerged from the depths, nodding to the one who had sent him down. It was OK, ship-shape, fixtures and fittings still there, we could go, a jerk of the thumb towards the quay telling us so. Jérome slowly gathered up his holdall and made his lazy progress towards the slipway, head bowed.

'*Au revoir, Jérome.*'

One of them said it, Jérome ignored it but looked embarrassed, the others laughed. They knew him, and he knew them. He didn't look scared, though there must have been a reason why he'd been happy for me to face them initially rather than him. He threw his bag on to the land and hopped over to follow it. Jane sought my eye for her instruction. I told her to follow and took her hand to steady her as she left the boat. That left me standing on the lolling deck, possessions slung over my shoulder in a piece of knotted cloth like Dick Whittington. Something kept me there. Something made me speak. I tried to sound like a native.

'You guys travelling far?'

'Perhaps.'

'She's a beautiful boat.'

'*Oui, bien sûr.*' Sure thing, someone said. This was almost like a conversation, although none of the new crew seemed to be paying undue attention. One of them jumped on to the quay to let loose the last of the ties. They were casting off.

'I think I've left something behind, can I look?'

None of them answered, at least, not immediately. I heard the engine being revved to a new level and realized this was it, goodbye *Anneka*, goodbye stash. Except it wasn't.

'*Vous comprenez les bateaux?*' You know boats, came the question after my question. We were beginning to slowly ebb away from the quayside.

'*Mais oui.*' Of course. Of course *not*, might have been a more honest answer, all I knew was how to sleep on one.

'*Nous allons maintenant.*' We're going now. That's what was said, literally, but again the meaning was slightly different, slightly longer. We're going now, this is your last chance to leave.

'*Ou?*'

'*En Turquie.*'

I couldn't really tell you why I was still there at this stage, or why sailing to Turkey with three complete strangers might have seemed a good idea, nor why I lied about being a yachtsman. All I can say is that I was still just a twenty-year-old dickhead from Greenock, that I was annoyed at Jérome for not letting on for whatever reason that he knew these men, that I couldn't be bothered explaining to Jane why we had been evicted, and that there was about a thousand pounds' worth of my hash still hidden in the first-aid box on the bridge.

On such sound foundations decisions are made. I put down my gear.

'*Turquie bien.*'

I chose not to look but was aware of the shapes of Jane and Jérome in the gloom, further and further away. What would they make of me, would they run into Paul, and tell him I'd absconded? All three of my new shipmates were busy. I watched them examining the rigging – perhaps we would set sail once out of the harbour. I half-expected them to hoist the skull and crossbones. I knew I'd done it at last. I knew I'd joined a pirate ship.

I had left a note for Sarah, asking her to open up the bar once she arrived and to wait for me. She had only been working for a couple of weeks but I was sure she could cope, she was a bright girl, beautifully bright. I had seen that from the first moment she came into the Arena just the month before, looking for work. It was why I had taken her on when I hadn't really required anyone else, and couldn't even afford someone extra. Maybe I knew that someday I would pay anything for that brightness, anything to lift the heaviness of everything else going down. Sarah with her flashing eyes and weather-girl smile would have the place buzzing with positive energy soon enough, and would have taken everything else in her confident stride – making the espresso machine whistle perkily, putting the froth in the cappuccinos, making the toast pop up with an exuberance bordering on the unnatural. She would be doing all this so that whilst I was there in an empty abandoned house in the mountains, struggling to cope with a loneliness that I'd been working up for a lifetime I could at least console myself that my latest screwed-up fuckhead staff recruitment decision might have actually come good just when I needed it most and that if I could just make it back to Puerto Puals there would be that smile to greet me. A woman's smile. A girl's fresh smile. A comforting smile. If I could just make it along that road I could be a customer in my own bar, sitting there gathering my thoughts and she could bring me a coffee, something light to eat, and she would notice how down I was and would ask if I was OK. *Martin, is everything all right, what's happened, what can I do*

76

for you? Maybe I would tell her, maybe not straight away so that she could watch me struggle manfully with the weight of the world on my shoulders until she teased the reluctant truth out of me with her feminine guile.

The truth.

Just feeling her bright eyes upon me would be enough to take some of the pain away, just watching her cotton dress float from table to table, taking her lithe limbs with it but leaving its citrus and sandalwood perfume trail in its wake would be enough to take my mind off the mess that made up the rest of my life's rich tapestry. Maybe she could give me the will to start again. Maybe I could lean on her until the strength that had deserted me came back.

I wandered around the house for twenty minutes or so, it seemed a lot longer, roaming absently from room to room, looking for an answer, like a rat in a laboratory maze, twitching, nervy. Eventually, the walls began to close in around me, and I threw a selection of clothes into a suitcase, together with some music and toiletries. I lifted a bottle of aftershave and a picture of my daughter from the bedroom, the gathering of essentials becoming more and more hurried. I had to get out, shock was giving way to an anger that I was struggling to cope with, an anger that made me want to wreck the place. So this was not good enough for her, after all I'd done to make it possible, after how I'd slaved to sustain it. Why the fuck was I working so hard when obviously no one was happy? So she didn't want a home, well fuck her, neither did I. I'd clear out as well, let's see where that gets us, bitch. Wouldn't it be great if I could just walk out of things as well and leave some other poor fuck to sort it all out, but that's not the way it works is it? Hardly part of the plan that says you screw it up, I clear it up. Not this time though. Come back for the rest of your things and you'll see I've left it all to you for a change.

I threw my case into the jeep and took a look back at the house, wondering if I could remember all the alarm codes. They were in my head somewhere, the problem was calming down sufficiently to find them, and doing that I guess meant losing some of the sense of righteousness that was keeping me going. No codes, the fucking building would have to fend for itself, like me. I didn't have the energy. I could barely move, suddenly aware I was wheezing like an asthmatic. I climbed into the front seat, ever more short of breath, ever more desperate to get away, dizzy to the point of nausea. What the fuck was wrong, was I about to have a heart attack? The problem was worsening with every breath despite my attempts to slow down and just fill up my lungs. Then the panic made it all go faster, and I wondered if there was so much cocaine still in my system that that was the problem, but this was all new to me and I had taken much more in the past to nothing like this effect. I thought of Sarah at the other end, and how she could take care of me, how she would insist on calling a doctor, and then he would check it out, give me a shot to stop the pain. I put my foot down hard and heard the gravel crunch and go flying under the spite of the wheels; this and a full lock on the steering sent the jeep spinning into a turn as it pitched into reverse.

And I looked into the mirror more by instinct than anything else, safe driving wasn't really high on the agenda. I tried to look out of the rear window but it was my own reflection that drew me as the mystery was solved. I was crying, crying uncontrollably, another new one on me.

Two o'clock, maybe a little later by the time I eventually made it to the Arena Bar. This was later than planned, breakfast had been and gone, and lunch was winding down. There was no Sarah, no welcoming smile, no words of comfort. It had all been a fantasy. The place was a shitheap and no one seemed to give a fuck, other than the half-assed jerk who presumably parked his dick in her on a regular basis, who presumably she had a thing for, presumably in a half-assed jerk thing kind of way. Jesus, his very presence on the planet, let alone in my bar irritated me so much I could hardly sit with it. What the fuck was she doing with him?

I'm referring, of course, to Alexander, Sarah's other half, and the other half of my latest lunatic recruitment drive. I hadn't meant to take him on but I had, it just worked out that way, there was an inevitability to it. There's me, ageing fucking swinger, killing an already dead after-

78

noon in a dead bar at the end of a dead summer season. She walked in, radiant, vivacious, and somewhere maybe fifteen years my junior. There was nothing especially unusual about her, sure she had her happiness button switched on, the way some of these young student-traveller-year-out-types have, the attractive ones at least, going around greeting the world with such innocence and delight that even grizzled foreigners like me will yield to their insouciant charm. Want a job? Sure baby, it's your destiny to light up my bar. Never worked a tab system before? No problem, you'll pick it up. Don't speak Spanish? Ditto. I'll pay you just to be the person you are, right here with me, and you can write home and tell them they were all wrong, that you are having a great time and that everyone you've met is actually very friendly and helpful, and finding work has not been a problem. But hey gorgeous, just remember, your ugly friends might not be so lucky; see, what you don't realize is that a pretty face is its own passport, the world only opens up like this for the young and beautiful and one day you will go to try this again and find that same world suddenly shut. Then you will realize you've grown old, so old that even sad and older dickheads like me won't employ you on the off-chance. *The off-chance of what?* What do you fucking think, darling? Oh, relax. Want to get a little high?

Sarah breezed in one day, tanned, upbeat, laughing, and I wanted her. I was vain enough to think that I could make myself attractive to her once I'd worked my magic, and stupid enough to believe that if I could bring her into my life it would be some kind of answer to everything else that was bringing me down. So I offered her a job, determined not to let my impending bankruptcy hinder the process. And she asked if her friend Alex could have a job as well and so I duly offered her one too, again not letting the grim realities of the bar's financial situation stand in the way. Only Alex wasn't a she, Alex was Alexander, her fucking boyfriend. No matter, he wasn't really competition; bookish, shortish, jerkish. I was going to do my thing and he would soon be history, it almost seemed fair to compensate him somehow.

'Martin . . . You OK? Couple of people been looking for you while you were away.'

Alexander was loading the dishwasher, trying to make some kind of inroad into the pile of plates and rubble stacked by the side of the sink. He had the knack of making even the simplest menial task appear taxing and intricate. Alexander looked at me through half-moon glasses misted up with steam. The front of his shirt was soaked with hot water too, obviously he had been wrestling with the hose that was meant to flush the debris from the crockery before the machine did its business on them. I looked to the floor; his soggy footprints made their own abstract pattern, like a child's potato prints spreading like a rash all over the ground. Hapless cunt. The simplest of tasks. The shit we find ourselves in.

'I'll fix that, leave it alone. Clear the tables, give them a wipe. There's not a clean setting left in the whole bar. Did you change the lager barrel? Where's Sarah? You deal with the bakery, did they try to overcharge you? All these customers happy, you checked they're not waiting for something, how long you been fucking around with the washer instead of serving customers?'

Customers. There are three, and one of them is under five, gurgling in the lap of his mother whilst a proud, handsome Spanish dad looks on. Beyond them, at the extreme of the bar's quayside patch though still under the shade is a middle-aged man reading a newspaper. He takes no interest in the yachts glistening in the sun right in front of him, he's seen it all before. He sits at one of my prime tables but he's not a customer, despite whatever Alexander thinks.

'Sarah is not feeling so well this morning, she's planning to come in later this afternoon, we thought it would be all right if I covered for her. The bakery delivery went fine, I put the receipt in the till somewhere . . . I didn't know the lager –'

'OK. Shut up, stop. I'll sort it later. Who was looking for me?'

Alexander's pale face flushed momentarily. He took off his glasses and wiped a sleeve across his forehead in boyish embarrassment. One of the few good things about him was how easily he was offended. Strange how infantile he could look, rubbing his eyes like a four-year-old, skinny and clumsy; everything about him seemed borrowed, as if he'd lifted a job lot of gestures, hair, teeth, stubble and voice and was still working out how he could use them all together, like an actor improvising with new props.

'A few . . . I . . . took a note.' He turned and fumbled his way through a pile of receipts on a spike at the counter. 'Yes. Two men, spoke hardly any English . . . Miguel Carcera and Torres Carcera. I think they were brothers.'

'Yeah, and you figured that out by yourself?'

Alexander stopped and folded his arms, letting his chin drop to his chest. The gesture of a sigh, even if he didn't make the sound. I knew he was waiting for me to apologize, or show him I meant the last remark as a joke, this was his way of showing me he could only be pushed so far. I let him wait until he couldn't stand the silence any longer and began to recite once more from his notes.

'Some Frenchman, said he was an old friend of yours . . . Gerald?'

'Black guy? Jérome?'

A straightforward question this time, and still he looked affronted.

'I suppose . . . coloured, yes. Jérome, that was probably it . . . And that man over there . . .' Alexander nodded to the newspaper reader '. . . I told him I didn't know where you were and he said he would wait anyway, been there over an hour, says his name –'

'Save it. I know *his* fucking name, I'll see to him . . . whenever. No one else?'

He shook his head and crushed the note into a ball which he dropped sulkily into the waste. So a whole galaxy of stars had been on call but no emissary from my newly estranged wife, not even a lawyer's demand for the cash to keep her in the lifestyle to which she had become accustomed. The realization left me feeling deflated and weary. I really was alone. That was bad but what was worse was not being able to do anything about it, anything at all until she gave me something to react to. Right now, nobody seemed capable of giving me anything worth-while to kick against. Alexander stood next to me, running a hand through his short wiry hair in a gesture that spoke of nervousness. I wished he would swear at me, or point, or maybe just slam a fucking glass on a table. Anything to show me he had balls, anything that I could square up to.

'How was business anyway?'

'Five breakfasts, about fourteen lunches, double that in coffees. Didn't stop until about half an hour before you arrived.'

'How did you cope with that lot on your own?'

'I had to get your cleaner to –'

'*Oh Jesus fuck* Alexander! Don't tell me the fucking cleaner was out there on parade you dick . . .' I hit top volume from more or less a standing start. I was surprised how easily it came and by the force behind the words leaving my mouth. Not surprising that he tried to halt the flow.

'Just to clear and take the food to the tables . . . seemed better than turning business away – like, most of the time it's so quiet.'

'OK fuckwit, OK! *Stop! Just fucking* . . . stop.'

My shouting was so loud that some of the crews cleaning decks in the marina were looking round. I could feel the dryness gripping the back of my throat, making it hard to swallow. My eyes were going too, the same arid shame. I could hear the noise better than most and recognized the sound of some poor harassed bar-owner berating his hapless staff, but shouting at himself more than anybody, shouting so loud to cut through the shit in his own head, to push the bloodstained trousers, the empty house, the dreams about water, all of it to the back of his mind so that he might have a chance just to think about what the fuck was going down. It was that moment in the car again. This was the sound of a man beginning a nervous breakdown. I wanted to cry.

'Listen . . . Alexander, Alex. Anyone ever call you that? Alexander, I mean. Thanks . . . Can you excuse me?'

I would be surprised if he heard more than two words of what I tried to say, and I'd spoken with my eyes closed whilst I tried to pull myself together so I couldn't tell if any of it registered. Maybe it didn't matter, if I was talking it had to be better than screaming, so I tried to keep going, talking as normally as I could to make my mind think normally, to kick-start everything back into gear. It didn't really work, other than to remind me that there were more obvious methods, like the one hidden under the change drawer in the cash-box. I pushed past Alexander and retrieved the envelope lying there. Time for a visit to the toilet, the same toilet I had stayed late cleaning the night before when I'd been so delightfully interrupted. Time to finish off the other gift besides soiled trousers that the girl who had been doing the interrupting had left. Four lines of white powder pick-me-up, finest Devil's fucking dandruff. She thought she was coming back to help me finish it off, she was in for a shock if she did. The way I was feeling there was only enough for one.

There's a stage when you're doing coke, probably the stage when you're doing too much, it's when you find yourself craving some just to calm you down, when the high you are looking for is a mellow one, when all the excitement and novelty of using it is a long-distant memory and you want to take it just to chill, not to charge-up for some party where you're going to work the room like a politician or chase some gorgeous lay; no, you're in a toilet ignoring the smell of shit and snorting up half of Peru just to soothe your soul. Just to be yourself. Probably the stage when you're doing too much. Then again, only the connoisseur will understand what I am talking about here, because most will associate the hit from a line being like a rush of energy, a smack right between the eyes, a rush. Yet the more coke you do, and the better the quality of coke you do the more you'll find it the way I've described. Nature's balm really, something to glue you back in touch with the universe. An injection of high-octane hope and confidence with which you can feel ready to take on the world, or at least some of its more challenging inhabitants. Like Herman the German, the man who has been waiting patiently for me all morning. All through my tantrums, my absence in the mountains, my sojourn in the toilet this man has waited. Like the grim fucking reaper, he knew he would eventually meet his quarry. He knew I would come to him. He knew I would have to.

I wonder if Alexander noticed that a different person came out of the cubicle from the one who went in. I wonder if he knew what was in the envelope or indeed the plastic bag inside the envelope. Maybe he thought the mood swings were another symptom of my madness. Maybe he didn't notice, maybe he was more stoned than me, after all, he had to have something going for him. No matter, I asked him as politely as I could if he could bring a fresh pot of coffee and clean cups to the table with the gentleman reading the foreign newspaper. I asked and saw that he was still up for it. Fine. Thanks Alexander, really appreciate it. One day you and I should have a proper chat, I would like that, really. I better see to Herman. Fresh pot. Any time you're ready. Appreciate it. Hey, listen; you make the *best* coffee, seriously. *You really do. The* best.

Then I walked over, sat down, shook hands and had the conversation, the one I would replay over and over in my head in the days and weeks to come. At the time there were so many other things to take in: the effect of the coke, the look on Alexander's face, the memory of the house that had just ceased to be home in the mountains, the gravel chips sent flying by the wheels of the jeep. And the heat. Coming up for three o'clock, the hottest part of the day. Herman sat in the full shade and I pulled my chair round to his side. I sat with a hand tapping my thigh and the next day it was burned like I'd been dipping it in sulphuric acid. The heat of the moment lingered, like the sounds of the moment; flies buzzing around the empty plates on the table beside us, the revving up of motor launches in the marina just in front, the radios pounding out the relentless Eurodance beats as the open-topped cars cruised up and down the street to the side. Herman's voice was in the mix too, or rather his words. They weren't as telling as they might have been, only when I hit rewind in my brain did the meaning begin to emerge from the camouflage. Yes, it's worth lingering over the detail in those words because this was a conversation that was going to cost somebody his life, most probably mine. I didn't know it at the time, it just turned out that way.

By now you are maybe thinking about me and the women I've mentioned. You have heard me talk about the treatment, or the magic, or how I do my thing. You'll have understood that what I meant was seduction, and you probably wonder how it works. I can tell you how, or at least, how it works for me, believe me, it's relevant, relevant to everything. So let the lesson begin, let this teacher face his empty classroom and tell it like it is. First the basics; there are easy ways to seduce women, you can do it by offering them what they want, and that, usually, is commitment. Most women are in love with this word, promise them that you'll stick around, that you can be sure that what you are offering now will still be available in ten days, months, years; tell them that and you can get laid. A lot of hearts are broken every day as the next generation learns to perfect this trick, libraries are full of works written by women who found themselves on the receiving end and were taken. This was never my style though, my style is more subtle, or is it? In truth, I learned how to screw on the beaches of the south of France on my first and only student holiday, and as I also said, my initial technique owed a lot to what I had encountered whilst selling donuts. Later, I copied the skipper of the *Anneka*, Michel; not an especially handsome man but one who never struggled in this regard. What I learned from him was simple and stays with me to this day, that if you are a man and you smell beautiful – his was Hugo Boss – and have an attitude then you can fuck all you want, the only how you're left to decide is how many. Simple.

It stays with me to this day.

What is an attitude? Well that's something that can be hard to articulate; I guess I mean a mixture of coldness and vulnerability that signals that you are there to be loved but you can also be cruel. Not giving a fuck coupled with occasional flashes of something aching deep down inside. Never underestimate how much a woman can love a cruel man. The shelves of the libraries I mentioned are full of it, every woman's Anna Karenina complex spawning another epic tale of passion and betrayal, good love after bad being hurled at broody, taciturn, tortured men. What they want to be is the one who cures him, the one who sees the tender side and coaxes it out with her love. That's what my magic is then, giving the signs that I could be that man.

Then there's being a sexy man. Every woman can tell in an instant whether a man will be a good lay, even the innocent ones. One glance is all they need, and what they are looking for is a mixture of things rather than a massive bulge in your trousers. No, to give them credit, they'll go beyond that, they want to see a self-confident man, one who will seize the initiative, they want to see some kind of sensitivity, someone with a love of beauty, and the patience to wait to find the beauty in them. You can show these with your eyes, the way you study things, the way you show yourself taking them in when you meet. Let yourself linger on her eyes, let yourself smile, but slowly, as if you have noticed something even her best friend wouldn't recognize, something deep in her soul. That's good for starters, then the best sign you can give that you have what it takes between the sheets is a kind of display of applied concentration. It doesn't really matter on what, as long as it's not anything vain, or half-assed, like wrestling with the dishwasher hose. It has to be something you are in control of, that way you show you can dominate, but that you can also give attention. Women love attention. They love it more than just about anything else.

Sonia came into my bar two summers past. Blonde. Mid-twenties, I found out later twenty-seven. She was Scottish, a highlander, she had moved to London when her modelling career had taken off. I've known a few models, they all have those cheekbones and full red lips. Usually skinny. Long legs, nothing on top. Sonia was different in that she had breasts. They are also well-used to being told they are beautiful so you have to modify the act to an extent. They usually have expensive tastes. Sonia was no different in that regard, she came in with her boyfriend, an American, well dressed but older. Forty-two he said. You could tell that he took care of her, and that he was a bit of a man himself, used to expressing himself through the power of his wallet, and one of the few to cross my door with a finer scent than me. She was bored with him though, she had a gleam in her eye that spoke of feeling trapped, a resentment at being his trophy rather than his partner. Maybe that's what he had promised when they started, that it could work that way between them and then like any successful man he'd reworked the deal so that he would provide the wealth and intellect and she could concentrate on providing the elegance and beauty. She wasn't really my league, these women are high maintenance, and there are better-looking men with more money than me willing to take them on, like the guy she was with for instance. What would she have seen in me? Mid-thirties, tanned, reasonably lean after years at sea had honed some kind of physique and killed any outrageous appetites. A full head of hair, cut short and expensively so that the carefree look I sought would never look so carefree it was plain fucking messy. I've got grey-green eyes, I can look at people for a long time without blinking. I don't know where that trick came from but it can be useful. I tend to wear either black or white, nothing in between, no colours, no Hawaiian shirts. Your clothes can look more expensive than they are if they are simple and well cut. She should have seen that, coming from her world of real glamour, should have seen that I was papering over the cracks, should have seen she was above my league. Anyway, I wanted her, that was all there was to it. So, let the lesson *really* begin.

I saw them arrive and went over to meet them, they were at the table overlooking the very front of the marina, at the point where the quay begins its curve round to the ivy-covered rocks that mark the harbour wall. Back-lit, magnificent. Sonia took it all in; the warm evening air, the flags on the yachts, the dazzling clarity of the stars in the sky above. Her partner chose to look through the cocktail list for his inspiration. I noticed his watch, a dazzling chain of gold strangling a puffy forearm, shiny against a mat of inky-black hairs. I chose to make a fuss over her and her Scottish accent, right there from the off, in front of him, all in the name of Caledonian kinship. I spoke to them both, though it was her remarks, her background and her jokes that I let myself be most taken with; nodding encouragingly, smiling warmly as if she was a close friend recounting a shared intimate memory, closing my eyes as proof that I was really listening, focusing on the wisdom of her words rather than the superficial beauty. Also to hide what I was really thinking, to make her try to guess what that might be. Women are always fascinated by your analysis of them. *So Sonia, do you miss the bright lights of Inverness, do you get misty-eyed like me when you hear the sound of the bagpipes? I came here for the usual things, the heat, the culture and language, and the hills; have you been on the road on the west coast, past Valldemossa, to Deia? More enchanting than Speyside, as romantic as Glencoe. You can feel something magical in the air, a beauty that isn't just . . . of that moment, do you know what I mean? These places, and there are only a few on earth, where you realize that all this will still be there after we're gone. But that's a joyful rather than melancholic realization because others will let it touch their hearts like you have, for generations to come. Sorry, you must be thinking I'm talking utter nonsense! Are you? Come on, trust me on this one, try it, that's the real Spain, the real Mallorca.*

Then I leave them, or to be more specific, her. I never let her catch my eye or show that I am in any way interested in them other than as customers. I concentrate on the rest of the things I'm involved with; like if I'm pouring a lager I'll fix the glass with a stare, I'll idolize it as if my life depends on the presentation of this beer. Women notice these things, and they hate being ignored, they want to feel reassured that you have found them attractive, not necessarily because they want to fuck you, but just because they like to know they have the power to attract men. Sometimes, if you are clever, you give them no signs so that they *have* to fuck you just to prove to *themselves* that they can attract men, or more specifically, you.

Eventually, Sonia cannot stand it any longer and she has come over to perch on a barstool to watch me do my thing. I begin to show off, speaking in Spanish to the other staff, putting a brotherly arm around my assistant as I explain in quiet passionate detail how I want him to operate the espresso machine. Sonia's man is reading some business magazine back at the table, she's left him behind, bored, and her head is resting in the palm of a delicate hand, elbow on the bar top. She smiles slowly, she wants me to know she's intrigued. Fine features, long fingers, silver rings. It all gives an impression of intelligence. If her half of the deal was that she supplied the elegance she was living up to it. Yet she still wanted to be taken somewhere, she wanted to sacrifice that beauty for something other than to satisfy a rich meal-ticket. When she speaks it's in a neutral tone, newsreader-style, only a hint of the Highlands left in her accent. Class, the real thing.

'Martin . . . can I ask . . . What the fuck is it you're doing here?'

I didn't even look up, I might have pursed my lips as the head on the beer slowly rose to the top of the glass.

'I'm pouring a beer.' Deadpan. The radar in my eye detects the beginnings of a smile on the full red lips. Model lips.

'You know I don't mean that. I mean *here*, on the island, a man of your talents . . .'

I lift my shoulders, almost as if I'm yawning because the question bores me. My T-shirt is a V-neck, black, cut short. I'm flashing half an inch of my midriff, by accident, or perhaps not. The scent of the Herrera for men is let loose from under the fabric. She's leaning forward, close, she should catch it.

'I'm running my bar. That annoy you in some way?'

I speak slowly, wryly. Now it's me that's showing the faint signs of amusement in all this, Steve McQueen to her Faye Dunaway, a coldness and a cruelty but also a hint of tenderness. A mystery that demands to be solved. She can't decide if she's enthralled or plain annoyed.

'And that's it? That's what you left Scotland for? Is there anything else, I mean, what's next?'

I get the impression these are questions that she asks herself, a good sign, it means that she thinks I might have all the answers for her but I'm just not telling. I feel so good with her gaze on me at that moment that shit, maybe I do, though I won't make it look easy. A shrug, a shake of the head, a deep breath, anything to show that I'm shy with this, that I'm going to share something personal. I speak even slower, more quietly, more directly.

'Well . . . Maybe the plan is . . . I give it all up and write some kind of book and buy a yacht and sail off into the sunset.' Staring full-on into her eyes, not blinking. I've cut the enigmatic shit and I'm giving her the full treatment, it's almost as if she's pissed me off, robbing me of a prized secret and I'm daring her to live with the consequences.

'Where to?'

'Doesn't fucking matter, Sonia, are you going to come?'

The curves of her lips straighten out as she thinks about what I've just said and tries to figure if I mean it. At that moment, I do, and that's why I can hold it, the look, the eye-contact, everything. She's silent. She knows to let the moment hang there, a good sign. I wait long enough to take that for an answer in itself. A sigh, time to bring down the curtain, to cut short the supply of attention.

'You better get back to your man, he'll be wondering where you've gone. What did you want, espresso? I'll get them sent over.'

I speak quickly and then break off, striding down to the other end of the bar – the show is over.

She left that night without saying goodbye, the table was suddenly empty. Her man left a large tip.

Two days later. Early afternoon. I'm haggling with the bakery man, I see her walking through the heat haze towards me. Cream silk, sleeveless, white sandals, metal-rimmed sunglasses. You wouldn't take her for Scottish, she's left all that behind. There's a stage when you've done too much beauty, so that it almost makes you unreal, a fantasy pin-up, stateless. This time what fascinates me about her is the poise in her walk, the way her head and shoulders are carried with the grace of a schoolgirl high-jumper, her collarbones as alluring as any jewellery, offering a perfect symmetry.

'I need to talk to you.'

She cuts right in. I close down the baker's man in Spanish. Bill me and call tomorrow, we'll sort it then. Then I shout to the staff, cover for me, I'll be half an hour, going to the town hall. They smirk; why do I always take a beautiful woman with me every time I need to discuss my drinks licence? Sonia doesn't understand any of it though, doesn't even understand that we're leaving. Doesn't complain about it either.

We walk in silence to the flat, two blocks away. I unlock the door and let her in first. Inside, she turns as if to ask which room she should make for but finds my hands both brushing back the hair from her cheeks and gripping her head so she can't avoid the kiss that's upon her. The kiss comes back at me although she keeps her hands by her side. So I step forward, pushing her back against the hall wall, we still haven't made it more than three feet inside the apartment. I make the kiss less intense by taking my fingers from her hair, they can carry the passion elsewhere, independently, like they belong to another man, the coarse hands of a sailor intent on violating her, running up and down the front of her dress, squeezing her breasts with an urgency that borders on the savage, then dropping right down to scratch the back of her thighs, lifting her dress in the process, higher and higher. Then my hands are back in her hair, this time pulling and tugging, bringing her on to me. There's no dignity or tenderness here, a hand claws its way behind the waist of her white panties, a tiny exquisite lacy thong with an expanse of gorgeous material no bigger than a mouse's eye-patch, snatching to tear the material apart at the hip. It falls to the floor as the same hand circles in on the parting her legs open to expose, the tops of her thighs are soft, softer still as the hand makes its way inwards. The skin of every woman is different, different kinds of texture, of feel; some like velvet, some like silk, each one unique to its owner. My fingertips brush along the length of her lips, from the back to the front. Every woman I've been with is different down there, when they are excited; every woman gets wet differently, gives off a different scent, holds a different wetness within her. Some have a honey sweetness that draws you in and won't let you go; for some there it's like a lotion, a balm, a coconut oil to be rubbed in with an urgency to pacify a raging skin. Some women though, like her, can make the finest perfume, concentrated but light like the air, giving you a sign to take time, to spread the fragrance around every fold and crevice so that all of her can enjoy its soothing properties. You use it to cast its spell on everything it touches so you go back along those lips only slightly deeper, helping the perfume flow wherever it is needed, the mouth of her vagina, and then back, deeper again, all the way to her clitoris which now has such a thirst to be touched, to be moistened, to be relieved of its isolation.

Her eyes are sometimes open, sometimes shut. She tugs at the belt in my trousers, tears open the fly so that they can fall. She does the same with my boxer shorts though I have to work one side in tandem with her as the concentration comes and goes in waves. She is trembling, shaking as she unbuttons my white shirt, pulling on the chain around my neck, almost breaking it as she gasps aloud. I push my chest on to hers, there is a thin film of sweat covering her body from head to toe. Her eyes are closed all the time now. One hand is still working her, the other I cup around the side of her face, stroking a cheekbone, a model's cheekbone. I let one finger drift to the lips of her mouth and she snatches at it, biting as she reaches her orgasm. I pull it back and draw it down her chest, roughly and quickly, almost scratching her breasts as I drag my clawed fingers across from nipple to nipple. She tugs at my silver chain one last time, throwing her other arm in a lock

91

around my neck as her trembling shudders to a halt. After a moment that hangs in silence she loosens her grip.

I turn her around and then fuck her, taking hold of her so that I can pull her on to me as I stand still, pulling her faster and faster, taking hold of the straps on her shoulders and pulling them down as well so that the whole dress is bunched in a hoop around her waist, something else to be gripped and tugged; no bra, her breasts are firm though they can't help but slap against the cool plaster of the wall, such is the force she must accommodate. There isn't a rhythm to it, just a quickening, an ever-quickening intensity until it stops, until it stops for good.

I didn't say another word to her. We washed separately, one after the other, her first. I came out of the bathroom to find her fully dressed, smoking a cigarette. She didn't smile. I guided her out of the flat with an arm around her waist but when we reached the street we didn't hold hands.

Goodbye Martin, she said, I hope you get your yacht, that you make your voyage to wherever you want to go. I hope you don't do it alone. It took a while for me to realize what she was talking about. I was thinking of the bar, of that night's staff arrangements. Cheers, Sonia. All the best to you too. Why do I get the feeling you're all disappointed, why do women fucking do this to me?

Where to? *It doesn't fucking matter.* True enough, the last part of the lesson. These women adore words that speak of freedom and escape, even the ones that lead them into traps set by cold and cruel men. Never underestimate a woman's willingness to love a cruel man.

It was the 21st of April 1698, according to the log, the day they made their first sighting of Africa, appearing as it did, a monster rising out of the water suddenly upon them. An impossibly verdant, lush and forested landmass, cramming as much growth as it could within its bounds, right up to the water's edge, or at least up to the golden sands which would glow with a whiteness that would blind at high noon. Nature gone mad, said some, a devilish expanse, home to heathens and the strange creatures that made for their bedfellows. What struck Martin most was not the spectacle but the sound of this alien landscape; the ominous and relentless hissing that would emanate from its reaches by day, and the creaks, cracks and humming that would replace it by night. *Devilish*? Martin was not sure, for him Africa was always somehow meant to be blank and barren, a canvas waiting for him to express himself upon it. Its dense bush gave the opposite signal, that it was closed, impenetrable, as if it were trying to ward off newcomers for their own good. A country with a will of its own, a country making a warning sign for those willing to read it.

Captain Henry took *Anne* in close but not too close, staying out somewhere between two or three leagues so as not to court whatever danger there might be lurking amongst the giant palms and conifers of the jungle. As the ship crept in soundings would be taken from the sea bed below, a lead weight coated in tallow lowered over the side. Once retrieved, the particles of sand embedded in the congealed animal fat that served every purpose on deck from sealant to staple foodstuff would be examined, and then compared with the detail recorded already in the captain's charts. The ocean floor would guide them from now on, becoming the means by which they would feel their way along the shore, like a blind man, thought Martin, a blind man using someone else's memories.

Although he did not confide in his crew as to where exactly he wanted to take the vessel, the captain obviously had a particular place he sought to locate, most likely a trading fort which he had reason to believe would treat his ship fairly, perhaps even one that he had already entered into correspondence with. Thus it was that a new routine became established in those early coast-hugging days; tacking in to two leagues from the shore on a stifling draught, laying anchor, sounding with the lead and tallow before raising off and moving south again.

After three days the *Anne*'s longboat was lowered and trailed behind her. The men took this as a sign that trading must be imminent, despite the apparent lack of habitation in the land before them. Some sailors spent the long days studying the wooded horizon for any evidence, fear and trepidation gradually giving way to exasperation and frustration as neither trader nor native materialized. The jungle had a restlessness to it, Martin noted, one that seemed to have affected the ship as much as the buzzing interior of its leafy skyline. Paradoxically, he himself had no doubt that there were men out there, with eyes that were watching them. This was not so much an observation as a premonition, one that gripped him with an increasing certainty. Sometimes at night, in the sweltering clammy heat of the cabin, he would hear the sound of distant drums echoing out from the hinterland across the water and would be tempted to wake the others. Yet something would always halt him as he struggled to discern the faint rhythm. The noise of his fellow officers' snoring would then be enough to perturb him, enough to persuade him to keep it all to himself.

So the days went by and then the questions began to arise, muttered between men on the decks, passed around furtively at breakfast, whispered even amongst men at their toilet in the jardines. *Where are we going . . . Who is it we are to meet . . . Are the negroes already bought . . . Can they be loaded in one stop?*

Different questions but all probing for the same thing; how long will we be here, when will we leave this God-forsaken place? Soon they were aimed directly at Martin, albeit discreetly. Many thought he should know; after all, he would be one of the unfortunates that would eventually have to set foot on the fever-ridden land and confront the savages. That was their job, Martin and the captain, to step ashore and inspect the merchandise, to make the deal which meant they would be on their way to the Indies.

'Mister Law . . . begging your pardon, sir.'

Martin turns. The blinking eyes of McKnight the bosun face him. A kindly face, somewhat out of place amongst the permanent scowls of the hardened crew. McKnight is red from his days in the sun, his leathery skin adopting a new scarlet hue, the straggles of his hair bleached white.

'Yes, Stanley?'

The deference the wizened seadog shows the novice sailor seems sincere. There is a bashfulness to him when he speaks, and he seems unable to look Martin in the eye, though not through any underhand motive.

'The lads were wondering sir . . . been asking . . . I said it would

94

be acceptable to approach you, sir, rather than trouble the captain . . .'

'Yes?'

'Of course, sir . . . Would it be correct to say that the captain's aim is not to go as far as Cape Bojador sir, or beyond it?'

Cape Bojador. Martin had heard this name mentioned more and more in the last few days, usually with dread. He had come to learn that it was not the place itself that the men feared, it was what it represented: the end of the world. In the taverns and whorehouses of the home ports the word that was passed on Africa was always the same, that a good man may chance his luck travelling as far as the Guinea coast, but there was a limit where you no longer enjoyed an acceptable chance. If these were devilish lands that they looked out on, beyond the Cape was the abyss, where madness was waiting to strike the sanest of men, where fever was sure to grip the strongest. Those that dared to sail to Africa were the few, those who ventured beyond the Cape had only themselves to blame.

'I am sorry, Stanley, I do not honestly know. The captain has not shared his plan with me.'

McKnight nods, ruefully. 'Thank you sir, I would be grateful if you did not mention my enquiry to the captain.'

'You have my word.'

Another nod and the exchange is over. McKnight leaves to pass the news to his mates, their speculation can only but grow. Martin looks out to the stern of the ship. Captain Henry stands next to the helmsman, instructing his every move. Beyond them, the turquoise sea has a disappearing wash in their wake. And still the longboat trails behind. Martin can only hope it is sturdy enough to withstand long journeys.

After a full two weeks of anxious waiting, the crew finally had sight of some fellow men. Unfortunately, these were of a breed with which they were well familiar; not caboceers – African chiefs – nor even the staff of a remote trading fort. No, here on the fiery underside of the world they happened upon another ship, another Guineaman on the long voyage from Europe. Captain Henry trained his glass on the pennants and markings of the larger vessel coming into view, fearful lest it be a pirate ship using subterfuge to inch closer. Eventually he was satisfied, and folded the instrument away.

'The *Marguerita* . . . A Spaniard's ship,' he said softly, in a way that Martin would later recognize spoke of his disquiet at this discovery, even if the pronouncement seemed to come as a relief to those around him. Before long though, Martin was aware that the presence of such a ship in these waters represented something of a puzzle to all of them. This was Royal Africa Company territory, surely? The skipper however refused to be hurried into any meeting, even when every move closer seemed to confirm his initial judgement. Instead he ordered the mainmast sail to be taken down to slow them down further and that the batteries be loaded behind the gun ports. He did however, stress that the ports themselves were to remain closed unless he gave express permission to open them.

Thus it was that the two ships drifted together on a becalmed sea in an atmosphere of mutual suspicion. When the Spanish flags signalled an invitation to board the captain remained cautious. He would not draw alongside. Instead he requested Martin to join himself and the first mate, Wells, in a rendezvous with the crew of the other vessel.

Martin found he was the last to join the party after clambering down the rope ladder to the longboat. He realized as he did so that this was the first time he had left the holds, decks and cabins of the *Anne* for over four weeks. He settled on the front thwart and let his gaze lift itself to admire the ship that was at once both prison and gateway to him, puzzled to feel a real affection for the hulking brute of timber and sail confronting him, surprised to see a heavy glowing growth of algae and moss clinging to her hull revealed whenever the gentle waves ebbed away from her.

'Crew, take up the stroke,' he heard the captain say, followed by a shout from Wells, 'Heave!' – the first of many as he tried to impose an order and urgency in their progress across the water.

Martin recognized the two men working the oars in response; they were the Spanish recruits they had taken on in Tenerife. Perhaps the captain was taking them along in order to translate the words which might be uttered in a strange tongue on the *Marguerita*. Even if this was to be their future role, it obviously did not spare them from more menial duties in the meantime. Martin smiled almost apologetically at the pair as they laboured, the commands of Wells still ringing in his ears; 'Heave!'

On the other side of the oarsmen the captain sat regally as they began to glide over the water and approach their fellow craft. Martin eyed the sweat forming on the brows of the men as they toiled to pull the blades through in the heat. Two cups of water each day, that was the ration for each crewman, regardless of weather, work or constitution. Perhaps he should recommend that this pair receive more after today's efforts, perhaps he would even give them some of his own. Yes, he thought, it would be dangerous to lose so much perspiration and not replace it; a half-cup extra with a generous portion of lime juice to freshen the taste after weeks in a stale barrel, would be beneficial, and would help these men retain the health God had blessed them with, even perhaps to ward off the scurvy. He would insist. Looking at them as they moved in graceful tandem, Martin wondered how he had failed to notice that they were brothers when they had first come aboard; both handsome men, both with deep-set olive eyes that hinted at an intelligence above that of the average deckhand. He recalled how McKnight had been more than complimentary when asked as to their worth. Martin had been given the impression that far from being of no consequence in the ship's running and maintenance both men had proved worthy additions to the crew. Opinion was that the elder brother, José, was the more outgoing, and in truth his ready smile was now as much of a fixture on deck as the rigging, masts and rails it adorned. His younger brother was altogether more shy, and may well have been several years younger than the twenty he had claimed. Nevertheless, he took his lead from his sibling, and it was difficult to think of him displaying anything other than an obliging demeanour. It was a curiosity to Martin, considering all that he had been told about the Latin temperament, that there was not a trace of vanity in either man, everything about them suggesting a straightforward and open disposition. Both wore long dark hair, tied back into a tail, both wore simple shirts under leather waistcoats, again to prevent any fanciful detail from catching in the wind or a rope, and both wore plain sturdy breeches. Here they were, travelling to meet their countrymen on a larger, more stately vessel. Yet neither had altered his appearance or sought out his best hat and coat in order to impress, as he himself had. These are good men, thought Martin, they shall have their share of water and lime.

The *Marguerita* had the same fetid stench that seemed to go with a life at sea, the same chaos of rope, rigging and canvas that held mast and sail together, and the same air of forced reality whereby a chain of command stretching down from the King through to the captain down to the cabin boy still held sway so far from home. Aside from these similarities Martin recognized that this was an altogether different breed of boat. For him, stepping on board was like setting foot in another country, the immediate differences all being to do with size, scale and splendour. Here was a vessel embellished with hand-carved crests and founts at every turn, where heavily varnished beams shone like silver ingots in the mid-afternoon brightness, and where the raised quarterdeck lifted the captain and his men so high that they were almost above the trees on the shore they spied upon. Martin was also surprised to see livestock being kept on the deck; chickens and pigs in their cages almost cooking already in the heat, fed and fattened to supply fresh meat *en voyage*.

From what he could see of her crew, they seemed to share the same weatherbeaten countenances as their English counterparts but were, Martin felt, better dressed, embroidery and lace common features in the rather effeminate shirts and waistcoats on view. There was also, as if to balance this, a greater preponderance of beards and moustaches, although none more luxuriant than the captain's. Captain Hernandez himself was a small man, a good inch or two shorter than Martin or Captain Henry at about five-foot-five. There was however, a natural air of presence and authority about him, and Martin could only be impressed at the way things happened around him and for him without ever an order being spoken. Thus doors would be opened, salutes given, views and vantages offered in a continuous display of silent respect and discipline that he was not aware of witnessing on board the *Anne*. Captain Hernandez of the *Marguerita* also proved a convivial host, smiling broadly and proposing a brandy toast to the party as soon as they were on board, and happy to indulge Captain Henry's request to view the other asset that set them apart from the *Anne* at that point; the human cargo they had bargained for and loaded, their Guinea slaves.

The request had been relayed via the elder Conera brother, José, Captain Hernandez' command of English proving as limited as his counterpart's knowledge of Spanish. It was José who was led first into the dark stinking hole that was the main hold. As they descended behind, the putrid fetor that hung in the still air made Martin's stomach turn. He was to be glad he had not partaken of the alcohol proffered earlier. Captain Henry came alongside as he struggled not to retch, though it was not to enquire as to his well-being.

'Be sure to make a good inspection, Doctor. We should become familiar with the quality of the stock, and the value these Spaniards have achieved. Take a considered study . . . Are they sound of body, have any the fever, will they command a fair price in the Indies?'

He whispered, even though there were few present who would understand him if they heard. Martin nodded vigorously, anxious to break free.

He stooped low to avoid the beams that marked the roof of the deck. He took off his hat, unable to see through it when cramped forward as the four-foot height demanded. And then, out of the gloom, a forest of eyes, flashing in the dark then disappearing behind blinking black lids. Martin had never seen a negro before and was at once engrossed and aghast at their ebony skins. As his eyes became more accustomed to the dim light creeping in between the gaps in the ship's timbers he saw that there were row after row of them chained together at neck and ankle, head to toe, all lying prone like a field of corn newly flattened by a storm. Some lay silent, some sobbed gently, some wailed more openly without anyone appearing to notice or take heed. Pots of urine and excrement lay between the lines, slopping with the movement of the boat, spillage everywhere. Flies buzzed around the groaning mass of bodies like insects busying themselves round an animal carcass. Again, Martin moved to cover his mouth. Captain Henry was still close.

'Are they healthy? They say the negro is naturally listless, happiest when freed from labour . . .'

Martin stepped forward to tug the arm of José. 'Could you ask Captain Hernandez how many they have here, how many are stowed in total, and how many they lose?'

José did as told. Martin heard the answer being relayed through the dim light.

'They say two hundred on this deck, one hundred and fifty more below. They lose one, maybe two each night. Some refuse to eat, they will themselves to die.'

'What do they feed them on, the pork and chicken from the deck?'

Laughter erupted amongst the Spanish crew as the question was translated. When the answer came back Martin understood why.

'The pigs and fowl are for officers only, the negroes are given beans, beans boiled in fat. Sometimes fish.'

'Fish?' interrupted Captain Henry.

'Shark meat.'

'Is that hard to catch, does this ship carry a large amount of nets?'

There was a prolonged pause before the captain received his reply, José and Juan struggling to understand and then rephrase the question. Evidently, a special technique was employed to catch the fish; in the shadows Martin could make out one of the Spanish crew using extravagant gestures to demonstrate it to José.

'They say it is easy . . . It is possible to use the dead negroes as bait . . . They say the sharks follow slave ships by habit, the fish wait for the bodies to be cast over anyway.'

Captain Henry nodded appreciatively. 'Good,' he said, squatting down beside a chained quartet of lifeless souls. '. . . Good . . . seen enough?'

The last remark was aimed at Martin who was showing less appetite for the close inspection than the captain enjoyed.

'Aye.'

The captain stood up as far as he could and then turned to compliment his host. '*Gracias*, Captain, *gracias* . . . Hearty fellows all, good stock, tell him José . . .'

Captain Hernandez bowed slowly when the compliment reached him and then led the party back up to the deck. They emerged one by one, stiff and dazzled as they straightened themselves out and adjusted to the sunshine. They followed as they were taken up more steps to the quarterdeck and then into the captain's cabin. A crewman appeared with a tray of brandy glasses. Only the captain and Wells partook.

Captain Henry forced his best smile as he supped. 'Ask him if there is anything he would want from us.'

'Nothing . . . He say where are you headed?'

Captain Hernandez had unrolled a chart at his desk and gestured for his opposite number to mark his spot. Captain Henry pondered for a moment but eventually could not resist giving the Spanish map his scrutiny.

'Fort St George,' he said quietly, running a finger along the coastal outline. 'Ask him if he called there and how far he reckons we are now.'

José spoke briefly to the Spanish captain and his entourage. His question seemed to have ignited considerable debate, and within an instant four of them were huddled around Captain Henry at the chart. Their raised voices obviously irritated the Englishman who remained ignorant of the cause of the commotion.

'What are they saying?' he barked angrily at José.

'They say they have not heard of Fort George . . . except for the one which is two hundred leagues west. There are no trading missions in this region other than the one at Point Colou.'

Captain Henry made to push the throng away from the desk in order to prove his case.

'What? Here man . . . here!'

He stabbed a finger at a detail on the map. This too provoked heated words from their hosts, words which were directed at both Conera brothers. When José eventually spoke, it was with a hesitancy that spoke of embarrassment.

'They say we are here . . .'

His finger indicated a point on the map several inches to the right of Captain Henry's asserted position. Martin looked on in astonishment. Each inch on the map represented about a hundred leagues. The Spaniards were saying they were off course, well off course, beyond Fort St George, beyond even Cape Bojador. That was why this ship was so well equipped, he thought, it was a deep voyager, an exploratory vessel. That was why they were being so friendly, they thought they had met fellow adventurers, not a boatful of lost Englishmen.

'Tell them they are wrong.'

It was, Martin would later reflect, probably the only option left to Captain Henry at that moment, coming to terms with his humiliation in front of such an audience; outright denial. Perhaps he even believed that it was the Spaniards who were wrong, they who had located and loaded their cargo, they who had been here longer, hugging the shoreline for months already. Or perhaps he thought that they were simply lying in order to confuse him for some other dastardly purpose. Whatever the case, José's hesitation in translating the last remark showed clearly enough whom he believed to be correct. This only served to goad Captain Henry further.

'Tell him, damn it! Tell them now man!'

The skipper's fist was clenched, shaking, ready to punch. José took note and began to speak, his delivery of the words somewhat less impassioned than his captain's. Martin sensed it was unlikely he was saying exactly what had been asked of him; no, he was in no rush to insult his hosts and countrymen. Instead he might have been enquiring if they were sure, and if this was the case, what made them so. This exchange went on for some time before an English translation was given. José eventually addressed his own party.

'They say it is possible there may be a mistake. They will study their map further because of what our captain says.'

Martin doubted that this was what the Spaniards had intimated. His respect and trust in José was hardly diminished by the realization though. Here was a man, he thought, helping them negotiate a difficult passage, steering them through a potentially dangerous situation using the disparity of their languages. Thanks to his subtle diplomacy, both parties had saved face. Not that his captain seemed in any way grateful.

'We should return to the *Anne*,' he announced, draining the last from his glass. 'Thank them and bid them *adiós*.'

There was a heavy silence in the longboat as they made their way back, only the sound of Wells shouting the stroke rising above the gentle chop of the waves and the mocking cries from the seagulls. Soon, even that was gone as Captain Henry indicated a halt.

Puzzled, José and Juan lifted the oars clear of the water. To Martin though, what came next was entirely predictable.

'Men, it is clear that the Spaniards are in error as to their navigation. Nonetheless, I want no word of what was said on board our ship. Any man guilty of passing on gossip or any harmful detail will be punished severely. If I hear of any innuendo I will know that it could only have come from those here now. If any man is coward enough to seek to spread word and hide behind others I will punish all of you ... *All* of you, hear me?'

The cry of 'Aye' which followed the captain's speech was hardly enthusiastic, but seemed to suffice. A wave of the skipper's hand had the stroke raised again, and the journey recommenced, albeit with all the joy of a funeral procession. Martin let his hand drag through the water. *Shark meat.* He let his arm in further, up to the elbow, wetting his sleeve. There was much to ponder. The *Anne* was miles – hundreds of miles – off course, not that this was to be acknowledged. Yet how could it remain secret to the rest of the crew when the trading forts failed to materialize on the shore? What were the options, to turn back against the little wind there was and make for Fort St George? Surely the trip would take weeks, months? But what chance was there to trade if they stayed in their current vicinity in the absence of forts, how were they to converse with native caboceers without a knowledge of their language and without an established system of barter? *Colou Point.* That was where Hernandez had told José they had bought slaves, that had to be where they should head now. Yes, Colou Point, they could yet retrieve the situation.

He withdrew his arm and shook it dry, returning Captain Henry's stern glance. Was there wisdom in approaching him with these thoughts, was the captain aware of his crew's restlessness? Perhaps. Why else hold it concealed that they were beyond Cape Bojador? Perhaps Mr Henry thought they would not notice the unrelenting, sticky, suffocating heat of night and the burning sun of day. Nor the constant whine of mosquitoes ringing in their ears. Martin cast an eye to the brooding landmass which was beginning to throw a shadow over their craft. He did not relish the prospect of stepping ashore, no. It was inescapable though, and surely best done soonest. Everything told him that the best plan had to be to load up and leave as quickly as possible and escape the Guinea coast and its dangers. The premonition was stirring in him again; this land would consume them all if they loitered. He could only hope Captain Henry was moved by a similar force.

Barely were they back on board the *Anne* when the nature of their predicament was made clear through the advent of a more pressing problem. McKnight hauled first the captain then Martin over the deck rail before taking them to one side.

'Nisbet, Harrison and Anderson from larboard watch . . . O'Kane from the starboard . . . all sick with fever, sir. All down. There's many more lads say they are none to the good but are still at their posts, sir, meantime.'

Whilst McKnight had barely whispered his report, Captain Henry lifted his head to the quarterdeck and mizzen-mast, as if addressing a crowd from a stage.

'Aye . . . and I say they will remain so! I will tolerate no malingerers on my ship, you hear?'

Martin chose not to stay whilst the captain gave vent to his sudden anger. He made to seek out those who were infirm. McKnight pointed to the stern. There were more words from the captain as he walked over, he guessed these were again intended for the crew rather than himself.

'Bleed them, Doctor . . . Bleed them, then have them back on their feet. I will have no malingerers.'

Martin didn't turn to acknowledge the command, striding forth to the companion-way instead, for once eager to duck under the deck parapet and be welcomed by the dull and rank innards of the boat. There was only one thing malingering he saw, with bitter realization, and that was the *Anne* herself, cast adrift, without a plan, without a purpose. And with Africa so near, yet further away than ever.

Shit moments in my life. Glasgow airport, goods to declare, September '93. I've come back on a holiday charter for my father's funeral. Before I left I was asked if I would carry some extra baggage. I'm feeling cool, although maybe a little self-conscious as I cart the stuff over to the desk, I'm thinking about what's waiting for me on the other side, family I haven't seen for years. Why do I feel so bad about it, when did they ever come to see me? I have an enormous nylon holdall that takes all the gear. It looks battered and sorry, like its owner.

'What have we got here then, sir?'

'Diving equipment, bought it in Spain, brought it back rather than leave it behind. The breathing apparatus is the expensive stuff, for specialists. Means you can go down deeper. I've kept the receipts.'

'Can I have a look at your passport, sir?'

'They're in Spanish of course, I don't know . . .'

'Travelling alone? Any other baggage? Passport please.'

This is a new one on me, being interrupted by the normally better-mannered men of customs. This one looks keen, almost my age, he's got an attitude, he's looking at me like an army captain eyeing a deserter. Was there was a hint of adrenaline to his voice? Yes, this is something he's enjoying, these Gestapo undertones, they seem to come easily to him, I almost expect a click of his heels at the end of every sentence. What if I say no, you can't see my passport, what the fuck has it got to do with the duty due on diving gear? I can't of course, I must comply, I want to give a signal that his attention doesn't concern me.

Mr Customs Man studies my papers like they are written in some kind of code, one that a professional like him might crack.

'Mr Law . . . Mr Martin Law?'

Yes, at least, that's what it says on the cover, dickhead, you expecting someone else?

'Could you step this way?'

He points to a door. If I appear bemused, it's genuine. I go to lift the holdall. He stops me.

'That's all right, sir, we will attend to that later, this way please.' He points again and I know this is serious shit, they don't even want me to touch the stuff in case it turns out to be evidence that I'm trying to tamper with. I try to hold my nerve, to concentrate on signals. I scratch my head, you guys want to lift that? You're welcome.

We arrive in a windowless room and are joined by two of my man's chums. They exchange looks like nightclub bouncers about to do over a drunk who's been giving them lip. I suppose you think we like doing this, son, their expressions seem to say; well actually, I do, and I'm dead fucking right.

'Could you unpack the contents of your personal luggage if you would sir, on the table, one item at a time . . .'

One of them has a video camera, he's pointing it at my bag. Serious shit.

'. . . and in your own time.'

My own time. As if. All right, cunts. Let's try it in my own time.

105

We go through the bag slowly, item by item as instructed. They are relaxed at first, not tense until later, happy to leaf through shirts and underwear in their polythene gloves in a matter-of-fact way, like friendly doctors looking for symptoms at some African field hospital; is there a tell-tale rash, spots on the tongue? By the time they are squeezing the toothpaste out of its tube though, and sniffing the deodorant that they've sprayed out of the aerosol it's obvious that they want it bad. Then they talk about the suit and the oxygen tanks.

'We would like to take a look at it all . . . Get the tanks x-rayed, sir, is there anything unusual in there, any surprises waiting for us?'

As it happens, yes, one big fucking surprise: oxygen, there's nothing in the oxygen tanks but oxygen, like there was nothing in my soap box but soap, or nothing up my arse except the torch you were shining. Sorry to disappoint, it wasn't meant to be like this, it just turned out that way. You see, this trip was different, my father is dead and I'm all mixed up because I don't really know how I feel about that. So when I get all this hassle before I leave Spain to come back here, you know, hassle to take a package, hassle to say when it is I'll be leaving, even hassle about how I plan to bring it in, it pissed me right off. Hassle, I should add, the likes of which I hadn't really had for any other trip, so I wasn't used to it, so it ended up pissing me off so much that I decided not to fucking bother, not to mix business and pleasure, just to do the funeral and see where that got me.

That should be out of here, shouldn't it boys? Maybe it gets me an apology as well. And it gets me to thinking about Michel, my skipper on the *Anneka*. Maybe because he was more of a father to me than the man I've come home to bury. He was the hardest man I ever knew. With attitude, ship-loads of it. What I didn't learn from him I copied, right down to the aftershave.

So I met Michel when he came to take over the yacht that I had been partying on. He and his crew came to take the boat to Turkey, to its new owners. I stayed, I don't know why, mainly I suppose because I had over a kilo of hash stashed in the bridge that I was reluctant to say *au revoir* to. And they were OK about taking me along, for no pay, no reward, and instant acceptance as the lowest form of life on board.

So we set sail for our two-and-a-half-week voyage to Bodrum, seventeen days and nights of seasickness, homesickness and other unmentionable kinds of sickness that only four men in the enclosed space of a pitching yacht for that length of time can generate. As newest crew recruit I had all the choice jobs once at sea; it was here that I learned about cleaning toilets, cooking up fish stew, and the impenetrable language that sailors speak, the language of boats, of *pétards*, *brouillards*, of *vent mistral*. After a while I like to think we all warmed to each other, me to this strange sullen threesome whose modus operandi seemed to be getting through the day whilst uttering the fewest number of words they could, and them to the naive but willing youngster who had lied about his knowledge of seacraft in order to join the voyage, like a cabin-boy stowaway from a different age.

All the while this slow bonding was taking place over plates of fish stew in the galley, and endless games of cards in the lounge, my stash stayed where it was on the bridge, ticking away like a time-bomb, never far from my thoughts, because as we neared our destination I began to get plagued with visions of some kind of *Midnight Express* scenario being played out once we docked, and these poor guys being dragged down screaming their innocence as they took a smuggler's rap having been betrayed by the stranger they had taken aboard. Every day I would wake knowing we were a day nearer, wondering how to solve the conundrum; struggling to convince myself that the gear was best left where it was, and my shipmates best left in the dark. I held this line for sixteen days, seven hours and thirty-five minutes until I couldn't stand it any longer.

Three miles from the port, a sunny early afternoon. The *Anneka* is making her measured, stately progress towards the shore under the proud and watchful eye of her skipper. The sails have come down, we glide in under motor, Michel silently contemplates the formalities to come, he is resting on the starboard side of the deck when I interrupt his meditation. *There's something you should know.* I tell him about the extra cargo and he draws a breath. *In the first-aid box?* Yes, about a kilo, maybe slightly more. He nods and stands up, pushing himself erect against the guard rail. Another deep breath as he surveys the full panorama around him; there are no other boats near, and the tiny scorched islands we are passing are uninhabited apart from the odd goat clinging to the rocks that merge into the turquoise sea.

Everything is calm, for the first time in my life I can smell land the way sailors can, the scent of the thyme growing wild on the hilltops above, dried mud and dung all combining with the briny salt of the water to create the sense of an alien landscape coming closer. We are explorers drifting toward uncharted lands, silent lands surrounded by a still sea. Michel takes a step towards me, he draws back an arm as if yawning and then punches me full in the face with the force of a head-on car crash. I can hear him shouting to the others but not what he actually says, I'm flat out sprawling on the deck, the blood from my nose vividly scarlet against the polished white wood. I look at the strange palette of colours without it registering that some comes from me. Luc emerges from the galley with the casserole pot, together with other heavy items. Michel has made a grab for the first-aid box but it's not to tend to me as I waver on the verge of passing out; no, he's breaking up my stash and taping it on to the items, working quickly as he makes up a series of bound-up parcels. I watch my prized investment being lobbed over the side to plummet to the depths. This whole scene is like a dream, I begin to wonder if the fish that feast on it will get stoned, my mind drifting away with shock when Michel turns to admonish me, muttering angrily under his breath, lips straight and tight as he spits out his anger. Stupid *imbecile*, he says, stupid stupid imbecile. When we get ashore, you fucking pay for a replacement dish and anything else we've had to waste because of you. You got that? I nod, still dripping everywhere. Good, he says, good, you fucking imbecile.

I thought he had broken my nose, as it happened he hadn't, but he might as well have for the pain and trouble he caused. I would bleed off and on for another three days, waking up to see a pillow caked in the stuff. He also gave me two black eyes your average panda would have been proud of, thank God for wrap-around shades. What really hurt though was the thought of the entire summer's graft lying on the floor of the Aegean Sea, priceless yet irretrievable, slowly dissolving into nothingness. So I was broke as well as beaten, leaving more and more behind. Welcome to Turkey.

We were in Bodrum to swap yachts; Michel's task was to take the *Anneka* to her new owners who were based out there for the winter, bank their cheque and wait for confirmation that it had cleared, hand over the boat and head off with another one which had been earmarked for a German dealer – as in boat dealer – a fine sixty-foot-plus craft that was slightly older and heavier called *Sea Princess* or something equally banal. I'm sure the Krauts will have rechristened her to suit whatever purposes they had in mind. The new boat was more decorative both above and below deck, stained oak features abounding. I remember seeing a porn movie years later, something someone brought into the bar, and there in its full splendour, hiding behind the throbbing orgy of sucks, fucks and multiple penetrations was the antique woodwork of the *Princess*. I couldn't help but feel guilty about the part I might have played in reducing her to this, how strange to watch this stuff and be more interested in the background furnishings than the up-front action so carefully choreographed for the more immediate viewing pleasure.

Anyway, all this took days to come to pass, more days of card-playing, morose chat and time-killing, except this time without the entertainment of having to keep the boat upright and on the move. And except this time there was an atmosphere between me and the rest whilst they decided whether they could trust me after my shock exposure as a smuggler. No one ever mentioned it, even though the episode hung over me like a cloud, even though the red spots on the handkerchief I kept stuffed under my tender nostrils remained a constant reminder of the altercation my activities had caused with the captain. One night he got especially drunk, we all did, I can't remember why but there we were, finally opening up like we had threatened to do in the last days before coming ashore. Michel asked me how my nose was, I could tell he liked to see me suffer with it, not from any sense of sadistic delight, no; where he was coming from was that he hoped he had taught me a lesson, one that I wouldn't forget. As it turned out, I never did forget it, and that's why it sprang to mind that day at

Glasgow airport, because that day's events proved that Michel was right, right in his theory, and right about me.

His theory? He explained it to me that night, in a booth in the town's only open bar, an arm around my shoulder keeping me close in case I missed any of its more salient points, face pushed up to mine, a gentle spray of spittle hitting me as he made his conviction known. Understand, he said, that smuggling is no game for the amateur. Smuggling, he said, should be left to the professionals, to the teams who made it their profession, their work. He had known many men, some intelligent men, many good men, who had thought otherwise and paid the penalty. He drew deep on his cigarette and pulled me so close I was almost embarrassed. Better men, he said, blowing out the smoke on to my sunglasses, much better men than you. The point was, it was a game, a game played out every day around the world between the two sides, the smugglers and the customs men, the hiders and the seekers. And both sides knew each other more than they would like it to be known so that at the highest level they knew each other very well indeed, well enough to rig the whole game between them so that everybody was happy, so that everybody could continue playing. Had I ever heard the expression 'street value'? They use it every time a seizure is made. It means the value of the haul, except it's not of course, it's the value of the haul the customs or drug-enforcement people choose to go public with. They might mention a weight, say, half a kilo of cocaine, but then they can give that weight a 'street value' by estimating how much that initial capture would have been diluted or cut before it was sold to its users down the line. And since no one is ever in a position to argue, they can be generous in their estimates, saying that your original half-kilo would be cut tenfold with whatever filler but still sold at a premium price so that its street value is over a million fucking dollars.

You can see why they do it, he said, it makes them look good, makes it sound as if they've caught a big-time player when all they've got is an amateur, some poor illiterate African fuck, or sweaty Colombian waiter praying for mercy but unaware that they've been given up by the very people who put them on the plane in the first place. Why would they do that? Simple, to keep everybody happy. To keep the opposition occupied whilst they get on with the bigger game that keeps whole markets supplied whilst the amateurs tinker at the margins. All these men, he said, loners convinced they could beat the system; arrested and taken to court to discover they were carrying goods with a 'street value' that in reality a fucking crane would struggle to lift and who is ever going to argue for the poor shitheads, to point out the absurdity of it all? Even if anyone did, who would be believed, the man in the dock or the man who put him there – would the forces of law lie to a judge?

Everyone ever caught has been set up, said Michel, *everyone*. Anyone ever tapped on the shoulder anywhere in the world already had the mark put on him. Sacrifices, *amateurs*, all volunteered to keep the professionals happy. *Better men than you*. Besides, taking hash *into* Turkey, what the fuck was I thinking of, didn't I know the trade was meant to go the other way? He took a swig of beer as Jean and Luc began to lose themselves in laughter, how stupid do you need to be to risk that one? Michel eventually joined in, tears welling as he struggled to contain himself. He tightened his grip on me one last time, wrestling me close so that he could shout into my ear above the raucous bar-room din. You remember this, he said, now and for ever; you let yourself be someone else's set-up and I'll fucking kill you. *Comprenez?* I nodded, allowing myself a smile at my own expense. He made a playful grab for my nose which I managed to duck away from, still too sore, tired of the open season that had been declared on me. Michel's mood changed, suddenly pissed off, he turned to speak to the others, talking fast, indecipherably, bitching, no doubt. I pretended not to care. Then Jean and Luc were off without saying goodbye, leaving me and Michel to finish our last beers in virtual silence. The bar was filling up, hotter than a sauna, and with the same stilted atmosphere, everyone looking round and trying not to catch another's eye. A bearded guy in a skip-cap came in and stared at Michel. Michel didn't make any show of recognition but something was up all the same, something brewing.

We left together and stepped out into the early morning gloom. After the stifling confines of the bar it was like walking along the Clyde.

That's where my mind was when Michel announced he was taking a piss, cutting in behind the quayside in search of an alley. I hung around for a while and then grew impatient, what was keeping him, had he fallen asleep? Then, like a fool I followed, round the corner, pacing forward into the dark, calling him.

Up ahead there were three guys in outline, right up in the break of the lane. Before them stood one man, his back to me but facing them in the stand-off. Oh Jesus, Michel, what's up? None of them was moving or even saying anything but an atmosphere hung there and I knew it was a good time to get scared.

'Michel . . . A problem?'

'*Pas de problème.*'

The words weren't Michel's but came from one of the other guys. The same guy who had eyeballed him in the bar.

'No problem for you, kid, it's him we want, you can go.'

I took a glance backward to see if we could run for it. The exit was closed. Another three had arrived to close us off.

'*Sortez!*' said a voice, go.

And my nose hurt more than ever just at the fucking thought of what might happen, yet this wasn't an option.

'Six of you, two of us . . . OK, but as we say in Greenock, that's your lookout. We know the score.'

There was a chivalrous nod to acknowledge my little speech and then nothing. I tried to imagine if I could land one serious punch on one of these men, and if I did, would it hurt or just plain irritate them. I thought of the absurdity of what I had said, what use was it to actually know the score. Then I noticed Michel's shoulders were twitching, not like he was limbering up to throw a hook, more that his sides were going to split. Then it spread to the other guys and they were suddenly all smiles, laughing away, pissing themselves. Michel turned around and locked me in an inescapable hug.

'I knew you were one of us! One of us, yeah?'

I could feel the hands of the others suddenly on me, not punching, patting my back, cuffing my head. It had all been a set-up, a test, our deadly enemies recruited on the spot by Luc, the same Luc now pointing at my nose, and my eyes in their black rings. The laughter rose again, I pulled free and pretended to be annoyed, disappointed that there would be no fight. It took an effort not to run, the adrenaline flowed like I'd just won in twelve rounds.

A happy memory then, one which you might have thought would have cheered me as I repacked my case at the airport those years later. The camaraderie of that moment was not what my mind lingered over though, it was the detail of what I had been told, a particular detail within Michel's philosophy. Everyone a sacrifice, he argued, everyone ever caught had the mark already put on him. You can only trust those who would make a stand with you, he said, and men who would do that in this world were rare. He would be there for me like I had been prepared to be there for him, I should never forget this. I promised I would not. As it happened, I didn't; and this would be a favour I would have to pull in so many years later. I couldn't have known this at the time, but it was always going to end that way.

The conversation with Herman went something like this, I think. Maybe it might be relevant to introduce him before telling you what was said, maybe that way you can get the full story about what went down between us, and why it has to end the way it will.

So who is Herman? He is Herman Ungerer, or Herman Schmidtpeter, or Herman Zieglemeir. Surnames aren't that important, I've heard him called all of these, and worse. These are just the inoffensive ones. So let's just call him Herman the German, everyone else does, the polite ones at least. Herman the German from Berlin. Or Hamburg. Or Munich. I've heard him claim all three as his home city. Places aren't really important either.

Herman is somewhere in his forties but could pass for years older on account of his rotund shape which is in itself on account of his fondness for food. Hot weather can be a problem for Herman, with his wispy white hair and blotchy skin, not to mention all that excess weight he carries all over his six-foot frame so that on particular days he can bear an uncanny resemblance to an enormous oily bratwurst, one about to explode with a sizzle under the heat. Happy Herman

113

loves it on Mallorca though, I know this for fact, he never tires of telling me. Indeed, Herman looks fondly on life although on days like today you might not guess that, days when he's adopted his stern demeanour, when he's constantly pushing his glasses back to the top of his nose and then pointing the same finger in the air just ahead of you in one flowing movement that speaks of the distance between you and how he intends to fill it. On the whole though, life is good for Herman; it could be better for sure, if we all could follow his lead in adopting a Teutonic efficiency and thus live in a state of maximum harmony, but life is good all the same. It's just that we should continue to strive for the best, whatever it takes.

I first met Herman two years ago, he was a late arrival to Puerto Puals, replacing another German, the original owner of the bar that corners the end of the marina and the main exit road. The rest of us had bought into the development when it was still a building site, me taking a gamble I could barely comprehend, paying top-dollar for the largest retail space at the centre, full on and flush with what would become the glorious waterfront. I didn't know it would turn out that way, I was just lucky; lucky that the development would grow into something chic and beautiful when so many others went so resolutely tacky, lucky that the property deeds were genuine and not part of some elaborate con, lucky that Puerto Puals for some reason steered clear of the gangsterism and protectionism that had taken over entire strips of bars and clubs in the main resorts in and around Magaluf. Then one day my luck ran out; Herman had a lot to do with this, but more of that later.

If you listen to some you would think that Mallorca is the Las Vegas of the Mediterranean, Las Vegas circa nineteen-forty that is, a Mecca for hoods and their dirty cash. I guess all that's missing are the casinos, and instead of desert we've got sea. I can't say it's a comparison that I was ever really taken with. I went years without any knocks being made at my door, and the tales you would hear would strike you as just that, tales or legends designed to attach some kind of spurious glamour to otherwise dreary resorts and drab bars. So Fred's disco in Magaluf is coveted by two different Berlin gangs, big deal, why the fuck would anyone want it? But what was undeniable was that the villas going up around the coast were becoming bigger and bigger, higher and higher up the hills, with fences that were ever-taller. Money was pouring in, and those bringing it wanted privacy. Then there were the names that would disappear, owners and bar names that had seemed like permanent fixtures suddenly vanishing, and you would ask yourself where or why they had gone. The rumours went in cycles; it was all the doing of the German underworld, then it was the turn of Spanish drug syndicates laundering their money into leisure outlets. Latterly all you would hear about was the Russian invasion, a new eastern Mafia with the largest duty-free scam in the world. And they were meant to be the worst, the filth of the Black Sea washing up on our shore, Chechens, Georgians, Muscovites, all bringing their own feuds and ruthlessness with them. Yes, you would hear all this and let it pass without thinking until you noticed the number of shops selling fur coats springing up or how every second car around Palma seemed to be a Mercedes with dark-tinted windows. Maybe the prospect became a little more scary but you could always reassure yourself that the gangsters tended to pick on their own kind, criminal or compatriot, that all of this would never touch you.

Puerto Puals was built on legitimate money, mine included, or at least, built on money with legitimate aspirations. When Herman arrived, things began to change in some kind of way; as you might have guessed, one is never quite sure where one stands with Herman. First he buys out his countryman to become a bar-owner like myself, one welcomed by myself, welcomed as a fellow entrepreneur. I didn't ask him where his money came from for fear he would ask about mine. What I did assume though, was that it was his, and he never gave me any impression otherwise. In those early days we would call in on each other, sharing tips and rivalries as one landlord to another. Then I hear that Herman's interests have widened somewhat, that he owns the restaurant next door to him, then the one next door to that. And so on, until a year and a half later, out of twelve units he seems to be in charge of ten with the eleventh about to follow. He never admits to this, no; he owns his bar, and he keeps an eye on everything else on behalf of the organization back in Germany, whose plans, desires and instructions for the future of the units are passed exclusively through Herman. At times it is difficult to tell where Herman ends and the organization begins. He is always keen to convey the impression that this is a position he has never sought – mouthpiece to the faceless new corporate owners – and that he is as much at the peril of their capricious wishes as I am. Herman would have me believe that he alone acts as a brake to some of their more outrageous demands, that I should be grateful that he acts as a buffer, so to speak. Perhaps I should, and not be so cynical and suspicious. So what that Herman says direct contact with these people is out of the question, so what that they have no name whatsoever apart from *the organization*, so what that in any conversation Herman skips between *we* and *they* and *I* with a fucking abandon more gay than Paris. No. Maybe it's just his problem with the language. Life is good, Herman is here to tell me, *why be difficult*? You tell me Herman, you're the one with all the answers.

'Marty . . .' he says, '. . . look Marty, we both want the same thing.'

There's no one else on this earth that calls me Marty, yet this cunt has the gall to do it not once but twice in succession. I'm really high, really mellow, my brain is buzzing with positive thought and still he manages to rile me. All I can do is stare at him and marvel at the amount of contempt he can generate, how much does he have to inspire before he realizes this chat is not going down a storm? At the same time the drug-induced weirdness in my mind makes me wonder if you can measure hate, like on a scale of one to ten, could you do it by weight or in gallons? Herman wouldn't like that though, the use of an old Imperial unit, it would have to be to a European standard, an index of loathing in metric litres. At some point, presumably, you would move to a dangerous end of the spectrum, like when your Herman indicator points to overload. Like now. The man himself however, is unmoved.

He takes his glasses off so that he can wipe his forehead with a napkin, one of my napkins. He grimaces, giving me a quick flash of teeth in the process. Maybe something is troubling him.

'Marty, you have pastries here?'

'We sell croissants.'

'No, like sweet pastries, with icing. Like strudel. No? You must meet my supplier, I will introduce.'

Herman wants my place to run like his place on the other side of the development. Something about it being different, being run to a shambolic Scottish regime of haphazard croissants instead of regulation strudels bothers him. Let me explain. Much as he loves life in Mallorca and tries to smile at all it can throw at him, Herman has one problem: me. Acting on behalf of *the organization*, which may or may not mean acting on behalf of himself, Herman now runs all except one of the bars, cafés, restaurants and shops at Puerto Puals, with a single unit left outside the new empire, namely the Arena, my bar. Herman has made what he thinks is a good offer for this, and likes to press me for an answer. Was it a good offer? It might have been, but then I haven't really thought about it, not because I don't want to sell, more because I've been busy with other things. I didn't set out to stall Herman, it just turned out that way and this has been dragging on for six months. Unfortunately, Herman or his organization have taken this badly, for whilst this is a sort of secret organization in that no one knows who they are or what they do, they certainly don't like being ignored. That's why they, through the good offices of Herman their fellow German, have turned the heat up, so to speak. The prices of food and drink in all my neighbouring attractions have plummeted of late, you can practically dine and swill for free anywhere on either side of the Arena. I don't know what this has done for their business but it's certainly grabbed a hold of mine and fucked it right up the ass, and that's not even the worst of it. For some reason it seems that since I'm the one to blame for the situation, I should meet the cost of this cut-price extravaganza by the sea. The good price offered to me for my place has gone down every day, to the extent that it barely covers half what I paid for it three years ago when it was nothing more than a muddy hole of clay and sand and an architect's sketch. And if I appear bemused and at a loss as to what the fuck to do, it's genuine.

'Do you want a croissant, Herman, feeling hungry?'

It transpires although he might be, he wouldn't.

'Coffee,' he says, by way of reply, meaning no, I decline your kind offer of a snack and will limit myself to another cup of your fine coffee. This is an order in every sense, in Herman's English 'coffee' becomes a verb rather than a noun, a verb meaning, 'Get me one, Marty.'

I turn around to wave to Alexander, to gesture to him to rustle up another and realize that things really are so bad, no matter what signals the cocaine is giving my brain. Here's Alexander, my expensive new recruit, my unfailingly inept staff recruit. Here he is, eager to please, relentlessly upbeat though fuck knows why, happy as a pup, fucking around with the espresso machine wasting copious amounts of time, energy and milk. The same Alexander who fucks Sarah. So this man is on the case, preparing a drink at my expense for the man there, Herman. The one I hate being served by the one I loathe, or vice-versa, it doesn't matter. What does is that I'm being squeezed in the middle between them and there's no one who really understands what's going on. My wife has left me and nobody knows or cares. Does this include me? Does anything *include* me? I need to get more stoned to cope, I've got more anger and confusion that I can handle and only one sure way of dealing with it. I can feel those short breaths creeping in on my lungs again and hope to fuck I'm not crying. It's OK, I can't be, Herman is droning on without any show of obvious alarm, acting perfectly normally, that is to say threatening me, or telling me that the organization is threatening me which I'm increasingly sure is one and the same thing.

'What can I tell them, Marty? You said you would think about it and they ask if you have decided in the affirmative. They are saying, we make a good offer, why does Mr Law insult us so? I tell them to be patient, Marty, but I'm afraid they are becoming angry. No good for you if they become angry. Not good at all. Things are bad today. You know this. You can change, you can decide.'

Yes, somehow I've become a real fucking nuisance, and should feel more ashamed, a fly in the proverbial ointment or maybe more a gnat on the windscreen of the otherwise smoothly purring Mercedes-Benz that is *the organization*.

'I need more time. I've got things to sort out.'

'There is no more time, Marty. I have to tell you this.'

I am being honest with Herman, even if he does not appreciate it. I need time to decide what to do. I need time to raise money so that when I sell I can cover the debts incurred in running at a loss for the last six months. I need time to straighten out, get less high. Over Herman's shoulder a boat is setting sail as it leaves the marina. Perhaps that is the answer, a yacht making for an open sea. I've dreamt of the sea for so long now, every night I hear it calling. When I say the sea, I really mean the sea, not the boats that glide upon it – I was never a natural sailor with a love of the discipline and dedication it takes to keep afloat and moving from one port to another, no. It is the sea itself that draws me, the flat horizon, the emptiness of the sky above it. The best thing about being out in the ocean is diving into the waters when they are calm enough to accept you, or rather calm enough to give you back. If you dive in naked, then it hits you as you break the surface, the certainty that for all we gather around us as we go through this life, the possessions, property and partners, for all that we have nothing but what is inside us, the skin and bones and whatever memories we have in our heads. All we have. I would dive into the sea just to enjoy that thought, just to prove that you can leave everything behind and be swallowed by the water that asks no questions about what it is you are trying to escape from, just diving in to rid myself of the baggage that weighs you down. I wanted to buy a yacht so that I could enjoy that feeling again, enjoy it for ever. I wanted the yacht drifting out of sight behind Herman so that I could use the sea to come to terms with being alone, truly alone for ever.

Herman must have guessed I was day-dreaming – maybe he was annoyed that I didn't seem to appreciate the seriousness of the situation. He leant forward, pink skin suddenly glowing with a red rage as he exposed himself to the full glare of the sun.

'Marty,' he said, 'you must decide in the affirmative. Think of your wife and child, have you seen them recently?' He shook his head. 'It would be good for them for you to decide soon.'

With that, he got up and left, he didn't wait for the fresh coffee that Alexander had just about finalized. He left me to dream about boats and the sea. I was about to cry, to surrender to the irresistible pull of self-pity, unaware of the implications of what had just been said – that would come later.

Everything was coming to an end. I didn't realize it at the time but it was. Herman had raised the stakes so that there was only a way out for one of us.

To the roll call of Nisbet, Harrison, Anderson and O'Kane were soon added the names of Irons, Wilson, Spens and Stewart. Eight men incapacitated by fever. All were crew, used to sleeping wherever they could find a space. Martin had them moved together to the open hall underneath the highest part of the quarterdeck, this being the best ventilated area that was still in the shade. Collectively, they made an even sorrier sight, sweating profusely, drifting in and out of sleep, most not eating, many vomiting their water as soon as it hit their stomachs to leave a syrupy mess by their sides on the boards. None had died as yet, though surely that was to come.

Martin scanned the room. All were on the floor, not a blanket between them. He was surveying for opportunities to hang a hammock when he spied the captain approaching. For a moment, it seemed to him that he was joining them as another casualty, such was the ghostly sheen on the face of the skipper. Here was someone else who was suffering, someone else with eyes bulging under a sopping forehead, thin cheeks and distracted demeanour. Martin felt a brief sympathy for him. The captain was not a man to give in easily, however; if he was infirm, he did not mention it to Martin.

'So then, Doctor, you have gathered our weaklings in one spot. I would have preferred it otherwise. I do not wish to encourage any man to report sick.'

'I could not believe you would have been satisfied had they been left

120

scattered around decks. Word amongst the crew was that the sick were everywhere, I moved to avoid this.'

'Aye,' mused Captain Henry softly, uncharacteristically softly, mopping his brow with a yellowed handkerchief. He seemed to be taking Martin's point. The latter was encouraged to probe further.

'If I may sir, I would welcome your guidance on another matter.'

The captain nodded magnanimously.

'Water, sir. These men require a generous allocation. As you can see, they are burning up. I fear there may be others soon to join them. I would not wish to unfairly ration any future victim of fever, but unless we take on board a fresh supply our own stocks will be exhausted too soon.'

'We . . . we will take on more water at Fort St George.' The voice was weary, the voice of someone suffering.

'Of course, sir. Only we do not know when that will be. There may be somewhere close at hand where we might accomplish the same.'

Captain Henry's eyebrows were raised in query. Martin continued.

'The Spaniards, sir. They spoke of a place they called Point Colou, that is where they had recently taken on supplies. Now I appreciate that they are wrong in their navigation, lost, indeed; yet were we to head for the place they *believed* to be Point Colou we should find water, perhaps even slaves, perhaps the true location of where it was they were. I am a novice sailor, sir, that is why I seek your counsel. I am only concerned with drinking water, and to avoid rationing its provision to new cases. Therefore I merely question, in the most respectful terms, whether sounding with the lead or setting course for Point Colou will reach it the quicker.'

The captain blinked slowly. So slowly that Martin wondered whether he had fallen asleep on his feet.

'They are wrong, aye. Mistaken . . .'

'Their error could still lead us to water.'

'Aye . . . aye lad. There is that. Point Colou . . .'

The captain had more to say but the sound of O'Kane retching interrupted. The sight of it then caused a further pause, almost as if the skipper was unsure as to whether he should join in.

'. . . I shall consider it with the bosun. Perhaps there is a way.'

*   *   *

Martin knew his advice had been taken when he saw that the *Anne* was stretching steadily further away from the shore. This meant more light tacking out into the sea in order to catch the prevailing eastward wind that would send them speeding back towards the Guinea coast twenty leagues along. It also meant more fears in the men that they were heading too far towards Cape Bojador, or so they would have thought, unaware as they were that they were long past it.

For all this it was noticeable to Martin how much morale improved; sailors were happiest when sailing, happiest on the move. Making for open sea meant respite from the flies and mosquitoes of the land too, and also somehow alleviated the fever in some. This comfort came too late however for O'Kane and Spens, their bodies finding themselves wrapped in tarpaulin and surrendered to the cool ocean. Another ceremony, another reading from the Bible. Martin listened with a weighty heart as the captain slurred his words; if only he had tested his scheme earlier. *May they rest in peace, Amen.*

Two days at sea then back to the coast. The captain's fever subsided, the crew were singing again as they homed in on the shore. Up atop the nest on the mizzen-mast the smoke from the fire that led them to the settlement was spotted and a course duly set. José had relayed his information well, his conferences with Wells and Captain Henry had been fruitful. Under normal circumstances, thought Martin, all three should be commended. It was a matter of no little irony that they would remain unsung heroes.

Again, the *Anne* was moved in close, to within two leagues. This time however, the land opposite offered more to observe than dense vegetation. At the beach edge was a collection of huts and enclosures, and a larger wooden shack which was fenced off. Black faces looked out to them as the crew spied on them from the water. Soon there were canoes being introduced to the waves, soon the canoes had progressed beyond the breakers that rolled in a continuous barrier thirty yards from the shore, testimony to the skill and dexterity with which the natives manipulated their craft and paddles. The canoes appeared at the ship's port side. Martin leaned over the rail to smile down on them. Then, something even more astonishing; in amongst the negroes a white face, darkened by the sun yet distinct from those around it. This white face was smiling too.

122

'Captain and crew of the *Anne* . . .' came the shout from its lips, '. . . Welcome to Point Colou!'

It was a strange voice, one with an accent Martin could not place. No matter, they were here, they had arrived.

The trader was taken on board. His name was Harold. He spoke with an accent that was difficult to place and Martin was sure he had meant something else, *Haraldt* perhaps, but those around him leapt to hear it as the former and to the man himself it did not seem to matter. It was not, Martin would have admitted, as if he would be mistaken for anyone else, the only white man on the coast for hundreds of miles. The captain greeted him in French and received a smile for his efforts, the first of many.

Although old, at least in his fifties, the trader gave every impression of enjoying a rude health unaffected by the solitude that was his existence. To all, he was respectful and cordial, if a little crude in his affable joking with the crew. He told the captain he had been at Colou for over four years and his deeply lined skin and ruddy nose certainly bore testimony to this. He had contacts, he said, a network of suppliers working deep inland, a range of grommetoes – free natives – working exclusively for him. How many slaves do you have available for trade? asked the captain. Do you have water? asked Martin. Women? asked the crew. To which he smiled, a smile for everything, a smile that said everything, everything at a price.

He came on board to offer his invitation for the crew to join him ashore. Captain Henry agreed in principle but decreed that the initial party should be small, just himself, Wells and Martin. Eventually it was agreed that there would be four, Martin suggesting that José join them to corroborate the quality of the merchandise in comparison with that carried by the Spaniards. And so the trip was confirmed to take place at daybreak. They would not rush in, no; it was an historic occasion, 30 April 1698. The captain announced this fact as if expecting a fanfare.

Martin was briefed in Captain Henry's cabin at midnight. Although it was now acknowledged that they were at Point Colou, there was to be no mention of the incident on board the *Marguerita*, nor information given to the men as to the incorrect theory of where Colou lay in relation to Fort St George. Haraldt himself could well be wrong, said the skipper, the years of isolation could have disorientated him. As far as the men were to be concerned,

123

they were some way east of St George. Indeed, added the captain, warming to his theme, this had always been the intention, the avoidance of Royal Africa Company territory in order to enjoy better trading terms with independent operators such as Mr Haraldt. After all, had he not the same the goods?

Dawn, and the men climbed down from the *Anne* into the longboat to the perimeter of the sea ledge, where they clambered aboard the canoes of the natives to be steered over the cascading fall of the breakers rushing to the shore. The waves and paddles carried them on to a gliding finish on the sands. Martin swung a leg over the side and found himself in Africa, a hundred faces peering at him with a curiosity that reflected his own. Captain Henry bellowed instructions relating to the canteens and ledgers to be brought ashore but Martin was deaf to them, taking in the sensations of the landscape and the fact that he had made it to another world. It would be a full five minutes before the smile of wonderment would leave his face.

The captain's judgement proved sound in one respect: Mr Haraldt had the goods and the means of exchange. He showed the party round his outpost with an amicable pride. There were over two hundred souls living within the flimsy walls of the compound; all of them displayed a deference of sorts, particularly some of the women who, Martin noted, were most free with their smiles and kisses to their outsider king. Was it his imagination or did some of the younger children cartwheeling barefoot around the settlement have paler skin than their cousins? His eye was drawn to them, drawn to them all in their unashamed nakedness, some men covering their genitals in a calico loincloth, others wearing nothing but a belt. The women were bare-breasted, free, nipples darker than stained oak, broad and pointed as if swollen by the heat. Martin was not used to the sight of flesh, especially the female variety, though he tried to study with a medical rather than prurient eye. He could not help but conclude that the vision before him was ungodly, the lack of gentility and refinement troubling him.

Captain Henry meanwhile was concerned with the military aspects of the garrison; how many carbines and cannon, how many defenders, how many raids had there been?

To which Mr Haraldt's lips gave nothing but a slow grin. A beaming smile to say you are asking the wrong questions, we are happy here, we have

124

harmony, we are not attacked because it suits the caboceers to let us be, to provide them with an outlet for their goods, to help them make money. Why would they attack us, Captain?

Anne had set sail loaded with firkins of gunpowder, guns and muskets. Captain Henry would have assumed that these weapons would fuel a conquest but made a poor show of hiding his astonishment when he learned that the conquest would not be made by the white man but by black tribe against tribe, those on the coast moving inland using European guns to take slaves to trade for guns, to take more slaves. It was God's will.

Not that there was any sign of such conflict within the encampment. Here all faces were friendly, here the drums played out only a dancing beat. Here all eyes sparkled in anticipation of the riches that would flow from trade with ships like the *Anne* which were beginning to find their way there with increasing regularity. Martin already found himself wondering if he could live there as Haraldt did, taking a wife, many wives, siring children by the dozen, taking his money from the trade. It was worth considering, especially once the mainland heat had the captain's brow drenched in a feverish sweat again and his powers of reason and his temper grew short.

The party moved on, guided by Haraldt, followed by a throng of children, towards the guarded cages housing the slaves. There were eight in the pens, although they were told they had housed as many as one hundred awaiting transit to the Guineaman ships. Captain Henry insisted on an option to purchase those that were there immediately and thus the unfortunates were led out for inspection. Sorrowful men, thought Martin, hanging their heads more in shame than in fear, hands tied behind their backs, chains linking them neck to neck. Martin prodded the first in line with his cane, feeling that this might appear more professional than touching the negro with his bare hands. He wanted to appear professional to everyone, the captain, Wells, Haraldt, even to the negro himself. So it was he probed with the stick, pushing and poking and prompting a startled look in his victim's eyes, eyes suddenly alert, shining white amid a dark countenance, like candles lit inside a pumpkin head. A response, murmured Martin in his embarrassment, a satisfactory test, his reflexes are alive. Next, he lifted the man's arms aloft, checking for swelling and growths around the armpits; none were apparent. He proceeded down towards the groin, trying to make the subject open his legs but meeting more resistance. Improvising, he stuck out his tongue so that the negro might copy, he did so and a vibrant pink tongue reached out to him. The negro's front teeth were filed, all of them to a point, ivory spears in a wild and tamed creature, captured trophies in the white man's hunt.

'He's good,' announced Martin, 'A good . . .' he paused, searching for the word, '. . . specimen.' He felt himself flush as he said it, felt the attentions of the others crowding in on him, much as they must have been on the negro.

He offered to inspect the rest on his own whilst his host continued the tour with the party. The captain insisted on staying close though, determined to scrutinize every detail of each examination, leaving Martin to wonder whose eyes felt worse on him, those of the slaves or the almost salivating skipper. His routine grew shorter and shorter until all eight were done, all passed fit. The first of over three hundred, it could only be hoped they would eventually appreciate their place in the proud history of the *Anne*'s trading mission. Martin was astounded to hear the captain insist the men were loaded immediately despite the mild protestation from Haraldt that they remain in their pens until they were set to sail, but no; Captain Henry's face had its sheen of sweat back, his eyes were no little wild. He would have his way, no matter that the eight might stew for weeks below deck whilst the holds were filled, before they would leave for the Indies. They would be loaded immediately. May they rest in peace.

If the *Anne* was to take immediate possession, there would have to be an exchange of equal value until payment in goods was made, explained Haraldt. This would normally take the form of hostages, members of the moored ship's crew, to prevent their vessel from leaving. He proposed Martin and José stay overnight to fulfil this. The captain agreed without a word, nodding briskly whilst gazing at his exotic new purchases. He walked behind them, enraptured, as the departing party were led back to the canoes.

One of the grommetoes led Martin and José to their quarters, a pleasant and cool room within a straw and plaster hut. There were two beds and a matted floor. Through a simple mime, their guide indicated they were to sleep until called to dinner which would be after sundown. Martin would have preferred to walk to the beach and to enjoy the waves from the perspective of land. However, this would have brought the ship and her captain back into view. He lay down on his cot, suddenly tired. Soon he was drifting into a light sleep, hypnotized by the deepening rhythm of his own breathing. He lay there for a while, consciousness fading in and out of focus, his ears picking up sounds that would prompt images in his mind; children playing, women singing, running water, *Africa open*.

The noises continued, rousing him further, water being poured, splashing and squeals of pleasure to go with it. Intrigued, he slowly raised himself to his feet and followed the sounds outside. Out in the settlement's main square, in a collection of wooden tubs, some of the grommetoes were washing with unrestrained pleasure. As naked as they were by day, emptying buckets over each other's heads; unashamed, unworried, unencumbered with the travails of bathing as Martin knew them as part of his life in faraway, cold Scotland. When had he himself last washed? Weeks, months ago, when he had dived into the flooded hold. His clothes were the same ones he had worn since they left Tenerife. Martin cupped a hand under the sleeve of his shirt, feeling the rancid damp that accumulated there each day. He found himself peeling off the same shirt, almost without thinking, and continuing his strip as if in a trance, not pausing as his hands peeled off his boots, socks and made to untie his waistband. Soon he too was naked, and had found a tub to immerse himself in. His pale form immediately drew shrieks from the children playing around him, and in an instant he realized how dazzlingly white his body appeared in comparison to the others, and thin too, a skeleton amongst the living. Although he was now the centre of attention he initially felt no shame at the strangers espying him in this state; reminding himself that he could not credit them with the same powers of discernment with which he would credit his own kind, thinking of the situation as akin to being naked before a pack of dogs. The volume of the high-pitched squeals which accompanied his every movement rapidly forced a reappraisal of this stance however, and a hurried duck of his head under the water. *A pack of dogs.* Friendly dogs. Two old women came close and began to scrub at him, using some kind of bunched dried flowers. Even they were taken with giggles as they went about their work. Martin closed his eyes and tried to concentrate on the scent of the perfume with which they cleansed his skin. When he opened them again he felt an alarm as he saw his clothes were gone, the heap at the side of the tub having been moved to an unstated destination. He tried not to panic, not to think of the jeers of the crew were he forced to return as bare as a savage; the discomfort galloped away within him at speed regardless. At last a voice behind him, one that might help restore order.

'So . . . Mr Surgeon, you choose to take your bath with the grommetoes . . . You have startled them.'

The tone of the voice was one of joviality rather than admonition.

'I am keen to understand the ways of the savage; after all, I will be responsible for their welfare aboard ship.'

Martin found himself talking to a shadow in the fading evening light rather than the sight of the man standing behind him. Haraldt now came forward to address him directly, the mirth in his face showing more mischief than any of the natives surrounding him.

'Ahh . . . Of course, sir. *The ways of the savage . . .*' His voice found an easy target to mock in the absurd scientific timbre Martin had tried to affect. 'Well then, you should know that it is the habit of the savage to wash once a day, in fresh water. At sea, I am told, they yearn for this and will scrub themselves down with the ocean, if permitted. And the teeth, sir, you must have noticed? They clean them daily too, using the bark of a tree, polishing them to the whiteness one observes. Their food? The savage is fond of the fruits that abound in Guinea, happy to eat from trees, bush and the ground; shrubs and egg-plant satisfy their stomachs in a way an educated man might find perverse. A most unusual breed, Doctor, as I am sure you will discover.'

'And your breed, sir?' Martin heard his voice become more arch in its delivery as he wrestled with the absurdity of the situation, conversing whilst naked in a tub with a man who seemed to never stop smiling, a convivial man who knew he had the greater knowledge, the advantage in every respect.

'I do not understand.'

'Your country?'

A fresh smile, a nod of understanding.

'Africa.'

'You told our captain France.'

'Then why do you ask again?'

'Because I did not believe you.'

Still the smile lingered. 'And this matters?'

'It matters if a man lies.'

A pause. Haraldt's face gradually becoming more solemn. 'My father was German. I have lived for many years in Denmark and also London. What does that make my breed, Mr English Surgeon?'

'Scottish.'

'*Scottish* surgeon . . .' As Haraldt said this, Martin saw the twinkling devilment return to the older man's eye. 'So concerned with nationalities. Tell me, Doctor, the Englishman and the Scotsman, are they different, do they share the same bones, the same eyes and ears . . . is it not the man that counts, not his country?'

'You said France.'

'If you recall I said nothing, your captain assumed this and I did not move to correct him – for which you must forgive me. I merely thought it may perhaps reassure him to believe this as I took him to be a . . . *limited* man in these matters.'

Haraldt did not elaborate further, there was no need. Martin realized it was not only himself who was now exposed. By strategy or accident, his host had begun to build a bridge of confidence between the pair.

'How many wives do you have?'

The question caused Haraldt to snort in shock and amusement and again the conversation returned to a jocular theme.

'Wives! There are women here, Martin, perhaps you should learn of their ways too!' At this Haraldt's laugh threatened to overcome him, reducing him to convulsions. Martin knew the humour was at his expense but found it hard to take offence.

'Where are my clothes?'

The older man wiped his brow as he calmed down. 'They too are enjoying a bathe. I will organize items for you to wear whilst they dry. Unless of course, you wish to adopt the ways of the savage?'

Martin did not reply, shaking his head instead, as if mildly exasperated. At this point José emerged, staggering out of the hut like a drunk. He had been sleeping, his eyes, narrow from fatigue and his arrested slumbers, becoming wider as he took in the vision of Martin sitting naked in the water of the tub.

'Good evening sir,' boomed Haraldt. 'Will you join your companion in enjoying a bath?'

José nodded and began to take off his shirt, exposing a torso noticeably darker than Martin's. The difference between a Spaniard and a Scotsman. Within seconds he had dropped his breeches and was stripped, bounding over the side into another unoccupied tub. As two old maids approached bearing their washing implements he glanced across to Martin, his face a comic mixture of trepidation and anticipation. He winked and then was gone, ducking his head down beneath the water level but blowing off like a whale as he descended. Bubbles rushed noisily to the surface, causing the native women to dissolve into outraged shrieks that were so loud Martin wondered if they could be heard back in Garachico.

So by now you have heard all about my women, my endless successes, my triumphs. You will be impressed, you now know the secrets, the inside story, but maybe you are still not satisfied; maybe a part of you is wondering how it could be that all of these people were so easily impressed, so submissive. Didn't he ever meet someone who wasn't impressed with all this transparent bullshit, someone who tried to engage him on equal terms? Well, truth be told, the reason all the women I've described fell so easily owes more than a little to the fact that they put themselves in the frame to start with by some kind of demonstration of their susceptibility to my kind of thing. Yes, it's true, they were pre-selected; I try to avoid the other kind of women, the ones that might challenge me, ask me what the fuck all this chasing is about, avoid them like the plague. I did meet one once though – predictably enough, it ended in disaster. I married her.

It was in America, in Key West, Florida, to be precise, that she came into my life. Seven years ago, summer '93. An overcast day, our second in the port. I was crewing another yacht, as I had done ever since stepping aboard the *Anneka* in St Raph at the start of my odyssey in my abortive student days. I had crewed in a variety of guises –

simple ligger, cabin steward, first mate – and on a variety of boats – sixty-footers, luxury cruisers, liners. And all this for a lad from Greenock with no great love of sailing, a love of the sea for sure, but a different kind of love from the rest on deck; none of them loved it the same as me, for the water itself.

So this was another voyage on the circuit that Michel had introduced me to at the beginning, taking the ships over to their seasonal cruising territories – the Med in the summer, the Caribbean for the winter. Moving from one ocean to the next was the easiest part of this life, the rest was fraught with frustrations. Waiting weeks for cheque clearance to come through for the yachts that you would then be asked to vacate at a moment's notice so that the new owners or tenants could take possession, living off bread and cheese and the emergency supplies in the galley whilst you waited for your wages from the same bank, or waited for new instructions to be faxed to your skipper from some important boss's harassed PA half a world away. A glamorous life. If you had the time to hang around. So we hung around getting pissed and stoned and hoping the weather would improve and one day another European yacht arrived and berthed next to us. I had been out on my own for a wander and had sussed out the town bars – most of which seemed to be gay – and returned to be greeted with the news of the latest arrival. The rumour had it that there were girls on board and that some of our lads had already fixed up a date. I don't know why but I was in a mellow mood, and I declined the opportunity to join in. I had no money and was lonely, a loneliness made more acute by being in company, especially the company of the boisterous younger men who were going to join the young ladies on their introductory tour. So I watched them all leave, and saw the girls join them, and sat gazing at an empty yacht as the early evening light faded. I don't know what I would have been thinking at that precise moment, but later it would seem as if I had *willed* her to be there, that somehow I had asked the gods to give me a sign that they had not forsaken me and could grant meaning to a life of endless journeying. But maybe that's just me post-rationalizing the miracle that was about to happen, because the yacht next to ours wasn't empty; one more head emerged from below

131

a full hour after her giggling colleagues. This was Johanna, with the most exquisite face I had ever seen. And the miracle wasn't that she was so beautiful, or the way she carried herself was so serene, or that she knew right away that she was being watched and smiled over to whoever it was that seemed to give the signal he was longing for her. No, the miracle was that from the first moment I laid my eyes upon her I knew that this was someone different from anybody I had ever met before in my life. This was someone I could love, and I could let love me.

A blast from the past. A gangling, languid, laid-back blast from the past. Yes friends, Monsieur Nonchalance himself is in town and appearing in a bar near you. Your bar.

'Nice place you got here, Martin. Very nice.'

There is a silence that follows his comments whilst I try to figure out a couple of things, the first of them being just how serious he is. Deadly, probably, given that there was no grimace or even empty-eyed smile to go with the words, certainly no air-guitar being played by his ebony hands nor shadow-boxing actions that would have previously been the accoutrements to show that he might not have been entirely sincere when dishing out the compliments. No, Jérome isn't fidgeting today, hopping around like a ferret has been put into his trousers and has managed to get right under his skin; no, this is a mellow Jérome, a well-dressed, Italian-besuited Jérome, as lean and swanky as a catwalk model. A mature Jérome, mellow and thoughtful, he has grown up. *The man* has become a man. *The man* though seems on a downer. Welcome, join the club.

'Your ideas, or did you buy it like this?'

Again I'm thrown. Could this be Jérome speaking like a normal person, not leaving interminable gaps between sentences, following up one comment with another, within the same week?

'All mine. Or mine and my wife . . . Johanna's. I chose the name, the overall concept . . . colours. She did most of the detail, logos and menus, the smaller design. All hers.'

'A good team. I would like to meet her, is she coming today?'

132

It's my turn to squirm and let my body language broach the unmentionable. I don't fucking know Jérome, do you, is that why you're here all of a sudden, or am I being paranoid? Who is this guy, is he an impostor? *A good team.* That isn't the kind of thing Jérome would say, and why is he speaking in English all the time?

'*Tu parles en anglais tout le temps, Jérome; pourquoi?*'

A smile and a shrug that erupts unilaterally in one shoulder before rolling across his chest to the other. An impossibly broad smile, a Cheshire cat smile with gold teeth and a coffee-coloured face. A blast from the past.

'I've been doing a lot of business with English. Good business. You should have stayed in touch, very good business. Good for you. But your bar . . . very nice. I understand. Anyway, you prefer to talk in French?'

'English is cool. My French may be rusty. It's been such a long time. What brings you here Jérome, apart from my fine bar?'

'I have a present for you. I wanted to see you, friend. I thought you might be interested. You miss me, yes?'

Well, yes and no to be honest, Jérome. I didn't miss you when they held me at the airport for four hours because they were convinced I was carrying. Convinced because someone, somewhere had put the mark on me, accidentally or on purpose. But I miss the friendship we had before that for sure, when we were two young blades on the make and take in those halcyon Riviera days. And the bit in between when we were couriers for hire, working the routes for your Arab friends and my Spanish friends, I could take or leave. Then again, friend, I suppose we are like a married couple, and we've been through the stages like one; intimate and caring at the start, sharing everything, tolerating everything in each other because we know, *knew*, that despite whatever petty jealousies and feuds that might develop between us, ultimately we absolutely had each other's best interests at heart, and no matter where each other was, we could depend on that as a certainty, that we were looking out for each other. I would never have let you down and you were the same. And I thought that it was rather wonderful for a Greenock boy to have reached out into the world and found someone from a background so different from his and made such a bond, a *brotherhood*, with him, a closeness I had never come near with any woman. Maybe you saw it that way too, or am I just being romantic, me with my dreams of pirates and water, and a nation of outlaws living by their own noble code. We lost it though, didn't we Jérome, just like a sad married couple, until we never knew for sure just where we stood. You know, when I made it out of that fucking airport and stood outside the crematorium waiting for my father's service to begin I cried and cried, Jérome. Cried for the first time in years, a fucking new one on me. And everyone got it wrong, trying to comfort me, telling me that he loved me but couldn't find a way to show it, and I, well I wasn't going to tell them what the hurt was *really* about, was I Jérome? And the strangest thing is that I'm hurting again like that today but cannot discuss it because you'd never understand, you just never let yourself be touched like that, you live your life avoiding it. Now I envy you for that. How I envy you for that, my friend.

'What kind of present?'

Jérome disappears momentarily behind his smile. 'Here?' he laughs.

OK. Let's consider the evidence. Let's think what might be going on. Item one, the reappearance of Jérome, an Anglified Jérome here in Mallorca, far from his home beat. Number two, the rushed manner, the accelerated speech coupled with sentimental references to the olden days inviting me to bypass our recent history and dwell on the past. For points three and four we can ponder on the freely-given references to *business*, and how good that might have been, and presumably still could be, for me. Plus the fact that he doesn't want to give me my *gift* here, as in out-in-the-open here. This is a private present. I don't think you would need to be Einstein to figure it out, or Sherlock Holmes. No, even Inspector Clouseau could piece the charge together from these tell-tale clues. Jerome is high on his own supply and wants me to share the action. Whether this is because of a sincere desire to make up for fucking me over seven years ago, or just a simple way of doing business with someone he knows in an alien environment, or some form of entrapment with us being wired and recorded as we speak by the police or Herman's goons, is for me to figure out. That is, if I choose to accept the mission. For the moment, I borrow my old friend's trick of communication by shrugs and grimaces, keeping any future escape route clear by way of throwing this cloak of ambiguity. *What did he say when you offered him the drugs, did he consent to buy them? . . . Couldn't say . . . Didn't say anything, just pulled a face, just kind of slumped in his chair. Is that enough for you?*

Jérome looked around as if he was looking for something. I didn't make it easy for him. Without excusing himself he was up on his feet, pacing towards the toilet; yes, pacing, another word I never thought I would live to use in any connection with him. Crazy days. The end was indeed drawing near. Clouseau could have read the portents. Then Jérome was back at my side.

'In there,' he said, 'quickly, before anyone else finds it. For you. Special. Try it.'

He was nodding encouragingly, although I went in more from a sense of curiosity than any urge to indulge or please him. Inside, once I'd locked the cubicle door behind me, I smiled at the sight of the lines he'd laid out for me, two of them in shaky parallel. There was a note, a hastily written user's guide, weighed down by the silver quill so kindly left to help snort the shit into my system. *Good quality*, it read, *New supplier – pure. Try. Trust me.*

As hard though I tried, my smile faded as my eye lingered on the last two words, words I never thought I would live to use in connection with Jérome again. What was he here for? What sense did it make for me to be standing there staring at this stuff, when there was so much else falling down all around me, when the only certainty in my life was that I would be back in this same fucking toilet six hours later, only this time so I could clean it up, to make it ready for another day of this garbage. Were the lines safe, clean cocaine, not heroin, not cut with poison so that they would find me here, slumped over the fucking toilet bowl, another sad junkie loser? Another sad loser. I bent down towards Jérome's presents. Poison? I hoped it was. Maybe he'd come to do me a favour after all.

★   ★   ★

Of course, the shit was so fucking good that any scheme to be involved with it seemed a good idea. *The best idea ever, honestly.*

'You want two, three kilos?'

'I don't . . . travel any more, Jérome. I can't. They're looking out for me. I'd have to be crazy.'

'Then you get someone else.'

'I can't think of anyone else I would let . . . It's tougher now, Jérome. They've caught up with our kind of scam.'

'Then here. It doesn't matter. I sell to you, you do what you want. I tell you, this is good stuff. Business is good, good everywhere. You be my man in Mallorca. I can get it to you, you decide from there. Your business. I'm trying to help your business because you are my friend. Will you be my friend?'

'It's not as simple as that, Jérome. I have no money, everything is tied up, in this bar or whatever. I can't pay you.'

'Then you pay me when you can. That's why I do business with friends, I trust you, buy three kilos, pay me in two months. Three months. Twenty thousand dollars. Friend's price. You can do what you want with it, your business. Cut with something, deal yourself, sell on at fifty a gram and you have ten times your investment. *Good business.*'

Maybe looking to multiply my money that much was pushing it too far, but there was sense in what he was saying, especially since I was high, and that my own business here in the bar was anything other than good. And especially since I had a need for money, a need more desperate than anything I had ever known. Jérome was now smiling, relaxed, sanguine. I needed some of that, maybe this was where it came from, why turn away an opportunity when it presented itself like this, with a bit of clever planning the shit would be in my possession less than an hour and I would have doubled my money, or rather made money out of thin air since my outlay would be fuck-all. This had to be the way. Maybe I was wrong about Jérome, maybe he wasn't the one who betrayed me. Maybe he really was my friend.

'Can you let me have two days to check something out? Two days, Jérome. You call me, I'll tell you what business we can do. You want another beer? What about the old days, Jérome. Do they still work the beaches, ever see Henri and his van, ever go to Les Acacias, ever run into that old bastard Michel, my skipper?'

Jérome rolled his eyes and tapped a twitching thigh. As ever it was hard to know whether this was my answer in itself or a prelude to another series of jerks, tics and gestures which would serve as clues. Maybe if he could be persuaded to take another line of his own product we might make progress in a real conversation. *Plus ça change*, Jérome, *plus ça change*.

The plan was simple, and there is a beauty in simplicity, a beguiling beauty that maybe takes your eye away from the detail that should concern you, especially when the shit you find yourself in has the potential to become especially heavy shit. My plan was simple. Beautiful, so long as everyone played their part, behaved honourably. Beautiful in that everybody could have got what they wanted; Jérome his new distributor on Mallorca, the Carcera brothers their new opportunity, Herman to buy my bar, and me, well, I was going to sail off into the sunset and leave it all behind.

Behind.

As it happened, nobody won, nobody. I did take a boat out to sea, but it turned out to be a very different voyage from the one originally intended. Not my fault. I tried. I honestly tried. A simple plan. The cocaine would be in my possession a matter of hours. I wasn't going to be greedy, wasn't going to cut it, dilute it with anything to bump up its weight and value, no; if it came to me pure then I would pass it on as pure, it was up to Miguel and big Tony what happened next, what state it would be in before it finally rushed up the noses of the island's sniffing elite, and the boys were confident enough that they had a demand to satisfy in that regard. Not my problem then, I would buy from Jérome and sell to the brothers. Jérome had given me a month to pay my twenty thousand dollars whilst the boys were under strict instructions that their money was required up-front, all forty-five thousand. Cash-flow. Simple, beautiful. My only risk was the time the shit was in my hands, it didn't take a genius to work out that this was a lot of gear to have on one's doorstep, and that there would be one awful lot of explaining to do if the stuff was in your lap were the police to stop the music during our little game of pass the parcel. Going into it, waking up on the day in question, this was my overriding fear, that this was a set-up, or that Jérome himself was being set up and was too dumb to realize. But I was small fry, why would anyone want to bust me in the middle of my one and only deal? And Jérome? For all his faults, he was a survivor, he had stayed in the trade all this time, all the time I was screwing and cleaning toilets in my island speakeasy joint, he had been giving himself an easier ride by working the business he knew best. *Good business.* Maybe, he certainly looked good on it, and had obviously kept out of the wrong sort of mischief and avoided the worst kind of luck that can blight the best-laid plans. Bad luck? Not this time, please Jérome. Everybody is going to get what they want; at least, that was the plan.

A sultry day, at least to start with. May 28th. The morning had begun brightly, one prolonged dazzle of brilliant sunshine forcing its way through the apartment blinds though without the angry heat that would blister everything and anything left exposed to it. I woke early and in good spirits. I remember ironing some pants and a clean white linen shirt. Shaving whilst facing something other than a scowl in the mirror, whistling in the shower, coughing on the heavy fumes of the aftershave I hit myself with in a series of generous squirts. I was in control today, I would look good, smell beautiful and have an attitude. Even the sight of the blue sky clouding over around ten-thirty didn't dampen my enthusiasm for this particular day and what was about to be done. I would head down and open up the Arena for breakfasts, brief the staff on my requirements and wait for Jérome to arrive around twelve. He would then follow me back to the flat – I wasn't going to walk with him whilst he carried the gear, that was still his risk until he handed it over – where I would test it before agreeing to buy. I had tidied the flat in preparation the night before though in truth there was hardly anything there to tidy. I tried not to think of how long I'd been living there and moving more and more fixtures in somehow troubled me, as if having basic living items – a kettle, television, furniture – would serve to remind me that this was now my permanent home rather than a temporary one-night stop-over where I had somehow passed away the best part of the last year. No, I still had a home, a family home in the mountains. I would sort that out once that bitch of a wife finally got in touch and made her pitch to settle. She could take whatever she fucking wanted and then we'd be able to split properly, her presumably to go and be fucking miserable in Sweden, and me? I was going to sail away to freedom. That's what today was all about. Whatever I had done, and I knew there was plenty, I couldn't think how that deserved the sudden walk-out, the total lack of communication for over three weeks, no contact with my daughter. How much did she have to hate me to do that, didn't even prisoners have more family visits, didn't even fucking condemned men? Maybe this was why I didn't mind living in primitive conditions, in this solitary cell of a flat with its brown wallpaper and musty air, its echoes when your shoes clicked along the dusty tiled floors. All of it gave me a sense of righteousness about the situation, a resentment that however bad things might have been, at least it wasn't *all* my fault. And that resentment gave me the something to kick against and the energy to kick hard, the drive to do what I had to do, what I would do today.

Jérome arrived early. It didn't unnerve me. He walked into the doorway and stood still until I noticed him. Then he took his sunglasses off and winked. I knew everything was going to be all right it was that kind of wink, it said as much and more, something like – OK Martin, I understand your nervousness, with this being such a big day, but chill, relax, it's all in hand, it will all go fine, your ship has come in my friend.

I turned to Sarah who was next to me behind the bar, mopping up after me as I went. A good team. I found her presence comforting, her so lovely and fresh in her white vest top and short skirt. Everything about her gave signals of how she belonged here; the tanned legs and arms, lithe, supple, so comfortable in the late spring heat, her scent, hairband, she was born to Spain, born to be here at this moment, so carefree for her yet heavy for me. But that is a man's lot, to take on

139

the world, to go out hunting for the meat that will feed us. She belonged to me, I wanted to kiss her, not in a sexual way, just a kiss and an embrace, maybe on her bare shoulder, so that I could let my lips reassure themselves with the softness of her young skin. The sort of kiss a man might give his wife when he hears some good news, a promotion, a lottery win, when your tiny daughter tells you she loves you. I wanted to kiss Sarah for luck before heading out but I couldn't and didn't because Alexander was there; I would have to find a way of dealing with him later. For now, with Jérome standing waiting, I told her I was going away for a while, that any messages could be left here at the bar, and that if Miguel or big Tony showed they were to be sent to the flat, but only after three o'clock.

Then us two hombres made our move, black and white, walking together into the high noon glare, sleeves rolled up, shades on, a swagger in our walk. Not ordinary men, more gunslingers heading off to the shoot-out. Jérome was looking cool, you couldn't see he was carrying a package but I assumed it was on him, tucked away under his suit jacket. He had a mobile phone, and an earpiece from it in place like it was a radio, as if he was a secret serviceman, a highly trained ex-assassin protecting an oil prince on his tour of the fleshpots. I asked him to follow me. He nodded, sauntering after me during our five-minute journey. When I arrived at the doorstep to the apartment block I was careful to leave the front door ajar so that he could follow me in, then he was pacing around the hallway and stairs, looking out for anyone hiding or any concealed cameras, now acting as if he *was* a secret security man. He eventually made it inside the apartment and was soon repeating the act, not uttering a word, not a sound, not even a chuckle at the new set of kitchen scales I had set up on the lounge floor.

I saw him punch a number into his mobile and then he turned his back on me to peer through the blinds on to the street outside. He murmured in English, I could hear the address and number of the flat mentioned. This was the first time I realized he wasn't carrying the gear himself; naive as it might seem, I honestly thought it was hidden under his clothes, maybe strapped to his back beneath his shirt. Because that was part of the attraction of the transaction to me, that it would just be us, the two friends, a private matter. But when he spoke into the receiver he became a different person, transformed so that *the man* who hung aimlessly around Les Acacias, *the man* who was my shipmate on the *Anneka*, *the man* who winked at me in the doorway at the Arena Bar was so far away. Instead here he was now, another dealer, a big-time dealer. He finished speaking and waited, still looking out, arms folded. He didn't turn to face me or explain who he had spoken to or what would happen next. A different man. This was business.

Moments later, his movements became more agitated, he began to talk into the phone – the line had been kept open. He walked to the door, muttering as he did so, part of the same private conversation. He reached the front door and held it ajar. My eye lingered on the part of the hall and wall where I had made love to Sonia two summers past. I had thought that there was tension in that moment but it was a simple affair compared to this, and I found myself wishing I had just stuck to what I was good at, the screwing and fucking, the bullying of staff. I almost felt nostalgic for those days that I realized were now going to be locked into a different age, an age of innocence.

Jérome meanwhile was totally focused on landing the catch, steering in the next arrival, welcoming him to the secret landing plot. Soon enough, the newcomer was here, out of breath, drawn and furtive, a strange-looking kind of guy who reminded me of Henri from those years ago on the beach, a blonde version of Henri with dirty white hair and moustache but equally as greasy and badly dressed. His khaki shirt sported dark stains around the armpits with a smell to match. Welcome to the sophisticated world of international drugs, welcome to the stylish players in this exquisite game. He didn't look Spanish for sure, but neither did he look British with his sharp features and narrow eyes though it was English the pair conversed in once he was inside with the door closed behind him.

'Cool?'

'Yeah it's cool, you cool?'

'I'm cool.'

Jérome didn't bother to introduce us, preferring perhaps to get on with more pressing matters. He pointed to the case our guest was carrying and jerked a thumb towards the lounge. We followed his lead, me last. When I arrived the package was produced, a large white block, as brilliant under its cellophane wrapping as Procter and Gamble's latest soap, engineered to bleach your jaded whites beyond brightness. The stranger threw it down towards the scales; it hit the floor with a thump, hard like a brick, tougher than the tiles it landed on, a builder's commodity, an industrial pack of icing sugar. Vacuum-packed, I hadn't expected that, vacuum-packed in its wrapper and with a stamp moulded into the contours of its side, welcome to quality control, welcome to the big time.

It lay on the floor, two flies buzzing about it, curious and crazed, looking for a way in to check it out, round and round, hovering frantically in the stale air. I almost winced, this stuff was surely too precious to be treated this way, God alone knew what price had been paid just to bring it here, to this apartment through however many sets of customs hurdles and however many pairs of criminal hands. Jérome and his friend both stood back from it, waiting for me to do whatever I wanted with it whilst they were still there, until I formally acknowledged receipt of the quality goods that had been ordered. Jérome glanced at me, eyebrow raised quizzically; was I going to test it? Yes, I nodded, I was.

Ridiculous as it might seem, now that it was my turn to do my thing I felt a twinge of adolescent shyness begin to take a grip. What was unnerving me was the realization that this deal was always going to be way beyond anything I had ever been involved in before, even when I was a courier taking the shit from one place to another. This time I was straying miles away from that safer ground, this time I was a buyer, part of the commercial chain, an investor rather than a delivery service. I was out of my league, but trying to carry it off, something that would have been easier if I was just dealing with Jérome as planned. Would this new guy realize that I was bluffing, that I was strictly small-time, or did he not give a shit either way, was the joke on me, was this the real thing or fake, like me? I had to try to find out, armed only with the most basic grasp of what I should be looking for. Yet here I was, staring at a twenty-year-sentence-worth of shit on the ground, and, as ever, thinking about the *signals* I was giving. OK, I told myself, begin for fuck's sake Martin, get this over with.

And so I came to begin. Weighing the load was easy, even an idiot can look in control toying with the balance and counter-weights. Three kilos, easy. Was it pure? Here I was in unfamiliar waters, relying on what I had picked up in conversations in smoky bars way back. What if the talk had just been to fool me, a joke back-firing ten years later, what if the industry had moved on since then? Jérome's friend was staring impatiently at me – what had he been told, that I was a player, big-time, worthy of the generous terms of credit that had been agreed? And was I about to spoil all that with my half-assed tests, fumbling hands and sweaty lip? It was hard enough to open the fucking bag, it was packed so tightly, with a solidity that would vanish once the air got to it, and for one second the thought that it might all end with me spilling the lot across the floor crossed my mind, on to tiles so dusty that the bag would weigh more if we ever managed to get it all back together. Eventually, I managed a tear in the polythene and looked up to the folded arms and tapping feet of my business partners.

'Jérome, could you get me a glass of water?'

It wasn't because I was thirsty that I asked him to fetch it, I asked because the first test could tell me two things. Pure coke dissolves in water, usually before it reaches the bottom of the glass. Adulterated coke won't, unless it's been helped perhaps, like if the water is hot to aid the process. If Jérome is trying to screw me, he might try to up the temperature, so I'm almost as interested in what he brings back from the kitchen as I am in what he's leaving me with. After an uncomfortable delay, he returned, handing me a chipped beaker. The water, as if I couldn't have guessed, was lukewarm, it might have come out of the tap that way, perhaps not. It would have to do anyway, time was passing. I spooned some powder into the glass and watched its progress through the liquid into infinity. This seemed OK, we could move on, on to the burn test.

Under the scales I had a couple of pieces of aluminium foil; I heaped a small amount of the coke on to one. I lit a match and held it underneath, knowing that if this stuff was what they were telling me, then it would bubble with the heat, eventually leaving behind just a light-brown film. Anything darker and with more substance would indicate the purity of the stuff was dubious. My hand was shaking as I tried to hold the flame steady. Would they notice? Here I was, again not knowing exactly what I was looking for but almost more concerned with impressing a slovenly-looking creep with mousy hair that I had never met before than attending to the deal that could set up the rest of my life one way or the other. The first match went out too soon, then the second wouldn't light. They must have thought I was fucking around; they looked to each other and then Jérome's unnamed friend took the sheet of foil from me, bringing out his cigarette lighter as he did so. He held the flame further away, soon the coke was smoking. He stopped and handed it back, not saying a word, leaving his brusque actions and impatient expression to tell the story. *See, fuck-head, that's how you do it, that's how it should look, it's good stuff, can we go now?*

Almost, guys, one more thing, the only test I've probably got more experience than either of you at, sampling the goods. I took a couple of pinches from the bag and placed them on the tray of the scales, shaping two lines with the edge of my credit card. I was about to use the shell of a Biro pen to do the business but this time Jérome intervened, handing me his smaller metal nose-flute, as if this stuff deserved the appropriate respect, like the finest crystal glasses for the finest vintage claret. Snorting the lines in front of them was harder than I would have imagined, almost intimidating. The whole situation was new to me, taking a line not in search of a high, but like a wine-taster, checking for quality, checking the investment is sound. But the wine-taster spits out his mouthful afterwards – I had to drink the whole bottle, see if it got me drunk, see if it got me the right kind of drunk, and then conclude the deal whilst under the effects. The right kind of high from this shit would take time to come, an instant hit would indicate some kind of amphetamine mixture, a numbing of my nose might mean other impurities. I was looking for the mellowness that connoisseurs crave, yet my own nervousness might make that an impossibility. I finished the second line and invited my guests to partake; they declined. Maybe I had offended them, maybe at that stage the stash was still theirs and not mine to offer. Anyway, things were looking OK, I wasn't getting the immediate high that would have alarmed me, no; things were normal, reassuringly normal. At least, they were until there was a knock at the front door. Shit. I wasn't expecting anyone. I never expected anyone. Not once in seven months of off and on living at this apartment had there ever been a caller. Shit. Who the fuck could it be? I looked at my watch; two o'clock. The Carcera boys weren't due until after three, but fuck, even then they were meant to show at the Arena. As this thought hit my mind I realized the extent of my panic. They didn't even know of this place so why was I bothering to check the time?

I tried to calm myself lest I scare my guests, maybe they had an idea who it might be. I sought their lead, trying to see it in their eyes, wiping my nose and top of my lip, what to do guys? Jérome and his friend were close to the wall, hanging in close behind where the door would open from the hall should anyone burst in. I hadn't heard them move, they must have just glided across by instinct, criminal instinct, like professionals, cat burglars shifting ground without a sound. Jérome was squinting through the tiny gap between wall and door, peering in concentration as if with enough effort he might see not only through that but also the front door itself beyond it. I threw a glance to his colleague behind him and saw that he had drawn a gun. Shit, shit, shit. How had I got into this, why wasn't I down towards the shore, serving up fucking beer? It was only a small one, a revolver, almost ordinary, nothing flashy, just dull metal and black handle. What was scary was the thought that the hand holding it might actually use it. I couldn't stop staring at it, hoping it was part of the trip the drugs were sending me on, but it was there. The real thing.

The knocking started again. This time there was a voice to go with it. A female voice. It sounded like my wife. I wanted to cry.

'Martin. Are you there?'

The man with the gun caught my anxious glance. He shook his head; no, he made as if to say, I wasn't there.

'Martin . . . Martin?' This time I shook my head. Fuck the bullets, I was going to answer it.

145

'Yeah. Hold on.'

I tried to ignore their expressions as I got up and went past them, they would just have to trust me, just have to be fucking cool. I went to the main door, rubbing my nose. I hated the thought of seeing Johanna with any traces of the powder still showing. There would have been no way to explain.

'Hold on . . . Oh.'

I had opened the door expecting to be greeted with the face of my wife. Whether it would be angry, sad, conciliatory or plain confused would only be apparent once I saw it, as would my reaction to it. Instead there was someone else standing there, Sarah.

'Martin, you OK? Did I disturb you, were you trying to sleep?'

'Something . . . something like that Sarah, something came up, that's all.'

Her eyes on me spoke of a mixture of concern and bewilderment. She knew I was in trouble. A beautiful girl. One hundred per cent beautiful. I couldn't keep my hands from my nose, she must have wondered what I was trying to cover up, why I wasn't inviting her in.

'Look, I'm sorry, Sarah, I'm kind of busy, did you want me for something, is there a problem at the bar?'

Her smile was so hesitant it must have lasted less than an instant. A beautiful smile, what couldn't I do with a girl like this at my side?

'I don't know, it was just that man, he was round again, looking for you, said it was urgent.'

'What man? Miguel, big Tony . . . One of the brothers?'

'No. The man from the other bar, the German guy, Herman.'

'What the fuck did he want?'

'Look . . . This is difficult Martin, and I would hate you to think I was being intrusive, but I know, well Alexander and I both know that there is . . . something going on with your wife . . . that you've separated or something. Anyway, it's just that Herman was around and he said to tell you that you had to make a decision . . . soon, that if you wanted to see your wife it had to be soon . . .'

She stopped and looked over her shoulder, embarrassed at what she found herself saying, embarrassed on my behalf that she could have been heard by anyone on the stairs. She swayed on her feet, uncomfortable with my silence, rocking away like an errant four-year-old pretending she had done no wrong.

'Anyway, that's what he said, and I thought it might have been sort of urgent.'

Sarah. Beautiful Sarah. What would I give for some of your innocence? Can't you see, right now, *everything* is urgent

'Yeah, sure. Don't worry about it. I'll go see him later this afternoon, when I'm not so busy. You did the right thing. You're a good girl. I love you. Listen Sarah, I'm sort of trying to sort things out . . . things have got a bit crazy, you know? But I'm going to fix it all, and then I'm going to go away somewhere . . . and . . . would you come?'

'I don't understand. Go where?'

'Well, sort of . . . on a boat, you know, sailing somewhere . . .' No wonder she didn't follow, I was mumbling, trying to make the sell, trying to do my thing whilst a man with a fucking gun was tuned in, tuned in with radio Jérome and half a ton of highest-grade coke by his side, the same coke that was beginning to chill through to my brain, fighting with the words Sarah had just said that would have had me spinning in confusion. No wonder this wasn't a vintage performance, no wonder the magic didn't seem to be working.

'I really don't know, Martin, I would have to discuss it with Alexander. Are you sure you're OK? Is there anything I can do?'

I replayed what I had just said as best as I could in my head. A sense of horror came over me, I must have sounded like a complete cunt. Signals, Martin. Think signals, for all the audiences.

'Sarah, thanks. No, nothing. We can talk later. You go back to the Arena, I'll be there in twenty minutes. Like I said, things are a bit crazy but it will all be sorted. Thanks for coming round, you did right, you always do right.'

I closed the door on her before she had even made to leave. I would make it up to her later. The two hiding in the lounge had to be my priority right now. I went straight for the room but didn't speak until Sarah's footsteps were a distant echo.

'Sorry.'

'Problems?'

I gave Jérome the best smile I could find. 'No problems, friend. Your stuff is good. Seriously good. I'll take it.'

I offered him my hand as if we would shake on the deal. Maybe he didn't see it, it wasn't taken. His friend stuffed his gun back into his waistband.

'Twenty thousand,' he said, closing the door.

'. . . and in the English forts on the Guinea coast they think of England, of King and country – you have been told this, you believe it, yes?'

The scene was dinner, at Haraldt's table, Martin's first night on the shore of the Dark Continent. His host was speaking in a voice laden with irony, enjoying the opportunity to air his cynicism to two such innocents as Martin and José. He shook his head at the absurdity of it all, laughing silently, pausing only to sip generously from his brandy glass before answering the question himself.

'Do they think of England? Listen. In the English forts are Englishmen . . . men, yes? They think of what men think about. They think of surviving Africa and its dangers and fevers, of some day making the journey home, of saving enough money to make their sacrifice worthwhile. What would you think of, Martin, how to line the pockets of those who have not made the journey, those who stay at home and enjoy its comforts, those who are with their families, in the safety of port? I tell you this, Martin; I am a man, I do not think of this . . . I am a trader, I think of trade, of my personal situation, why else would I be here?'

Martin had been able to listen to the older man whilst holding Haraldt's gaze, albeit with a frown of wry detachment on his brow, for whilst the latter was intent on paying him the compliment of sharing another confidence,

Martin preserved the right to play Devil's advocate in response, to leave it open to question as to whether he endorsed the opinions being offered him.

'Surely it does not matter what they think. They trade with Royal Africa Company ships, the transactions are logged by both parties to ensure His Majesty's Government is not defrauded of monies it is rightfully due. There is no room for deceitful manoeuvre.'

A dry, stony laugh emanated from somewhere deep inside Haraldt's throat. He would know, thought Martin, that the remark had been made with sarcasm equal to those of his own, earlier. Still, Haraldt could not prevent himself rising to the bait. He shook his head ruefully and began again, speaking in an earnest tone.

'Listen to me, Martin. This is Africa. There is no room for *honest* manoeuvre. You and your friend here must beware of assuming that those you meet have the integrity you may possess yourselves. Every man you will meet out here thinks first for himself, himself only, understand? You have a personal venture? I ask you to guard it, to think how any other man, were he dishonest, might seek to deprive you of its worth. This way you will stay on guard against those who may cheat you. Africa changes men, and never for the better . . . Something in the air, the heat, the black skins of those we sell, who knows? Africa darkens the soul, turns any man into a liar. Any man. Remember this.'

Martin gently shook his glass, slowly spinning the last of his brandy round and around.

'I have no personal venture.'

Through the candlelight he saw the creases of another smile, a tired smile.

'Then you are indeed a strange man for these parts. I hope you may leave these shores with those values with which you came still intact, sir. I salute you.'

Haraldt raised his glass in a toast. Martin followed suit, as did José.

'I salute you too, friend, and I thank you for your advice. May I never be deprived of its worth.'

Once more he returned the trader's look; this time there was not a hint of irony in either's words or gaze, the silence a bridge between them.

*   *   *

His first night ashore in Africa. Martin could not sleep. It was not that he was uncomfortable; no, the opposite. It was the absence of the petty tortures he had grown accustomed to over the past months, men snoring, passing wind, raising out of their hammocks to spit and urinate through the door and over the side. Most of all it was the smell, or rather the lack of it, the stench of the *Anne* with her three months' worth of bilge water festering deep in the holds suddenly gone. It was as if someone had lifted a clothes peg from his nose and he was now free to appreciate the true aromas around him which had long been drowned out by stronger and more foul odours. The smell of grass, some freshly cut, was in the air, mingling with the scent given by the harvest of apricots drying out in the yard. His nose could even discern the lemon-hinted starch of his linen sheets, the suggestion of perfume on his own skin left behind from his bath earlier in the evening. He lay back, eyes open, taking it all in, enjoying the cool freshness of a room which had been shaded all day. He took it in as a child might on its first day after birth, with a sense of a simple creature overwhelmed by the range and depths of the sensory assaults pitted against it. In the darkness of the room's far corner, the sound of José's breathing, ever deeper, lent a rhythm to his observations, gave a count to his pleasures in making them.

Thus it was that he was awake when the visitors arrived, awake to hear the sound of feet on the matting carpet, a muffled sound; naked feet, thought Martin, his heartbeat quickening. He lay still, determined not to panic, not to make a fool of himself should the situation be harmless. Thus it was that he did not move when he was joined in his cot by a new companion, female. Nor did he stir when he felt the softness of her breasts brush against his chest and she threatened to light up the room with her smile. An innocent smile, at once familiar, *did you feel that?*, at once shy, *you do not like me?* Martin blinked hesitantly in the gloom; was this really happening? How was he to respond, was it a trap?

The stirring he could hear elsewhere in the room spoke of José's more obvious shock at being wakened in this way. Yet Martin for once had no concern for his fellow sailor, his own mind too absorbed with the new sensations presenting themselves to him for any other considerations. He could feel soft feminine thighs intertwining with his, hands caressing his shoulder-blade then circling down, down and around ever lower with an exquisite

150

touch. His senses were swimming in a delight that was overwhelming though still he sought vainly to remain detached; was Haraldt the architect of this, was he about to enter and demand another barter by way of apology? If he let himself surrender to his most basic urges what would be the penalty, was it right to make love to a savage, to give the precious gift of his seed to one who was so free with her love? Again the noises reached him from the other side of the room, José's bed creaking as if it were under assault from a company of men; evidently his progress in familiarization with native ways was not being halted by any qualms similar to his crew-mate's. And still his own dilemma grew ever more immediate, his head being pulled close to hers, a forehead gently rubbing against his, then their noses meeting, then her smile edging forward to kiss his lips. He could feel fingers deftly wrap themselves around the base of his stiff penis, like a vine wrapping itself around a trunk in the jungle. He thought of the tropical forest outside, the giant palms swaying in the wind. The force of nature, it had to be stronger here, nature untamed. Was it pointless to try to resist? She had climbed on top of him now, and was drawing him to her, like a flower, a beautiful flower with a thirst that was even more sweet. The tenderness of the moment gradually dawned on him, a real tenderness that needed no translation. His hands caressed the smooth skin of her back, falling down to cup around her waist. He looked up to her and pulled closer, to listen better to nature's demands.

Two nights moored at Point Colou and the captain was already impatient. After delivering the bales of flax and firkin of gunpowder that marked payment for the eight slaves taken aboard earlier he announced that the ship was moving on. Inland, he said, a remark that had Martin wondering if his ears were deceiving him; what kind of conversation had the captain shared with Haraldt? To his dismay, as the method behind the madness was gradually revealed, Martin came to realize the comment had been offered in earnest, Captain Henry's ambition would take *Anne* to the brink.

The balance of the quantity of slaves required to fill the ship's holds would come via a commission given to Haraldt's caboceer associate. A message pertaining to this was already on its way to the interior, asking for over three hundred slaves to be supplied within two weeks. Captain Henry also however reserved the right to cruise the coast and purchase any slaves available which represented a better, or more immediate, deal. Haraldt had counselled against this plan, stating that it was unlikely that any of value could be located in such a haphazard way. Martin wished that the captain would heed this advice, yet the more he was implored to do so his inclination to employ good sense seemed to lessen.

'Where will your man gather the cargo, at the coast?'

Haraldt fanned himself with his straw hat. Martin knew him well enough to detect a hint of exasperation with the captain and his questions.

'Inland. Goods from inland make their way along the Odoro river.'

'And if we were to sail up the Odoro, could we receive our slaves the sooner?'

'I do not know, sir, I do not know if the river is grand enough to receive your vessel, no ship has ever ventured beyond the estuary.'

'This will be our mission. I would be obliged if you would advise your partner in trade of our intention to pick up the cargo on the river itself. We will make our way along the coast to the mouth of the river and turn inland, heading as far upstream as the banks allow. We will meet your man within two weeks or the deal is cancelled, and we will strike a local deal.'

Much as Haraldt again tried to dissuade him, Martin saw that the notion was fixed in the captain's mind. Somehow, his vision was of an African interior bristling with slaves, slaves gathered by the riverbanks eager to be traded, quality slaves at bargain prices, obtainable without the costly interference of the merchant middlemen, available to those with the strength of will to travel to them. Who was to blame for this delusional optimism, was it the captain's own wishful thinking, his fevered greed? Or had Haraldt unwittingly stoked the fire by speaking of the ease with which the three hundred souls could be conjured together by his associate? Martin wondered how the crew would react to this latest plan, once the reality of the cloying, swamp-ridden land as described by Haraldt was upon them.

'What is your contact's name?'

'Fela,' replied Haraldt, running his tongue along his lower lip in distaste at the line of questioning.

'Feller? You send a message to him that we are on our way.'

The glance that Haraldt threw furtively to Martin served to increase the younger man's sense of foreboding. Captain Henry remained steadfastly

ignorant of others' misgivings, beaming with satisfaction at his decided course
of action. Indeed, Martin would never see him look happier than at this
moment, eight slaves aboard, a commitment to buy more at an opportune
price with the possibility of a free-for-all in the heart of the country they had
skirted for so long. Days after arriving at the Point, here they were, off again,
this time steering into uncharted waters.

I had taken possession; next came the re-sale, the hand-over to the
brothers. Another transaction, another sweat, another plunge into
unknown waters. Jesus, would I be glad when the day was over. Originally, according to my deceptively simple plan, I would have waited
with the gear in the apartment until the scheduled time, and then have
made the brief journey to the bar to rendezvous with the boys, bring
them back to give them the goods and count their cash. Somehow,
things weren't working out that way, and already the sunny optimism of
the morning had been overshadowed by something darker, something
poisonous going on, unnoticed by the island's holidaymakers filling up
the beaches or lunching amongst the cafés and bars for sure, but there
all the same to me, a black hole in my universe, sucking everything in
around it, there was no escaping its pull.

So Herman wanted me to decide, and he knew about the sorry
condition my marriage was in. Hadn't he let slip something about that
before? Every cunt seemed to have heard about the situation but what
exactly did they *know*? Herman liked to drop his hints, first to me and
then through my staff. As luck would have it I'd been stoned both
times so it was difficult to know what he wanted me to understand from
his talk; maybe it was a language thing, something lost in translation from
German making it sound more sinister than intended, maybe he meant
nothing. I needed to think straight, to rewind it all in my head, maybe if
I could do that then I would see that the worst of it was not happening.

153

My feet led me into the bathroom, where the warped reflection in the mirror had me still wearing the matching whites from earlier, but looking clammy and sickly underneath, the crispness of the clothes disappearing somewhere along the way since I'd dressed, stolen by the heat, ruined by the steady trickle of disquiet eating away at me. I would have studied the symptoms in more detail, would have if I hadn't started to retch and vomit at the thought of what was going on, spasms erupting out of nowhere as the thought of my wife and child in danger because of the shit I'd put them in took its grip. And I would try to deny it to myself, to calm down and concentrate on the deal, but then my whole body would shake as if to throw out the excuse and I'd be puking again, choking as the convulsions tried to evacuate an already empty stomach, nothing in it except coffee.

Coffee and cocaine.

Half an hour left before the pick-up was due to take place – it would have to be enough to compose myself and go see Herman, to tell him what needed to be told. I threw some water on my face and fled, grabbing keys on my way out. I couldn't afford to fuck about any more, couldn't hang around and hide the stash, it was left where it was on the lounge floor. I was trying to think clearly, *Martin think straight for fuck's sake*, to think it through and realize that the only people likely to break into the apartment would have been set up one way or the other, either by Jérome and his friend, or the police, or even the Carceras; the point being that anyone breaking in at that moment would have to know the coke was there and would turn the place over until they found it, so stowing it somewhere clever would be a waste of time and effort. Herman had to be told. *Martin, go tell him.*

I think I ran over to his place, through a heat so thick you had to swim your way along. Fuck knows what I looked like when I arrived, probably like some kind of accident waiting to happen; all sweat and snot, stringy bits of sick clinging on to my shirt, tenacious and greasy. Not the kind of clientele Herman must have had in mind when he launched his marina empire. Herman liked his place to be formal, he had his staff wearing uniforms, white short-sleeve shirts and bow-ties. Black trousers, women in short skirts; all his, or his organization's, attempts at setting the highest standards at Puerto Puals. Everything here was bigger than the Arena, Herman having knocked through from his original bar into the next-door restaurant he'd bought later to create the cavernous bierkeller atmosphere, on the inside at least. On the outside, which was where everybody sat from March to October, he was as restricted as any other operator would have been at the development, only thirty settings per outlet. Maybe he'd screwed up by spending so much refurbishing an interior that nobody would use, maybe that's why he wanted the Arena so bad, just so that he could increase the number of his exterior covers. Just so that he could own every piece of the jigsaw.

There were about twenty customers spread about the alfresco tables when I arrived, all of them resting under the shade of Herman's brown, black and gold canopy rather than studying his interior collection of Fatherland memorabilia in air-conditioned splendour. I walked past them all and looked for him in the heart of his den. His head waiter motioned me over, I waited at the glass frontage. It was cooler here than out, like walking into a fridge. There were two others from Team Herman looking across, checking that I had closed the doors to keep the heat out, one girl working the tea and coffee orders, a barman at her side, polishing glasses and wiping things down, a strapping guy busying himself with effeminate tasks. I wondered if that did something for Herman; maybe it did something for his lieutenant who had come across to interrogate me. Another German, mid-thirties although dressed older, probably gay, someone who revelled in the authority Herman had granted him over the others. I think he must have recognized me as the Arena's owner – he certainly didn't greet me as a customer, even one who had wandered in by mistake looking for the toilet. No, I got far less respect than that, what I got was a look, delivered in silence. *What is it you want, make it quick, we're busy people here.*

'Where's Herman?'

'He is not here.' He spoke his English in a clipped and precise way, taking either pride in his command of the language or pleasure at telling me I couldn't have what I wanted.

'Look, he was round at my place half an hour ago saying he needed to see me straight away.'

'Not here now.'

'Tell him he can't do that, if he wants me, I'm right here.'

'I will tell him you called.'

'Tell him now.'

'Not here.'

It was obvious I was failing to impress the urgency of the situation upon the audience of restaurant staff now listening in, particularly their robotic chief who was leading the negotiations. I paused to consider my position. *Think it through, Martin.* All the customers were outside, on the other side of the ceiling-to-floor windows and glass doors, most of them at the furthest extreme, as close as they could get to the harbour without getting up and heading for my place. *He's not here.* Perhaps we can change that. Herman's tables were copper and wood, his seats were heavy, not the canvas deck-chair efforts that the rest of us had. Herman's standards meant they had to be solid, German oak. I lifted one and took two steps towards the entrance, then threw it as hard as I could at the ghostly reflection of me and the head waiter shimmering on the pane. The glass shattered immediately and spectacularly, shards raining down from on high like confetti. For one glorious moment the noise of it breaking was loud enough to drown everything out, every sound, every word, every thought. I had assumed Herman would at least be double-glazed, maybe even reinforced. The ease of destruction was as surprising as it was satisfying.

Everyone had turned to see what the cause of the sudden commotion might be; I was aware of heads and shapes turning my way but didn't see them, only the next chair waiting to be plucked from the floor.

'Not here? You find him, tell him what's happened, tell him Mr Law is here.' I stopped to nod at the door on the right. *This one, yeah?*

It was easier to hit than the window next to it had been, although I still used just as much force. Again the whole thing came down, like a rock going through the windscreen of a speeding car. People were standing up at the tables, peering at the spectacle, unsure whether to be alarmed. I could hear a baby crying somewhere in the marina, I could hear shouting, voices raised in different languages. What's going on? Herman's man was bawling to his colleague behind the bar; he came bounding out as ordered, running towards us.

'Tell him if he touches me I'll rip his face off.'

I have no idea how you would carry out what I had just threatened. I had a large piece of broken glass in my hand but no real concept of how it might be used in the process. Having said that, the actual mechanics didn't seem that important, the intent was there, and I knew that however useful this new guy or any of them were at fighting, they would be in an unequal match. I could hurt them. They couldn't hurt me. I was beyond pain.

'Just get Herman, *now*, please.'

I seemed to be making some kind of progress. The two men in front of me exchanged some words in their native tongue, and the barman was off, sprinting out through the gap where the door had been. I was left to wait in a silence interrupted only by the shuddering of the air-conditioning unit which now had the task of cooling the entire island. Eventually Herman's man put the machine out of its misery.

Then Herman himself arrived. Enter stage left, looking typically flushed, reluctantly hurried, waddling like a duck being chased on land. He took a deep breath, studying the wreckage with silent consternation. The indignation seemed to give way to a despondency I had never thought him capable of. I was surprised, almost disappointed.

'Hmmmmm . . . What *is* this shit, Marty?' Maybe his doctor had warned him to avoid stress, that could be why he was so intent on keeping a lid on things. He couldn't control the colour of his skin though, it was always ready to betray him, turning redder by the second, more scarlet with every crunch under his fat feet.

'Bit of an accident, Herman. Where's my wife?'

Herman tried to look preoccupied, stepping up close to the window to examine the damage in detail. He said something in German to the one I'd kicked off the show with, probably something about calling the repair man, or looking out the insurance policy. He tried to sound resigned.

'I don't know, Marty, don't you?'

A bad answer, one that had the adrenaline flowing through my veins again, so much so that finding the strength to lift another chair was no problem, not a problem at all. This time I turned and twisted on my heels, like a discus thrower searching for the momentum that will hurl his attempt into the record books, or in my case, carry a solid wood chair clean over the bar top and into the mirrored shelves behind it, like a bowling ball aimed at the bottles that substituted for skittles. I wanted to bring them down. Bring them all down. As it turned out, it was a fair attempt – only six or seven bright phials of ready-mixed cocktails remained standing, the rest of the scores of assorted gins, whiskies and brandies now the froth of their own free-style punch on the ground. It still wasn't enough. I had another seat in my hands.

'You can't threaten my family then pretend not to know what I'm talking about. You know where they are. You better tell me or I swear to God I break this fucking thing over your head.'

Herman took a handkerchief from his pocket to wipe his forehead. If he was nervous, it didn't show. He looked for a dry corner to wipe his glasses with, not intimidated at all, no; he'd been here before, this was no ordinary bar-owner, this was a player, the real thing.

'It's not me Marty, understand?' He sighed. 'The organization, they are the ones. You sell and you see your wife and child again.'

I put the chair down. It felt heavy and the perspiration on my hands made keeping a grip more and more difficult. I needed to think, no distractions.

I looked at my hand. I noticed that it was bleeding.

'I'll sell when I'm ready. You tell your organization that if they so much as harm one hair on their heads then it's you I'll come looking for. You fucking tell them if they are harmed I'm going to take all of Puerto Puals down to the ground, brick by brick, and then they won't have anything left to buy.'

Rip his face off. Brick by brick. This wasn't the coke talking, this was me, these words came shooting out *despite* the drugs. This was me talking. Beyond pain. A part of me wanted to start now, part of me was waiting for a sign from Herman that he wanted to tough it out, to see if I was serious, so that I could be justified in demonstrating the depth of my sincerity. But no, Herman must have sensed the danger in doing that. He didn't look at me, didn't show any interest in what I was saying. He mopped his chin with his handkerchief and the moments passed.

Without a word between them, his staff began the first attempts to clear the damage. His customers wandered cautiously forward, partly to settle up, partly, I guessed, to ghoulishly examine the scene of the crime, perhaps hoping to see the police draw chalk outlines and photograph the victims' bodies. There was almost a tangible sense of disappointment that it hadn't ended that way. Not this time. All that was left was me and Herman standing in silence, surrounded by the debris of a Wild-West saloon brawl, both of us looking spent yet unharmed, as if we had ducked under the bar once the fists were flying.

It was becoming hotter, the dusty choking street air following the flies on a path inside, both wafting around us. I glanced at my watch, a quarter past, I was late for the brothers. Still, Herman had been told. It was right to be calm. I started to walk out. As ever though, he wanted the final say.

'You are stupid man, Martin. You make too many enemies.'

He said it as if he felt sorry for me, he might even have meant it. I shook my head, it was too late for that. Besides, things were only just becoming clear.

'No, Herman, that's the whole problem, I've just realized. I don't make enough.'

I have told you all about my fantastic success, how I manage to score. Score relentlessly. So many women, endless conquests. I've given detail on the different shapes and sizes, colours and contours, the cunts and grunts that have made up my sex life. I've told you about how it was done, from start to finish, from the way I'd introduce myself to how I washed my cock afterwards. I hope you've been impressed.

There is something else though, something that would shock you for sure. It's relevant, so why have I left it until now; my secret? A dark secret. A guilty secret. You see, I've fucked a lot of women.

Fucking, screwing, I've had a lifetime of it. Self-taught, I learned how myself, never depended on anybody. Until I met my wife.

I looked at her and saw the future, saw everything at once.

'What is your name?'

She would tease me later how I didn't even say hello first, and tell me that was why she laughed. Diving straight in like that made her wonder, it made it all daunting, I didn't know it at the time, but that was the reason for the slight pause, the demure girlishness, the hand through her long blonde hair, the downward glance.

'Johanna.'

'I'm Martin. You are beautiful, you know that, don't you?'

You must know that. I hadn't meant it as an accusation, the girl really was beautiful. One hundred per cent. I was simply stating a fact, thinking aloud, thrown by her sudden appearance. I wasn't thinking of where this might lead, of the next line, the next clever thing to say or what might impress her. None of this. You see, I can think back and it is all still so vivid. She glowed, radiated some kind of serenity, everything about her presence spoke, screamed, of a loveliness inside and out. So I really wasn't thinking of seduction, or how she would look under her clothes, or how she might taste when kissed, or how soft her skin might be to my touch or even how her hair would smell first thing in the morning on my pillow. I didn't need to concern myself about any of that because it was so obvious that everything about her would be exquisite. One hundred per cent.

She smiled and held my gaze as the harbour waves gently lapped around the hull of the boat. We looked at each other. It was easy, as if we had already had a past together, one that we were so comfortable with.

'Thank you, Martin. Do you know you are a handsome man?'

Her English was good, slightly halting, but all the more charming for it. And she could say that and be wrong and I still loved her for it. I wasn't a man at all, I was a twenty-seven-year-old cabin steward, a boy who had run away from home and never really gone back. Never faced up to the hurt I had caused as a man presumably does, or asked myself why it had turned out this way. I was a boy with some money in the bank as a result of some moderately successful puerile escapades and scams, money but no clear idea of what I was going to do with it or how I was going to make my life count for anything other than one long wait between deals.

When I looked at her I saw a future, a way of curing the emptiness that always seemed to have me in its icy grip, I saw the way it had to be. I began to feel an entirely new sensation stirring deep inside, and I began to think of what I could maybe give to her, something she was capable of drawing out of me. I would give her devotion. I would be anything she wanted; decent and dependable, dangerous and desirable, all in the same instant, if that was her call. I could have signed up for it there and then.

So we started talking, in this strange mixture of the guarded and the bold, the cool and the warm. Two strangers who knew each other, who recognized the importance they might have in one another's lives. We started to talk with me on the solid concrete quay and her swaying with the gentle rocking of her boat, talking intimately as other crews went by.

When Johanna eventually joined me on the shore it was time for us to go on our walk; talking, talking, talking as the harbour front, the benches and palms, the streetlights and boats all passed by unnoticed as we began to part with the experiences and routes that had brought us together here, at this place, at this moment. A new one on me, beginning by sharing, no secrets, no pose or pretence. I wanted to take in everything about her and nothing else; *tell me everything, Johanna, tell me what made you the woman you are and I will love you for those influences and experiences, every one.* We settled in a bar, looking for privacy and finding only a procession of intrusions and then straining to fend them off, everywhere suddenly a conspiracy to stop us from building our bridge; the waitress telling us the menu − *It's OK we're not eating,* shifting seats for the boys gathering around us − *Sure, take it, no one sitting there,* being recognized by members of a previous crew − *Look, guys, could you fuck off? This is the girl I'm going to spend the rest of my life with, I'm trying to get to know her and I might not have that much time.*

She was in Key West for one night, this was it. I didn't want to scare her by pledging my all there and then but I had to know I had connected, that there was a space for me in her heart and that we would meet again. This was the most important thing, understanding her, and letting her understand me. I didn't try to make love or even to kiss her, I just wanted her to know what she meant to me. I did hold her though, and whilst she was in my arms I persuaded her to promise that she wouldn't forget and would see me at the end of our trips.

A promise.

I never doubted that she would keep her word, and, in my own way, tried to make sure she would; staring at her photograph every morning and night the oceans kept us apart, silently repeating the Swedish words she had taught me as I did so, saying them over and over, like a mantra, *du är vacker* – you are beautiful. You are the one for me.

She kept her promise. Johanna and her all-girl crew sailed up the Atlantic seaboard and then crossed over back to Europe. I had another two lovelorn weeks to endure at Key West before heading south for a Caribbean excursion in a new boat once the other was finally sold. I made it back to the Mediterranean two months later and made contact. We were to meet somewhere convenient, and the plan was to see if we could take up from where we had left things the night we met. Of course, the pressure on us was intense; time had passed, we both must have wondered at some point whether we were deluding ourselves, if this was a simple holiday romance that we were overloading with all our hopes and dreams. That was why we met on neutral ground, to give room for escape if it proved to be a dreadful anti-climax.

The venue? Mallorca, Cala Fornells to be precise, a quiet tiny harbour where we could work it out and I could gaze on that face I had studied so long in the photograph. Would it all be for real, true love, or just an illusion? We gave ourselves two days to get to know each other properly and decide if there should be a next step.

As it happened, I put my arms around her and knew again in an instant, knew straight away. I didn't need the other forty-seven hours, fifty-nine minutes and seconds. I didn't say so because I wanted that time to last for ever, to never let her go. So the two days became two weeks, then months and then years. In fact we never left the island, at least I didn't, we were married after the first year ended, and our daughter, Amy, was born five months later. Even then, we could have done all that sooner, could have made our plans as soon as we started sharing our pasts on that Florida quayside, there was that kind of certainty to it all, a certainty I thought we would never lose.

I remember all these details with a sadness. Sure, every newly-wed thinks it will last for ever, never imagining how the romance could ever wither and die until one day you question what the fuck it was you ever saw in the person you married, what it was that made you want to commit the rest of your life to them. But for me the sadness isn't that at all, I can remember all too easily what it was I was buying into, and when I think of the past the craving which I once felt for Johanna isn't so hard to evoke. Give me that photograph and I could still make the same dedications, still mean it almost as passionately. You see, that's the real secret, my guilty secret. I'm still in love with my wife.

It took a further three days to reach the estuary of the Odoro by which time the fever had returned to take a grip on the *Anne*, nine men too feeble to move, gasping for breath in the sticky heat of the night. After two more days travelling inland on the river itself that number had more than doubled, with scarcely a man left who did not dread the arrival of nightfall and the clouds of mosquitoes that would descend into the ship, choking those who would dare to breathe with mouths open, hovering above those who did not, eager to feast on the exotic fruit that was white flesh in the jungle. The insect bites produced lumps in some and angry red weals on others, and men begged

Martin to lance the huge boils that grew like some evil seed planted within them in the dark. One man with six such sores on his arm requested that Martin amputate the limb itself. At the time he may have been joking, making a show of bravado to his crew-mates. Two days later the sight of the grotesque swelling had Martin examining his saw in preparation. In the event the operation was not required though he was hardly glad to be relieved of its burden; Seaman Gibbs died on the third day.

The *Anne* continued to crawl upstream despite losing, on average, a member of crew every second day. Progress was so slow and the wind so light Martin wondered if more headway would be made if men disembarked and dragged the ship along from the riverbank. Wells was now conducting the funeral services, Captain Henry, presumably bored with the ritual, preferring to rest in his cabin, examining his charts, avoiding an increasingly dispirited crew, a crew being taken to boiling point in every sense.

And on the land? Nothing. Absolutely nothing except thick growth that seemed impenetrable to any creature other than the insects and birds who were free to rise above it. No natives, no traders, no merchandise. Nothing but the reeds attempting to keep a slippery grip on the ship's bow, parting as she ploughed doggedly through. Martin hoped Captain Henry would abandon his scheme and head back to Colou Point in the absence of any contact yet there seemed little hope of this, each setback serving only to strengthen the skipper's resolve.

With over half the crew incapacitated, however, this commitment was not being matched by those around him; even in the officer quarters that Martin shared the talk was of the dreadful consequences of the foolhardy decision to turn inland. Within these ranks the fever had taken its toll too; Fotheringham the purser already dead, Gardiner gravely sick, Wells weakening by the day. Even the precious cargo that had been so eagerly loaded at the Point was looking vulnerable, the eight slaves barely still alive. Poorly though they were, these captives still had to be guarded, and the task of standing over them through the heat, torpor and stench of filth and vomit was the least popular of all crew details. Not that there was less work elsewhere; those men still capable of moving woke daily to a new reality, that there was more work to do on a near-stationary ship than on a fast-moving one. In the still air, duties multiplied, firstly in deploying all sails to catch what little wind there was, and then keeping watch for any signs of slatting – when the sails rubbed aimlessly against the mast and shrouds because of the lack of breeze – and hauling them back up again to secure them with buntlines to prevent such wear and tear. All of these actions would fill the daily log, though the effort required to carry them out in the sapping heat would not be recorded.

Four days in, high noon, and the *Anne* is inching her way along the narrowing banks, Captain Henry atop the quarterdeck, spying the land around through his glass. He scours the landscape as if expectant, but there is nothing stirring except the men on the deck below him.

Reid, one of the crew summoned from the sickbay to man the deck, has finished rigging out the foremast. He has glanced over the side at the bow and wishes to speak to the captain. Wells is leading the skipper away, determined, for whatever reason, to keep him in quarantine from the thoughts of his crew. Reid though, shivering and red-eyed with sickness, demands his skipper's attention, shouting up to the nest of officers at the stern. Martin watches dispassionately, the heat and a melancholy longing for a return to the pleasures at Colou Point inducing a languid stoop in keeping with the vessel's morale. Reid had not been the most patient of patients when presented for treatment, his temper and abruptness almost a match for the captain's. As Martin lets his mind meander back to his conversations with Haraldt and the delight of the evenings on the coast his focus is gradually brought back to the shouted exchange between Reid and the captain. Words that were merely washing over him are now stinging like the heat. He realizes the crew have halted all their work to listen in too.

'Just look over the side, Captain, the moss and growth have spread all over the hull, we are picking up weeds because of that, dragging them along ... there will be teredo worms in there too ... eating their way through the timbers. We must move to salt water soon sir, otherwise we will take a forest with us when we do leave.'

Martin glanced down to the waterline; it was true. From what he could see, a thick coat of green slime had attached itself to the ship, as if she had grown a new coat. He could only assume that deeper below the problem would be the same or even worse. Nevertheless, the captain did not trouble himself to view the spectacle.

165

'We will remain on the river until I order otherwise, and you, sir, will keep your opinions to yourself regarding the worm, algae, or any other facet of the ship's management, understand?'

'Aye, Captain. The growth on the hull will slow us down, sir, that is my only concern . . . slow us down when we do leave . . .' Reid's voice had reduced to a mumble, with a stronger west-country accent as he saw he had lost Captain Henry's ear. '. . . *if* we ever do leave this God-forsaken land . . .'

The last remark drew a muted round of laughter from those still listening. It was this that had the skipper turning and bellowing back at Reid.

'What did you say, Seaman?'

Martin watched with mounting anxiety as Reid toyed with the notion of denial, scratching his head as the silence grew heavier, clawing at a scalp turned red and peeling on the bald patch surrounded by his straggly red hairline. He sighed; the men were watching, he could not back down.

'I said, it would slow us down, if we ever leave, Captain.'

The skipper nodded, satisfied that this was an answer of accuracy, although his stern demeanour meant there was no repeat of the mirth the comment had elicited first time around.

'I see,' he said acknowledging the crime. 'Wells, have him flogged, twenty lashes.'

Martin felt a bead of sweat trickling down his cheek, almost like a tear. The sun was directly above, imbuing every dark surface caught in its rays with the silent resonant heat of hot coals. He felt his boots burn as he shifted his feet on the boards. Nobody else moved. Wells stuttered into life, seeking to confirm the order.

'Tw . . . twenty lashes, sir . . . Now?'

'Yes, man, dammit! Do it now!'

Wells moved slowly, almost reluctantly, his expression one of puzzlement as if he was at a loss as to how he might accomplish the assignment. Down the steps to the main-mast, across the deck and main holds, throwing a glance of mild scorn at Reid as he passed by; *look at what you have got me into, yours is the easy part, I have to organize this thing.*

Martin's mouth was dry. Now he heard another voice calling for the captain's attention, his own, even though he had no idea what it was he meant to say.

166

'Captain Henry, sir . . . Captain Henry!'

'What is it, Doctor?'

'Captain Henry . . . If we could speak in confidence, sir . . . I would be grateful.'

'Speak now, dammit.'

'I wanted to mention our water consumption, sir – a lashed man will require more water than his allotted share. I would move to advise, as ship's surgeon, that the punishment be postponed until we return to the Point, where supplies are plentiful.'

The captain shook his head. 'What is this nonsense, man? Let Reid worry about his precious water, let that deter any man from insubordination. On with the whip.'

'But sir, it is all crew who will suffer if the water –'

'Silence, man! Enough! Now will you be quiet or do you wish to be lashed as well?'

Captain Henry turned briskly, heading for his cabin. Martin felt it imperative to make one final plea for clemency and moved to reach him before he disappeared, pushing his way towards the quarterdeck. He reached the companion-way to see McKnight blocking his path. In desperation, he cried out once more.

'Captain!' Again he was unsure as to what exactly he might say, thinking only of securing the dialogue. In an instant however, this was no longer a problem, nor an issue, the blow from McKnight's spindly fist knocking him clear off his heels and sending him sprawling on to the deck. Captain Henry gave a brief backward glance as he opened the cabin door but Martin was now out of view. The door closed behind him.

Martin rubbed his chin, raw and throbbing. Why would McKnight assault him?

The same man offered the same fist to help him back to his feet.

'I'm sorry, sir. But one man's plenty enough for a lashing.'

Reid's flogging was marked in the log as having taken place on the afternoon of 15 June. Whilst Martin was sure the captain would have written of the crime and its punishment in all the self-justifying detail posterity would require he was somewhat less certain that the disastrous effect on the *Anne*'s morale

167

would have been similarly noted. Captain Henry might have had his taste for blood satisfied in the twenty minutes of hard labour it took the weary Wells to administer the penalty, yet the toll on the men who witnessed it lingered for days after Reid was untied and dragged away from the lattice work on the deck; men unable or unwilling to look one another in the eye, men barely acknowledging an officer's order with a nod let alone a hearty cry of aye. Martin wondered if the crack of the whip as it made contact had echoed out into the wilderness beyond the riverbanks on either side of the ship. What would the sickening snaps and accompanying shrieks of the victim have told any listening native? That here were strange invaders, that here were the pale men who had travelled so far just to beat each other, that here were the men who did not die fast enough, that they could afford to grant the reaper a helping hand?

Reid was unconscious for the best part of the day, rousing only to whimper or vomit as his wounds woke with him. Martin thought his death inevitable and was both surprised and relieved when the stubbornness that had been the cause of Reid's punishment manifested itself anew for Reid to cling on to life in its aftermath, despite the legions of buzzing flies and mosquitoes come to feast off his fresh cuts.

The *Anne* came to a complete halt two days after the beating, when the banks finally converged enough to halt any further progress upstream. Even the captain was forced to concede that there was nothing to do now but wait, wait and hope that the agreement they had felt free to renege upon would still be met by Haraldt's associate. Fela's arrival the next day was therefore greeted as something of a miracle by those crew strong enough to witness it, to have spied the procession snaking its way through the bush and scrub that had replaced the thick jungle as the river narrowed, a procession winding towards them like an ant chain busy with grotesque industry about a decaying carcass on the bush floor. A long chain, Martin mused, hundreds strong, captured and captors who, if they had chosen to combine, could have easily overwhelmed the dwindling energies on the ship. Yet rarely could the sight of a mercenary slave-trader have been greeted with more warmth by an English crew, men to whom such an arrival meant the possibility of leaving these poisoned shores behind, of going back to the sea they yearned for. Here was a Messiah to lead them out of this abundant and lurid wilderness,

168

a black Messiah from the black land. Everything would be simple. They would trade, load up and go. That was the plan. The beautiful plan.

The first thing that struck Martin about Fela was that he was not fully black like the men he sold. He was more akin to one of Haraldt's bastard children with a mixture of breed in him, light brown in skin tone, with the sharp features of a white man greeting you in his face, together with a manic stare that spoke of a distant European lost in the alien jungle landscape a generation ago. There was an arrogance too, although this was difficult to place in terms of race or geography, perhaps this was merely an acquired habit, a consequence of being surrounded by a fawning entourage paid, presumably, to admire his every move. Fela first addressed the captain in what Martin took to be Spanish, then switched to something sounding like French before smiling with effortless condescension and replying in English to Captain Henry's increasingly loud enquiries. Surely, Martin deliberated silently, he would have already known that the *Anne* was an English ship, surely then, this was all for show. *I understand about you and your culture, I understand more than you will ever know about me.*

'Three hundred. Finest quality, fresh from the interior. Jubana tribe. Ready for your vessel now. You wish to count them, inspect, take possession now?'

To Martin, Fela had a more regal bearing than that of a trader, even though his conversation took him directly to the heart of the transaction. What was undeniable was the impression he gave that all this was somehow beneath him and the dignity of his rank, as if he were being reluctantly dragged into such commerce by the avarice of his white guests. Martin found himself fascinated by this, and by the unease Fela's posturing seemed to engender in the captain, the proud Captain Henry, once confident of trading as an independent on the banks of the Odoro, now reduced to accepting the terms of a young negro barely half his age. A young black surrounded by a retinue of flunkies, whose devotions, smiles and fanning of their leader showed none of the surly cynicism that had become the crew routine for the mighty captain of the *Anne*.

'Possession? Of course, immediately, understand? As soon as our ship's doctor . . . medicine man . . . passes them fit for sale . . . we will then make our bargain.'

'Good!' shouted Fela, clapping palms together, 'Good!' He turned to share his joy with the circle around him as if letting them into his private joke with the captain. 'That would be most agreeable.' Agreeable. His voice echoed inside Martin's head. *Ah-gri-abble.* Fela pronounced the word with singular emphasis, drawing it out, stretching it towards parody. 'Where is your doctor now, let him commence!' The hands were slapped together again, this time with a hearty laugh that was swiftly joined by his lieutenants. Captain Henry smiled hesitantly, unsure as to where the humour lay.

'Mister Law . . . *Doctor* Law, will you come forward and . . . *commence*, if you would.'

Martin moved towards Fela. To his astonishment, a hand was offered to him, a black hand reaching out in a white man's gesture.

'*Master* Law?'

'Martin.'

'I am pleased to make with your acquaintance, Martin, it is most agreeable. My name is Fela. And you are to do us the honour of inspecting our stock?'

Martin was dazzled by the ferocity of the friendship being aimed at him. Fela had yet to release his hand. He shook it once more.

'I would be glad to, sir.' Like his skipper, he found himself beguiled, smiling without quite knowing why. He realized too, that the creases in his face felt somewhat unnatural. Not forced, no, it was more that they had become so rare for him, so unusual that it could appear so, it was more that it was so long since he had last worn a smile the expression had almost become extinct in him and he struggled to fight the urge to thank Fela for reviving it in such an unexpected manner. Fela turned, Martin followed, walking at his shoulder, mesmerized by the sparkling stones sewed into the trader's elegant shawl, a new follower basking in its reflected light. This stranger had only been in their company but minutes and yet was already established as the new situation's dominant personality, the force that all others would adjust to.

'See my men, Martin, you will see the finest of Africa.'

Martin was led to the first in line of the stock, the first of the three hundred, shackled in rows of nine or ten, all kept on their feet by the guards whipping them to order. A vast crowd, intimidating when viewed as a whole, as a single entity by a boy from Greenock. Up close though, seen one at a time, a different perspective was offered. Martin instantly recognized the cowed, broken stoop of a defeated spirit, as he had seen in the eyes of those chained below deck on the *Marguerita*. He made to prod the first man with his cane; Fela stepped in first, however.

'See Martin!' The voice had lost none of its arresting diction – *Mah-tine* – nor its laughter. 'Good man, fine slave!' Fela ran a hand across the man's forehead, almost caressing him, stroking the face in a downward motion. The subject did not flinch, but his eyes flickered slightly to reveal the fear Fela inspired in him. The man's cheeks were marked with scars; tribal emblems, Martin guessed. Fela pinched the skin on the left side of the face tightly, pulling it towards himself and the ship's surgeon.

'Most agreeable, yes?'

Martin nodded. Was he agreeing? No; although the gesture might have said as much it was an empty one; he realized he was sauntering along in a trance, like a sleepwalker. The experience was proving overwhelming, so much to take in with such limited experience behind him. Would Fela know this? Probably. How many would be used to viewing three hundred slaves in one session? And yet despite this and all the efforts to distract him, there were details right before him that once they had been taken in by his eye, took all of his concentration so as to countervail the trader's showmanship – details that caused Martin's heart to sink with despair. The man before him was older than the eight previously loaded at the Point, older than any man he had seen aboard the Spanish ship. What made this noticeable was not the ageing in the man himself but the attempts to conceal it; the shaved limbs, oiled and gleaming like a newborn foal, the dyed hair, an incongruous reddish brown atop an ebony forehead, the narrow waist, drawn tight by a vicious belt dividing the man in two.

Martin looked to the next in line; he too was made up like an actor, blinking in embarrassment at the folly of his appearance. Martin stopped, holding his ground, ignoring Fela's progress further down the column. He didn't bother to touch either man with his cane. A parade of mutton dressed as lamb, he thought angrily, a joke being played upon the *Anne*, whose crew had risked death to get here. His rage grew rapidly, a strange vexation, a curiosity, like something he had never known before. Resentment at the captain for leading them on this fruitless mission, against Fela for taking them to be fools, against the flies buzzing incessantly in his ears, against the slaves themselves for – for what? He did not know except to wish that they could stand taller, with more youth and vigour, that they be decent merchandise.

'I want to see under the arms, arms and groin, understand? Between the legs.'

Fela almost jumped to attention as he heard the change in Martin's tone. He relayed the order to the entourage, obviously passing on the full urgency of the request. Two guards drew close and hoisted the arms of the first man in line, performing this so abruptly as to almost wrench the limbs free from their sockets.

'And the legs now. Open them.'

They screamed at the man, who showed a reluctance to comply as his knees were pulled apart. A guard struck him smartly on the side of his face and he was persuaded. Martin peered at the sight thus presented.

'All right. Next.'

He passed the first four – mutton dressed as lamb. Not prize livestock but good enough to get them out of here, good enough to trade for damp gunpowder or lice-infested muslin, good enough to eat the rancid fat and boiled beans that awaited them aboard ship. Shark meat. The fifth man bore swellings around his inner thighs, growths flourishing there like strawberries. This was what Martin had been checking for.

'No. Out.'

Fela accepted the verdict and the man was released from the line and led out to one side. He seemed to want to complain to Martin and make his own deeply-felt case for sale. Martin wondered briefly why this should be but was soon on to the rest of the inspection. Hundreds to see, all with Fela by his side, and the same unprompted commentary. *Very good. Strong man. Obedient. Grateful.* And his rage never seemed to subside, simmering as he went through batch after batch. There were nearly two hundred done when he saw the first members of the rest of the cargo: the women slaves.

That they were different to the men was obvious to his momentarily shy eye. Smaller, less inclined to be herded together in neat rows, more akin to cats, preferring clusters. It was the behaviour that was so dissimilar, the dry, dusty sobbing and whimpering that set them apart, unrestrained as they were by the need to display masculine stoicism and pride whilst they were being bought and sold. An unruly gathering, more in need of a beating to force compliance with the demands of the examination. Martin's ire began to boil again; he was irritated by the endless weeping now before him, disgusted by their nudity, by their sagging breasts, exasperated that the decisions he had to make were made by him alone among the whole crew of the ship. He halted, raising a hand to silence Fela. *Good woman. Good for breeding. Good milk for children.*

'What happens to those I have had taken out?'

'Out?'

'The ones I have rejected, the ones suffering from yaws.'

'They are taken away, Martin . . . Taken away.' Fela bared his teeth, lips parting in a cruel smile. 'Do not worry, they will not be sent to your ship. Sent away, yes.'

'Where?'

Fela kicked his sandals at the dusty earth, lost for once, unsure of his words or perhaps baffled by the question. *What does it matter?*

'Taken away, Martin. Not come back, no worry.'

'I will take all of the rest.'

'All!' Fela snapped, elation surging through his veins.

'All of the rest. I do not wish to inspect them. I have seen enough.'

'Very good. Most agreeable. And at the price we have agreed, yes?'

'Speak to the captain.' Martin realized he was struggling to speak at all, his eyes and concentration drifting to the crowd of thirty or so he had rejected. Men he had earmarked for murder. 'Speak to the captain. He will tell you everything about the price.' Martin turned to the *Anne*, the ship that was being transformed into a prison as the holds were being cleared for their new cargo. For an instant he wished her destroyed, that she would burst at the seams as she made her gluttonous feast. He turned back to the wretched landscape on his side of the river and the hordes awaiting their fate. The captain had been alone in his resolve to bring the ship here, but he was no madman, more a pioneer. Where *Anne* had come others would follow; Martin knew he should be glad that he would not return to witness it. Much as he felt the need to abscond, to abandon his station in favour of some kind of solitude, he also understood that the ship represented the one route out of

173

there at that moment. With a dread heavier than anything he had ever known, he let his feet trudge the path back towards the vessel.

There are a few things that are required to make it as a dealer: guile, a cool brain, an ability to keep one step ahead of trouble. Then there are the essentials: a mobile phone, a fast car, a network of friends and clients, and of course a ready supply of merchandise to supply them all. As far as I could tell, the Carcera brothers were lacking in most respects when it came to any kind of suitability; maybe they hoped to make up with enthusiasm what they lacked in general experience. They did however have a shit-load of drugs to sell thanks to my connections, and whilst they had that and hadn't been arrested there was always, in theory, a ray of hope. Not that it bothered me either way when they came to the apartment to claim the gear. How they made out would be their problem and theirs alone. In theory. As with everything though, there were problems, and whilst I didn't fully appreciate it at the time, I was obviously in the market for problems, becoming a fucking magnet for them, hoovering up anybody's to add to my impressive collection. This had already been a day of rare vintage, when a complete fucking stranger had pulled a gun on me in this very flat, when I'd more or less been told to fuck off by Sarah when I had tried to articulate my dreams of escape with her, and when Herman had grudgingly admitted that my wife and daughter were being held somewhere by his groovy organization after my one-man demolition job on his now – completely – open-air gin palace. Yet this day was not done, there were other dilemmas floating in the air ready to circle in and sting me. Like the Carcera boys not having their money. Not the full forty-five thousand dollars or even a half deposit. Not even forty pesetas for a half-hearted deposit. No, and it didn't seem to matter to them either. What was even worse was that they gave every impression of being pissed off that it mattered to me. I would get the cash for sure, eventually. So they had said they would pay up-front, sure, and they still would, eventually. They would pay once they had found buyers themselves, like I would. Like Martin *relax*, for Christ's sake, *had I forgotten we were partners, yeah?* The shit we find ourselves in.

I had three weeks to repay Jérome and his pistol-packing pal. Three weeks, unless I just gave them back the three kilos untouched and with my apologies for wasting their time. That would have been the sensible option. I didn't take it. Why? It was that day. I was tired, not thinking straight and the boys were wearing me down. Grinding me right down through the ground with their stupidity. It was easier to go along with than fight against, because fighting it would have meant teaching them and I didn't have the energy. I just wanted them out, out of the apartment and out of my life, and the cocaine out, everything out of my sight.

I was also wired. Wired to the fucking moon. My own quality control experiment had done more than merely convince me that the goods were good. It had taken me higher than I had ever been before or since. So high I was in orbit. So high any thought in my head was just the best thought ever, so clear, so lucid, so obviously perfect for the tribe that is humanity. The Carceras were here and being their own glorious selves and I didn't care because it was me that was actually controlling them. Yes, I could see where all this would lead to and it suited me fine. I smiled because I had the wisdom of King fucking Solomon right then when I looked at them and saw the world would be a better place without them and their kind, and the kinds that were a blight on my life. And hey, yes, the world would be a better place without me. I wanted to hurt myself, to write my own suicide note. The short circuit flashed in my brain and I saw the end right there for all of us.

The brothers were in their own world too, and not ready to leave it, or my apartment. Miguel was in effervescent form, wiry hands lighting cigarette after cigarette, explaining how he hadn't wanted to insult me by showing with a suitcase full of cash. That was for the movies, that wasn't how friends did business, no. We would do it by trust. He would give me my share in manageable amounts, so that I wouldn't arouse suspicion. He was saving me from myself. A real touch of class. *Nice place you got here Martin, yeah?* He flicked his ash on to the floor without thinking. I thought he just had to be taking the piss, there wasn't even a chair for him or his sulking lump of a brother to sit on whilst he gave me the lesson in money-laundering. Anyway, he went on, finding the gall required to shoot his particular line of shit didn't seem to represent any kind of significant challenge. Meanwhile big Tony remained more reserved, scratching his balls and yawning, propped against the wall, contributing nothing to the moment but the stink of a particularly disgusting body odour. Yeah, works for you, doesn't it Tony, smell bad and have a psychopathic attitude, it'll get you through the day, that's how you get problems to just melt right away. That and an equally psychotic older brother, it helps if he's a compulsive liar who can rant endlessly about the great deals he's pulled in the past. None of which had probably ever happened. I saw the end, I wanted to make it happen, Jesus how I wanted to bring it down. *Hey Martin, you ever bring girls back here?*

Of course Tony. There's no fooling you, is there? Maybe we can talk about that later, once we've figured out what to do about the three kilos and the forty-five thousand you were meant to have. *Hey Martin, why don't we have a party tonight, fiesta, yeah? Get some girls round, let them score, they'll be as horny as bitches after a shot of this stuff, what do you think? Come on Martin, you know lots of girls, English girls, Germans . . . say you fix them up and we let them have some lines, on the house. We can spare a few lines, can't we Miguel?*

If I hadn't already spent so much energy throwing chairs around at Herman's I would have been tempted to have a go at knocking big Tony's empty head off with the kitchen scales. The gear hadn't even been paid for and he was already talking about giving the fucking stuff away as if it was his. Wearing me down with stupidity. Didn't he realize that the whole point of his and his midget sibling's presence here was to take this away, as in off my hands so that I could stop sweating about it being in my possession? Probably not. Then again, big Tony probably didn't realize much about anything, no. He tended to leave that side of the business to his brother and concentrate on doing the one thing that he did best. Being a cunt.

I tried to figure it out once more, to consider the options, but clarity of thought was in short supply with Miguel's routine going on non-stop, the stink of sick in the bathroom from earlier in the day snaking its way into the bare lounge, with big Tony being big fucking Tony and the bag of coke sitting there like a dismembered corpse. I should have asked them their plan, demanded a guarantee on payment, given them only a sample of the gear until they had proved they were up to it. Should have. Instead, it was me pushing them out the door, the precious stash in a supermarket carrier bag; go on, get out of my sight, useless fucks. This was the moment I could have hit reverse and got out, yet here I was wading in deeper and deeper. So deep I was digging my own grave. I knew it but couldn't stop. I was rushing toward the end, going out on a high. If only I could concentrate on what to do, how to get Johanna back, how to make her safe. Somehow, the Carceras and the three kilos were meant to be the way out of it. And the irony was I thought big Tony was stupid.

I watched them laugh and whistle as they made their sweet carefree way down the apartment block stairs, white polythene bag slung over Miguel's shoulder. I felt relieved. I also felt a churning in my stomach and knew I was about to throw up again. Be careful boys, that's my future you're holding there, and my wife's and my daughter's. Yeah, I've given it away. *Go down deeper.*

The price was met by a variety of means: gold coin, carbines, Zanzibar cloth, brandy. The captain had sought to negotiate a lower tariff but the simple fact remained that to make room for the incoming slaves goods would have to be off-loaded from the holds. Far from moving off quickly then, Fela's arrival, and Martin's rapid curtailment of the inspection process, merely marked the advent of a new phase of the *Anne*'s inland stay. With so many crew sick and feeble, the clearing of space aboard ship became a protracted affair, the sluggish waters of the Odoro becoming no more than a cesspool for the vessel to float upon.

Fela entrusted his landbound cargo to some of his personal aides and elected to travel back with the ship to Point Colou where he would disembark with the balance of his payment and reacquaint himself with Haraldt, who, presumably, was due some form of commission from the proceeds of the sale. Martin too longed for a return to their former anchorage and was grateful when the *Anne* was eventually on the move once more, beginning her cumbersome backwards crawl, the first stage of the torpid journey to the estuary. He had begun to wonder how much longer he could masquerade as Captain Henry's surgeon, how long it would be before he was tied to the deck lattice and flogged. *Twenty lashes.* What price a clear conscience?

'How many are dead this morning?'

'Two, Captain.'

'Seventeen in total then; how do you propose to stop the deaths?'

'Sixteen.'

'I include the three from our original eight purchased at the Point.'

'Sixteen, all told, Captain. Eleven crew, sixteen slaves. Eighteen crew if those who were lost before we reached Cape Bojador are included.'

'I am talking about slaves sir, they are all that concern me.'

'Quite.'

It was 4 July, some time early morning. Captain Henry had had to seek out the increasingly reclusive ship's surgeon in the officers' cabin. Where once his had been an almost constant presence on decks, observing the ship and men at work, it was now rare to sight him at large; the crew would have to summon him to attend the slaves in the holds. If the captain was curious as to the reasons for the change, however, he chose not to show it. Martin took from his silence that the exchange was over and returned his attention to his reading matter.

'What do you find in your books, sir, what do you find that is of use to us here?'

Martin recognized the voice as that of a riled man but took pleasure in the contempt it stirred within him rather than the fear that it was doubtless intended to provoke. *One hundred lashes*.

'The journals have little to say regarding yaws, other than how to spot its symptoms. On the fever they are more forthright.'

'How?'

'Fever lurks by the African shore, Captain, and from my own observation grows even stronger inland. The more we linger by the shore the longer we are at risk; if we move, the risk will reduce.'

'And do your damned writings explain how the savages can live happily on these shores where the fever is ever-present and then drop the minute they are on a vessel such as ours, do they explain that, heh?'

The voice of a man riled. A man who, Martin pondered, would have had the bodies of the slaves flogged for their impertinence in dying before tossing them over the side.

'Fever affects them on shore but there is a difference between their existence there and that which they enjoy on board. On land they are free to escape from the heat, to partake of water. Here they are cooked in our holds by day, bringing the fever to the boil so to say, and watered only occasionally. It is the combination of captivity and proximity which fells them, Captain. That is the explanation.'

'I have never read this in any damned book. Where is it written?'

'Partly written, partly theory.'

'Whose theory, yours?'

'Aye, Captain.'

'Then I would thank you for not mentioning it, I will not have your wild fantasies upsetting my crew, hear me?'

'Captain, please understand me. Unless we move swiftly to the Indies we will have no slaves left alive by the time we do get there.'

'Silence! We would have more left living if you had carried out a proper inspection of those we have taken aboard and rejected the diseased then. We will move when I command it, once we have our full complement and not before. That is right and that is how it will be and you, sir, will be charged if you prove obstinate or insubordinate. Be warned! I will not be lectured by a mere boy on how to run my ship, do you hear me?'

179

Martin heard but remained unconvinced. Unconvinced and unintimidated. He thought back to the day he had first stepped aboard the *Anne*. *A last throw of the dice*. He thought of how things had changed, day by day, land after sea. Everything had changed so that he would arrive at this moment, when he would realize he no longer cared, that he had nothing left to lose but his own sense of worth, his own humanity. And how he was not going to surrender that without a fight.

When they arrived back at the Point, Captain Henry sent for Martin. He wanted him to go ashore and scrutinize whatever slaves Haraldt was holding in his compound. Over thirty of those loaded on the banks of the Odoro had perished by then and it was obvious that the skipper was desperate to replenish the numbers. Martin did not realize at this juncture just how desperate, and swiftly reported to the longboat, excited at the prospect of renewing his acquaintance with the trader he considered his friend. When he stepped ashore however, Haraldt was to greet him with a question rather than a welcome.

'Where is Fela?'

'I don't know. Perhaps he is supervising the unloading of his cargo. You heard of our trade by the river?'

Haraldt nodded. Martin noticed the smile was missing and felt an uneasy atmosphere between them. As if Haraldt thought that he was lying when he had no means of proving the contrary, and also his own disquiet at being taken as duplicitous.

'Haraldt, I am sure he will join us later. How are you?'

Martin offered his hand, eventually it was taken.

'Your captain made no further trade?'

'No, as you said, it proved fruitless. I am here to enquire whether you have any others to be offered for sale.'

Haraldt stood motionless, not flinching even when a breaker rolled in to soak his boots as he stood on the sands, his eyes fixed to the horizon, and the ship that hung somewhere in the space between ocean and sky.

'Then let us wait for my partner, since he should be concerned with such matters.'

'Of course.' Martin sought Haraldt's eye but the latter was still absorbed in the activity aboard the distant ship. His impatience grew until he could stand the silence no longer.

'Haraldt, what is the matter, why are you behaving like this?'

'I am . . . .' Haraldt paused as he peered into the glistening waters out ahead of him. '. . . I am disturbed that Fela is not here, I would have thought he would choose to join me upon your arrival, or at least send a message. I must warn you, Martin, it would be no good for your ship to attempt . . . You should all understand that there are laws here in Africa too, that harm will come to those who do not keep agreements. No good will come to those who ignore this and are not honest and straightforward with other traders. I must warn you, you must tell your captain.'

Martin listened intently to the words as they were spoken yet still found it impossible to follow what it was that Haraldt sought to articulate. Was this the same man who had been such a convivial host only weeks ago? If he was suspicious of something, then what? Was he perturbed that Captain Henry had ventured inland via the Odoro against his advice?

'I do not know what you mean, Haraldt. Forgive me, but I am lost. What is it that you are afraid of, how have we offended you?'

Haraldt pulled his feet from the pits of wet sand they had been sinking into, his face showing nothing but displeasure.

'I am afraid that I am dealing with those who would act in bad faith, those who would act with duplicity. I may be wrong, I would be delighted to be. I am one man alone in Africa treating others as I would hope they should treat me. Now, as I said, we should wait for Fela to arrive.'

Haraldt walked off towards the compound without inviting the others to join him, leaving Martin and José unattended by the shore. The longboat which had taken them to within the beach perimeter waited out beyond the breaking waves, and the natives who had brought them into the sands by canoe had dispersed back to the huts that lined the compound. Martin felt abandoned, an orphan again, cast out into the wilderness, denied a welcome in a place he would have been proud to consider some kind of home. He looked to José, trying not to betray his hurt at the treatment given to them by Haraldt. José stared back blankly. *I do not understand either.* Martin sighed and began to walk toward Haraldt's settlement. Ten paces in, José moved alongside to tap him on the shoulder, inviting him to turn and look out to sea. He did so and saw the flagged communication between the *Anne* and Wells upon the longboat. A message given and confirmed as received, what was going on? Astonishingly, the longboat was realigning itself for a bid to come ashore, negotiating the breaking waves with flailing oars so that for an instant it could pass as an upturned cockroach struggling to stop itself drowning, an insect being toyed with by a cruel hand. The boat was being steered to straddle the breakers sideways, stabbing out against the malevolent energy dragging her hull from underneath. Eventually she was through, surging in on the surf to a sliding stop on the sands. Wells leapt over the side, immersed to his waist in the warm frothy waters. He moved with an urgency, wading towards Martin as if he were an invader, come to stake first claim to the land.

'How many slaves in the compound?'

Martin did not make ready with an answer, more intrigued by the somewhat charged arrival of the crew at the shore. Wells was joined by three others now, slipping over to sink into the sand beneath the surface, some of them carrying carbines, guns that they took care to keep high above their heads as they made their way to dry land.

'How many and are they fit to travel?'

Wells' tremulous voice betrayed an edgy impatience that puzzled Martin all the greater. There was an urgency to everything these men were doing that added an undertone to the question already asked; why won't you speak and give us the information we need to do the job?

Martin stayed quiet, trying to think all of it through, this strange situation that was gathering pace all the time; Haraldt's demeanour, Fela's absence, the carbines, the longboat being brought right into the shore once the canoes of the natives had been berthed. When it struck him it was so obvious he wondered why he had not seen it sooner. This was no visit, this was a raid.

'No slaves.'

'What . . . none?'

'There are no slaves here . . . in the compound.'

Martin held José's face fixed as he replied, drawing him into complicity. Wells was either suspicious or plain uneasy at the answer. Martin could guess at the reason for his apprehension.

'I will explain it to the captain. There are none worth taking aboard.'

Wells nodded, relieved at the burden being taken elsewhere. Martin wondered if they had been ordered to loot any other valuables.

'You should rejoin the ship at once.'

Martin threw a look in the direction of the compound, as if to say he had knowledge of imminent reprisals, of a pressing danger to the longboat's crew.

'Captain says we are not to leave without you.'

Martin had no doubt that Wells took the implied threat seriously and had no desire to loiter, yet his deeper fear of Captain Henry's fevered moods meant there was no chance he would depart without himself and José. Martin looked towards the settlement again, this time to satisfy his own interest. There had to be every reason to expect retaliation from Haraldt. Here were the men who had cheated him, enslaved his friend, gone against their word. Martin asked himself what he would have done in the same situation, would he meekly accept such treachery? No, he would fight, he would go down fighting if need be, take a hostage if possible, to be used in future exchange. The irony was that his plan had been to stay here, to abandon the *Anne* and watch her leave for the Indies without him, to make a new life as a free man here in Africa, at the Point. Now he understood in an instant that if he attempted to do so he would merely bring ruin, and be seen as a stooge or captive; Haraldt no longer trusted him and the captain would bring force to bear in order to return him to his own notion of freedom, a version as warped as the heat-seared boards on the decks of the vessel he sought to escape.

Martin made to speak but found his throat strangled by the emotion sweeping through him as the realization became overwhelming.

'We must . . .' He paused and sighed deeply. He knew tears were not far away and it was important that he did not surrender to them. '. . . We must return at once.'

His voice was trembling; Wells would later report to a scornful Captain Henry that the young surgeon's nerve had failed him when confronted with the execution of the skipper's audacious plan, unaware that the truth was somewhat different, that here was a man with more daring in his veins than any of them, yet a man whose plan was perishing before his eyes.

They waded back through the wash to clamber aboard the longboat.

Haraldt reappeared, a gun over each shoulder as they began to pull away. He was flanked by gromettoes carrying arms. They came forward slowly, making no effort to take aim nor indeed move into the range of the visiting crew's weapons. No, the advance was a gesture, the slow silence of the elderly trader giving a simple and dignified message to the exiting marauders. *You have wronged me, no good can come to you thieves.*

José lifted an oar though Martin displayed no inclination to share the labour in fighting the incoming tide in order to return to the ship. He too kept a brooding silence, hoping that somehow Haraldt would decipher the reason behind his own sad and languid bearing. *This was not my plan, I have returned to the ship to save you, to save your friend.*

The longboat was toiling to make headway and Wells began to call a vigorous stroke. Martin could feel all eyes upon him; perhaps they were angry that he chose not to join their efforts. He was beyond caring though, eyeing the vacant oar with contempt as he let his arm trail in the waters over the side. *Shark meat.*

Making love with my wife. Afternoons spent in a sun-filled room making love with my wife. Kissing her on the lips, kissing her on each eye, one after the other, and then her forehead, like the Pope giving a blessing. Letting your actions, the gentleness of your touch, the delicacy of each caress and stroke say all you ever need to say about your feelings. Never having to say anything, just lying there on your side, face to face, slowly blinking, a warm and lazy smile in each direction as the summer breeze softly blows the curtain back into the room from the open balcony doors, so that the dazzling blue sky is a momentary backdrop to the two pairs of bare feet on top of the white cotton sheet and you can move your head and imagine that this bed is floating high in the air, floating in heaven.

Afternoons and early evenings. Lying on the same bed, now firmly planted on the top floor of our new apartment in Cala Fornells, watching her study herself in the mirror, drying her hair, putting in earrings, following each curve of her mouth with her lipstick. Does she see herself as I do? Is she immune to her own beauty or blasé after years of living with it? What does she see in me when I feel her gaze on me whilst I'm reading, how could it be the same for her, looking at my ordinary face, a Greenock schoolboy's face. Doesn't it strike her as unfair that there is such an imbalance, how could someone so perfect love me?

Late evenings, in a bar somewhere in the bay. The same beautiful face is surveying the street scene, looking on serenely at the endless parade of gaggling young girls under the predatory eye of the men following in their white jeans. I wait at the counter to settle the bill. I like being removed from her like this, not that I haven't enjoyed sitting hand-in-hand as we sipped our beers at the table; no, but here at this distance I can allow myself a little fantasy, that she is not my wife, that I am just seeing her for the very first time, seeing her like the others around me, so that I can be captivated anew and set myself the imposs-ible task of making her mine, the one I have achieved already.

I walk back slowly; she is far away from me, maybe thinking about a memory of cold Swedish winter, although I don't need to ask what train of thought she's on because she's happy to break away from it when I stand beside her chair to place her linen jacket over her golden shoulders. She smiles, it's as if a light has been switched on, a glow; she takes my arm as we walk along the street. We are in no hurry, the path back to the apartment is all uphill, narrow and winding. I have my arm around her waist as we climb. We pass old widows dressed in black sitting out on battered chairs whiling the night hours away in solitary silence, we pass open doors revealing families squashed together on couches peering at blaring TV sets; skinny cats accost us, trying to charm food from the perfumed strangers moving amongst them. Then we are home, pulling off shoes to walk barefoot to the bedroom, then opening the wooden shutter doors to stand out on the balcony and survey the moonlit scene below, to watch the rippling silver waves far out in the harbour, to hear the same blasts of hillside radios and tele-visions that we have passed on our way here, now sounding so distant, the echoes of the Spanish voices on the airwaves ever more frantic and vaguely absurd, alien yet comforting, reminding us that we are exiles in a strange land, exiles with nothing except each other. Johanna steps towards me, soft arms pulling me close, closing her eyes as she kisses me. Exiles of love.

I've never been one to bury my head in the sand when it comes to problems, you know, just ignoring them and hoping that they will go away. No, I have never been so stupid as to imagine that if you ignore something then it will disappear, although, God knows, I've been envious enough of those who are. Running away is more my thing, taking off into the horizon and leaving everything behind, that's a plan, a *real* plan, that's what I was building up to. I only had to find a map to tell me where the fuck I was so that I could escape it, only needed time to think so that whatever scheme I came up with didn't take me straight back into the shit.

I took a short drive to Calvia, one of these inland towns that can look nondescript and dull under a grey sky, charming and authentic when bathed in sunshine. I took the trip not caring which I saw; for me Calvia was part of my past I wanted to touch again, my memory would fill in the colours and atmosphere as required. I parked and wandered around the quiet streets. I stood outside the council offices where I pleaded for my first liquor-trading licence, the registry office where I was married, and the square where the group shot of the wedding party was taken. Six years ago. This town looked exactly the same but I was a different person, a better person – what would he make of this mess?

I walked by the police station and toyed with the idea of going in. *Can I help you, sir?* Yes, I wonder if you can. My wife and child have been kidnapped, I'm being driven out of business by the people who have probably done it, I owe an old friend and his armed acquaintance twenty thousand dollars and the two crooks I had planned on hiring to kill the man who knows where my wife is want to take over my business as well. *And what can we do to help?* Well, if you could make sure the coke deal I set up to sort it all out goes OK I would be really grateful. *Yes, of course, señor.*

There isn't much to admire in Calvia for sure, the usual narrow streets in their own dusty ramshackle grid, white-washed walls and peach-coloured façades, it would remind you of the Mexican town they tried to defend in *The Magnificent Seven*, the place the noble outlaws chose to make their stand against the bandits terrorizing the honest toilers who made up the population. Not much to look at but still deserving more of my affections than I granted it, a better reflection of Spain than the bar I built here on the island.

Out from the town I headed further inland, further into the hills, higher and higher. Most new arrivals to Mallorca make the same journey eventually, as we did. They start off by the water, that's what initially brings them here, the chance to live on the coast. Then the charm of sea-level begins to wear off, it becomes too crowded, new developments like Puerto Puals spring up unannounced almost daily and on any available strip of land, squeezing you into a space which becomes tighter and tighter. So then, if you have the money, you move inland and build your home on a hillside, on a virgin patch of woodland that is big enough for you to fence like a ranch where no one will be able to encroach. That's been the story for the last ten years, more and more immigrants looking for privacy, carving out their territories, building the villas that keep their shutters closed, unaware that they are rejecting the culture that attracted them in the first place. We were no different, happy at first to live amongst the people, to be charmed and over-whelmed by the spirit of the island, every aspect of it, watching it bite the hand of the tourism that fed it. Then, slowly, without ever realizing or even discussing why, we sought out our privacy in the hills, we wanted our home comforts and to build the walls around us high enough to keep everything out. And us together.

Johanna and I were married in Calvia's register office off the main road. Tiny office, small wedding. A quiet couple. Content within them-selves. Her sister and mother came over from Sweden. I didn't invite any of my family to the ceremony, such as it was, it didn't seem appropriate. Too much time had passed since any meaningful contact, and I didn't want the awkwardness and effort of rebuilding whatever bridges were required to spoil the magic of what was happening with

Johanna. And what was happening *was* magical, believe me. I was in love with a beautiful woman, who was herself devoted to me. A flawless woman, every inch of her perfect, from her open brow and sparkling blue eyes to her small firm breasts to her narrow waist and gentle slope of her hips, smooth, tanned legs and ballet dancer's ankles and the short stubby toes beyond them.

Magical. I stood beside her as the prescribed words were read and slipped the ring on her finger, happy, grinning like a cartoon husband, thought-bubbles full of red Valentine hearts frothing out of my head; it's a wonder they never showed in the photographs. What they do show is the new Mr and Mrs Law smiling for the lens; Mrs Law looking like a model, Mr Law nervously holding the pose whilst he waits for the shutter to click. I can remember that feeling right now, blinking into the sunlight, aware of the shouts and waves of passers-by who had slowed down to take in the newly-weds in the town square.

What I did that day, that wedding, was another stunt, another steal that I pulled off by holding my nerve long enough so that the façade was never penetrated. Magical? A confidence trick, like walking through the goods-to-declare zone with three kilos of cocaine hidden about you, like pretending to be a knowledgeable sailor to the crew whose ship you want to join. I didn't know how she could love a man like me. I knew she couldn't love a man like me. I had an idea of the kind of man she wanted me to be so I had tried to be like that, someone better. I had kept it going so far but felt an impostor, that the full facts had been withheld so that I could negotiate a better deal, one weighted entirely in my favour. This poor girl was marrying with a hope in her heart that I could be the man I had promised her I would be. She had just married a fraud.

So I never knew how she could love me, and sure, for a while this didn't matter so much, I just blessed my luck on a daily basis that she actually did. Then the question began to grate though I never dared ask, and the more I didn't understand the more I could only assume she was faking it.

The Arena Bar was my dream, somewhere to put down roots, a chance to make something substantial, not a one-off deal. We worked on it together and it became our dream; up at dawn to cook the breakfasts, yawning together until way after midnight, mixing the drinks, pouring the shots. The dream became not a little mundane, a little confused, a little crowded. You see, the bar I originally had in mind would be a vehicle for me, my stage, my chance to star and draw people to me. The regulars would come in and give a warm handshake to Martin here behind the counter, maybe a rueful smile at being back and ready to drink so soon after the last memorable time. These customers would be more like friends, a gang I would be at the heart of rather than the loner who was for ever on the outside. This was the fantasy, quickly amended to include Johanna, expanded so that the bar would provide a comfortable living and generate the income whereby we would stay young and stylish for ever, like movie stars in their sunshine Paradise.

Yet with the two of us side by side it was hard to find the space in which to invent this new personality as well as playing the other new roles I had found for myself as husband and father. I didn't know it then but we were slowly mutating from being lovers to being joint managers of a demanding business. We would talk to each other as such in a working day, and then it became harder to switch it off once we had moved out from behind the counter. I guess eventually we stopped even noticing. The irony is, that at some level, we achieved the dream, we made money, lots of it. We bought the clothes, the cars, and the house in the hills we wanted. All of this before Herman arrived and his organization began to cast its envious eyes in our direction.

In truth though, things had turned sour already. The deal was that as the Arena's owner I would be surrounded by people who would be forced to love me; friends, staff, clients, wife. I would relax and open up to them, drop my guard and live a clear and uncomplicated life, be the same Martin Law to all of them. But the more you see of people, the less respect you can have for them, particularly when they are on holiday. You see them exposed for what they are once the straitjacket of work, neighbours and friends' expectations is removed. Stripped of the props that help them through their lives back home they'll get drunk, argue pointlessly, be selfish, insensitive, maudlin all at once. You begin to view them entirely in terms of their worth to you; wallets and purses to be emptied, mouths to be filled, hands to be occupied with your drinks. I became a host, a very good one, a *calculating* one. So good that I could do the act in my sleep. So good I could hardly turn it off. Far from being the star of the scene that everything revolved around I became more detached than ever, the reclusive director flattering his cast when it suits, gently easing those that don't fit out of the frame, manipulating everything to conform to his scheme, screwing the beautiful yet insecure female lead.

Yes, I was fucking the girls early on; couldn't tell you why, except that it was there, it was all available. Did I feel bad? Of course I did, as bad as I knew I would. From the moment I first met Johanna I felt terrified of letting her down. I also knew myself well enough to understand that I was capable of the worst and that this fear was a real one. So every time she looked into my eyes and told me she loved me, or held our child in one arm and pulled me close with the other I could feel this knot in my gut, this guilt – long before I ever did anything it was there marking time for when I would. The more scared I became the more inevitable it was that something would happen; when it did it was almost a relief because at last my suspicions were confirmed. Suspicions about myself. The shit I had become.

You maybe won't find screwing your staff in any management manual but you can take it from me that it is not necessarily a bad practice. If you want to get away with paying low wages, encouraging a fierce personal loyalty towards yourself and promoting a climate of secrecy whereby your interests are protected then you can hardly do better. If you want to stimulate competition amongst your team why not screw two of them alternately and divide your attentions between them? If they have come as a pair – as in boy and girl pair, like Sarah and Alexander – then you just split them down the middle, it adds to the challenge, besides you are doing them a favour by exposing the flaws that would have undone them in years to come anyway. In the meantime there is equal incentive for you and her to keep it all quiet from boyfriends, travelling partners, wives.

Didn't Johanna suspect? Object? Reject? Maybe. She never said. We had a child by then, she poured everything into her, and somewhere along the way she picked up on my trick, she learned to withdraw into herself, learned to watch dispassionately, began to view it as a process, me chasing my entertainment. She knew me too well to ever feel threatened by anyone in particular or worry that someone might attempt to take her place. She must have known that none of the chicks would ever get closer to me than she had. Maybe she saw me like a rat trapped in a laboratory maze, or a hamster in a fucking wheel, condemned by its own stupidity to go round and round. She was screwing one of the guys she met on the local tourist operatives committee, kind of a wet guy from Holland, ran a car-hire business just outside Puerto Puals. One minute he was round all the time, then the calls stopped, a bad sign. I think it was a German girl who once told me you can always tell if your partner is unfaithful because they fuck like the last person they slept with and you will notice the change. Well, I thought, not me baby, I'm too good at keeping everything in its right compartment, different strokes for different folks, literally. I was so busy concentrating on my performance that the fact it was a double-edged thing almost escaped me. Then I noticed a difference one night with Johanna, when I was deep into my own pleasure, enjoying the new side to her that had emerged out of nowhere, the biting, the scratching, her crying out loud enough to wake our baby. *Fuck me Martin, fuck me*. And I felt my grip on her shoulders slacken and my head turn from kissing her neck to face the window. Still pumping like a dog but by instinct only, my thoughts suddenly elsewhere, taking in the lights, sounds and scent of the moment, the moment I realized we had reached some kind of end. The one I had taken us to.

The captain was alone in his cabin. Martin saw from the papers strewn across the desk it was the inventory rather than navigational matters that absorbed him. Martin wondered what comment Fotheringham the late purser would have made; would he have congratulated his skipper on returning the whole venture to profit by his devious cunning, or would he have challenged the dishonesty that blackened the name of English merchantmen? Too many seemed fearful of speaking the plain truth. Martin had decided not to join their number.

'We must release Fela and his party. We cannot trade a caboceer as a slave.'

'You, sir, will knock before you enter my cabin; you, sir, will address me as captain, and you, sir, will keep your damned opinions to yourself unless you have a hunger for a lashing.'

'It was not my intention to be impertinent, Captain . . .' Martin's magnanimous statement brought a slight softening in his skipper's glare. However, it soon returned to its full intensity as he followed it with a further comment; '. . . nor was it my intention to be part of a buccaneer crew.'

Captain Henry stood sharply, snapping to attention like a trooper on the parade ground. In the confines of the cabin one step was all it took to bring his pox-ridden face an inch from Martin's. His breath stank like a dog's yet Martin did not flinch, determined not to give any ground.

'We are the ship that has been swindled, you bastard imbecile, we are the ones who have been sold substandard goods that perish before their journey has even begun. We are acting within our rights to secure a fair deal. We explain ourselves to no one other than His Majesty's Government, not to the braggarts and brigands who sought to take our money and goods in fraudulent trade. Understand me sir, I have long exhausted my patience with your pitiful medical skills, your worthless slave inspections and your constant air of whining grievance. If you care so much as to the fate of Fela and his companions it can be arranged that you join them, join them in leg irons in the hold. I will hear no more from you, understand?'

Martin waited for the captain to retreat, as he knew he would, the lure of the desk papers proving powerful. A venture returned to profit.

'Captain, I do have a final comment to make. I hesitate, but it may well be one you would wish to hear.'

The captain viewed him suspiciously; was he about to have his resolve tested so soon?

'Captain, I merely wish to relay an utterance made by Haraldt, as we spoke on the shore. He said no good would come to those . . . whom he felt did not adhere to a bargain. He said it with such certainty that I took this to imply he had some means of enforcing retribution, either himself or through allies.'

Martin saw that his quiet salvo had found its target as the captain fell still, eyes blinking in contemplation as the impact of his words was absorbed. Yes, this was something a skipper would need to know, although how to react was a matter of individual judgement. Now it was Mr Henry's turn to think things through.

'What would you suspect that he could inflict upon us?'

That it pained the captain to solicit an opinion from one whose thoughts he had so very recently derided as seditious and unworthy was apparent from the halting manner in which he had spoken. Yet the safety of his ship was at stake, the safe passage of cargo, and so he was compelled to investigate. Thus it was that he stammered out his words, with a voice alternating between anxiety and contempt.

'I would think that he would take steps to retrieve what he regards as rightfully his.'

'I know man, I know!' snapped Captain Henry, surrendering to the sense of affront induced by entertaining the conversation. He thumped the desk with a clenched fist, knuckles glowing white under the angry red skin. 'What I want to know is *how* . . . Understand? How many ships can he muster, does he have contacts in the Indies, does he have men aboard my ship?'

Martin remained calm, determinedly calm; a scheming schoolboy delighting in exasperating his teacher. Still, his conscience could now be clear, he was making his best effort to influence events.

'I do not believe he has any ships of his own, though he may have contact with those who may act on his behalf. If he were to offer a bounty for the return of his goods this could represent a danger. For this reason I would imagine that a provident course of action may well be to head for the Indies soonest, before such vessels have an opportunity to engage us. I would also

. . . speculate . . . that releasing Fela might reduce the perceived legitimacy of such an attack.'

Captain Henry curled his lips in immediate and sour disgust.

'We are eighty slaves light. We shall move to the Indies once we have completed the trade for them. We are legitimate traders and I will not set sail across the ocean in accordance with the fears of a cabin-boy.'

Martin saw that his audience was at an end. He made for the door, pausing briefly to bow to the skipper, another gesture resting in the uncertain border between insolence and respect. Cabin-boy, he thought, why should the term be given as an insult? One could be such and still be a better man than a captain. Such cheap jibes did not matter, he had done what he wanted to do. He had tried to relieve the suffering below deck. Captain Henry had been warned.

The *Anne*'s next intended destination? Fort St George, Martin guessed, judging by the western tack the ship now leaned to. Fort St George, for its sheltered harbour and safe trading after their adventures beyond Cape Bojador. Now, he supposed, they could pay a premium price for mediocre goods and still remain in profit, though of course there would be the problem of Captain Henry's wayward navigation and its concealment becoming apparent to the crew once they made the journey. How would he explain coming across the fort from the opposite direction? What would he say when they arrived? If they ever arrived.

Four days after their abrupt departure from Point Colou, another ship is spotted on the horizon. The captain stands on the quarterdeck and spies upon her, peering through his glass. Once more, those around him await the pronouncement; none is forthcoming, a sign in itself perhaps, certainly enough of a signal to send a frisson of excitement and nervous laughter through the decks. The *Anne* sits low in the water, very low, overloaded as a result of the one-sided trading that has taken place. Some of the slaves gasping for breath deep in the holds are below the waterline, starved even of a breeze through the sealed gun ports that would otherwise have provided a window on the world as it passed. The ship now gaining on them has no such concerns, she is high and proud in the water, carrying little, if any cargo, any crewman can see this, with or without a spyglass. *So she is not a*

Guineaman, goes the word whispered amongst them, *what can be her purpose?* The captain is not alone in his suspicion.

Martin had been loitering on the deck when she first came into view. The breeze that day had been gentle, and whilst the other ship gained it was a slow process. What seemed to Martin like hours passed before their apparent pursuer grew larger in image. Yet she drew closer all the same and with a relentlessness that affected all watching the process. Martin was aware of an array of emotions stirring within himself, none straightforward, some contradictory. What if this was after all just another merchant ship, eager to exchange local knowledge and chart positionings? Would he be disappointed? Yes, but for what reason? And what if she were a Royal Africa vessel, coming to inspect cargo and tax inventory, would this be more satisfactory? Hardly, however great the captain's discomfort. So what if she were a ship intent on confrontation and robbery on the seas, was that what he wished? Perhaps, with the fates finally free to decide the future for him; although surely the suffering and injury to the defending crew would make for the worst of all possible outcomes.

Activity on deck. Martin saw that the captain had instructed full sail to be set, manoeuvrability being surrendered to the quest for speed. Martin wondered how this would appear to those watching from the vantage of the other vessel; men crawling like ants on every spar, climbing high to unfurl the shabby canvas bleached yellow by months in the fierce African sun. The captain had made his judgement and would somehow seek to outrun those chasing in their sleek craft. No attempt had been made to flag even simple communications to this boat, but here, in this very act, was a message as clear as any; *we fear you, we are trying to escape, catch us if you can.*

Martin made to return to the officers' cabin; it was time to think. The moment was surely coming and he would have to be prepared for it. Time to think of the options, the strategies to be employed.

He passed through the crowded decks, through the whispering knots of men gathered at every mast and companion-way. Some sought to exchange glances, the ones they passed between themselves that told of their realization of the impending reckoning. Would they have to fight? How hard? To the death? Martin chose not to linger with any group, smiling courteously at McKnight, pretending to have no interest in the murmurs hanging in the air, buzzing like mosquitoes in the ear. Doubtless the captain would have had any instigator flogged for spreading panic had he chosen to mix with his men and listen in. He might even have had time to have one or more whipped to extinction before the *Anne* was stormed, beaten for airing their thoughts, for having thoughts. There was of course, advice that Martin knew he could offer his skipper in this time of crisis; that if he sought to reduce the ship's load there were at least eight more slaves whose lifeless bodies could be jettisoned in the quest for a lighter ballast and greater swiftness across the water, probably another ten whose gaspings in the still, stale air were so shallow that they could be discarded now rather than kept until their inevitable demise but hours away. Would the captain welcome such counsel? Probably not. Martin looked over the waves to the ship's shadow, still following, still threatening from a distance, closer all the time. Perhaps deliverance was at hand.

Darkness falling. Two lamps required to read. Time to see the captain, time to propose the plan. The pursuing ship has faded from view, receding like an apparition into the gloom. Some hope, perhaps Captain Henry included, that somehow it might be shaken off in the darkness, that their paths will no longer converge in the confusion of the evening shadows. Those of a logical mind understand that this will not happen, that the wind that moves them both does not change from one to another. The *Anne* is still under full sail, pushing forward on increasingly heavy seas as fast as she can, unaware of what lies ahead or under her; rocks, reefs? The first they would know of either would be when they smashed the weed-ridden hull.

Martin wondered if the captain cursed his inland adventures now that the vegetation sprouting from the bow dragged them back when the need for speed was so pressing. How would he justify such times and deeds in the log? No matter, his actions had sealed his fate, his obduracy had led to the chase. Martin knocked on the cabin door; time to speak to the captain.

There being no reply, he turned the handle slowly, entering cautiously. Captain Henry sat alone, slumped at his desk. Where others might have spent these moments locked in conference with trusted officers here was a man carrying the burden alone. Perhaps there was something to be said for such isolation, thought Martin, something even admirable in this, taking the burden of command as a solitary one.

196

The captain turned to face him, eyes immediately alert with suspicion at the sight of his troublesome intruder, voice betraying the fatigue of fever and frailty.

'What now, boy? How many dead?'

Martin cut to the heart of the matter. There was little time left.

'Captain, I come to offer my service, my support in seeking a means of escape from our current situation and ensuring that those who would wish to harm our ship shall face justice.'

The captain rubbed his damp brow wearily, showing no obvious appetite for Martin's sudden sycophancy. 'What do you mean?'

'If one is to assume that the ship trailing behind does so with harmful intent then it is pertinent to consider alternative strategies to be employed in the eventuality of that ship catching us, sir, strategies that I am sure as captain you are –'

'What do you have in mind, boy?'

'A scheme . . . fanciful perhaps, but worthy of your consideration if only to confirm the wisdom of your own intended action by comparison. I would urge you to listen, sir.'

The captain's pride duly flattered, he yawned and beckoned Martin to begin, pouring himself a large brandy and setting his feet up on the desk. His face settled into a scowl of sorts, although not, Martin guessed, aimed directly at him, more at the hopelessness of the situation. When a heavy ship is attacked at sea by a lighter, faster one carrying more cannon there are but two choices: surrender, and lose everything, or fight, and lose everything. Here was a man alone in his despair. Yet Martin knew he had news for him, he was about to tell him of the third option. Listen? He would have to. He pulled close.

If it comes to pass that you order the men to fight and they do we shall all perish at the hands of a greater foe. We would lose, heroically, but lose all the same. If it came to pass that the men refused to fight then we would also lose, yet you would lose the more, Captain, your reputation ruined by the insolence of a mutinous crew. If it were to be seen that you had sought to protect your crew, by removing the prizes that the thieves would kill to gain, our reputation would remain, become enhanced, an example to all of leadership, of protecting the interests of all who had invested in this ship. It cannot be said that the men would refuse to fight, no, Captain. Yet how can it be that our best course is to risk everything by gambling that they will? Who knows what lies they may be tempted with, who can predict how they might react? You must protect them, Captain, spare them the temptation that might entice them, us all, towards disaster.

'Martin, there's something I need to speak to you about, have you got five minutes?'

'Sure. Five minutes for everybody, why not.'

I lifted a glass and began to fill it from the lager tap. The drive back from the hills north of Calvia hadn't been so long and dry but the reality of finding myself back behind the bar at the Arena left me desperate for any distraction. The place was reasonably busy although it barely seemed to matter any more whether business was good or bad; the place was hardly mine now, however things worked out, and I had bigger fish to fry, a whole fucking shoal of them.

The froth gathered in a tight creamy head at the top of the glass as I waited for Alexander to tell me what it was that was bothering him. I could tell by the silence that he wanted some kind of sign that I was listening. I stopped pouring and drank an inch or two off my lovingly caressed masterpiece, then refilled it straight away, giving him a nod as I did so. Spanish beer, draft San Miguel. Not so bad, there was no denying it.

'You know those two guys who were round here the other day, the heavy guys . . . the brothers?'

'What about them?'

'The big one was in here this afternoon, while you were away – where were you anyway? I thought you were coming in . . . anyway, it doesn't matter, the huge one was round.'

'Looking for me?'

'Well, not exactly, I don't think that's what he originally came for.

He was just hanging out . . . Had a few beers, didn't want to pay, I don't know if you have some arrangement with him or what.'

Big Tony. The very thought of him here made me feel soiled somehow, giving me an instant need for some cool water on my skin, to go and wash the afternoon dust and melancholy from my face. Still, maybe Tony had been round with money, maybe even all of it. Maybe Alexander would get to the point.

'So he didn't pay for his drinks, that's it?'

Alexander sighed. I knew he didn't like it when I cut him off but what he had to sigh about in the greater scheme of things was beyond me, him with his simple life and beautiful girlfriend, easy job serving drinks in a quiet bar. What did he have to make him stutter and stammer his way through everything? At the end of the summer he'd be off, back on his travels, back to university, a step nearer being that accountant or lawyer his parents had conceived him to be.

'He was kind of hustling – the customers, that is.'

'*Hustling?*'

'Selling drugs, cocaine. Trying to put some on to the girls, English girls in over lunch.'

'I see . . .'

Of course, I didn't see, didn't *see* fuck all. Now it was my turn to grind to an embarrassing halt, as if it were me that had put big Tony up to it. I had to stop myself from asking if he had actually managed to shift some of the shit, it might not have been such bad news if he had, especially if he had money to give back as a result. Another thousand-odd deals and we would be able to pay off our supplier. Oh Jesus, everything was fucked, big Tony, big stupid Tony, what could I do with him, was this his own inspired initiative or was it part of a plan to drive me completely insane so that I would become a liability like him and his brother?

'That's not it, Martin. Not all of it. You see, you weren't around and I didn't know what you would have done . . . anyway, I threw him out.'

'You did?' I could feel my pulse quicken as if I'd just hoovered up a mound of speed the size of a slag-heap.

'I told him I would call the police.'

Faster and faster.

'How . . . how did he take that?'

'Not well. Said he wanted to speak to you.'

Back to me. Everything always back to me. 'Sure.' Yes, I bet he did. I took a hefty sip from my glass whilst I wondered what the fuck to do. Big Tony thrown out from what he thought was his own bar. Big Tony back here selling the very stuff I had tried to sell him. There had to be a joke somewhere in all this but I wasn't laughing.

'Anything else, Alexander? Anything else you want to throw into this five minutes we're having? How's Sarah?'

Alexander scratched his head, momentarily thrown. 'Oh fine, fine. She's on evening shift tonight. Here soon enough. Concerned about you actually. Look, we don't really know anything about whatever, you know . . . but if there's anything we can do . . .'

A conversation that had already proved disastrous was now turning distasteful. There was no way I was going to stand for this, this sudden outbreak of fucking niceness, not from this prick anyway.

'No. Fuck-all.'

'Well if there –'

'Fuck – all.'

Alexander nodded sagely, taking his time to absorb the message. At times like this he could look incredibly young, like a cub scout sixer who had just had Akela swear at him for not giving the right salute.

'Your other friend was round, the French guy, the black French guy. One of Herman's mob was looking for you as well.'

A galaxy of stars on my doorstep. It was nice to be wanted. I needed a line so bad just to cope with the excitement, sure the San Miguel had been good but not that fucking good that it could solace a con-demned man. The remnants of my previous stash should still be lurking inside the safe. Right behind where Alexander stood.

I looked at my watch. 'OK, Alex, why don't you knock off now, Sarah will be due soon, won't she? I'll somehow cope on my own until then.'

'It's all right, I'll wait.'

'Just go, would you?'

'You sure?' He had that wounded look again. *What have I done wrong, what is it about me that you hate so much, can you tell me?*

'Positive.' *No I can't, cunt. It's just that my world is falling down and you seem to be there every time it takes another downward spiral.*

'All right then. See you tomorrow. Bye.'

So it was that he shuffled off, having thrown his glasses, Walkman and existentialist paperback into his rucksack. *See you tomorrow.* Can't wait. What do you think will happen then, Alexander, will someone just lob a bomb in here and put us out of our misery? Any idea how close we are to that?

My hand rummaged through the contents of the safe. Shit, nothing there. I pulled out the piles of bills and receipts, tearing through them in turn in desperation. I dumped them on the floor and ran my hand along the cool metal walls of the safe; still nothing. I'm on my knees shaking every fucking envelope out when the first of the customers appear seeking their drinks. It took a real effort to abandon the search and become a barman once more. Even then I'm pouring out the gin wondering why the fuck I didn't help myself to a slice of Jérome's stash before giving it away to the brothers. Because, I suppose, I had wanted to be through with all this, at a time when it looked as if I could have been through with it all, when I thought I could pull off a twenty-minute deal. I hadn't helped myself to any because when the gear was in my possession I was high. A stupid bloody mistake, like going to the supermarket to buy a week's food when you're not hungry, then starving a day later when you realize that you've bought fuck-all. I held another glass to the tap and rubbed my nose. Was I an addict? No, no way. These were exceptional times and I needed something to help me through them. I needed to be exceptionally high. I rubbed my nose again, scanning up at the queue forming to be served. Where the fuck was Alexander? Why was it so fucking hot? Where had all these fucking people come from? I ran an eye along the line of bodies, offering a cursory nod and smile to each. All right, I'll see to you as soon as I can. Five or six people. I recognized the last man and my heart dropped low enough to join the crap kicking round my feet still waiting to be cleared up and put back in the safe. Here was the guy with supply. You might have thought I should be pleased to see him, though that wasn't the case. Showing up like this he was catching me off-guard, irritable, unreasonable. I almost knew it then that I was about to say something stupid. The end-game was about to start, the end to everything started right there.

Big Tony preferred to stand rather than sit. Yes, he meant business, not even leaning on a stool or resting his fists on the bar. I kept him waiting whilst I cleared up, not to piss him off, but to buy some time whilst I figured out my stance, what was my line on this going to be? I didn't know, other than to stall on the fact that he and his brother owed me an awful lot of money and should have been at least as nervous of me as I was of them. In theory. The problem with the theory though was that it took no account of big Tony's mad eyes brooding on the other side of the counter as he waited to have his say.

'Am I going to get some respect in here this time?'

He spoke quietly, in Catalan, as if he wanted no one else to hear.

'What will you have, Tony?'

I replied in the same tone and language, pointing to the beer fount. He ignored the gesture.

'That guy, the one in earlier. He a friend of yours?'

'Staff.'

'He's gonna get sorted. That's a fact.'

I put a glass under the tap and paused. 'You having one?'

'Sorted out. Yeah.'

I didn't know if he was agreeing with me or himself. I filled up regardless and handed him his beer. He didn't say thanks.

'Where's Miguel tonight, Tony? How are you guys doing with the money?'

He shrugged by way of reply. 'Don't worry about money. What's the guy's name?'

'What guy?'

'Asshole that was in here before.'

'Doesn't matter.'

'I'm telling you it matters.'

'Alexander.'

'Alexander what?'

'Fuck knows.'

'Where does he stay?'

'Don't know.'

'Find out.'

'Sure. You tell Miguel I want to see him.'

'What for?'

'I want my money.'

'You'll get your money, we told you. You deal with me on that, you don't need Miguel. You want to know what's going on, you ask me. OK?'

I nodded, holding my tongue. Mr Big-Shot was telling me he was in charge, that he could answer the questions.

'So when do I get the money?'

Another shrug into his glass. 'Soon.'

'And when is that exactly, Tony, any idea, or are you guys close to a deal, or a whole lot of deals like today's attempt?'

He swilled some beer round his mouth and scanned a professional eye round the joint.

'This place is quiet, Martin. Too quiet. You need more customers, you need a show, entertainment, something to bring them in. In Maga-luf the bars have a live show every night, girls fucking themselves with a candle, bottles, you know? A live act, that's what this place needs . . .'

'Thanks for the advice but right now all I need is my money, and I need to know when I'm going to get it, so maybe you can advise me on that, yeah?'

Tony slammed his glass down on to the bar. 'I fucking told you, soon. You just get me that guy's address so that I can sort him and we'll talk about the rest later. Unless you want me to come round here and rip his balls off in front of your customers – OK?'

I could have let the moment pass. Should have. But I was riled about my cash, riled by the fact that he was too fucking stupid to realize that the three kilos weren't given to me for free, too stupid to think of anything except the one thought that would occupy his brain at any given time.

'That's not an option, Tony.'

'Yeah? Well you give him up then, where does he stay?'

'I don't know and don't care.'

'What the fuck are you saying, Martin, why are you like this? Find out and it will be sorted. Nothing to do with you, I don't want any argument with you, we're partners. Him only, that's who I want, OK?'

There were others now waiting to be served, hanging back though, probably intimidated by Tony's raised voice. You wouldn't need any degree in linguistics to realize he was lecturing me. I glanced to the door to see if Sarah had arrived, and that made me think of Alexander and how they were probably together right now, maybe a quick kiss before her shift took her away from him for the next seven hours. Maybe he had her in his arms and they were talking about me, about what he had done earlier in the day and the hard time I'd given him over it. A pair of innocents. *If there's anything we can do.*

'I'm afraid it doesn't work that way, Tony.'

To his credit, Tony had enough sense to register shock at what he'd heard, hanging silent whilst his mind struggled to come to terms with it. *Did you really say that?*

'Don't be like this, Martin. It's not worth it. You don't have to be my enemy. Just him, that's all I want. It's your choice.'

'No, you're the one making a choice. I'm only saying leave him alone.'

Tony's smile spoke more of bemusement than anything else. He drained the rest of his glass in one long take.

'Well I'll see you later then, Martin. See you both later.'

He kicked a table on his way out; it was hard to tell if it was meant to be threatening or him being plain fucking clumsy. It didn't really matter either way.

Saturday. Eight hours or more playing mine host at the Arena passed uneventfully, the only drama being Sarah noticing my eyes following her as she made her rounds of the tables, lingering on every aspect of her from the openness of her smile to the firmness of her breasts hiding under her tight white T-shirt. Yes, I was staring at her, a lecherous sleazebag taking in what he could never have, what would be for ever denied him. She didn't challenge me though, didn't say a word; not because she was enjoying the attention, more that she was intimidated perhaps, or just feeling sorry for me.

I could see the end. The end didn't scare me any more. My thoughts went to Johanna and where she might be; did they have her locked in a tower somewhere, a fairytale princess waiting for her prince, or could it be that she was chained to a radiator like a Beirut hostage? Was it more a house-arrest thing, a personal chaperon monitoring her every move?

I was making a good job of fucking up, bringing it all down. But I had to find some kind of clarity so that she could be safe, her and our daughter. Of course there was no proof that the organization actually had her anywhere, Herman could have just noticed that she wasn't around and decided to wind me up. Then again, she could even be in collusion with them, enjoying the prospect of watching me sweat, intrigued as to how hard I would fight to get them back. Either way, Herman was due whatever was going on. Johanna? She would be rescued, I would have to find a way. The plan had mutated somehow, but there was still a simplicity to it in that everything was one great big circle, a circle of shit; Miguel and Tony wouldn't give me my money, especially now that I wouldn't give them Alexander's head on a fucking plate, and that meant Jérome wouldn't get his, nor would I get mine and be able to sell up to Herman. Everything depended on everything else and all of it was closing in on me. A way out? For her maybe. Never for me. That was the new plan.

First thing Sunday morning, a bang on the door, going on and on so long that I began to incorporate it into the dream I was having, the dream about water. The knocking became the sound of an outboard engine stalling, jamming with some sort of violent failure as everybody on deck looked on, sullen faces all merging into one. This was my fault. *What are you going to do about it, Martin?* This was my boat, I had brought the passengers here, the failed engine was my responsibility and they would make me pay some kind of dreadful price if I couldn't fix it. Yet I was helpless, all the machine would do was to repeat its shuddering, more and more frenzied until it was about to explode.

I opened my eyes. The sound had not gone, no; there it was, crashing away with an ever-increasing urgency. What was this, a fire? Was the block going up in flames, with this my last hope of rescue? I staggered through to the hall and opened the door. No smoke, no sirens. My confusion quickly lifted. There in front of me was the German delegation, the sight of Herman in his cream safari suit making me wake up fast. There was someone with him I didn't recognize; a hired heavy, could this be a representative from the organization calling to present his credentials? They didn't introduce or explain, didn't say anything at all. Perhaps they were waiting to be invited inside. *Some coffee or pastries, chaps? Go on, you know you want to . . .*

'What do you fucking want?'

'Good morning to you too, Mr Law. Do you want to discuss things here, or inside?'

'Right here's fine, Herman.'

He shook his head wearily and passed a glance to his companion. *See what I have to put up with?*

'Martin, you've been keeping some very bad company. If you choose to be friends with the Carcera brothers you should know that they are not welcome at Puerto Puals. We don't want their type at our establishments. You should listen to this, you have been warned.'

'*Their* type?' Herman's words deserved to be met with all the derision I could summon. 'Lowering the fucking tone are they, prefer a different class of criminal do you Herman, extortionists, kidnappers?'

'I have said what I came to say. Tony Carcera will not be allowed to sell drugs on our territory. You will have to stop him or it will be very bad for you.' Herman remained resolutely placid, blanking me out, refusing to compete against my sarcasm. He was good at that and it seemed to leave me no option other than to reach even higher.

'*Bad for me!* How much *worse* can it get? You have my wife and child somewhere, you're driving me out of business, you show up on my fucking doorstep to fucking terrorize me first thing in the fucking morning . . . What else have you got up your sleeve?'

He exchanged another look with his partner, two undertakers giving a professional show of dignity in the face of hysteria.

'You should listen more, Martin. This is a warning I have been asked to give. People are not happy with what you are doing. You are finished at Puerto Puals, your time there has passed. The answers are in your hands. Sell up, move out. Get rid of the Carcera brothers. That is what I have been asked to say to you.'

'Yeah . . .' I held fire on following up with a string of retaliatory insults, even though every instinct told me to. The reality of it all was that I — standing there in my boxer shorts, increasingly scared by what I was hearing from two fully-dressed men who seemed to have more of an idea of what was going on than I ever would — was in no great position to call the shots. *You should listen more.*

'Who's speaking here, Herman, you or the organization, and who's this, does he work for you or maybe *he's* the organization?'

'Not important. You should think about what is important before you run out of time. Think about your wife. Think about your little daughter. You can make things right for them. Only you. Think, Martin.'

Again I was aware of fighting the instant urge to grab a hold and throttle him until the great over-ripe tomato of a face he had burst all over the stairs and landing. Then came a strange sensation, not unlike exhaustion, a new kind of awareness sweeping over me; there was no point in fighting, what he was saying was actually good advice. I was making an excellent job of ruining everything, I had leapt from the top of a building and the ground was rushing up faster all the time. But if I could make things right for Johanna it might make for some kind of redemption. I had to give my child a chance. Every child deserves a chance, even the daughter of a shit like me.

'OK, OK Herman, I hear you. I'll think about it all. You tell me what your price is and I'll consider it.'

'Price? For the Arena Bar? You tell us you are ready to sell and we will tell you what you will get. Too late for negotiation, you cost too much time already. Just tell us you are ready to move and that you have told the Carceras to go.'

Instinctively my fists clenched tight, ready to punch. I relaxed them and kept them by my side.

'I'll think about it. I'll see my lawyer and then we can talk. In the meantime, I've listened to you so you listen to me; anything goes wrong, anything happens to Johanna and it's you I come looking for, understand? I don't know your organization so I've got no choice.'

Herman didn't even blink. Obviously threats only travelled in one direction as far as he was concerned. He took a deep breath that verged on a sigh and turned to leave. It was only around eight in the morning and I could feel the sickness and anxiety squeezing my stomach flat. I would have all day to struggle with it. Still, at least I'd told Herman where he stood, and had meant it. There weren't many I had managed to do that with, but at least it was a start.

From the ship's log, as written by Captain Archibald Henry of the *Anne*, 29 July 1698, Fort St George, Guinea.

Praise be to the Lord that we have arrived at a safe haven after five days' perilous voyage on the open sea. That we completed our journey is due to the grace of God and the steadfast courage of those men joined with me in our longboat after we left *Anne* on the evening of the 23 July. Therefore I note the names of officers Wells, Smythe, Greene, Gardiner, Owen and Brown as worthy of the highest praise as men of the utmost valour and unwavering loyalty. I pray that they shall have their reward soon, when justice is done and we regain possession of our fair ship.

As captain, I must also ensure that the extraordinary conduct of our surgeon is duly noted and recorded. It was Mr Martin Law, despite being the youngest member of our officer crew, who was first to volunteer for the dangerous task of remaining aboard, despite the imminent threat of attack.

Displaying a coolness of mind which has impressed all who have made acquaintance with him, it was he who suggested our chosen course of action; that we the officers make for the shore and hence Fort St George with the most valuable and immediately transportable items of cargo whilst our ship tacked a south-westerly line to the ocean, providing a decoy to our escape. The plan was conceived to take account of two contingencies, the first that the *Anne* was being sought as a prize by villains of the sea, in which case we would petition the authorities at the Fort to seek her immediate return, or second, that our followers had a more benevolent purpose, in which case the ship would return to seek out the longboat along the coastal waters. Thus the tactic of a 'precautionary diversion' was adopted by consent, with the former outcome apparently unfolding rather than the latter. We therefore pray for an early opportunity to reacquaint ourselves with our ship, whilst her remaining crew, cargo and surgeon are held in good spirit and that God grant us the strength to exact severe retribution should any or all be harmed.

Captain A. Henry. 29 July 1698.

Dawn, and the *Anne* wakes to a new kind of silence, no orders being bellowed, no threats issued to engender a snap and purpose to the actions of the weary sailors sleepwalking through their first tasks in the daily routine. The crew are awake and alert, alive with suspicions as to their fate. The captain is gone, some watched him go, some helped load the longboat, some merely awoke from their feverish, shivering slumbers to be told the sensational news. Gone. He had said he would be back, but when, and why take the rest of the officers with him, all except the young doctor; he was in charge now, yet what did he know of the seas, what was his plan?

McKnight had taken the tiller; Martin stood by his shoulder watching the men gather in clusters below, occasionally glancing to the outline of the ship stil following them, its menacing form silhouetted by the brightness of the sun rising behind it. Unlike the *Anne*, it had not employed full sail; Martin realized that this chase was taking place almost exclusively under the hunters' terms; they could close the gap between them at any moment of their choosing. As yet they seemed to want to prolong the hunt, to stalk rather than to kill. Perhaps they had long experience of softening the minds of their quarry by such tactics, perhaps the battle was already lost.

Martin did not bring the crew to assembly, though this happened soon enough when he offered a face to which they could address their questions. So it was that they came forward individually, in pairs, in gangs, to listen and enquire. *Why is the captain gone, when will he be back, are we to wait, are we to fight without him, has the coward gone so that we can be sacrificed instead?* Martin offered a soft voice in reply, soft and clear, a calm demeanour carrying more authority than an imploring one. He would not seek to lead them, that would be a mistake. He would instead explain their choices, and these were simple enough.

'We should not concern ourselves with the whereabouts of Captain Henry. The ship at our stern is a more relevant recipient of our attentions. If we do not decide how to deal with it and what it might represent then there will be none of us left to worry about our beloved skipper.'

The observation drew a few tentative smiles, particularly from the older hands. Martin had gained the silence and attention of his audience though some had obviously decided to remain guarded in their response lest any part of his speech be a trap.

'You will be aware that the ship following us may well be a threat. I believe we should be prepared to defend ourselves if this possibility becomes the case. Should they decide to attack they could well be upon us within the hour. Would any man disagree that we should be prepared to defend our lives and liberty?'

'Is that what the captain said?'

'It is the choice we have to make. It does not matter what the captain said or would say. Only we are in a position to decide.'

The early morning breeze dropped for an instant, long enough for Martin to feel the heat of the distant sun, long enough for the stench from the lower decks to rise up straight through the boards Martin stood on, filth and ordure snaking their way up from Martin's boots to his nose. The early morning heat. Who could feed and water the negroes whilst this meeting took place? Martin realized more urgency was required. Before he could speak again however, the crew were testing the limits of their new freedom.

210

'The bastard is off to trade more stolen brandy for slaves . . .'

'Dead slaves!'

'Off to buy a whip to flog the entire ship . . .'

'Gone ashore to capture Haraldt, to see if he's now dark enough to be a slave himself!'

Martin climbed up a step and turned to face the gathering anew, declining to join the wry, shallow laughter now spreading amongst them.

'The captain is gone and *we* remain. What are we to do?'

Martin nodded in the quiet that followed, and then returned to his softer voice.

'If any man has a plan, then let us hear it.'

No reply came, yet the silence was hardly a positive one, the resentment hanging in the still air above them almost tangible; a stubborn bitterness at their perceived abandonment, indignation at plots being hatched and not being part of them, reluctance at being led into any scheme that might have been fashioned by the captain's hand.

Martin started again. 'I would propose that we endeavour to protect our lives and liberty. Would any sailor disagree?'

This time the quiet that followed carried more comfort, enough to give him the confidence to continue.

'All must agree or there is no point, we cannot defend a divided ship, yes?'

Martin turned and climbed two steps to address them from a higher vantage, taking his time as he moved, granting every opportunity for an interruption from any of them. None was forthcoming, though he was aware that this was because of the bafflement at large within the crew at their curious predicament.

'Men,' he shouted, as if all decks below were packed, 'men, if you were walking down the street and found yourself being followed by a ruffian, what would you do, would you let him know you were scared of him?'

Martin gave a glancing look to the boat behind them on the horizon so as to leave no doubt to whom he was alluding. There were no answers offered to his question, no one seeming to possess the will or wit to provide them. This was not how he had imagined the scene would unfold when he rehearsed it in his mind; he had thought he might be challenged, that he might have

211

to earn his right to be heard, but to be listened to in a bemused silence was disheartening. Still he persevered.

'José . . . José, tell me, how long would you let yourself be chased before you challenged those who took you for a coward, who sought to play on the cowardice they thought had a hold of you?'

José did not speak, nodding slowly by way of showing his appreciation of the point. Martin looked to the other side of the crowd. He fixed on a pair of eyes staring back with cynicism and indifference, eyes still viewing him as the captain's man, a stooge left behind to carry out his bidding.

'Reid . . . Mr Reid sir, you notice the other ship does not employ full sail, they chase us yet hold back, I think they seek to scare us, to goad us into surrender. Some might say we should, though a man like you might say that perhaps we should give them a reason to be frightened of us – Yes?' Slowly, almost reluctantly, Reid's stony countenance gave way to a softening, a blink of the eyes, a nod of assent. Martin seized his moment. 'The captain is gone. He will not be back, unless you want him to return, or we let our enemies take us. We are free men. Let us fight to protect that, aye?'

The roar came back with a volume that startled Martin, almost robbing him of the composure he had striven to maintain.

'Aye!'

He let himself smile. There was still so much to do if all of this was to stand for anything, but he could not deny to himself that this moment was special. There were other decisions that would test them, battles to be fought, perhaps one immediately. Still, they were united. Free men. For one second he thought that his eyes were filling and was aware of the watery glaze through which he viewed his comrades. He swallowed hard. So much still to be done.

'Bosun McKnight . . . let us slow our ship down, we are tired of running for no reason. Have the sail reduced to a more moderate level, let us turn then turn around and face those who are so curious to make our acquaintance. Mister Reid . . . can you find some men who are familiar with loading and firing the cannon? Unblock the gun port on the bow-chaser, keep it covered from view mind – drape a sail or pennant over it, we might want our preparedness to come as a surprise. José . . . Have you or your brother any artistic talents? Can you draw, paint? I would have you prepare a special

212

flag, I will instruct you in the captain's cabin. First though we must attend to our negroes in the holds before any more expire. Who has the keys to the irons? The slaves are part of our plan too . . .'

The heady excitement of command was still dominating Martin's thoughts as Fela entered the cabin. He was sitting at the desk, filling the space so recently vacated. The captain had left only the larger maps, deliberately taking the more local charts with him. Martin wondered if he had been worried that his navigational folly would be discovered early, although it could simply have been that he was seeking to limit the treasures that the inheritors of his ship would find, whoever they proved to be.

Fela's anger was apparent from the moment he came in, a slow simmering haze burning red in his eyes, like the glowing embers of a fire; here was a man left incarcerated for days in the suffocating filth of the men he had sought to sell. Of the jaunty stride that had marked his walk and dancing hands that illuminated his diction when Martin had first met him there was not a trace. Instead he was hunched, almost as though he were still chained by the neck to the floor.

'You will pay for this insult . . . this . . . treachery . . . big pay.'

Fela pouted and pursed his lips as if about to spit, twitching his chin forward. Martin realized he was in fact retching, choking on a thin and dry form of vomit. Four days in the hell below deck had had its effect on his constitution.

'I did not imprison you. That was the captain's doing. You are free now.'

Fela drew his mouth tight, the normal upward curve of his broad lips folded into a flat line, the flared nostrils above telling something of the sense of outrage he was struggling to contain. His eyes took in the close-confining walls of the cabin, still retaining so much of the captain's presence; a braided jacket hanging by a hook on the wall, a leather-bound copy of the Bible, inks, quills and paper lying by the cot.

'My companions . . . You will release them at once . . . *Immédiatement!*'
In his anger he had switched to French; Martin understood all the same. He made no attempt to argue.

'They will be. Everyone below will be released.'

'You will put us ashore . . . I demand . . . *Immédiatement*. Take us to shore and make good the bargain that was agreed . . . *Everyone?*'

Fela's eyes returned to stare at Martin, studying him closely, as though confronting some kind of madman. A madman or a bluffer. Or someone planning a new treachery.

'You cannot do this! Slaves are mine . . . You pay for them or let me take what is mine. I do not permit this!'

Martin stared back; where did this command of the English language come from, what had happened to the simple caboceer of the interior, *most agre-able, good slave, strong slave man*?

'Every living soul on this ship is free. Free to do as they choose.'

Fela snorted, unwilling to believe what he was hearing. 'You free these slaves, they will choose to kill you, understand?'

He had moved up to Martin to be sure his words would not be lost, shouting louder the closer he approached. Martin suddenly became aware of the stink emanating from him, of how the rancid airs from below had become part of him, his clothes, his skin, his every breath.

'Everyone is now free.'

The repeated assertion had Fela shaking his head in disbelief.

'Ship of fools . . . Liars . . . You will pay.'

Martin stood, anxious to leave the cabin, eager to greet the open air outside.

'I think there is something you should see. Follow me.'

Fela hardly seemed inclined to move, wary as ever, reluctant to acknowledge any assumed authority. Martin tried to persuade him by gesture, dropping his arms by his sides, offering open palms to him. *I am hiding nothing, you need have no fear*. Fela slowly pulled himself to his full height, every effort, every motion infected with a lethargy that spoke of disdain. Slow though the progress was, eventually he followed Martin through the cabin door and out on to the deck.

Once there, Martin pointed out the ship following, now barely less than a league away. Again he noted how high it sat in the water, and for the first time saw the two tiers of gun ports on either side of its hull, all open. There seemed to be an abundance of men too; if each speck climbing like an ant on the masts, rigging and upper deck represented a man he could

214

count almost fifty, an ominously heavy crew for a presumably light load.

'This ship has followed us for three days. It is about to attack and take everything we have. You talk of treachery? Wait until they are upon us. It may be as well you grew used to being chained.'

'Pirates?'

'Undoubtedly. They choose not to show it yet.'

Fela peered through the brightness, leaving Martin to wonder whether he was trying to recognize the boat. It was not inconceivable that they would be associates.

'The captain has left to make safe his prized possessions and seek help. I advised him not to wait upon the inevitable. Our plan though, is to avoid bloodshed, to give any who would attack us no reason to do so. The men below will be freed. You will explain to them that they can fight to protect that freedom or be put back in irons and sold by those on the other ship. If we win our fight, they can go, they will have the liberty to do as they wish.'

'You plan to arm them? The first they shall attack are you ... It is madness!'

'We would die anyway, perhaps this way it may come sooner – unless you are successful in making your apologies and persuasive in urging them to fight only our common enemies.'

'We can surrender. Let these pirates take what they will, they would leave us something.'

'Leave us? Where? They would want our boat as well. Besides, why would they leave you free and not your countrymen, why would they believe that you are a caboceer?'

'I would tell them ... You would tell them –'

'If I was alive. The men would say you were on this ship as a slave.'

'Then perhaps I should become a pirate, perhaps you and your men – all pirates.'

Martin paused before replying, wary of who might overhear. Did it matter, wouldn't they all know soon enough? Perhaps he was inhibited by the mere thought of hearing himself say it. He took a breath and let out the shortest of laughs. He turned to stand face to face with Fela.

'We will be.'

José had arrived on the deck below, showing two hands aloft to indicate his task was accomplished. The *Anne* had now completed her turn, a full hundred and eighty degrees, tacking back to face the vessel approaching. Time was short. Martin knew he had to move to set the rest of the plan in motion.

'Mr Reid . . . Would you care to release the men in the holds. Mr Fela's companions, the slaves – all of them.'

Reid froze, staring at Martin in disbelief. *Why?*

'These men will help us defend our ship, Mr Fela will enlist their help. He will explain to them in their own tongue. I would urge you to release them from their bonds.'

Martin had addressed Reid directly, seeking out his eye to make his case compelling. He was aware, however, that the actions of those within earshot had slowed to a virtual standstill also. Here was another uncertainty, what was being said? Martin spoke again, casting his words and face to the wider group.

'If we do not release them we will be overpowered by the numbers on the other ship. There are too few of us without them.'

Reid's resolute inactivity told all he was unconvinced.

'Aye. And if we release them they will overwhelm us.'

'It is not in their interest to do so, not when they see the other ship. There is only one thing we can be sure of, and that is that we are damned if we don't. You may be right also, and we are damned if we do, but at least we have a chance. I do not pretend that I have the power to order you to do this . . . I cannot, nor would I have you lashed for disobeying me. I merely appeal to your judgement, I urge you to consider our only option if we are to be free men, not those who exchanged one yoke for another.'

Reid gaped at the quarterdeck, blinking as if smarting from an insult.

'Damn you, damn this ship,' he muttered, running a hand through his sweat-ridden pigtail. Martin suspected he was already pining for the life of cruel certainties under the captain.

'Think about it. Would you fight rather than be kept in chains? Why should the men below be different from you?'

Reid remained silent, as did those around him. Martin thought of the beating he had taken only three weeks ago, of the pride and obstinacy of the man. What could he achieve if these qualities could be channelled towards the good? A shout from McKnight at the helm interrupted his meditation; the ship closing in was now doing so at speed, under full sail as the breeze strengthened. Martin turned to see the enemy bow cut an effortless swathe through the foaming white tops of the pitching waves. She had had enough of waiting. On the top of her main-mast, for the first time, a new pennant, her true colours showing at last; a black flag, black with stark white markings, a skull with crossbones beneath, the Jolly Roger.

'Damn that bastard ship . . .'

Reid was still grumbling as the flag came into view; a collective groan from the others joined his lamentation, as if the spirit were suddenly flowing out of them. All eyes on deck were fixed on the fast-approaching mass, racing towards them like an apparition from their dreams, obliterating any other concerns of the moment, the vastness of the ocean immediately too small to accommodate the two ships, they would have to fight for possession of the horizon. A puff of white smoke materialized above the attacking ship's bow, a curiosity for one second, before the boom of the gun reached the ears on deck. Moments later, the whistle of a cannonball skipping over the waves towards them, buzzing like a wasp as it passed the *Anne* to starboard. Martin saw he could wait no longer. He could not lose the ship for the sake of indulging the men's appetite to wallow in their indecision.

'José! Raise our own standard. Make it high! McKnight . . . Have our bow-chaser primed, fire at will. Mr Reid, sir, make up your mind!'

Reid's stony expression slowly melted as he caught sight of the flag being raised on the *Anne*'s mast – its colours were black and white too. He shook his head ruefully. Martin saw him struggle to suppress his smile. As José pulled on the halyard and it climbed higher the wind pushed the cloth out to a fluttering horizontal and the others saw what Reid had guessed. A ghostly skull with a crossbones below. *We're all pirates now.*

'McKnight . . . Fire!'

An enormous roar set every timber in the craft quivering as the cannon gave off its counterblast and released its acrid sulphur scent.

Martin shouted for a reload and sought out Reid below. Reid was already moving towards him. He offered a nod, a salute of sorts that indicated his agreement. Yes, there is no going back.

'Fela, please join my comrade Mr Reid below deck. I hope you can explain well and fast. Mr Reid, find out where our remaining carbines are. Any man good with a gun should have one.'

'Aye!'

McKnight was holding the tiller, the attacking ship looming nearer all the while as the stirring breeze pushed its sails harder.

'Which way now?'

Martin pondered the question, determined to remain rational rather than become panic-ridden. The ships could hardly meet head-on and remain unscathed, so the opposing vessel would eventually have to pass to port or starboard. He had not ordered the gun ports on either side of the *Anne* to be opened; she would be defenceless against a broadside if their attackers had primed their guns.

'Straight ahead . . . When they veer in one direction, match it. We cannot allow clear water between us. Let us see how proud they are of their bloody ship.'

McKnight gave him a look which betrayed his misgivings. Less convinced than Reid, thought Martin, but less inclined to argue.

'Aye,' he said, warily.

Out of the foredeck companion-way the first of the slaves began to appear; cautious, measuring every step on trembling legs, dazzled by the sun, like insects dragged from deep in the filthy earth. Savages, yet determined to grasp any opportunity of liberty. Martin was lost for the moment as he watched, ashamed that he was asking them to fight when they barely had the strength to stretch their bent bodies straight. He wished he could communicate directly, that he could tell them that on his ship they no longer need fear any enemy. He wished he could convey the danger the other ship now represented to them. Would they understand, or would every white face embody a life under the whip in chains?

More men were coming up from below, Reid behind, carrying a case of guns.

'Is that all we have? How many are there?'

'Twenty, all told. Want me to surrender them to the negroes?'

'Give them to those who have skill with a gun, get them loaded. No one is to fire until I give the sign, understand? Not one shot.'

218

'You want to arm the slaves?'

Martin surveyed the numbers now milling around deck, around forty or so. There were still around another hundred and fifty in the holds, too weak or petrified to move. Those in view loitered alone, solitary men, no women, clinging to the ship's rails, as watchful of each other as they were of the crew, still dressed in the tribal rags they had been captured in weeks, if not months, ago.

'Give those that want them clubs, a spike . . . a bludgeon. Who can throw a rope? We need a good man.'

Martin wondered if anyone was still listening in the crowded mêlée that had engulfed the ship, cases being broken open, sticks and bayonets being thrown to startled negroes. A free-for-all. Some of the slaves had started their own search for weapons, breaking off handrails to arm themselves.

'Fela? Where is he? Find him and get him to stop this.'

Stop this. Martin paused, tripped by the lunacy of his own words. Who could hope to control this now that it had started? Anarchy, all of his making. Was he so sure this was the best defence, would surrender have been as ruinous?

'Mr Martin, sir . . . Mr Martin.'

Sims, a deckhand, stood before him with a docile expectancy.

'What is it? You have found Fela?'

'Rope, sir, I can use rope.'

Martin halted his dismissive wave. 'Rope? I need you to fasten a length of the strongest cable to our main-mast and make a noose at the other end. When the attacking ship sails past we will want to rein it in. If they cannot pass by then they will be less inclined to take shots as they fancy. We must pull ourselves close. Understand, boy?'

Martin wondered if the effort of explaining was worthwhile. Sims was a child, barely fourteen, a boy amongst men about to do battle. Would he have the strength required to hurl the rope? What if a musketeer hit him with a bullet as he made his attempt? Still, he had volunteered, to turn him down would offend at a time when everyone needed a sense of purpose. Martin fought the urge to wrap a protective arm around the lad as he prepared for his mission, grateful for the chance to show off his skills.

'Get ready, Sims . . . The moment will be soon.'

Out of the midships hold Fela appeared, arms aloft, the figure of Reid emerging from the darkness behind, prodding him with his rifle bayonet. At this prompt he began to address the negroes on deck, babbling to them in a strange tongue. The effect on their behaviour was minimal.

'No man is to fire unless I give the order, you hear?'

Martin shouted, but his voice suddenly felt small, strangled by nerves as the sight of the other ship began to dominate the view, blocking out the sun, an iceberg drifting towards them with a brute force that would listen to no reason. No matter, no time was left, no more agonies of waiting.

The opposing bow came close, close and closer, then swerved by on the starboard side, a splintering sound filling the air as the barnacles on each hull made their acquaintance. Sims sprinted forward past Martin, moving like a vagabond thief amongst the static figures of the market. Martin watched with a detached fascination as the rope was swung once, then twice, and once more before it was launched towards the swiftly passing timbers of the other vessel. For Martin, it was like being in a dream, the connection between Sims' actions and his orders to him only minutes earlier now vague, his connection with events all around him – the multitudes on the deck, bewildered slaves, tense crewmen brandishing guns, the skull and crossbones flag they all stood beneath – ever more tenuous as he watched the rope swing in a graceful arc, so absorbed that it was as if a silence had fallen over all of them, a silence broken with a vengeance as the rope landed, its noose hooking on to a hatch door on the other ship and clutching it tight as Sims tugged to make the connection good. Sims went about his business with a nerveless diligence as screams erupted around, wrapping the other end of the cord tighter around the Anne's main-mast, ignoring the shrieks and roars of the throng.

Martin sought to imitate his coolness, knowing that the young lad's grace under pressure should be the pattern for all their behaviour, most of all his own as supposed leader. He drew a deep breath. The ships were together, it was how he had wanted it to be, the situation was as he would have predicted, even if the battle to control his nervousness was not. Still, to calculate that he would stand on the quarter deck, looking up to a pirate ship grinding against his own ship's bow, to cast a glance and see another array of men, of every race, colour and age, united only by their expressions of ruthless intent and the weapons they carried as the means of achieving it; yes, to foresee all of this in the safety of the officers' cabin was one thing. The reality, now it had arrived, was another. Guns were trained on every inch of the *Anne's* decks. Only a special kind of man could remain resolute in these circumstances. Another breath. For the sake of those who had trusted him he would have to be that kind of man. A pirate captain. He could only hope he was convincing. In his heart he had already made the journey, a fact he tried to draw comfort from. It could be his protection, if, as he suspected, only a real pirate could tell the genuine article from an impostor.

I made it over to the bar as soon as I could on the Monday morning after another night of no sleep until the early hours. Each day was now starting out with a cramp in my stomach so bad that I could hardly straighten out to stand upright, my knees just seemed to want to hide under my chin. There had to be an ulcer festering inside, probably not improved by the diet of whisky and beer that was helping me through the day. Anyway, I dragged myself along the short walk to Puerto Puals hunched like an old crone with a walking stick, up and out without showering or shaving, leaving the squalor of the flat behind; the sheets that hadn't been washed for months, the piles of discarded underwear and clothes strewn across the floor, the solidified carton of milk in the kitchen and a fossilized cup of sugar next to it, the permanent thin black line of ants that carried away whatever nutrition remained in them. Left behind again until much later, not important, not worth thinking about. I wanted to be in early, there were calls to make, like one to my lawyer in Calvia.

Maria the cleaner was waiting for me outside the bar, sitting in the shade from the strong morning sun. *Hola.* She drew on her cigarette and watched me unlock the doors, raising herself to her feet without any great enthusiasm once they were open. We had barely been inside five minutes when the first of the day's callers arrived, a delivery man wheeling a barrow carrying several cases of booze, trying to dump it on us. In amongst the scheme of things, this was a minor irritant, someone to be thrown out, no matter what invoices and order forms he was waving, just someone else trying it on. How wrong.

The first guy was trying to offload five cases of vodka, Smirnoff vodka. I say first guy because to my alarm it turned out that the grizzled midget charging merrily into my space was the first of many. Behind him was another man with another five cases, and then another after him, this one with cases of whisky. They meant to empty an entire fucking lorry-load into my bar; it made no sense at all, until I saw the last man in the line, the supervisor organizing the drop. It was Jérome.

'What the fuck's the score, what is this shit?'

Jérome swayed, his broad mouth alternating between a smile and a grimace. 'What you mean, Martin? It's good stuff. Smirnoff . . . Johnnie Walker –'

'I don't care what it is, I didn't ask for it and I don't want it. Take it away.'

Jérome sagged, crestfallen, his long arms almost touching the ground.

'What do you mean? I told you it was coming.'

'When?'

'Before. I've been round before. Saturday, I told your man. Good stuff, very good prices, just go with it, Martin. Good business for you, you don't have to keep it, you can sell it to your friends, we will help you.'

'Who's *we*?'

'Me. Me and Sasha . . . You met Sasha. He's got supplies of everything. He likes you, wants you to be our man.'

Struggling as I was to think clearly through the fog of sleeplessness and anxiety there were at least a few fixed points I could steer by: one, I didn't know this guy Sasha. Two, I didn't want the booze. Three, I didn't want to be anybody's man. I went over and stood in the bar doorway, blocking the path of the next barrow-load. The delivery man stopped and sought Jérome's next instruction. Perhaps a wave of the emperor's hand would have him bulldozing his way over me. I put a hand to a case and tore open the top, studying the label on a bottle.

'This stuff for real, duty paid?'

Jérome's shoulders rose in unison. *What does it matter?* 'It's the best, Martin . . . Good stuff.'

'Sure, Jérome. I'll bet it's fucking wonderful. Just take it elsewhere. I don't want it and I'm not going to pay for it.'

'But you are our man here, you have the contacts, you can move it on. We don't want anything for it right away, man, have this lot on us, you can pay from the next load, it's cool. Sasha's a cool guy, good business.'

There were now three men lined up outside the bar in the ersatz loading bay that I was blocking, all three sweltering in the early heat as the stand-off continued. I couldn't have given a shit about the snide glances they passed amongst themselves, I only wanted rid of them and their cargo.

'Jérome, listen. I'll tell you one more time and then I'm going to start lifting these fucking boxes and dropping them in the fucking water. I don't want them, I didn't order them, I have no intention of moving them on for this Sasha or anybody. Get them out of here, Jérome, I mean it.'

Jérome's eyes went skywards as he offered his face to the sun as if wanting to turn his black skin even darker. He shook his head and motioned to his men to stand down. *Five minutes, OK guys?* It was then my turn for some up-close personal charm. For this, he adopted a more serious demeanour, solemnly putting an arm around my shoulder to lead me away from the doorway, a friendly doctor breaking bad news to his patient.

'How are you doing with the three kilos, you ready to pay yet?'

He might have felt me stiffen as we walked towards the boats moored at the waterfront.

'Soon. You said I had four weeks.'

'Sasha says he wants his money now.'

'Who is this fucking guy, why is he so important all of a sudden?'

'You met him. We brought the three kilos round to your apartment. It was his supply, his connections, like this vodka.'

I thought back to the drug drop and the sharp-featured gunman lurking around my flat. *Sasha*. What kind of name was that?

'Where's he from?'

Jérome blinked as if blinded by the bright reflection on the water. I let the question sit with him until he was ready to give me an answer. It took more than a while before one was offered.

'Russia.'

With that single word it was as if someone switched the lights off in my universe. I should have taken three more paces and leapt into the sea right then. I tried to keep my voice steady but the words must have come out as a gabble. The end was coming ever more near, close enough to touch. Too close, too fast.

'You told me you were dealing with English connections, Jérome. *English fucking business* you said. Jesus Christ! Is this guy Russian Mafia? Is that what you've got me into? *Good business* . . . How could you do that to me?'

'Hey, relax Martin, Sasha is cool. He likes you, wants you to be the man. If you can't pay the twenty-thousand right away why not take the drinks he's sending? Show him you're cool. That you will help him. You should try to be his friend, Martin.'

'Yeah? And how much does he charge his friends for delivering a ship-load of dodgy spirits their way. Is this all added to my tab, do I pay in fucking roubles or what? For fuck's sake, Jérome . . .'

He seemed happy to let me grind to a halt. I saw him nod towards his team. *Steady boys, almost there.*

'Martin, it's OK, simple stuff, no need to worry. Pay the twenty-thousand now or take the drinks. You don't want Sasha coming here, his boys can get . . . excited, you know? Better to keep him friendly. Take the stuff, it's no big deal, sell it to your friends and tell Sasha how much you got.'

As simple as that. Another brilliantly simple deal that would see me knocking on doors and becoming a travelling salesman for the new Russian empire, another business partner, another *organization*. In the process I would establish a new Mallorcan distribution network for the drinks arm of the conglomerate to work in tandem with the drugs wing for which I also had the island gig. And if one day I didn't make the sales target I would presumably have to hand in the keys to my company car and take my retirement gracefully, contract terminated, time to head off to the great vodka bar in the sky. Still, I had a chance to prove my worth before then, it was no big deal. I was losing control, that was all.

Taking their cue from Jérome, the men had started to dump their stuff in the bar. I looked inside to see Maria resting on her mop as the cartons were stacked in the middle of the wet floor; her face didn't register any kind of reaction, not even when, one after another, sets of dusty footprints left their pattern on her handiwork. I'm sorry, Maria, sorry that it has come to this. Someone put the mark on me, I'm being used as someone's set-up. Again.

'Jérome,' I said, ushering him back towards the boats, 'do you know whatever happened to Michel, my old skipper on the *Anneka*?'

He scratched his head, a caricature of puzzlement, a mongrel on a leash catching the scent of something intriguing downwind. 'Michel . . . Michel Descourax? Last I heard he ran a yard at Port-Vendres, fixing boats. Small-time. I don't think he crews yachts any more, but it's four years since I heard anything about him. Not my kind of guy.'

No. I could have guessed, but what better recommendation.

'Where is Port-Vendres?'

'On the coast somewhere, south-west from Marseille, down towards the border with Spain. Why do you ask?'

No reason, just curiosity. Something and nothing. I know where I stand with you, my friend.

The last of the delivery was laid to rest. There must have been at least fifty cases taking up most of the space inside what had been my bar. Jérome offered me his hand.

'See how you get on. I'll come back in a few days. You are doing the right thing for now. But, as I said, don't forget the twenty thousand, Sasha doesn't like to wait, he don't want to be anyone's fool.'

We shook hands and I tried to fix his eye. Who does, Jérome, who does?

Alexander arrived about ten o'clock. I saw him study the pile of bootleg spirits which had taken over the bar. I waited for the questions to come, waited to tell him it wasn't his problem. Yet when he spoke he was helpfulness personified, upbeat and ready for my command. Another fixed point in a crumbling world.

'Do you want anything done with this lot?'

I had planned to fire him as soon as he showed, but the fact was that something had to be done if the Arena was going to function as anything other than a fucking warehouse.

'Could you find somewhere for them all, Alexander?'

'– Here?' He was hesitant in reply, doubtless waiting for the punchline that would tell him I had been taking the piss.

'It'll have to be. We will have to spread the cases around wherever we can, maybe some in each toilet, if you stack them high so that the top case can't be opened, you know, really squeeze them in . . . and some under the bar if they will fit, and some in the fire exit. What's the word? Improvise. Can you do that? I want you to count them as well, put a note in the till with today's date saying how much there is of everything.'

'Where did this all come from? Didn't know we usually carried this much stock.'

'Don't ask.'

He nodded, a hint of exasperation leaking into the gesture. *Stupid question, stupid answer.* 'Anything else?'

I wondered if he could read my mind, if he knew that me being civil to him was a prelude to something else.

'Yeah, actually. We need this stuff cleared as soon as possible. Then maybe we should have a chat.'

'About what?'

'Couple of things.'

'Should I worry?'

'*Worry?*'

He was about to lose his summer job, maybe not great news, not a tragedy either, at least not compared to what would happen if I kept him on. Still, his question had me floundering. I didn't want to tell him before I had had the benefits of his best efforts and muscle. 'Not exactly, Alexander.'

'Then what?'

You could see how his persistence would get on someone's tits. Like a dog with a fucking bone. A stupid, gormless mutt that has to go when it bites the fucking postman believing it's guarding the home. Persistence, forcing the issue. Now I was faced with the choice of telling him straight now, or waiting until he had done his stuff, cheating him out of his labour.

'Well, Alexander, it's like this. You are going to have to go.'

'Right . . .. I see . . ..' His school prefect eagerness suddenly vanished. '. . . Today?'

'Once we've sorted all this shit, yeah.'

'I see.' He was stung, however manfully he tried to mask the pain. He drummed his fingers along the top of one of the cases, a minor flash of petulance. It didn't bother me but he was either going to help me shift the boxes or piss off. I didn't have the time to let him down gently.

'Sarah?'

'What about her?'

'Is she finished too?'

'I hope not. I still need her.'

'But not me, obviously. I suppose it's too much to ask for an explanation?'

How much to explain, how long would it take, what would he think of me if he knew? We stood staring at the pyramid of boxes. *Yes, Alexander, I'm afraid it is too much to ask.*

'Don't ask. Are you going to help me move all this or not? I'll square up your wages, it's up to you.'

He didn't make a move either way. He was building up to something and needed time, so we stood there whilst he worked up to his moment, until it came, more words in one go than you would have thought him capable of.

'Just tell me, for fuck's sake, Martin, just be straight for once, so that I can leave here and remember the one time you and I had a normal conversation where you said what you meant and I heard you. What is it about me? Is it Sarah, is that what it is, still trying to fuck her, think this is the way? You'll have to come up with something a bit better. Or do I cramp your style when you'd rather be snorting up Peru . . . . Making a deal . . . . You seen yourself today? Any idea what you look like? I don't really give a shit what you get up to, I just wanted a job but it's never that simple with you, is it? We would have tried to help you but you're just never straight. Why is that so hard for you, how much longer are you going to go on like this?'

Cheeky cunt. I knew I should have fired him as soon as he arrived and wished that I had. I moved over to the till and counted out what was there, not enough to meet what he was due, the rest could be sent via Sarah, if she showed again. *Straight?* How straight did he want it? Try this.

'You know the guy you threw out last night? Tony Carcera. Turns out he took it badly and that's bad news for both of us. Especially you. He's not the kind of guy you want to have gunning for you but that's what we've got. That's why you're finished here, for your own safety. Probably a good idea to leave the island too because he's looking for you and you wouldn't want him to find you. If that means Sarah has to go as well then so be it. Now will you help me move these fucking cases or not?'

'What do you mean it's bad news for you?'

'Alexander, it doesn't fucking matter, it's not your problem.'

'If I've done something to put you in the shit then it's my responsibility and it is my problem.'

'But there's nothing you can do, nothing I want you to do other than not get killed on my fucking premises, OK?'

'That's my choice.'

'No it fucking isn't. Grow up!'

'Listen . . . . I can get killed any time I want, for whatever I want, *wherever* I want. Nothing to do with you or your poxy bar.'

Youth triumphing in an insane argument. I was wasting my time

228

in a pointless debate that had turned increasingly bizarre. Still, within the terms of what we had discussed, his last point was a valid one. Irrelevant, but valid. I felt a smile creeping on to my lips, the first time I could remember smiling in weeks.

'Fair enough. You got me there. Be my guest.'

He was still angry enough to try to resist, but eventually he gave up and the smile came back at me.

'Are you really in the shit?'

'Completely.'

'What can I do?'

'If we could shift these fucking boxes it would be a start.'

'Then what?'

'I really don't know . . . I'm going to go see my lawyer. I guess I need to check on my house. Could you do that? Take the car over to Andraitx, see that I haven't been broken into; if I have, call me. If not, I want you to move in for a couple of days, keep away from big Tony. Do you dive?'

'What, scuba diving?'

'Yeah.'

'I have . . . In the Red Sea, when Sarah and me were in Israel. We did the course —'

I cut him off as the plan crystallized in my mind. 'I need you to check over the gear and make sure the regulator is OK. I'll need a full bottle, for maybe an hour below. Whatever you need to fix, just do it, I'll give you a credit card. Then we'll have to figure out what to do with the bar whilst I'm away. Maybe we'll just close, maybe Sarah could manage. I don't know . . .'

'Where are you going?'

'France. I need a boat. I want to see an old friend. Now, for the last time, can we move this fucking mess?'

I made an effort to clean myself up for Michel. I needed his help that badly. A shave, a visit to the laundry. No haircut though, no new suit, no cocaine. No cocaine for over five days, but more by accident than design. I had run out and hadn't made it a priority to stock up; cash-flow, time constraints, Alexander's steely fucking gaze all playing their part, all getting in the way. The irony was that I looked worse for being off it than I had when permanently stoned; constantly agitated, restless, paranoid. Still, I had every right to be paranoid, events were closing in.

The journey to Port-Vendres would be a simple trip, first across to the mainland by air to Barcelona, then a hire car at the airport to take me to the French border and the drive about an hour beyond back to the coast. The cost of all this was going on plastic; at one time or another I had opened up six different credit card accounts for various deals to do with the bar and the his-and-her clothes and lifestyle non-sense we had indulged in when the going was good. Now I was topping up the last of these to their credit limits, never really knowing if the debts would be paid off.

My flight had been fixed for three o'clock. I was in the flat waiting for Sarah to arrive and give me a lift to the airport, her other half having already completed stage one of his assignment by phoning in from the house to confirm it was untouched. The bar was shut; Sarah would open up later if the help from Maria's sister materialized. I was contemplating a shower when I heard a knock. I thought it had to be Sarah, early as ever.

'Hey, Martin . . . The bar is closed, yeah?'

Ten out of ten for observation, Miguel. I left him at the door and returned to the lounge, throwing the fruits of my laundry visit into a leather holdall. I turned to see he had followed me in, despite the lack of invitation.

'You got my money?'

Mr Carcera major was happy to let the question float by. That wasn't why he was here.

'In a hurry, Martin, leaving, yeah?'

'Going to buy a boat. Leaving right now. When will I get my money?'

'So who looks after the Arena? You should have told me, me or Tony. How long you going for?'

I stuffed two pairs of boxer shorts into a side pocket of the bag, anxious to hide them. Even having Miguel's eyes on them would be enough to soil the wash they had just enjoyed.

'The bar is sorted out, I don't need any help. Look, I'm out of here any second. What about the money?'

'That piece of shit who insulted Tony works for you, yeah? Is he going to run the bar? If he is we got a big problem. Next time Tony sees him he's dead – unless I see him first, I want him just as bad. You need to tell me where I can get hold of this guy, he ought to get what's due, yeah?'

Anyone else might have used their partnership with a heavy-handed, slow-witted but quick-tempered brother to form the basis of a good cop/bad cop routine. *Hand him over to me and I can protect him.* Maybe Miguel lacked the imagination required. Bad cop/bad cop. Maybe Miguel lacked imagination full stop. Maybe not. I was nearly finished packing. I lifted the bag and tried it for weight.

'Anyway, Martin, this guy's finished at the Arena, you fired him yeah?'

'Finished at the Arena. Yeah.'

'You know where he is now?'

'Out of town. He was in Palma. Gone now.'

I pulled the zip closed and rose to my feet, squaring up to Miguel. I felt a good five inches taller, felt angry that I had spent my time answering his questions whilst he had answered none of mine.

'Miguel. Where the fuck is my money?'

Miguel stared back, raising his eyebrows by the merest fraction. *There's no need for that.* 'You get your money soon, Martin. You get what the stuff was worth.'

'*What it's worth?* It's worth forty-five thousand dollars, as agreed.'

By now I was right in front of him; he would have seen my gaze narrow, would have heard my voice take on its righteous charge, and felt my pointing finger poke him in the chest. He would have noticed it all but kept his own face straight. That was the problem with dealing with genuine low-life, however much I might flatter myself as to how intimidating I could make my act it didn't score a single point with these guys. They were professionals, immune to it, they could face me down any day of the week.

Miguel put his hands to my shoulders in a brotherly embrace. *OK, let's relax. Let's be reasonable.* His voice turned unexpectedly solemn.

'Martin, the three kilos were shit. They are not worth forty-five thou and we won't pay that. We won't let you pay twenty thou so that the bastards who tried to sell at that price can say they screwed you, so that they can't piss themselves and say, "*We fucked Martin over, we got twenty thou for shit.*" Not going to happen, no. You better tell your people this, give them a chance to realize who they are dealing with.'

Miguel didn't blink. I could stare into the whites of his eyes, or what would have been the whites of his eyes had they not been so bloodshot and jaundiced. I could smell him, his breath, his sweat, his greasy hair. I could get the full physical experience of the man as if we were making love, taking in the hairy knuckles, the shoddy cowboy boots and all in between. A small man. Impossible to spot any similarity between him and big Tony other than their ability to view the whole world and all its events in entirely their own terms. I wondered if Mrs Carcera was proud of her boys, I wondered if she had loved them, whether either had ever had love in their lives and what they thought the point of it all was. Did they really live for this creed of honour or was it a convenient prop to justify the thuggery that was their bread and butter? Did Miguel really think he was protecting me by insisting he wouldn't let me pay an inflated price for sub-standard goods, was it really so bad to be a laughing-stock in the criminal underworld?

'What do you mean it's shit?'

'Shit . . . Rubbish . . . Mixed up with all kinds of crap, Martin, less than twenty per cent pure. They were trying to take you my friend, they thought you were an easy touch.'

They thought I was the easy touch. I thought of the package being delivered in its ultra-tight wrap, its stamp of authenticity moulded on. There was practically a freephone number to call if there was any cause for customer dissatisfaction, without affecting your statutory rights as a dealer. I thought back to the frantic tests I had carried out in this very flat. Imprecise, yes. Amateur, yes. Less than twenty per cent, could I really have got it so wrong? Unlikely, though not an impossibility. But did it really matter? Somebody was lying, either Merry Miguel or

Secretive Sasha. I was in the middle, fucked either way. I gently pushed his arms from me, a lover no longer in the mood.

'I've got a flight to catch, Miguel. I'm out of here, got to go.'

'What about the Arena?'

He was still close enough to punch, but when I reached out it was to stroke his stubbled cheek.

'Don't you worry your pretty little head about that, Miguel. It's not your problem.'

My display of affection wasn't entirely appreciated. He didn't want to return my smile.

'This guy then, you find him and tell us. He's going to get what he deserves.'

I steered Miguel to the front door, almost pushing him out over the threshold.

'Sure Miguel. Everyone's going to get what they deserve.'

I panicked when I arrived at Barcelona airport and the car hire company told me that there was a problem before asking me to step into a side-office. For a moment it was as if they knew the plan in my head and were about to arrest me on a conspiracy charge. Then I calmed down, fractionally, and let that absurdity fly off on its own harmless flight of fancy, only to replace it with the fear that the credit card had bounced. As it happened, all they really wanted to tell me was that they had no cars left except at the very bottom of the scale. *A Renault Twingo*, the girl said, *will that do? We'll make it up to you, I promise.* She had dark, melancholy brown eyes that seemed to show she took the heavy weight of meeting customer expectations entirely on her own slender shoulders. A nervous smile and the air of a contrite twelve-year-old whose dog had just shat in your garden. They had her in cherry-red uniform with a ridiculous hat, some kind of air stewardess get-up that was presumably meant to speak of glamour and efficiency. *A Renault Twingo. How small is that, can you make love in it, could we make love in it, give each other some kind of comfort for these troubled times?* I took the car, letting the waves of relief wash through as I signed the form. Still free, free to fight on.

Two hours of whining engine drone on a bumpy Spanish motorway later, a jail sentence didn't seem such a bad option compared to travel by Twingo. Then there was the queue to negotiate customs and cross the border into France. Then there was the search for the road to Port-Vendres. Then there was the prospect of seeing Michel again after so many years, assuming he was there and easy to locate, assuming that the trip wasn't one last delusion, the final straw to be clutched. Jail, how would I cope with that, all your decisions made for you, time just drifting by out of your control instead of chasing it, would it really be so bad?

Time.

Three hours to find Port-Vendres, for what the nondescript coastal town halfway to nowhere was worth, since landing on the mainland. Add to that the forty minutes to find Michel's yard, and then the hour to wait for him to arrive. Six hours after the confrontation with Miguel at the flat. I'm in another room facing another man. A different kind of man.

'Remember me?'

Michel raised his chin for a fraction of a second, more a twitch than a nod, but an acknowledgement all the same. His concentration was focused on his arm which was rummaging deep into a drawer in his desk. Eventually it emerged holding a lighter. Michel offered me a cigarette before lighting up himself. You might have thought I was a troublesome customer, back to complain again about a late delivery, or maybe a cold-calling salesman, round to hawk varnish or other boat supplies, perhaps even an employee back after an unauthorized afternoon off. No, not much of a welcome. That was Michel's way.

'I need your help.'

This brought more of a response as he drew on his cigarette, tipping the ash straight on to the floor. This was the office in the yard, a wooden shack strewn with litter and the debris of a solitary life; empty beer cans, sandwich wrappers, last year's calendar on the wall. A black and white picture of a forty-something woman, probably his late wife. I noticed a dog basket in the corner. It was empty.

'I need a boat.'

His eyes were on mine, a typical blank intensity that betrays nothing of what's going on inside, a priest listening to your excuses for missing

234

confession. I stayed silent, waiting for his invitation to continue. He might have been about to speak when something buzzed – a mobile phone in his pocket, one he pulled out to blow smoke on in frustration as he struggled to locate the answer button.

'Michel Descourax . . . *Oui* . . .'

The conversation on the mobile seemed to be equally one-sided; we sat in a silence punctuated by his gruff interjections into the small black brick held close to his ear. The office had no other phone, no computer, nothing electrical. I stifled a yawn and rubbed my nose, snapping out of both as I realized I was under scrutiny. Michel looked older, brow and cheeks incredibly lined, like a picture of an elderly Samuel Beckett, with a beard more grey than the hair on his head, knots of muscle visible under the veins and tan of his arms.

'So. A boat?'

He spoke, as I had, in French. *Un bateau*? He said it slowly, mimicking my clumsy pronunciation. Not affectionately, not as I heard it anyway, more like a headmaster taking the school dunce to task. I began to wonder if it had all been worth the effort, whether it had been too long or if he resented me for never keeping in touch. Were there any other means of getting what I needed, any other forms of credit that could be tapped? A free trial, could that be arranged?

'What kind of boat?'

'A launch, a power-boat. Take maybe seven or eight people.'

'Berths?'

'No, day trip. Open top is fine. Power is the thing.'

'You mean speed?'

'Yes, I suppose so.'

He took no obvious pleasure in correcting me. He walked to the window and threw his cigarette butt out.

'Anything else?'

I turned to face his back. 'I need it to carry something, underneath, a compartment large enough for a suitcase. I need it to be secure, but also easy to release, so that the whole thing can come away and sink when required.'

'I see.'

No you don't, Michel, you think you see. You've already made your judgement, already decided that this is trouble, another half-assed smuggling caper. You give me no credit for what I might have achieved in my life since we last met, give me no credit for learning, for being a man instead of the boy who sought your advice. You give no credit to the notion that I might not be in the market for advice and that that might be why I can't tell you what I'm planning, because you might try to talk me out of it and I can't let that happen. I can't let that happen, Michel, because it's all I have left. You see, I'm like one of those cartoon characters that has run off the end of a cliff but won't start falling until he looks down and realizes it. I can't let you point that out, I can't let you make me fall. Not yet.

Michel turns. His face is sceptical. I don't have the energy to challenge it.

'There's one other thing you should know.'

'What?'

'I can't pay. Not now, anyway.'

He sat down, running his hands slowly through his hair.

'How is your wife?'

I cleared my throat and wiped my lips clear of the sweat I felt forming. 'Fine. We have a daughter, did you hear?'

'Give her my best wishes.'

'I'd love to. This is for her. All this.'

'When do you need the boat?'

'As soon as you can . . . As soon as possible.'

'When?'

'Thursday.'

Thursday. That too soon for you, too late for me? Does that give you the out you are looking for, are you about to tell me about the work you have lined up before then?

'This compartment – does it have to be watertight?'

'No, I don't think so. In fact, definitely not.'

'If we could fit one of those luggage racks, the ones used on the roof of a car, would that do?'

'As long as it held when the boat was moving but could be released quickly enough afterwards.'

'Released from where?'

'Underneath.'

'*Underneath*. Of course.' Michel's voice was deadpan. I almost regretted giving so much away. 'I'll see what I can do for Thursday then.'

I could feel tears welling up and struggled to get the words out before my voice completely broke. 'I will pay you back my friend, I swear it, myself or Johanna, we'll make sure . . .'

Michel shook his head, uncomfortable, not interested. '*Non* . . . Let's go for a beer. It's been a long time. Can you pay for that?'

I can't pretend it was easy that night with Michel, that we clicked back into the old ways, that we bonded once more as brothers of the sea. No, there was too much that had to be kept from the agenda, too much that was non-negotiable, not up for discussion. I didn't want to lie, but wasn't ready to tell him just how bad things had become. I think he guessed that and was sensitive enough to it not to probe. There were fenced-off areas in his life too; the wife lost to cancer, hints of other relationships that had soured, the fact that he was no longer in touch with any of the rest of *Anneka*'s old crew. So we were reduced to swapping the odd reminiscence from the golden days of the Côte d'Azur. Jérome merited a mention, as did the boat-owners, as did a host of girls from my youth. Michel remembered everything. I guessed that was all he had.

We got drunk on beer, and then more drunk on Armagnac, then whisky. We were still drinking at about three in the morning in the kitchen of his harbourside apartment. I woke up on a lumpy couch in the lounge with the hot panting breath of a dog in my face and no recollection of how I had got there. There was no sign of Michel or the previous night's debris so I pushed aside the expectant beast and tried to remember what had been said. There was a point when I had been tempted to lay everything bare. I didn't think I had, although the memory of insisting to him that what I had planned was for the best of reasons and not what he might have assumed was a strong one. How much he would have believed or even understood through my blurred French was questionable. The thought of him waving me down when

I asked if he still thought of his wife and what he would have given to save her had my face flushing with shame. *Non, non.* Not up for discussion. He had seemed disappointed when I told him I wouldn't be back to pick up the boat in person. Someone else would have to make that call, there were too many other ends to tie. I tried to convince him that I would return afterwards, once things had settled down, but the truth was that the scheme I had in mind meant it was unlikely I would ever see him again. Maybe he realized this, maybe it was written on my face or there in the quaver in my voice when I told him how much his friendship had meant to me.

I made my way into his kitchen and found a cup and jar of instant coffee had been laid out on the table. Beside them was a note, written in a captain's hand. *Revoir Martin,* it read, *I have to be busy to make everything ready for Thursday. Thank you for letting me help you.*

I folded the note, kissed it, and started to cry.

'Who is your captain?'

'I will speak for the ship.'

'Your ship . . . the *Anne* . . . It has cargo belonging to another that we will take possession of.'

'Our ship has been renamed, it is now the *Liberty*. It has nothing on board that belongs to anyone other than those who sail with her.'

'You are the captain?'

'I speak for the ship. And you, sir, your ship?'

'The *Tomasz*.'

'You are not an English ship?'

'We are a free ship. We sail under no flag.'

'You fly the Jolly Roger.'

'As do you, sir.'

'Who are you?'

'Alexi.'

'You are the captain of the *Tomasz?*'

'I speak for our ship.'

Whilst the conversation was balanced, Martin knew any other contest would hardly be equal. He craned his neck to speak directly to his counterpart standing on a deck at least three yards proud of his own, trying to ignore the latent threat of the cannon pointed directly at his chest. There were other guns trained on his person too, at least half a dozen barrels of iron levelled at him by strangers who had no doubt killed before for lesser reason. Yet safety, for him and, more importantly, his crew, depended on his ability to treat all of this as a mere distraction, a buzzing of a fly in the ear; any acknowledgement of danger would be seen as a sign of weakness, and would be seized upon without warning by those looking down on him. That was why it was important to look his opponent in the eye, to hold steady and not attempt to move out of the line of fire, for while he felt like no equal, he had to pretend to be one.

Alexi seemed older than himself, maybe aged around thirty years. He held himself with an obvious assurance and high self-regard; Martin felt half his age, a schoolboy once more. He persevered regardless.

'You sound foreign, Mr Alexi. German perhaps, am I correct?'

'*Foreign?*' Alexi replied scornfully. 'We are all foreign out here. You think this is England?' Alexi turned to share the joke with his shipmates although few seemed inclined to join his laughter, preferring instead to concentrate on the good aim of their guns. Not that this seemed to matter to Alexi, content to enjoy the humour of his remark on his own, unconcerned, unembarrassed. It took a special kind of coldness to act this way, thought Martin, that which belonged to the superior or the insane. He felt his hands begin to tremble and pushed them into his sides to hide it. No equal match. Three to one, he counted, three shots to one their advantage. Surrender came to mind – would it be the rational move?

Alexi's guffaws came to a halt. He began again, face relaxing, his eyes losing their manic glint against the light of the sun, a man suddenly sober.

'I am a Pole. The best Polish man you will be fortunate to meet out here.'

'You are a long way from home then.'

'I would say the same of you, Mister Englishman.'

'Scottish.'

Alexi shrugged, as if summoning the energy for another sarcastic reply was too much effort. *We are all foreigners here.*

'So, my Scotsman friend who speaks for his ship – what is your plan, you wish to board our ship?' Alexi looked to the rope which Sims had thrown to tie the two vessels together. He affected an air of bemusement as he renewed his observation of the link.

'Not unless you give us reason to. Do you wish to board ours?'

'Only under invitation sir, though I would not choose to speak like this . . . Shall we tell our men to stand down, to lay their weapons to rest?'

'Gladly . . . On your word as a man of honour, as a Polish patriot, that you will not attack our ship or seek to harm us in any way.'

The creases that marked a smile returned to Alexi's thin face. Martin found it hard to judge whether the expression was genuine or a mask for yet more contempt.

'I give you that, conditional on your word as a Scot, as an *honourable pirate*, that you will do likewise.'

Martin knew he had been shadowed word for word, equalled in every exchange, as his ship had tried to match the *Tomasz* when she had closed in on her. Three to one. Yet when Alexi spoke, he had the luxury of the full weight of his crew behind him, and he could look down on to a smaller ship, decks littered with broken wood and half-naked savages. Was he being toyed with, drawn into a conversation simply to prolong the spectacle, so that the tale could be the richer in detail when it was told in the taverns long after he and his men were gone? The tale of the rag-bag of a vessel attempting to pass herself off as a pirate ship and paid for her impertinence. In his mind Martin rehearsed the order to fire. They could all be gone in an instant, in a flurry of flying lead and gunpowder. They would give *Tomasz* something to remember them by in the process, and a different story would be shared in seafarers' inns.

Young Sims clutched his cutlass and turned to hear Martin's eventual answer. Fourteen, thought Martin, catching sight of the youngster's drawn countenance, feeling old and weary with the burden of responsibility.

'You have my word. I invite you, sir, and one companion to join our ship. We shall release our tether to you once you are aboard and will lay down arms once your crew have done likewise.'

'Well, then . . . gentlemen of the *Liberty*. May I join you?'

Alexi's gestures were those of a relaxed man. Martin was envious. The raised eyebrows, one hand through his fringe of weather-bleached blonde hair, one on his hip rising to wipe his mouth as if cleaning it of any disrespectful mirth. A man at ease, even though the weapons all around were drawn, a man whose charm was disconcerting. Martin found himself wanting to give in to it, to be seduced; everything would be so much simpler if he could take this man at his word, everything less exhausting, less humiliating. Yet he had to think of the crew, had to look out for them against any potential danger and one still remained; that this could all be an act, a ruse by which Alexi could gain first possession of the ship before giving the signal for his hardened shipmates to storm across and over. A throw of the dice.

'Men, lay down your guns. Our brothers on the *Tomasz* will do likewise.'

The moments passed in silence save for the squawks of the seagulls floating on the warm breeze above. Martin heard the slow movement of his men as their carbines were lowered, though he kept his eyes fixed on the opposite decks, watching to see the gesture being reciprocated. Gradually it was, even if the crews of the cannons remained vigilant. It would have to be good enough, now they would be safer with Alexi on board. The invitation was not spoken, a curt nod indicating he was welcome.

Alexi strode down the steps to his own main deck and then veered sideways, vaulting over his rail down and across to join Martin on the *Liberty*. He took the three-yard drop with ease. The crowd on the deck parted as he thumped the boards on landing, another fact that seemed to cause no little amusement. He shouted back to his ship, something jovial Martin judged, guessing by the way he tapped his boot against the wooden beams of the decking. See, not so heavy that I broke it. Another sailor from the other ship landed shortly after, a different kind of man, yellow-skinned, shaven-headed with a kerchief tied over his scalp to protect it from the ferocity of the sun. His eyes were dark, darker than a gypsy's, his movement in leaping over every bit as graceful as his captain's. Martin wondered where he came from, a curiosity he would not attempt to satisfy. Alexi was right, he realized, studying the pierced ears of the exotic newcomer, we are all foreigners here.

They would need to give two men in exchange to show good faith. Men of a quick mind and even temperament, men he could trust.

'José . . . Juan?'

José stuffed his pistol inside his shirt, the briefest of glances as good as a salute before he began his climb, his brother following close behind. Good men, thought Martin. The best we have.

Up close, Martin was to discover that Alexi was a man of only moderate stature, not the giant he had expected to tower over him. He was barely five and a half feet tall, his bones fine and feline, features sharp on a face that could have been fashioned for a porcelain doll. A modest size though immodest manner; he strode the boards like an emperor. Martin had long fancied that his own mind could race as fast as any other's, a conceit that he had let lead him into confrontations big and small. Yet here was another whose very presence rendered such an assumption dangerous at best, and right now, downright foolhardy.

Martin watched the Pole's eyes scan rapidly, devouring every image in an eagle's hungry sweep. As he tried to follow its path he found himself taking in the detail from a new perspective, that of the predator, come to enforce the King's justice with the savage authority of the assize judge. When Martin viewed the scene as his visitor, the case for the defence looked anything but proven: the freed slaves on deck, loitering in their soiled rags, unconvincing as pirates, implausible as free men; the ragged sails and warped boards of the *Liberty*, an absurd imposture, fortunate even to fool the waves she rested on. In contrast, everything about the *Tomasz*, gracing the same water and mere yards away, spoke of authenticity. It had not occurred to Martin before, raised to believe that piracy meant a permanent state of desperation, that a pirate ship should represent the very best in seamanship. Here were men whose very existence depended on maintaining an ability to outrun, outgun and outmanoeuvre any target or foe, who could appropriate the best attributes and features of the ships they took. Martin felt a sense of shame at the state of his charge, making a mental note to make for the shore if they broke clear of the *Tomasz*, maybe Colou Point, anywhere that granted the opportunity to release the sick and dying, to overhaul the ship and rid her of the barnacles and growths on her hull, a place where she might regain her dignity.

Liberty and *Tomasz* were still bound together, stretching an increasingly taut rope, one that also held Alexi's scrutiny. Martin gestured to him that the connection could be released.

'We have no longboat. You have one, or any means of returning to your ship?'

Alexi nodded, though hunting the deck for the sight of one, as if verifying Martin's claim.

'You sail without a longboat?'

'We cast our captain and his officers adrift in it some time ago.'

'How long has *Liberty* been a pirate ship?'

'Long enough.'

'We have not heard of you . . . You fly the black flag yet have no captain, how can this be so? You have articles?'

Martin felt his burden grow suddenly the heavier. 'We are a pirate ship, sir, we follow our own path, our own rules.'

Alexi bared his teeth as he smiled; uneven, short, black spaces between yet forming a regular pattern all the same in matching top and bottom sets. He shook his head at the disorder surrounding them on deck and spoke through the gaps in his laughter. 'So I see . . .'

There was more than a hint of cruelty in his amusement, thought Martin. *Shark teeth*.

'. . . Yes, so I see my friend. We on the *Tomasz* follow our own rules. One of them is not to attack other pirate ships. So we would need to be sure that this is the case here. We would need to see that every man here has signed your articles.'

Martin blinked. Checkmate. He had been caught out of position, the plan had been so simple, beautifully simple, yet it was taking him down, deeper and deeper. José and Juan on the *Tomasz*, the savages on the brink of death below, the unruly ones on deck, the crew he had begged to follow him; their fates all in his hands. He needed time to think again; such a short day, so many decisions.

'Please, we should discuss this inside. I would prefer to speak free from any distractions, will you join me in quarters?'

Alexi assented, a sideways glance telling his companion to remain on the quarterdeck whilst he retired for the closed session. He followed Martin down the steps. Martin did not wait for him, seeking out McKnight instead. Time for action. Sailors are happiest when on the move.

'Stanley . . . please set a course for shore. We need to restore our vessel. We shall survey a spot where we may careen our hull.'

McKnight acknowledged the order, paying scant attention to Martin's nervous demeanour and more to the mesmerizing figure of the grinning pirate captain alongside him. Martin spoke, aware of the need to break the spell.

'We will move towards the shore. I take it you will wish to follow? Perhaps you want to relay this to your ship?'

Alexi shouted to his companion on the quarterdeck above. A foreign tongue, strange in intonation and structure, as if he were speaking backwards. His instruction was in turn relayed back to the *Tomasz*, again in an indecipherable language, possibly the same even though Martin struggled to recognize a single word being repeated.

They entered the silence of Captain Henry's cabin, Martin walking into the gloomy interior first and heading for the seat by the desk. Martin wondered for a second how the fates were treating his old skipper, realizing he would not be surprised to hear of his death; already this room felt as if possessed by the dead, a haunted chamber with a ghostly presence whispering of treason, the captain's last fevered words carried out to sea by the wind, speaking of how he was duped to surrender his command.

Martin pointed for Alexi to sit on the cot whilst he tried to rid his mind of his previous confrontations in this space; the exchanges with the captain and Fela, how his plan had taken shape within these same wooden walls. Those triumphs were in the past, another scheme was required now, one to better anything conjured before. The *Liberty* had no articles, it was out of the question that Fela could persuade the multitude of slaves aboard to sign allegiance to the pirate code, even less likely that Fela himself would sign and risk the wrath of the Royal Africa Company that he might yet seek to trade with. Then there was the crew; what kind of future could he offer Reid, Sims, McKnight and them all as outlaws of the sea, the real thing? None. It would have to be their choice. That was the reality, that would have to be the plan.

'I would offer you a brandy but our former captain believed it fit only for trade.'

Alexi did not show any particular disappointment. He had crouched forward on the bed to fight its natural inclination to lay him out flat, swallow up his small frame in the dip between pillar and post. He did not take to squatting low, Martin noted, did not seem comfortable at a lower station. Martin continued.

'We have no articles ... As an exercise, it is not something we have granted priority. We have only recently established ourselves as free of captain and officers. We will have articles in due course.'

'We must witness this.'

'You are welcome to. First we must put those ashore who wish to leave our ship. We have many below who are perishing and must be returned to land. Men ... women ... those who wish to stay on the *Liberty* will sign articles, you have my word on it.'

Alexi stood abruptly, stamping his heels into the floor. Martin was startled, though he sought to hide it; was his word not enough?

'Women?'

It was as if, thought Martin, he had let slip a mention of buried treasure, or an unguarded galleon laden with gold; at the sound of a magic word instinct seemed to take over. He thought of the wretched souls languishing below deck, too weak or weary to venture into the open air. Women? By definition, yes. As receptacles for the lust and demands of a love-starved pirate crew, no, decency surely stood as a barrier to that. Martin floundered, lost for words as he thought through the situation. These are women you cannot touch, they have suffered enough.

'Men and women ... returning to shore as we promised.'

'You were in no position to promise them anything, were you? They are the property of others ... stolen property.'

'They are dying and will be no one's property but the Lord above. You and your ship must realize that you will have to fight to retake them, to fight the *Liberty* and the slaves themselves.'

Alexi moved close to Martin, one hand on the desk, the other on the arm of his chair, embracing the air around him.

'You have men who would fight for the freedom of savages?'

His tone was one of utter disbelief, as if Martin had decreed that his crew would take arms to defend the stars, or the fish in the sea.

'We will not stand aside and let them be retaken.'

'Your ship is a mess. It could be taken any time.'

'Perhaps . . . Though not without cost for whoever tried to do so.'

Alexi shook his head, as if the futility of such a battle was beyond pointlessness.

'Yes, for sure. And you speak for your ship.' The deep lines in his face kept their pained crease. 'And your men will fight for . . . this? You court disaster. Men are indifferent to the plight of the savage.'

'Most men. Yet none will ever fight for indifference.'

Alexi made to speak but halted, tripped by the measure of what Martin had said. His mood was changing, he seemed tired by the debate, a debate he may have been realizing he could not win.

'We will follow you to the shore, we will help you unload. You will need to pay your craft some attention, it is not fit to sail or fight under the black flag.'

'We would be grateful for your help and will pay for your labours and advice. In the holds we have brandy, linen and fine cloth.'

Alexi's features were still for an instant, as if frozen in shock. Eventually a grimace formed, one which in turn gave way to a rueful smile as Martin held out his hand.

'Cloth?'

He studied Martin's hand, pausing like a man confronted by a gesture so new as to be completely alien to him. Martin's offer lingered the while; eventually Alexi took it.

'*Fine* cloth. You make a strange pirate, Mister Scotsman. You sail a different sea. I think my men would prefer to know how much brandy.'

Tuesday. I returned to the island sometime after one o'clock. Early afternoon in June, emerging from the belly of the plane into the empty glare of the runway at Palma, like walking into a concrete sauna, maybe the first time that year that the breeze had completely died and the temperature had hit the high eighties. Things were stifling, hotting up, as if a monsoon storm was about to burst. Not much of a homecoming but then it hardly felt like home any more.

Another hire car on another credit card had me back on the road to the house, bypassing Puerto Puals and the Arena and the pack of hyenas who were presumably circling the territory. Alexander would fill me in, if he was still there, if he hadn't fucked off with Sarah and left the madness behind. I couldn't really blame him if he had, he hadn't been fully paid for weeks, had been threatened by one maniac, was living in semi-exile whilst house-sitting for the other maniac who had got him into all this. Then there were the attempts to steal his girlfriend though these were all now in the past. She was off the agenda, I didn't have the time or energy any more.

I made the drive up to and beyond Andraitx in a little over an hour, taking it easy, not wanting to draw attention to myself, constantly checking in the mirror to see if there were any Germans, Russians, Frenchmen or psychotic Spanish brothers on my tail. Maybe a whole posse. Yes, I was starring in my own third-rate spy thriller, like Roger Moore as the Saint, shaking off the dastardly foreigners whilst finding time to smooth down his hair and smooch up to the girls. Roger Moore so depressed and paranoid and desperate for a line of coke that both eyebrows are disappearing off the top of his forehead. Roger Moore becoming clammy and nauseous when he pulls into the driveway of his home and sees that the car he had hoped would be there isn't, wondering who, if anyone, is in his house.

'Alexander?'

The door had been locked and the house was still, the alarm switched to off. I hoped to fuck he was still around, things would be so hard without help. What if the Carcera boys had caught up with him?

'Martin? . . . in here.'

Thank you Jesus, thank you God. I followed the voice through to the kitchen and the stairs to the garage beneath it.

'*Hola.*'

'How you doing?'

Ça va, Alexander. Want a coffee? A drink of any kind? Let me feed you, let me build you up. There's something else I've got to ask you.

'I'm OK. You? Going stir crazy yet? How's Sarah coping with the bar?'

'Ended up closing it, Martin, it was just a bit too heavy, a lot of people looking for you. She thought it was the best thing to do. . . .Is it a problem?'

My eye fell to the spaghetti of pipes, tubes, tanks and mouthpiece surrounding him on the floor, some of it spilling under the car which he had brought in from outside. You could have been forgiven for thinking that some kind of alien octopus had been wrenched from the heart of its engine. Alexander really had taken this undercover thing to heart, hiding the motor indoors, living a quiet life. The bar was closed, was it a problem? No, of course not, in the greater scheme of things not a problem at all.

'As long as no one has tried to break in, set up and trade under a flag of convenience. No overtures from Herman to do with that?'

He shook his head. Obviously not that he was aware, or wanted to be. His face was a study in concentration, completely absorbed in the diving debris around him, far more at home here than he ever had been pouring pints for the hoi polloi. This garage, spanner in hand, vest and jeans was where he was at, somewhere he could be happy, transformed back to being a five-year-old with his plastic bricks in the play-pen.

'Anyway, this gear's got bit rusty; long time since you dived, yeah?'

I suppose so. But then again it had mainly been used for other things, less obvious things. In fact this might be the first time bits of it would go under the waves.

'Is it salvageable? What about the navigation stuff?'

He nodded eagerly. We were moving on to his specialist subject.

'Your boat, will it have some kind of system on it?'

'Probably not. I'll need another way of knowing where I am, anyway.'

248

Alexander stood up, abandoning the open-heart surgery he was carrying out by pen-knife on the breathing apparatus.

'Well, the good news is that technology is on your side. Five or ten years ago you might have struggled but now there's a thing called GPS – Global Positioning System – based on a military thing, I think it's how they guide missiles, using satellites. You can buy a ship's compass with it built-in, can even buy it on a watch. They take a fix from whatever's in orbit to give you coordinates. Infallible, seemingly.'

'Complicated?'

'Shouldn't think so, whatever you buy should have instructions.'

'Expensive?'

'Yeah . . . Well, that's the bad news. Anywhere around a hundred thousand pesetas.'

'How easy to get hold of a watch?'

'Not a problem, maybe about the same price. We could look at getting it secondhand if you've got the time . . . shouldn't be any less reliable.'

I wondered how much more credit my assorted plastic cards held between them. I needed one watch, maybe two, though if more than one was required the decision wouldn't be mine.

'Thanks, thanks for your help with this and with everything. I think I'll need one new, you'll need to tell me where I can pick it up. Alexander, there is one other thing, another favour. A big one.'

'What's that?'

'You're good with boats, aren't you? Could you pick mine up in France and bring it across here?'

'What kind of boat?'

'It'll be a speedboat, a launch. It's being worked on just now. Ready Thursday. Could you do it?'

He took a deep breath and held the metal of a spanner to his lips whilst he pondered.

'Do you know what you're doing, Martin, is all this under control? What's going on anyway, what is the plan?'

His tone was quizzical rather than confrontational. I think he was genuinely baffled. It was back to the scene with Michel. I had all the answers, good answers, but they were no use because I couldn't share them. I had to let the silence speak for me, had to let him go on.

'I'll help you Martin, sure, if I can. I just don't want to be part of anything. What I'm saying is that I'm not a courier, not some runner . . . If you've got some scheme to bring something in then fine, best of luck . . . but count me out, I'm not a smuggler, it's not what I'm about.'

Me neither, not any more. What I'm about is doing the right thing, what I'm trying to be about. For once. Takes a bit of getting used to. Takes a bit of believing, doesn't it?

'This is nothing to do with drugs, Alexander. I know it might not look that way but that's the truth. There might be a pick-up at sea, sure, that comes later though, if it comes, and that's got nothing to do with drugs either.'

His eyes were locked on mine, testing for sincerity. I was worried that he might have mistaken my nervousness for deceit, and suddenly aware of how fucked I must have appeared. Would I have trusted someone looking like me? And yet just about every other time in my life when I had had to put on an act to get my way it had never been a problem. Now, when everything depended on it for the best of reasons I must have been coming across as a con-man. I couldn't even stop my stomach from rumbling, the noise robbing the moment of its last fragments of dignity. It was time to beg, to speak from the heart, however difficult that might be.

'You've been a great help to me so far and to be honest I don't really know why – I don't know why you've stuck with it when I've hardly been fair with you in the past. I can only thank you for it, can't even promise to make it up to you because I don't really know what's going to happen . . . Look, if you don't want to do this then it's OK, I'll have to find another way, but I'm not asking you to do something that's wrong, not setting you up in any way. Alexander, you've done more for me already than I had any right to expect so whatever you say is cool.'

Alexander. Cool. Who would have thought the words could sit together? The man himself showed every sign of being lost in concentration again, chasing off on his own tangent.

'When that man – the dealer – Tony . . . came round looking for me, did he ask you where I was? And you didn't tell him, did you, was he pissed off?'

'I can't remember, is it important, has he been round here?'

'It's just that you said before that he was pissed off and that it was bad news for both of us, remember?'

I'd have been lying if I denied it; somewhere in the catalogue of greatest hits in my mind there was a memory of saying something similar. Its relevance escaped me.

'Alexander, I don't really want to go into that.'

'It's just that it struck me afterwards that you could have just told him where I lived, or when I'd next be working . . . he must have asked. But you didn't, did you?'

No, I didn't. He had asked and I didn't tell him. I played the conversation over in my head, letting Alexander's question hang. This time the silence spoke for both of us. He had one more question.

'Why was that?'

Was this relevant? Damned right. Why the fuck hadn't I just told him, forgot about it, moved on to the next deal. Why didn't I want the Carceras as partners, to sell Sasha's contraband, to be at one with Herman? And no, Alexander, it hasn't gone unnoticed, no matter how hard I've tried, that I've had many years of success through being a bit of a shit and that the moment I stopped and did someone a turn it has brought the roof crashing down on my poor fucking head. Yes, so why didn't I tell him? Because I wanted to surprise myself. Nothing to do with you. I can get killed any time or place that I want to. And at that moment, when big Tony asked, I wanted to surprise myself, and fuck the consequences, and even now with all that's happened in between, when I replay the scene in my memory, I'm proud that I played it that way. Takes some getting used to.

'I don't know, Alexander. What are you getting at?'

His eyes were on me again, scanning for honesty. He shook his head slowly, very slowly. A smile came from somewhere.

'Oh, I think you do, but I'll let it pass. I'll fetch your boat, if it's a clean boat. You're telling me it is so I'll go and get it. Maybe one day you'll tell me the plan. I'd sure love to hear it.'

I tried to return his smile. *You are right about everything else, my friend, but wrong there, believe me.* My stomach groaned again, and I began to think about food.

And it hadn't escaped me either that the very thing that had got me into this mess was likely to be the one thing that could pull me out of it. I'm telling myself this as I prepare to go down inside, to look for the strength and the focus that I will need to turn this thing around. I thought of the plan, the great new plan that would rescue my wife and child and give them some kind of future. And me? If I was lucky I might be like the character from an old silent movie, was it Charlie Chaplin or Buster Keaton? The black and white sequence where the man is standing in the middle of a one-roomed house whose walls collapse one by one, falling inwards but because of the sequence by which they tumble, and the positioning of windows and doors within them, our favourite is safe as long as he stays still and ignores the disintegration around him, which he does, more by accident than design, emerging unscathed from the rubble, straightening a dusty hat as he walks free.

Could I be that man, a slapstick hero emerging from the ruins? If I was to have any chance I would have to concentrate, hold my nerve, be careful not to share anything with anyone that might let them see what was in my mind, to let anything and everything go that didn't concern the plan, let the walls fall in on me and not blink. Yet this was what had led to all of this; working alone, never sharing, never communicating, living life as a spectator, never taking a stand. If it did work just once again, things would have to change afterwards. One way or another, this would be my final performance, I was going down deep for the very last time.

Wednesday. I bought Alexander his ticket to Barcelona, figured out the buses that would take him from there to Port-Vendres and gave him instructions on where to take the boat and fit it out. I then went down to Puerto Puals and opened up the Arena in time for the lunchtime rush.

The bar had been closed for three days but it seemed so much longer, perhaps because it had never been closed for more than two before. Even then that was for Christmas and New Year breaks, national holidays rather than locking up when the season was about to hit the summer peak. Sarah and whoever had made a decent job of tidying up before the shutdown though the place still reeked with all the staleness of a ghost town. The heat does that to places like bars, even when they are hidden behind steel shutters to protect them. Rubbish, spillage, crumbs or un-emptied ash-trays suddenly acquire the power to stink out a space so that it's like a medieval town. Places like the Arena need circulation; air, money, customers. Without them the atmosphere hangs heavy. I opened all the windows at the back and the doors at the front, set the music to play and the coffee to froth. I gave out all the signs I could that things were normal and waited for them to come. Waited for anyone to come. Waited for the end to begin.

Herman came round first. Nothing surprising about that, no surprise that he wanted 'to get this mess sorted out, Marty', to get everything in order. I found myself looking at him, studying every pimple, spot and broken vein in his nose, thinking about what might happen to him, but without glee or anticipation, or even sorrow. Without anything. I wondered if I was psychopathic. I poured him a fresh coffee.

Herman scanned round to look over his shoulder. There was nobody else in and he must have known that, unless he thought someone had hidden in the toilets or glided in silently after he had taken his seat. No, he was doing it for effect. He wanted me to appreciate how seriously he was taking it all.

'It's a mess here, Marty, what's with all the boxes everywhere?'

'Mistake on my order form from the supplier. They've given me more than I need.'

'Mistake? You need a system. How often do you carry out a stock-take, you don't audit what you get through?'

I would miss Herman's concern for sure. Poor Herman could never stop himself, if he saw something broke he just had to fix it. Or tell you how to fix it. Or break it completely to save you the bother of even trying. Poor me.

'Fuck the stock, Herman, it's not an issue. It'll be gone soon enough. I've seen my lawyer. I'm ready to deal. I need to know your offer.'

'What's in them? Whisky? You'll never get through that amount . . . I told you before Marty, I don't like the way you handle things . . . not good, not good for Puerto Puals.'

'Your offer, Herman – I need to know your offer.'

'Offer? It's complicated now. We can make an offer but there are conditions.'

Of course there would be conditions. How could there not be? Why would Herman and the organization miss the opportunity to make me jump through one more fucking hoop? I stood up and sighed, tapped my hand against the tabletop in a show of frustration. A *show*. It was all a show today, I wasn't even interested in his fucking offer.

'Your friends . . . brothers, the Carceras. They have to go first. We can make no deal until you get rid of them. No good for Puerto Puals.'

'Then what? What will you offer if I persuade them to go? When do I see my wife again?'

I had hit good form at this point, snarling right into his hairy ear.

'You take it easy. You can sort this all out. All in your hands. You must get rid of the boys first.'

The script said I should calm down now and plead for clemency. I followed it.

'OK . . . OK, I'm sorry, I'm desperate, Herman. I need money as well, I'll do anything you want just to put an end to this. I've bought a boat, need to pay for it or else I've got more trouble. I need what you'll give me for the bar to do that. I have to see my daughter, have to see my wife . . . what can I do?'

Herman took out a handkerchief and mopped his top lip free from sweat as if wiping his mouth at the end of some sumptuous Bavarian feast. He was as easy with me as a disintegrating junkie as he was with me as a sober business rival. All the same to him. All just a bump to be smoothed out under the carpet of progress.

'I have told you, Marty.'

I tried to imagine anything that could take the performance to a new high. I thought of my daughter.

'Please, I need to see them, I don't even know if they are alive. If I don't see them tomorrow . . . if I don't see them tomorrow, Herman, I'm just going to die.'

The man was beginning to wilt, looking uncomfortable for the first time.

'Pull yourself together, Marty. I keep telling you what to do.'

Yes, and that's the whole problem, isn't it Herman, always you or your organization there to tell me.

'Look, I'll give you everything tomorrow. I'll sign over the bar, I'll get rid of Tony and Miguel, just give me my wife and baby back.'

'How do you mean "get rid" of them? They must not come back to Puerto Puals, understand? You cannot tell them to leave and then we see them back here a week later. Once we know they are gone we can make the deal.'

I turned the tears back on.

'I can't wait though. Can't wait that long and you know it, what do you want me to do?'

Herman slouched forward and shrugged his shoulders. He wasn't going to say it, no. I would have to volunteer for the gig.

'OK . . . OK. My suggestion – you bring my wife and child to Puerto Puals tomorrow and give me one minute with them so that I can see they are all right . . . My boat will have arrived, you see. So then you, me, whoever else you want, we all go out to sea for a trip, we'll take the Carceras with us . . . and I'll get rid of them.'

I looked up from my hands to see Herman nodding; this was obviously more in line with the organization's thinking.

Behind us two customers were waiting at the bar, having found their way inside, a man and a woman in their fifties breathing deeply to combat the heat, holding on to each other as if about to expire. I had to switch out of one role back into the more familiar one as host. Perhaps for one of the last times, a collector's item. The ease with which I made the transition scared me; again I thought of how the very thing that had got me into this could get me out. *Yes, of course, take a seat and I'll be right with you, is that enough shade, if you need more just tell me and I'll pull another parasol over, just give me one minute.*

255

'Have we got a deal? My wife and child must be let go before we head off.'

Herman's voice was low, he didn't want to be overheard.

'You will see them *after*, Marty . . .'

'No, must be before, I'm not going to go through with it unless I know they are well and free. I don't see your problem, Herman. I'll have signed over the Arena to you, the Carcera boys will be with us so you can see exactly what is said – and done. Even if anything goes wrong you'll still have me there, you can swap one prisoner for another. Have we got a deal?'

The old couple were looking round to us, wondering where their service had gone.

Herman was equally restless, wrestling with his better judgement, mumbling under his breath like a middle-aged father reluctantly writing the cheque that buys a sexy dress for his teenage daughter.

'Let me check with the organization.'

I stood up and smiled to the old-timers. *On my way, coming soon.*

'Don't give me that shit, Herman, don't insult my intelligence. Can you hear what I'm offering to do for you? Bring them here tomorrow for twelve o'clock, I'll get everything else together. Have we got a deal or not?'

He gave me one stern nod of his head. The first wall of the house had started to crumble; I hoped I would be standing in the right spot when it came down completely.

Two hours later, more visitors, two more to be precise.

'*Hola amigo*, where you been?'

'Away, like I said I would, making plans. You boys want a beer?'

Miguel and Tony had already pulled up at the bar, answering my question with a collective snort, as if it were so rhetorical it didn't really merit any proper reply. They stood before me, twitching, jerking, sizing up the joint once more like it was all new to them; taking in the decor, the state of the walls, the number of customers. They hadn't ever taken a seat at one of the tables, either in or outside in the shade. No, men like these preferred to stand, maybe half-balanced on a stool like a

crooner about to burst into song, like gunslingers about to leap backwards and draw their pistols. They liked to keep an eye on things, to
give out the signals through striking a pose, a pose that was far more
fluent and articulate than their gruff Catalan jive talk could ever hope
to be. *We are the Carcera brothers, we are players, we are here and we are
ready for anything.*

'Hey Martin, what's with all the boxes?'

'Stock transaction. I was offered a deal I couldn't turn down.'

'Whisky, yeah? You should have told me, we have connections,
you know.'

Miguel threw a sideways look to his brother, as if he'd been bounced
on to him by the scepticism he'd caught in me. Big Tony seemed even
less impressed by the Carcera drinks wholesaler credentials than I was.
He sniffed again and rubbed his nose, sticking his thumb right up each
nostril to clear out whatever debris he thought was lurking there. *We've
got connections? That's great news.* Big Tony's mellow demeanour had me
studying his runt of a brother; had he been indulging in the coke as
well? How much of the three kilos was left, had any of it been sold,
if its quality was so fucking bad how come you two show such a liking
for it? With Miguel it was hard to tell, he acted as if he was high all
the time. His delusions knew no bounds even without stimulants, wired
from birth.

'Can you excuse me a moment, guys?'

I thumped two glasses of beer in front of them and scurried round
to carry out a quick tour of the tables. I had about fifteen customers
in, all hiding from the sun, all sipping away as they studied the endless
parade of couples cruising around the bleached marina. I was working
alone today, as I had so many times before. A harder shift but preferable
in other ways, no one to answer to, no one to explain to, no one
asking for anything other than the next drink. So I left the boys and
saw to the clients, gathering up empty glasses on a tray and wiping
down the tables on autopilot. Inside I was going down again, digging
deep for the concentration required. Herman had gone well, one in
the bag, the most difficult one done. Or was it? This would be a
different sort of challenge in that whilst they weren't as smart as Herman

257

they were less predictable, always capable of some stupid stunt that would catch you off-guard. And they annoyed me. Their presence on earth pissed me off to such an extent that keeping up a front with them was in one kind of way harder than it was with Herman, playing out a role when all I wanted to do was smack Miguel right between his lying eyes, to rattle his brother's non-existent brain. A moment's satisfaction versus eternal regret. The kind of test I'd failed before.

'OK guys, ready for another one?'

The glasses were passed back for refill. Again the question didn't deserve further thought. Miguel took a gulp and cleared his throat.

'Ever see that guy?'

'Which guy?'

'The one we talked about, the one who tried to break Tony's balls.'

'Not recently.'

'Well you tell him, we haven't forgotten, we want him. You tell him . . . *if you see him.*'

In that one second, when Miguel fixed me in the eye, I felt a real fear, a surge of it telling me that he could see through everything, everything I had said and was about to say. Something else to grapple with. This wasn't going to be easy.

'So Miguel says the bar was shut, Martin, what have you been doing?'

Big Tony's intervention was as unlikely as it was welcome. I smiled at him, the warmth in my reply was almost genuine.

'I went away and bought myself a boat.'

'A boat, yeah?'

The generous helpings of cocaine didn't appear to have speeded the boys up any.

'Power-boat, a real beauty . . . Arrives here tomorrow, you want to see it?'

'You should have told me you wanted a boat. We got connections, could have fixed you up. It cost you plenty, yeah?'

'Cost enough, sure. But the money was no problem.'

Miguel's eyebrows rose in unison as Tony drained his glass.

'No, yeah?'

I stuck the glass under the lager tap yet again.

'No, I'm selling up, selling the Arena, going off in my boat.'

Miguel pushed his drink away from him, staring at me.

'Who you selling to?'

'A guy's making an offer tomorrow, the guy that owns the rest of the development.'

'You should have told me you were going to sell; what if this guy's offer is shit?'

'I don't think it will be, he's cool, he knows what I want.'

'What about us?'

'What do you mean?'

'Our cut, yeah?'

'I don't know what you mean.'

I tried to look as if this were the case, hitting him with my best gormless-though-shaky air. Miguel looked to Tony, giving him a look which I think was meant to say something like 'it's so obvious'. Nothing came back. Maybe nothing was obvious to Tony. Miguel ploughed on regardless.

'Martin, we have an interest in this bar. An *ongoing* interest. You should have thought about the help and effort we have put into this place before you agreed a price because now you are going to have to sort it out.'

Tony and Miguel's help and effort, yes, where would I have been without it? Without you guys I'm nothing, just another bar-owner fucking and snorting his way. With you I'm much the same, except with the addition of one great problem, you. What are my options, how about one baseball bat, one swing of the thing, right into your face staring into mine, what do you think I'd give for that?

One moment of pleasure. Now wasn't the time though. Now was the time to seem startled, like all of this came as a surprise, like all of this wasn't entirely predictable.

'Come on Miguel, this is my bar, always has been. Mine to sell.'

I made my voice sound small, as if I wasn't convinced myself. I wanted to give them a glimpse of weakness, see if they would go for the bait. Miguel didn't disappoint, he had scented blood. This time when he looked to his brother a nod came back.

'Your bar, yeah? What about the time we've spent here with you, yeah? We need to know what you are going to give for that, we're professional men, yeah? We don't mess about, we could have been busy doing other things but were here with you. We deserve a cut, yeah? We want to know where we stand with the new owner. Does he know about us?'

'He knows about you, yeah.'

'So he's going to make an offer for our services, yeah? We need to know what that is before we can let the deal go through.'

Sure, Miguel. I wasn't lying, he knows all about you. And I'll make you part of the deal, do you really want that?

'OK . . . This is too much for me. Maybe you should get something – I'm meeting him tomorrow, that's when we cut the deal, you guys should come along. We can sort it out together. Will you come?'

'Come where?'

Tony's question showed he was the man for practicalities, yes, they were his forte. Miguel kept quiet. Had he seen through this, had I made it look too easy?

'Out on the boat. We're going out for a trip on my boat, then we go to his bar for lunch and to discuss the business.'

'Is he expecting us?'

'Don't worry about that, I'll tell him before. That's not a problem, you are welcome on my boat anyway. Twelve o'clock outside here tomorrow, we can sort everything, what do you say?'

Tony slid off his stool, like he was ready there and then. I wouldn't have expected less, nothing about this would have struck him as odd, there was nothing that he should be wary about. Too brave, too stupid. The courage of an idiot. His brother was a different proposition though, and I felt exposed every time his eye was on me. He was still. Had I underestimated him?

He came towards me and pulled me close, wrapping his stubby arms around me in a stiff though brotherly embrace, whispering in my ear like a dying father to his son.

260

'You should have told me, Martin . . . We'll get it sorted, just don't fuck with us, yeah?'

He let one arm go and threw it over his brother's shoulder so that we were now a glorious team, the threesome that would conquer the world.

'Twelve o'clock tomorrow, yeah?'

I gave it the best smile I could and peeled myself away. A customer was waving for his bill at the far end of the bar. I moved towards him like a refugee taking his final steps to the West at Checkpoint Charlie. You can pay, no problem at all, sir, would there be anything else, anything on the house?

Miguel and Tony made their own exit as I dealt with him. I heard Tony asking his brother one last question as they passed by on their way to the door.

'Hey, any girls there tomorrow?'

It didn't get a response. Maybe Miguel had his mind on other matters. Two down and one to go. No Tony, there won't be any girls. Only one at the very start, and she's mine.

Martin let his elbows sink into the sand, feeling himself gently slip on to his back under the heat of the sun and the pull of the dune on his body. He had climbed to the sparsely-grassed peak to survey the scene in its entirety and the effort required had drained him almost as much as the vision he had encountered once he reached the top. He wiped the sweat from the end of his nose and peeled off his sodden shirt, eager to feel the warm gusting breeze blow and cleanse him dry. Down below, by the water's edge, the rest of the assembly congregated, a mixture of colours, labours and demeanours, all glittering like stony jewels against the backdrop of blue and gold. Over three hundred people, all here because of him and his decisions. He closed his eyes and took a deep breath, then waited for the wind to do its work.

There were two ships in the water, one out in the turquoise deep, one lying on its side in the frothy wash, a party of men scrubbing its exposed hull clear of the thick slime that had taken root. Some stood waist-deep in the waves, some balanced precariously on the shoulders of others reaching higher, a scream and a hearty splash interrupting their efforts at intervals. As Martin squinted into the light he could see them as anything other than men; perhaps ants breaking up the carcass of a beached animal, perhaps an army of dwarves attacking the underbelly of a stricken giant. *Liberty* lay at their mercy, as they themselves, thought Martin, lay at the mercy of liberty. Below him, in the pits at the foot of the dunes, lay the newly unloaded cargo of the former ship *Anne*; tarpaulin-covered pyramids weighed down with stones and sand. The heaps now represented the first spoils of the pirate craft that had usurped her, and Martin felt more than a passing guilt as his eye lingered on the goods soon destined to be split into individual bundles, the reward they had given themselves for taking up the outlaw code. He felt guilt when he thought back to how he had watched these same goods being loaded at the docks in Plymouth, the effort that honest men had put into placing them aboard, labour given in the belief that they were destined for honest trade. Would they have toiled so, and would the merchants have ordered it so, had any known then that it would end thus, on African sand, in bandit country rather than the secure land of the colonies in the Indies? What if one had said then that it was to be divided into lots, thieves' lots, spoils; spoils which brought an ugliness to an otherwise beautiful plan.

Still, the spirits of the men busy cleaning the hull seemed high; Martin heard their guffaws and wished he could join them. Sailors happiest on the move, men happiest engaged in constructive labour. Martin envied them the simplicity of their task; they were not thinking of the future, the price they would have to pay for signing up to their share of what lay on dry land before them. He would have to – he was the one who had brought them here, all of them; the survivors of the original crew, the slaves, Fela and even the men of the *Tomasz*. Brought them to this place, this situation, following him through every turn as events unfolded, demanding that he make the choice between good and bad and then conspiring to present the same choice again and again as the waters around went from blue to grey and the enormity of what he had started became as great as the numbers gathered in his wake.

They had come to this shore to clean their ship, to make her fit for the ocean, to release the slaves and return them to their land. A simple plan. But instead they had set up camp, some new kind of colony as exotic as the landscape it adorned. They had taken the slaves to the shore, some by the longboat of the *Tomasz*, the rest on *Liberty* herself, though all in the belief that they would flee into the welcoming growth of the jungle the moment their feet met dry land, that they would run and make good their escape from the treacherous grasp of the European. Perhaps, Martin had allowed himself to think, some might even thank him for the service he had rendered them before they vanished into the bush, thank their fortune that their Guineaman had changed its colours before it was too late for them. Yet this vision was to prove a dream. A beautiful dream. Reality was more cruel. Reality would prove to be more absurd. When they landed they did not run, they did not move or seek to hide. Instead they stood where their feet left the water, pleading for food, for shelter, for protection. Only then did Martin come to understand Fela's incomprehension when he had first stated his intention to deliver them here. Back then, in the fixed setting of Captain Henry's cabin, he had been able to wave aside any objections with the weight of the moral authority he had behind his cause. If Fela could not understand it had to be because he had no concept of justice. Yet his principled stand had proved to have less than sure foundations when tested by the slaves' arrival on the sands. Only then had he come to see what had perplexed Fela, for these were not Africans happy to make their homecoming, no; these were Winnebah, Quamboer and Kulti, tribesmen and women from deep in the interior, who had been chained by caboceers like Fela from the coastal regions. On landing they had no idea of where they were, except that they were in danger of being enslaved again, or worse. So they had stayed with the only certainty they had, that the crew of the *Liberty* had fed them so far and had offered some sort of protection to them, the three hundred souls stranded on a strange shore. Enough to seed a new nation, thought Martin, a country of the lost. What was he to do with them?

It would take a week to overhaul the ship, at which point the *Tomasz* would depart, though not before witnessing the signing of the pirate articles that would for ever damn them. Alexi had also intimated that some of his crew would seek to join the *Liberty*. Martin knew there was little point in trying to resist. *We are all pirates now.*

Three days after landing he gathered the remaining men of the *Anne* to tell them of Alexi's demands.

'Every man that signs will receive his personal share of the cargo we were left. Every personal share shall be written down in the articles and guaranteed. No other man on ship has any right to another's share. The articles will also attest every man's right to an equal share of any future . . . booty the *Liberty* acquires –'

'Will you be signing, Mr Martin?'

The question came from Sims, smiling, stripped and barefoot in his breeches, the skin on his shoulders red and blistered but elsewhere golden and bronzed from the sun. Sims, who seemed to have thrived since they landed, learning new skills and songs from the ruffians of the *Tomasz* who had adopted him as one of their own so that he had blossomed like one of the saplings on the edge of the jungle. What would he be, wondered Martin, all of fourteen or fifteen years old? It was hard to imagine he would live to a mature old age as a buccaneer. Pirates had to expect short lives, had to make up with intensity what they would lack in longevity. How long would Sims last before being brought to the gallows-tree, or cut down with a bullet as he stormed on to another deck?

'Yes, I believe I will . . .' *I have no choice, but you have. Think carefully, son. Just because I will does not mean there is any security or reason to this path. The opposite case is true. We court disaster.*

'You should all be aware that our King will regard the signing of articles as treason, a hanging offence. When you sign, you sign for life, the cross you mark will be witnessed . . . Do not make such a mark unless you understand and accept the consequences – I will have no man here do so under false assumptions. I cannot say where this road will lead us. Any man unsure of his position should be prepared to stay here until the next merchantman passes, or scouts from the nearest trading post find him. Perhaps these will be from Haraldt at Point Colou, although we do not know how far we are from that place . . . In any case no man should sign for fear of having no other choice but to be left behind and perish.'

Martin halted, realizing his talk was meandering, giving voice only to his doubts. For those slouched around his feet, distractedly swatting the flies and fanning themselves in the still heat, it must have seemed that he sought to dissuade them so that none would sign. How would Alexi respond were this the case?

It was a curiosity, thought Martin, how one piece of paper could change a man's life, a piece of paper intended to protect that life, so that he did not have his throat cut in the darkness of night and another steal his share of treasure. A piece of paper to guarantee fair play, yet also to take a man a step nearer the hangman's noose. For the kings and queens of Europe such an oath spoke of loyalty first to your fellow sailors, whom you recognized as equals, and not to the crown in the faraway land you had left behind. We are all foreigners here. It meant treason, treason to a distant and irrelevant authority, as absurd as the brilliantly coloured birds which screamed from the branches of the tallest trees.

'. . . Yes. I will sign. I make that choice.'

The election was carried out by a show of hands, every man who had signed or placed his cross on the *Liberty*'s articles being eligible to cast his vote. Juan nominated Martin. No other names were put forward and the decision was unanimous. Martin felt flushed with a strange kind of pride. Some of those who had voted for him could hardly have known him and must have based their judgement on his demeanour during his brief time with them over the last weeks and days. That such men would place their trust in him he found humbling, it was to them he would have to look to find the strength to achieve what they had asked. So he was now a captain, he mused, author-ized to rule, with a legitimacy the crowns of Europe could only envy. His only sadness was that he was now at war with them, a war logic dictated he would not win.

Of the thirty-one remaining members of the original crew, twenty-two had signed. The rest, including Roberts and Gardiner had elected to stay behind at the newly established camp, some by a rejection of the buccaneer code, others simply because fever had left them too weak to travel. Martin had noted how fever seemed less prevalent at this location, and wondered if this was accounted for by the coming winter months with their cooling breezes, or by the relative lack of flies and mosquitoes. There was also a degree of proof for his theory about the death of the slaves in the holds; none had died since being released. If only the captain were here now, Martin wished, here to witness how an abundance of fresh water and fresh air-flow had worked their miraculous effect. Perhaps then others might not have to suffer and suffocate in Mr Henry's next command.

Eight joined the *Liberty* from the *Tomasz*, of whom two, Luboniek and Deyna, had expertise in the science of navigation. Eight former slaves joined the new crew, as did Fela and the three members of his coterie. The latter though were designated passengers and were allowed to travel aboard despite not signing the articles. Indeed, it was one of Martin's first acts as captain to grant this concession, reasoning that Fela and his men were due some sort of recompense for their earlier wronging by Captain Henry. For whilst Fela had not expressed it, his predicament was obvious; he too was far from his homeland and any territory where he might enjoy influence; he could hope for transport from a passing ship back to Point Colou, but might wait months for such an opportunity whilst contending with the superior numbers of former slaves camped around him, men and women who were liable to seek revenge on the man who had captured and traded them. Thus it was that he and his kind were permitted to join the ship in spite of their qualms in declaring themselves pirates. A small compromise, Martin recognized; for all they had not made their mark, they were likely to be damned by associ- ation if *Liberty* were taken when they were aboard.

Martin began a new log as captain of the new ship, its first entry being on 3 December, his own estimate of the date when the *Liberty* was deemed fit to sail. His intention was to keep the log brief and factual, to record details of provisions, men and duties. He knew that were he to become a competent captain he would have to learn and that the log would be his best guide to future actions. Yet the first and most profound entries did not concern the ship herself at all, except to state that she did not cast off until 12 December, after her crew and that of the *Tomasz* had helped establish a more substantial camp on the section of Guinea shore that they had come to view as their own, a settlement more extensive than any would have first envisioned when they had initially dropped anchor. Martin's entry would note the name of the port of departure as somewhere never mentioned before in any other sea journal. And though he may have allowed himself a sly smile at the grandiosity of the name bestowed on the motley collection of huts they left behind, it was also noted in the log that they intended to return there at the end of the trip. Thus it was that the departure port and destination port were written as one and the same: Libertania.

Liberty herself was a vessel transformed. The process of careening her to scour the hull had also emptied her lower holds of stale bilge water and its attendant stench. Once the holds themselves had been washed clear of the accumulated excrement and vomit left behind from the slave cargo the craft was almost perfumed by comparison with her former state.

A fragrant ship, a willing crew, an elected captain. Sailing under a new flag, and in the new captain's cabin the manifesto which united them all, the articles which stated how each man should be treated; as equals, regardless of nationality, language, religion or rank. Martin would watch them at work on the freshly relaid and gleaming deck, men working in teams to haul the sails so that they could head towards the bright horizon. He would find himself wishing that this moment could be frozen in time, could last for eternity; to hold the course and never arrive. It was here that he had found Paradise. Happiest when on the move, they would head for Libertania, wherever that might be, recreating it every time they dropped anchor, every time they watched the sun go down, watching it as free men.

Three leagues ahead to starboard, the *Tomasz* carved a more menacing path through the waves. She was on her usual mission, hoping to make up for what she no doubt regarded as lost time on the shore. She was looking out for booty, spoils, any Guineaman overloaded and underguarded. Where she went the *Liberty* was honour bound to follow. All pirates together.

There were questions in Martin's mind, questions he could not answer. How would it feel to take another craft, to hear himself shout the order to attack? Would it sound like the voice of an impostor, would his men be at risk if their adversaries discerned his uncertainty? When the moment came there could be no hesitation, they would have to lash out with everything so that the struggle would be shorter; bullets and blades, cannon and cutlass. There was one choice, kill or be killed; after all, it was the rest of the world that had declared them pirates. That they had wanted to live outside of empires, to treat all men with honesty, respect and equality, that they had written this down had set the course for conflict. *We court disaster.*

After four days of steady north-north-west sailing in the brisk winter wind the longboat from the *Tomasz* drew alongside. Her navigators had bearings, the stars making their pattern known after hiding behind cloud for the weeks near to the shore. On board, they confirmed coordinates with Luboniek and Deyna whilst Martin and Alexi conferred, the latter not disguising his appetite for treasure, a hunger Martin tried to convince himself he shared. It was with relief that he heard Alexi's plan, that the ships should part and strike out in opposite directions, the *Tomasz* heading north, the *Liberty* due south, each to make its own way before turning back for Libertania to see out the January rains. Two directions, twice the opportunity, reasoned Alexi, double the rewards, which could be traded and shared at their new base. The plan was agreed, Martin shaking hands again with his new partner, wondering if their ships would ever cross paths again and what lay ahead for both of them in the time between were this to be so. New treasures, ones he would share and trade, aye gladly, once of course they were captured. First though, a southern course gave the opportunity to return his passengers, and renew acquaintance with an old friend.

From the ship's log, *in absentia*, as written by Captain Archibald Henry of the *Anne*, 30 November 1698, Fort St George, Guinea.

We thank the Lord that he has seen fit to help us in our mission to reclaim our ship, that he has ensured our petitions to the Governor of this fort have been recognized and acted upon. For we have warned that the fate of our good ship the *Anne* awaits any of His Majesty's trading vessels, be they humble ten per cent traders or Royal Africa Company vessels and that the danger in the pyrate infested waters presents a mockery to His Majesty's authority. Today, a Royal Navy vessel, HMS *Valour*, sets sail south to seek out the unlawful buccaneers who robbed us of our ship. We cannot be sure that our ship remains in Guinea waters but with no word of its arrival in the Indies it cannot be supposed that she does not loiter in these waters with evil deeds in mind. We have directed the *Valour* to the lawless stretch of coast beyond Cape Bojador, and to the outlaw post of Point Colou which we suspect is a place of habitual succour to the pyrate and as such is in need of reprimand and Royal Africa Company discipline. We have also advised the skipper and crew to keep watchful, and mindful of any word from passing craft of the fate of our beloved medical officer Martin Law and those crew left under his command. May God smile on him and his men and grant it so that he is with us anew or delivered from them that would harm a man of his honest intention. God speed the *Valour*!

Lining them up, a habit I suppose. Getting out by virtue of what got you in. Two meetings, two results. I was exhausted and the work was not yet complete. Around six o'clock the bar emptied and ground to a halt. Some days like this it would never recover, business wouldn't pick up, not even after ten when the beautiful people emerged to enjoy the cool evening. Maybe tonight would be one of those nights, maybe Jérome wouldn't show, maybe I'd got him wrong, and he was still looking out for me. I went into the toilet to wash my face, to waken up and study the face of the man who had found it within himself to set this whole thing up. Once again the only place I might find some companionship is in the glass of a mirror. I examine the image in reflection without affection. Happy? How can you find it so easy? And I feel ashamed, not because of what I'm doing, no; these guys were warned, they should have known what was coming. Ashamed because I'm good at this, I've had years of practice. Giving out the signs. Coming into this toilet to confer tactics, with myself. Coming in here afterwards to wash myself down, to congratulate the man in the mirror. Lining everyone up.

The screwing got out of hand after a year or so. I couldn't tell you why I did it. Couldn't remember who I did it with, or did it to. Every now and then an image comes to mind like a creature crawling out from under a stone insisting on making itself known, kicking and scurrying around until it's stamped out. Every now and then I want to come and face the mirror and ask that man why. Who was it all meant to please?

Why.

An image comes to mind. There were two girls in the bar late one August evening, I knew they were watching, knew they were talking about me. Not particularly attractive, one of them a redhead whose pale freckled skin had erupted under the sun so that you'd think she was covered head-to-toe by some hideous allergic rash. Still, this was the look she craved and had travelled and suffered for, so best of luck to her. Her friend was better; dark hair, cut very short and spiky, the whites of her eyes being very bright so that her face would sparkle when she smiled. I was taken by that. They were drunk and around thirty, both fairly plump but they didn't seem to give a fuck, squeezing themselves into sheer dresses as if they had the right to be proud of every paunch and stretch on show, voluptuous sylphs, sirens of the Med. Curvy, sure, too fucking curvy, sixty per cent beautiful, that was the better one, the redhead didn't merit a score.

So they were laughing ever more loudly and catching my eye as they poured down more and more drink and I began to flirt with them, out of habit rather than any desire stirring within. I had thought they were German and they turned out to be Swiss so I made some fucking awful joke about yodelling and all the usual cuckoo-clock stuff, and boy, did they laugh their heads off and hug each other like they were about to collapse with the excitement of it all into one great quivering mass of Alpine flesh. It was then that I realized that I could have them both, two girls, explore the options; boy on girl, girl on girl, boy on girls.

The redhead was called Karen. They both spoke good English but she was the one who was the more forthcoming, the one who would talk to me without clearing it first in German with her friend. Because of that the negotiations tended to go through her, though it didn't seem to matter. I started to pile the drinks high on their table. On the house, my treat. Cocktails, shorts, schnapps. *How would you two like to stay behind when we close, a little party, yeah?* When they locked in their giggling huddle to consider I joined it for one brief second, a friendly

270

but firm pat on the back for Karen, a lighter touch for her friend Marie, testing the water; *we're all friends together, girls, OK?*

Very late. After four a.m., the place is shut and we're inside. The bar is candle-lit, the blinds are drawn. The music that's playing is their choice, Fleetwood Mac or some shit, it only sounds great because of the coke. I feel like really going for it. *Hey Karen, let me try something, will you? Trust me on this.* I take her by the hand and lead her to the bar, helping her up on to it, laying her out flat along the top, like a magician about to saw his assistant in half. She's vaguely puzzled but goes with it; the trick is to have such total confidence in what you do that they are almost intimidated into playing along. *Voilà!* I'm hooking her arms out of the top of her dress, pulling it down to her waist. If I touch her, it's almost as if by accident, I show her I'm concentrating on something else; a surgeon perhaps, about to carry out an operation. Without anaesthetic. Maybe. I pull out the polythene bag in my pocket and pour out a small heap of the white stuff, plonked in a mound just south of her breasts. The landscape isn't firm, it wobbles as she laughs, the tremors becoming stronger as I reach for my credit card and begin to spread the mound out into a line, a thin line on a fat body, it must be ticklish. I act the stern professor. *Come on, be still!* How they love it when you're masterful. There's a glass filled with a host of dayglo-coloured straws, it's a step and stretch across her to reach one and then I'm ready to stick one end of it up my nose and run the other over half the line that's been so carefully created. Of course, having someone run a miniature hoover across your tits has Karen shrieking and quivering like a banshee and loving every second. I leave half the line and offer another straw to her friend. Marie hesitates for a second and then she's off, not as accomplished as me in clearing up the line, but the fact that she has to reverse to make sure every speck is consumed only adds to Karen's increasingly hysterical pleasure. The girls have let go. Everything is possible.

Without a word I help Karen down, she knows it's time to swap places with her friend. I hoped she would take on my act, strip Marie down, prepare her for the feast. She doesn't though – maybe she likes watching me do it. So I'm back into the ringmaster's role, up you go,

271

lie down, slip this off, that's right, good girl. Marie is a much more attractive prospect than Karen. When I pull her dress down I take in the relative firmness of her breasts; it's easier to tell what is there by shape and fullness rather than being bloated by fat. Sixty per cent, maybe higher. It's her beaky nose and over-sturdy thighs that count against her. Maybe she had to climb too many mountains in her school-days. Maybe skiing does that to you. Still, her eyes are bright, discon-certingly bright and sparkly, and I notice I'm becoming more and more conscious of them, I like to see them, to peer into them. I push her shoulders down to make her completely flat and there they are, glittering like stars in a night sky. If only they could be grafted on to a prettier face, a nicer body, like one of those taut Scandinavians that were my preference. Then would we edge closer to the magical hundred? With eyes like that there had to be a chance, however unlikely. Unlikely because of the nature of the system I observed. Sixty per cent or ninety-five per cent, the difference was immaterial, neither was one hundred, one hundred was perfection, and women need perfection. A woman can be ninety-nine-point-nine per cent beautiful but the point-one of her that isn't invalidates the rest of her beauty, because that's what men will look at, that point-one per cent. That's what's different between men and women, the things they choose to focus on. A man can be ninety-five per cent ugly with nothing to redeem him except the five per cent that isn't, yet that's enough to make him beautiful. Think of Bogart, Jean-Paul Belmondo, Steve McQueen, Clint East-wood. None of them handsome, none of them would ever make it as models, but all beautiful because of that tiny slice of them that is, maybe because of a look in their eyes, or an attitude, the way they pour a drink in a Spanish bar. A cruel world, an unequal world. I had only ever met one woman who was one hundred per cent. I married her and then pushed her out of my life because I was so afraid of letting her down. Letting her down like snorting coke off the naked body of a Swiss girl with a vulnerability about her that almost made her beautiful, a vulnerability and yearning for tenderness that almost took her to ninety-nine-point-nine. For what it was worth.

I marked out a line with my credit card. Marie didn't stir like Karen, lying still didn't seem to be a problem, perhaps she didn't get the joke, preferring just to watch. And when my eyes met hers I felt some kind of spark, some kind of indication that she wasn't really into this, that I had picked the wrong game. I turned and handed a straw to Karen, she grabbed at it and let out an excited yelp. I noticed for the first time that she was naked, she had stripped without any prompting from me, she was letting it all hang out and demolished the whole line with abandon. When she was done she gave me a smile and another irritating scream, then launched herself at me, throwing a freckled arm around my neck and locking me in a Swiss wrestler's grip whilst she kissed me. I had watched this girl smoke fag after fag all night, so the taste of her mouth whilst her tongue explored my teeth was no surprise but disgusting all the same. I tried to gently pull myself away but she was having none of it, her free hand patting my crotch, searching for the zip in my white jeans. Maybe I was waving like a drowning man, looking for a way for Marie to join in as per the original plan, the one that had been hijacked. Marie was nowhere to be seen, she had removed herself from the bar and had to be behind me. I wanted to bring her into the action, to kiss her and show them both that this was a me and Marie thing or a me and both of them thing, that that was the point of it all. Karen dropped to her knees and pulled my dick out, gobbling it up in her mouth and yanking my trousers down to my ankles. Instant fucking leg irons – between them and the toothy enthusiasms of her oral sex I found I couldn't move, however much I might have wanted.

A glance over my shoulder and my worst fears were confirmed, Marie was dressing again, gathering up her gear to clear off, I would be a gift to her friend's more ravenous appetites. She drifted to the front door and blew me a kiss before unlocking it. Karen didn't look up to say goodbye. A wistful smile is the last I saw of Marie, an expression probably reflected on my own face as I realized what was happening. I was about to have sex with a redheaded monster, one whom I didn't find attractive, sexy, or even particularly like. I would have sex with her because that would be less embarrassing than trying to talk my way out of it, explaining that it was her friend I had only ever been interested in, or both of them if they had cared to perform for me. No, I was stuck. I might as well get the fuck over with, switch on the autopilot. And so I did, trying not to confuse myself with the whys and the what fors, I was doing it, sharing the most intimate experience two human beings can share whilst trying to imagine I was miles away. Then I came and I stopped, and in that instant I was as lonely as I have ever been in my life, as if I had suddenly woken from a nightmare, a nightmare where a complete stranger is pulling you towards her in the belief that what you have just done has brought you closer together, when the reality is the absolute opposite. We were pressed together; sweat, saliva and juices all as one but I was miles away, cut off from every sense and sound. Like I had just dived under water.

Marie and Karen. Awful memories, as bad as it gets, as bad as finding her ginger pubes in my underwear the next morning. Jesus Christ, Martin, why? Lining them up, getting everyone to dance to my tune, pushed into playing the roles I gave them. Now it was my turn to experience this from the other side. That was why it had come to mind. Enter Jérome.

I had dreaded his arrival because this would mean a new level of deceit, because we had once been friends, because we still acted as if we were. Come on in, I've been expecting you. Hello friend. *Ça va?*

He tilts back his head, taking in a deep breath and then sighing like a horse at the start line.

'Sasha with you today?'

Something gets lost in translation, not that it matters.

'He's cool, he's OK.' Jérome raises both eyebrows at the sight of the stacked cases of spirits. 'How you going on with our stuff?'

'Struggling, to be honest. There's too much happening. I've been away, got all kinds of problems right now.'

'That's bad.'

This kind of observation was about as acute as you would expect. Still, Jérome being Jérome it wasn't exactly clear what it was that was being pronounced bad – was it me having all sorts of problems or me having not shifted his gear? I was tired, desperately tired. Making head-way with Jérome was like running up a sandhill, the more you put in the more it drained you, input of energy and upwards progress having no relation to each other at all.

Say Jérome, remember when we really were friends, or was that just a dream? And you betrayed me, didn't you? Tell me, was it easy, easier than I find this?

'I've got problems with the money for the three kilos, Jérome. The guys I passed it on to say it's no good, that it's not worth the price we agreed. They say it's shit.'

'I'll tell Sasha.' He showed me his palms as if to point out that the matter was now out of his hands. There was no hint of surprise in his voice or his actions.

'Will he want to see my people?'

'No, he deals with you.'

'What will he say?'

'Maybe he will try to work something out. You will have to pay. He will make you pay.'

'But you are his friend, can't you explain?'

Jérome looked around, more to take in a view of my assets than to check if anyone was listening. 'I don't know. Maybe he takes the bar and you work for him until he is paid off.'

The bar. The poxy Arena Bar, the most coveted piece of real estate on the island. Please take your place in the queue, Jérome. Why the fuck did everyone suddenly want it? Had it ever made so much money? No, it would be a front, wouldn't it, a centre of operations, a flag of convenience to sail the ship under. Nobody wanted it as a mere bar, not for the crummy dream Johanna and I had once had. My poor bar.

'Ever want to go out, Jérome, just me and you, away from all this? We haven't really talked since you arrived here, I don't even know where you are staying or even if you stay on the island. What do you say, why don't I close up right now and we head out somewhere, get pissed and remember the old times?'

You would have thought I was trying to sell him life assurance, not throw him a lifeline. I was desperate for him to surprise me, not to play the role that was carved out for him to follow. But something was

275

wrong, maybe he didn't trust me, maybe he just didn't care. The shake of the head said everything. *Nice try.*

'I better see Sasha. He wants to know everything.'

I poured him a beer.

Were we ever really friends, Jérome, or did I just imagine it? What was it like growing up in Marseille? Did they call you nigger, did they make monkey noises when you loped by? Did you fight back or just learn to live with it? To pass everything off as unimportant, to go down deep inside and think only of what was important, what was important in that very moment and nothing else. I would have fought for you, Jérome, shoulder to shoulder, but you never gave me the chance, never gave anybody the chance. That's your tragedy, our tragedy. Nothing sticks. Nothing and nobody gets close. If you let them it can only hurt you. My childhood? You never asked me about that, the only one who ever did was Johanna, she wanted to know everything. What was there to tell? Nothing as exotic as your history. Being bored fartless in a rain-sodden Greenock and being told to expect nothing else. Growing up with a stern and distant father who terrified you and whom you found you could best please by keeping quiet and going barely noticed. Best please by not being noticed at all. Playing the role that's been prepared for you, the silent son who does well enough at school and shows up at mealtimes. And a mother who loved too much to compensate so that any praise or appreciation is worthless because the currency is devalued, devalued through over-use on you, your brother, the dog. So you give up trying, go and play to a different set of rules. I guess we both did that, we both scorned the plans laid out for us and tried to invent new ones. But then we had to organize everyone around us to play the parts that would make those same plans possible. And we both became the people we were trying to escape.

'Maybe there's someone Sasha should meet. Someone who is interested in buying duty-free spirits, maybe coke. Buying in bulk.'

'Yeah?'

I would love to have fought for you, Jérome, all those years ago when I thought we were some kind of pioneers. Brothers searching for freedom. I would love to have fought and for it to have meant something, something pure, not the right to snort cocaine, or sell cocaine, or to steal yachts. The right to do whatever you want to do, to go anywhere you want to go. Shoulder to shoulder, Jérome. But it was never going to be that way, was it?

'Be here tomorrow, twelve o'clock. We're going out on a boat I'll have. Going out to discuss business. Good business. Should be quite a trip.'

Martin kicked at the charred remains of wood and metal hoops. From the roughly circular pattern they formed on the earth he guessed it had once been a bath, perhaps even filled with water when the blaze erupted in the buildings surrounding it, perhaps it was the same tub he had once graced himself in this very same spot. Now burned down, everything burned, nothing left standing save the iron bars of the slave pens to the rear of the former settlement. Fela waited nearby, presumably wishing to talk to him but Martin did not acknowledge him; it would be some time before he would feel like speaking with anyone. He bent down and reached for the charcoal with his fingers, its surface crumbling at first touch, the core retaining some resilience, a fresh and thick scent of smoke being given off to his blackened hand. He sniffed at it, as if the ash would also reveal some kind of secret up close, telling him who had done this, why there were no bodies, where he might find Haraldt. Few of the landing party seemed to join him in his fascination, the rest moving closer to the jungle's edge to seek out the plantain trees and their green fruit, a native food *Liberty*'s European crew had taken to with increasing relish since being introduced to it by the former slaves in their midst.

Martin closed his eyes and hid his brow behind the cupped palm of his hand. He felt an arm embrace his shoulder. He gave a glance, a sigh, a stiffening of his spine as he stood tall again. José nodded, maintaining his grip on his captain in silent acknowledgement of the happier times they had both once spent in this place. I understand. We must go now. There is nothing to be gained by staying, nothing we can do.

Fela came close, sensing his moment of intervention.

'Only one . . . two days ago. My guides tell me the ash is still fresh, not damp from winter rains.'

'Who did this, Fela? Another tribe, caboceers?'

'Not another tribe. Caboceers . . . why would they do this thing? There are musket balls in the sand, a fight fought with guns, white man's fight.'

'Caboceers have guns, guns traded for slaves, why not them?'

Fela swayed, rocking his head in a dance of denial. A shout from the trees interrupted his rhythm. Martin and José strode over to the centre of the commotion. In a patch of ground beneath a monster palm McKnight frowned at the evidence laid before them; a cannonball nestling like a giant egg amid the leaves. Martin turned back and matched his gaze to the *Liberty* out at anchor. How much closer could she come to shore, would the settlement have been in range of her guns? He tried to imagine a trajectory from the water to the jungle. One salvo could have been sent forth to drop in on the fences and huts scattering all before it like a lead bowling ball hurled towards skittles made of straw, then skidding across the sands and salty earth into the trees. They had not wanted to take Colou Point. Whoever had arrived here those days ago had sought from the first to destroy it, an ambition they had achieved.

That nothing remained of the settlement disturbed Martin, dominating his thoughts. That Haraldt could have established a peaceful way of life giving gainful employment to his helpers, that they should prosper and he should take some for his wives and have them bear children and develop some extraordinary kind of family and yet all of it stand for nothing and leave scarcely a trace behind weighed heavily on his mind. They returned to the ship less than an hour after landing; the helmsman requested a new course. *South*, stated Martin, absently. A sailor now, anxious to move.

And still their passengers remained, choosing not to be left on an uncertain shore, one turned inexplicably hostile from when they had left it, so that they had no option but to stay aboard the ship, in a dubious position, somewhere between hostage and pirate, although with neither's dignity or value. Soon, Fela too would have to decide, thought Martin; Africa abhors neutrality, demanding that everything be one way or the other, everything by extremes.

The disappointment of Point Colou and vague nausea of guilt stayed with him for days, sustaining his brooding mood in the gloom of the captain's cabin as his log began to fill with more and more words. The vellum pages soon contained more than the ship's movements and the commands that brought them about; soon they were a receptacle for his innermost thoughts and fears. Here he would write about Fela, portraying him as an obvious physical product of his environment, lithe-limbed, with the poise and elegance of a cat; a spiritual product of Africa, liable to side with the strongest in any argument, loyal only to those with access to the silver that would help him satisfy his vanity. One way or the other. Due south, the log repeated, three days after they left the Point. Martin did not know what they were looking for, though soon it would not matter. The situation would find them, forcing the issue, as the log predicted it would.

Sims was in the nest atop the main-mast when he shouted to those below. The ship he had seen remained invisible to most until it was within three leagues, closing fast under full sail, a shimmering presence on the horizon, a horizon which to Martin seemed almost on fire, as if burning from underneath and giving off a steamy haze. He looked up; the sky had turned from blue to grey, a sullen grey; no cloud, yet there was still no doubt that the heavens were angry. McKnight drew close to confirm as much.

'We're on the brink of a storm, Mr Martin, something strange . . . I have seen this once before – a hurricane they called it – wrecked everything and tore the sails from the mast. Can you tell the nature of the ship approaching?'

'No, sir, you? How long until the storm takes us?'

'She's a Navy ship sir . . . two gun decks, see? Four-fifty-tonner . . . That'll be the Royal Ensign she's flying. She'll signal for us to heave to.'

'You sure? How long before the storm bites?'

'Aye, sure, Captain. I cannot say . . . Could be a minute, could be an hour.'

Martin studied the vessel looming into view, a Navy ship, sailing close to the coast, travelling north, towards Fort St George, towards the Point. Had she already been there? What was her mission, search and destroy?

'Get Juan . . . Reid. I need their advice . . . yours too.'

'Aye.'

*   *   *

'Gentlemen, we are being confronted again. I would propose that we do not run. Our attacker is stronger, bigger, faster ... Yet I believe God is on our side and has blessed us with the better men and greater will-power.'

Martin paused to nod in agreement with his own sentiments. Those around could not help but smile; the flattery aimed at them was sincere and not offensive to their ears.

'I wish to form a plan that will utilize the elements to our best advantage; we have a storm coming – I expect it to be severe. I would wish that our opponent should experience the worst of it rather than we . . . the very worst of it, that is why I seek your counsel.'

'It will be the same storm for both of us, Captain.'

'Will it? What is the worst way to encounter such elements? With full sail or no sail?'

'Full sail, of course. There is no easy way to bring them down if the wind is intent on filling them and if it does there can be no control of the ship.'

'Then our plan should be to ensure they have deployed all sails when it least suits them, and is most advantageous to ourselves.'

'How?'

'Somehow ... I need your help to make it so. Somehow we will tease them, let them chase us fast and slow until we feel the storm will strike hardest, when we need their sails to be full. I would propose that we hoist the Jolly Roger now, fire our cannon so that they feel they must respond and impose the law of the crown.'

'Our shot will never reach them from this distance.'

'In which case they will think us impudent or just plain fools. Either way they will seek to teach us a lesson. We should stay still until they are upon us. If the storm is not on the up when they are less than a league away we should move, sharply. Is it possible to do so on one sail? I would want every man on deck to help so that we can bring it down in an instant, we must not be caught by the trap we set our foe.'

'Aye ... If we sit full square with no sail and the wind behind we can fire at them ... when they near we can hoist the foresail and be blown to their starboard. They would find it hard to turn into the wind and follow ...

Once they did we could veer to port ... We might be vulnerable to their cannon if we let them too close.'

'I'll be guided by your judgement on that, Stanley. Are we agreed? Juan, José ... take as many men as you need to stand by at the foremast. Reid, I would be obliged if you would raise our flag high, let them see our true colours. Please fire off a single salvo, let that be our invitation ... Have the gun ports cleared and all our cannon on the port side primed and ready. Give any spare men a gun, have them trained on our opponents. Aye, let's give them every cause to fear us and wonder why we would be so eager to engage. These are the men who razed the Point. Are we agreed?'

'Aye.'

Martin looked at his hand and noticed that it was bleeding. A curiosity – he could not recall cutting or injuring himself at any point during the engagement. There was no shortage of blood on the decks; perhaps he had picked it up as he moved about the men, he could not tell whose; white or black, Polish or English, it all flowed red when you opened a man up, when the bullets and cannonballs hit their target.

Martin looked to his hand in silence, in a quiet that seemed to belong to another world, as if he and the others left crawling were the dead and those lying inert were still living, living on the other side having escaped this still, stale hell. After the screams and roars, the explosions and cacophony of battle, itself amongst the thunder of the storm that ended it, this silence was the more terrifying, a silence which begged Martin for its end, that he might fill the void with words for the men, soothing, encouraging, words to take away the pain. He had none, nothing except an emptiness, a void that might swallow the entirety of the ship, or what remained of it.

He looked to his hand and its strange shape, the surface of the skin punctured by splintered timber, as if he had sprouted some kind of wooden growth from inside. He tried to imagine the force that had pushed this shattered piece of deck clean through like this, a curiosity, a result of standing too close to the firing line in the heat. A lesson he would never forget, not that it would be of benefit but a lesson nonetheless and given to few, that when ships stand close and let loose the guns everything dissolves, crumpling into nothingness, folding into itself so as to disappear, wood, canvas, rigging, men, *everything*. It was difficult to imagine a force great enough to do this but it had been all around him, the force that had felled the mizzen-mast, taken McKnight's leg clean off, bowled Fela and his attendants straight out of this world and into the next.

He could look at his hand with a detachment that bordered on the absurd so that it became the hand of another, a patient who would suffer as each splinter was pulled out, as the wound was cleared of its debris and allowed to heal. A doctor examining his patient, readying the tools that would kill or cure.

And he realized that it was better to look through the eyes of a doctor than those of a captain, a flawed captain who had led his ship to ruin, provoking a more formidable ship into action, ruinous action. The consequences of the engagement were still shrouded in the smoke, fire and chaos of combat, yet the images remained: the nimble *Liberty* teasing and dancing across the bows of the oncoming Navy vessel, swinging round as McKnight swung the tiller so that for an instant her guns had a clear sight of the defenceless pursuer; how his gamble had seemed to be justified as the stiffening winds pulled the ships apart and carried the the Navy craft helplessly adrift. And then how the winds had calmed unexpectedly so that they could be caught once more and he had decided, calamitously, to repeat the manoeuvre, dropping all sails bar one, turning sharply so that the *Liberty* might heel over and her cannon face nothing but the sky. Yet this time they did not surprise her foe and when the ship was righted the view from the gun deck was of the other ship doing the same with not one but two decks of gun ports, and cannon-crews readying themselves to fire. In this moment he realized he had placed everyone in peril with his misjudgement; he had not punished the other ship enough when she was at their mercy, nor had the men practise their drill so that their reloading could be quick enough to match the firepower of the decks facing them. All he had done was assent to McKnight's suggestion that the foresail be lowered so that their opponent would be pushed out of range when the wind returned since they had more sail to reef in and would not do so under the carbine fire that Fela and his men covered their deck with, firing with courage and resilience, having proved valuable if reluctant converts to the pirate cause. He had prayed that the storm would come down on them all and scatter the ships to the opposite ends of the earth. How he had prayed.

Morning. I watched the sun come up from a table outside my bar. I had washed and shaved and was as clean as the place itself after my nocturnal efforts. Immaculate. It was important everything was in order. I didn't want them to find a mess. I made myself a simple breakfast with endless cups of coffee as the gentle light grew. It was good, very quiet, breakfast in heaven. I wrote Johanna a note. I had meant to get some swimming practice in whatever time was left but it hardly seemed to matter now.

Sometime after dawn Alexander arrived, floating into the marina and mooring right in front of me. It was like a dream, his wave, his smile, a certainty about everything going to plan. When he stepped ashore I hugged him. In my mind I was embracing both him and Michel, embracing without a sound, like brothers. We were the only ones around in the long yellow glow. Like we had the world to ourselves.

The boat? Thirty feet, with a five-litre engine that had it purring across from France at forty knots, according to Alexander. A gleaming white vision that a millionaire might give to his mistress, space for twelve people on the recreation deck to the stern, navigation bridge with two seats forward, a galley below.

'What are you going to call her?'

A reasonable question — almost irrelevant, though. I didn't want to tell Alexander that the craft would have less than a day in whatever new incarnation we christened it with, especially after his efforts in bringing her here. I pondered for a while, scratching a sleepy head.

'*Anneka.*'

'Where does that come from then?'

'Somewhere in the past.'

'You being cryptic again?'

'It's not worth getting into. The navigation thing, the GPS, obviously it worked.'

'Yeah.' He looked to the enormous plastic bangle on his wrist. 'One fantastically expensive watch and a map of Europe and you're away. Want a lesson?'

'Later. Listen, the undercarriage, the compartment I told you about, did Michel give you that?'

'There's a box under the bridge. He gave me a diagram showing how it clips on to the hull. When are you going to fix it on?'

Here was the first glimpse of darkness in the day. For some reason I had assumed it would be an easy process to fill the box and stick it to the underside of the boat, yet obviously I would need a dry dock or more diving gear to do the job. I would have to snorkel below and do it myself, in the probably filthy but still water of the marina or the cleaner though unsteady waters of the open sea. I had more time to find.

'Sometime this morning.'

'And you still won't tell me what it's for?'

He didn't speak with any undertone of hurt or pique, more with a faint hint of ridicule at the secrecy involved. The truth was I wished I could have told him, he was proving to be a fairly safe pair of hands and I could have done with his input and reassurance that everything was feasible. It wasn't though, and that's what he would have told me. If I had told him he would have felt obliged to try and put a stop to it. He was honourable that way and I wasn't in the market for honour. I shook my head in what I hoped he took as a light-hearted way.

'Maybe some day, some day when we're old men.'

'As long as we're not old men in jail.'

I felt myself laugh. The least of my worries. I couldn't see Alexander in jail, except perhaps as a warder, or some liberal-minded governor.

'It won't come to that. I absolutely promise you.'

He yawned and rubbed his eyes. His face was still powder-white from the dried salt of the night's sea spray. His journey was over, sleep was his, mine had yet to come.

'I know you're tired, but could you be back here just before twelve? It's not to work, just to show me the boat's system, and I . . . I guess I want you to meet my wife.'

'She's back?'

Alexander and I had never discussed Johanna's being away. His only source of information would have been Sarah. What else had she told him? How I'd come on to her, promised her the world? *Too much to explain.*

'Should be . . . Yes, she should be. You can bring Sarah.'

'Are you all right? You don't seem yourself somehow.'

'I'm fine. Honestly. Thanks. Thanks for everything. See you at twelve, you go and rest.'

Yes, this is me. I guess you've only ever seen me when I'm high, or bitching at you, or trying to get laid, or being screwed by the motley crew of cunts that I've managed to gather around me. Or you've seen me being morose like this because I feel like a condemned man. And maybe if I could have one last request it would be to leave you with a memory of me just for once being something different, someone normal, someone vaguely likeable, that you tried to help.

'Want to hear a joke?'

He had been ready to leave, rucksack slung over a shoulder, eyeing up the walk home.

'Sure.' The weariness in his voice said otherwise but I went on regardless.

'This is an old one, OK, way back from school, a big joke at the time, world-famous in Greenock, OK?'

'Hit me.' He spoke through a hand that had been raised to cover a yawn.

'Shit, there's one thing you'll need to know, Scottish slang for bread, well, more a sandwich, anyway . . . In Scotland a sandwich is called a piece, so a piece an' jam is a jam sandwich, piece an' banana – well, you get it?'

'You're killing me.'

'No, fuckhead that's not the joke, that's just the bit of slang you have to understand to get it, all right?'

'Piece equals sandwich. I got it. Is this joke going to take much

285

longer? You want me back at twelve – I might as well just stay here.'

'There's these Red Indians in the Wild West and they capture this cowboy and tie him to a stake and put the firewood underneath him and start dancing around him before they set light to it. So the chief goes up to the guy in the middle of all this and says, "You got any last request?" and the cowboy says, "Aye chief, how's about giving me two slices of bread?" – so they do. And he gets out his dick and puts the bread around it and starts to jerk off frantically into it until he shoots his load right into the middle of it. Now the Indians are still dancing around him getting ready for him to burn but the chief suddenly puts his hand up and says, "Stop! We cannot kill this man." And the rest of the Indians are pissed off so they say, "Why not, for fuck's sake?" and the chief says . . . "Because white man come in piece."'

I thought the punchline had been delivered well enough but Alexander just stared at me like he was expecting to hear more.

'Why are you telling me this?'

'I don't know,' I sighed. 'Maybe because I thought it was funny, maybe I've gone fucking mad. Maybe I need some bread.'

I saw his shoulders sort of bounce in a strange way and then his face creased up and when that started I was away with it too. Alexander laughed in between the kind of grunts a pig would make at the trough and for a moment that laugh, and giving into it, and then trying to control it, was the only thing in our heads. Then the bag was back over his shoulder and he was off.

'I'll get you some bread,' he said, stifling another giggle, 'only don't expect me to hang around afterwards, OK?'

Yes, the cowboy had it sussed. Would my trick be as clever?

I bought myself a captain's cap. Captain Martin of the cruise ship *Anneka*, elected unanimously by its crew of one. The captain was quiet as he waited for the voyage to begin, taking in the colour of the sky and fragrance of the breeze. He studied the concrete, wood and glass forms of the buildings on the shore, some of them shining like jewels under the sun directly above. He found himself taking in the details like a stranger who had just touched down on another planet, concentrating as if experiencing life in this environment for the first time. Or the last. He cleared his ship of its safety gear; the distress flares, life jackets and radio equipment that he considered superfluous for the trip he had in mind, dumping them in the marina bins without ceremony. He disconnected the battery from the engine so that from the first moments of the day it was being drained, emptied, never to be replenished.

Alexander arrived, still yawning, around eleven-thirty. Sarah was with him. She took over the Arena with immediate effect whilst I had my navigation lesson. I was also talked through the bridge controls, such as they were, the motor was essentially an outboard. There wasn't much you could do other than steer and rev, and flood the engine. *Where are you heading?* Alexander asked. I didn't know. *Doesn't fucking matter.*

My guests docked in on time to a man. Jérome and Sasha first, I couldn't tell if they were armed although it was safer to assume that was the case. They had brought a friend, another impossibly pale weasel-featured man. I hadn't thought of that, didn't realize the trip would be so popular. Was he there as added insurance or was he the boss? Judging by the way they treated him, probably just a bodyguard. They had him going aboard first, performing some kind of security sweep in the guise of interest in boats. I was showing Jérome the wonders of the new toy. when Herman arrived, again mob-handed, he had a full crew as if they were going to row the thing. In amongst the scrum of people there was a blonde head and the voice of a little girl. I asked to be excused and jumped back on to the quayside.

Johanna looked small and somehow much older. Everything about her was drawn; her almost stooping stance, the way she held Amy's hand and kept it close to her, the anxiety in her eyes. Here we are again, I thought, another one of those surreal scenes that Herman has made his trademark, a family reunion on a sunny day. Please Mister, can I have my wife back? Farce notwithstanding, there was nothing about this scene that didn't hurt, nothing that warmed me to anyone who had brought it all to pass. *This is your captain speaking, we're all going down, together.*

'Johanna?'

I stepped through a gap in the cordon and moved towards her, finding myself facing her, wondering what the fuck to say. I didn't move to kiss her; the expression on her face was one of suspicion and resentment. I can't pretend it didn't sting to see her viewing me like that, but at the same time there was some kind of reassurance to this, obviously she held me responsible for what she was going through. If her reaction had been any different, like, for instance, a gushing concern for my well-being, then I might have been suspicious that maybe she was part of Herman's deal. None of that though. Her face for me had almost the same contempt that she had for the men surrounding her. *What are you doing, how dare you treat me like this?* In a way I welcomed it.

I made to kiss my daughter who was struggling to be free from the firm grip of Johanna's hand. She didn't show any sign of recognition, let alone affection, and in that moment I almost lost it, head swimming with a dizzying combination of regret and anger as if I'd hit the water already. I pulled back, blinking, trying to switch quickly back into a different mode, the one that would make them both safe, reaching for Johanna's hand, drawing her towards me and then with me away from the scrum surrounding us.

'You OK?'

'Yes.'

'I've got to go, it's part of this deal. Here.'

I handed her the note that had been written that morning, at this very spot though in a different light, in the first rays of dawn. An innocent light.

'Take this, it's important. See the guy over there, blond guy, dresses like a hippy?'

A flash of blue eyes to show me she sees him. No longer quite as angry, more bewildered, exasperated. Waiting for it all to be over.

'That's Alexander, remember him, was he around before you . . . ? Doesn't matter. He can help you, if you want help. I've got to go.'

Johanna nods, her guard is still up, Amy is still trying to pull free, a distraction at this, the most desperate of times. So much to be said, all of it standing between us, so much that neither of us has the will to even make a start to try and bridge it. And the pain in Johanna's eyes scares me more than anything else that's going to happen on this crazy day, it's what gives me the impetus to set my stalling plan back into action, to start pulling down the walls around me. One by one.

'Du är vacker.'

It's all I say, I don't want my last words to her to be any kind of goodbye.

I look over to the bar, nodding to Alexander that this is the woman I was talking about earlier. He can make his own introduction later. Herman is restless, clocking everything; Jérome, Sasha and their friend still on the boat; Miguel and big Tony loiter at the quayside, shuffling menacingly or as best they can. I clap my hands, slapping them together with a purpose.

'Come on guys, time to get the show on the road!'

Herman comes forward to hand me his piece of paper. 'For you to sign, as we agreed, Marty.'

I make as if to study it, then fold it and stuff it inside my shirt.

'I'll sign it later, on board. Let's get going.'

I extend my arm toward the stationary Carcera boys, herding the group together, pushing them towards the water's edge by a force of will. Tony is reluctant to leave the land – his eagle eye has spotted Alexander.

'Hey Martin, isn't that the guy . . .'

He's close enough for me to push on to the boat.

'Sure it is pal, I brought him back especially. He'll still be there at five o'clock. You sort him later, yeah?'

Our crew is at last assembled, everyone on board. The engine is revving and Alexander helps me cast off under Tony's watchful scowl. As we begin to leave the shore behind I realize that I've done it, I've brought them all together, there's no way out for any of them. *This is Captain Martin, welcome aboard the* Anneka. *Yes indeed sirs, we're all pirates now.*

They busied themselves with carrying out whatever repairs they could without returning to shore. Then they buried the dead. Then they went about their business in a state of numbed silence that Martin would later realize was a symptom of shock; group shock, like a cloud of melancholy hanging in the air over each and every one of them so that they breathed the same air and had no need to explain their quiet. There was no rancour, ill-humour, or mention of reprisals; instead, some strange kind of harmony, a sharing of sadness with each man taking his load.

Then Martin called for a vote. It was held three days after the battle, all hands called on deck, the survivors and wounded making a solemn and dignified audience as Martin offered them the opportunity to choose a new leader. It was an opportunity they chose not to take, twenty-seven voting in his favour as incumbent, but with eleven not exercising any choice and abstaining from displaying favour or displeasure. No other candidates were put forward. A part of Martin was disappointed; he had received neither a fresh unanimous mandate to carry on, nor the release from the burden of command that seemed to weigh ever more heavily. He thought of the funeral service he had conducted, returning his men to the sea, fighting the tremor in his voice and the trembling in his bandaged hands. He would not endure such a scene again. Next time, if there was one, it would be better to be among those being pushed over the side than those left behind. He would not ask men, his brothers, to trust in him and his judgement and give their lives to a cause he could barely articulate and then fail to match their sacrifice.

'I want to take us back to Libertania, to refit our ship and build a stronger base. If there is one thing I have learned it is that we need a home . . . a haven . . . where we can return and recoup our strength. I have also learned . . . I have also learned that there are no half-measures when fighting under the skull and crossbones. Next time, there will be no mercy, no quarter, these are the terms forced upon us by a world that seeks our extinction. So be it;

when next we fight, we fight to win at all costs, the memory of those who have fallen demands nothing less.'

We fight to win.

Martin handed the spyglass to Reid and waited for his judgement. Reid did not pass any comment before handing the instrument on to McKnight, the latter grimacing as he balanced himself on his wooden crutch and leaned into the railing for support. Martin noticed how every movement was a trial for him now, every step, breath and stride taxing him in a way ordinary men could never appreciate. McKnight's face was drawn, tight, lined; with new creases being added by the hour as testimony to a life with pain now that he had lost a leg and half his blood and learned to cope anew. The trouser leg tied in a knot, a stained scarlet knot just above the knee, could hint at the almost comical; a scarred pirate, the real thing. Here was a good man, thought Martin, stoical, battered yet not defeated, still determined to make his contribution.

'A Guineaman . . . Not English . . . No colours . . . Spanish perhaps, she moves slow . . . Heavily loaded.'

'Aye . . .' agreed Reid, '. . . Spanish.'

'Get Juan. Let us hear if he recognizes the type. What of her guns?'

'One deck . . . sealed . . . for now. You want to take her?'

'If we can. I have no wish to return to Libertania emptyhanded. She may have livestock, gold – even men that we might use. Though if we go in we cannot hold back. Ask the men if they are ready. We need every cannon primed, every carbine aimed and loaded, every cutlass sharpened. The world has proved hostile to the *Liberty*, it is time we were hostile to the world.'

'Aye.'

'Mr McKnight, I would be obliged if you would send us towards this ship with all the speed we can muster with our remaining masts. Mr Reid, I entrust our cannon to you, I would imagine we will engage on the port side . . . Juan, have those on deck at the ready with shot and sword, and hoist the black flag – let them have no doubt as to the challenge they are facing.'

Martin felt no fear as the ship loomed into closer view. Indeed, he realized how impatient he was for the confrontation to begin. Pirates, happiest on the attack. He wondered if the men shared the rage he felt when he thought of their fallen brothers, a weapon held inside but as powerful as any primed with gunpowder above and below deck. Pirates now, all of them, seeking a battle which they had to win. For their opponents there were many options: success, surrender, escape, even an adoption of the cause. For those on the chasing *Liberty* however, there were but two paths, victory or oblivion. It was this that made them invincible. Martin watched impassively as the wind caught behind the mainsail. More speed, he thought, let it all come down.

'You are barbarians . . . You bring anarchy and destruction to the corners of the world where others seek to impose order and law . . . brutality where others bring civilization . . . shame on you and your kind, *Monsieur.*'

Martin jabbed with a dagger, pricking the captain's throat.

'Silence! We bring silence, one way or another.'

He turned to José and Juan. They stood at his side, still brandishing their pistols at any who dared approach them.

'You speak French?'

They shook their heads.

'A little, not good enough.'

'Find someone who can. Bring them aboard. Find out how many slaves they have in the holds. See if any of our men speak the tribal languages. Understand? Make it quick.'

Make it quick. The *Laetitia* had surrendered without a shot being fired. Martin wondered if her captain had the safety of her crew in mind or some treacherous scheme. He had been almost disappointed that the *Liberty* had lost the chance to prove herself in the aftermath of her struggle with the Navy vessel though he reminded himself that there was still time for hostilities to erupt. Nevertheless the *Laetitia* had been an easy conquest, a lumbering, slothful presence on the ocean, desperately vulnerable to any form of attack. Perhaps they should be grateful that it was the *Liberty* that had happened upon them first.

The *Laetitia* was a French ship of large enough size but limited crew. Martin guessed her ranks had been decimated by fever during her stops along the coast; there was more than a hint of Captain Henry's obdurate denials of the dangers of the African shore about her skipper. Martin smiled when he thought of the similarities; here was a craft laden to the point of sinking with plundered treasures of the continent, a craft toiling to escape with her own ill-gotten gains, straining under the weight of her own greed and crying out to be robbed herself. So she was. And whose fault was this, her captain's, her officers', those who had presided over the deaths of men and slaves for the sake of the gold they were about to lose? No, it was the pirates' fault for not observing the law and order that the guilty had hoped might protect them. The law and order of imperial Europe lying another world away.

'Two hundred or so below, Captain ... Many lying dead ... much sickness.'

'And this is the civilization men like you seek to bring?'

The French captain held his tongue. Martin tucked his dagger back into the scabbard on his belt. *Go on, you can speak now, defend yourself.*

'Does anyone speak French?'

'Aye, Captain. The Pole. You want him?'

Martin nodded. He could feel the rain beginning to fall, the gentle winter rain of the African variety. For one instant he thought of Scotland on a summer's day, of walking out of church as a boy into a summer shower and the smell of wet grass in the graveyard, of his parents' graves by the drystone wall and how he would hope that their bodies would remain dry, dry and warm in the earth that held them. How the minister would tell him they were in a better place, meaning heaven, but how he knew, even as an eight-year-old, that the better place was down, not up. The better place was the soil they had been returned to. *Free at last.*

'Captain?'

Deyna was a slender man, with a skin as pale and untouched by the tropical sun as the congregation in Greenock a lifetime away. Martin smiled at him, the surviving navigator of the pair who had joined from the *Tomasz*. A pirate did not look for sympathy though, and Martin tried to turn his thoughts to more immediate matters.

'Can you tell this crew that any man is welcome to join us on the *Liberty*, or to journey with us to the new settlement at Libertania. You can tell them this in their tongue?'

Deyna began to speak, drawing an immediate reaction from the French captain.

'*Non! Non! N'écoutez pas!*'

293

Deyna halted, seeking Martin's eye; the two exchanged a look that seemed to both define the problem and its solution. Martin took a step forward and drew his pistol, pressing it tight against the Frenchman's temple, as if his barrel were sharp and capable of boring a hole through the skull. He took hold of the other man's arm, clutching tight around the wrist. Martin's hand stung under the strain of the grip – there were splinters still lurking under the skin there that he would be drawing for days to come. Still, the pain only served to make him clasp tighter, as if he could transfer the agony. Deyna had gripped the captain's other side, and together they led the quaking skipper to the rail at the edge of the quarterdeck. They made to push him over, and the Frenchman began to crouch and employ any means to resist, backing away, trying to twist out of their hands.

'One more word – one word – and we will watch you swim to Africa, yes? These are not your men to command any more . . . That ended when you let us aboard, when you surrendered. These are free men. One more word . . . *Comprenez?*'

Martin let go with his hand but kept his gun trained on his target's face. He nodded to Deyna to start again. He did so. This time there were no interruptions.

Martin listened to Deyna's words; there were few that he understood yet there was an undeniable poetry to what he heard, more so than when he himself addressed the men. Deyna came to his conclusion. *Liberté! Égalité! Fraternité!* Martin withdrew his pistol and waited for the response. To his astonishment there was none. No volunteers where he had thought they would be overwhelmed. No applause, no cheering, not the slightest acknowledgement. A curiosity. Perhaps the French could never be moved by the power of words. The rain was becoming heavier. Time to move on. He called on the boarding party to gather.

'We will take all livestock that we can carry across to our ship, any gold you find, any coin, weapons . . . Anything heavy we will have to consider carefully, we should not linger here, I cannot believe a ship such as this would travel unprotected and I wonder if there are other French craft nearby. I want two men to lower their longboat, another two to release their slaves.'

'They will have them back in irons as soon as we are gone.'

'Then so be it . . . At least we will provide the chance and the means for some to make their escape should they choose. We have but a short time to achieve much. Let us begin.'

From the ship's log, *in absentia*, as written by Captain Archibald Henry of the *Anne*, 13 April 1699, Fort St George, Guinea.

We have endured here eight months now, praise the Lord, and the months will soon be a full year of waiting as the passage of time since we were parted from our ship grows the longer. There are three officers of the *Anne* remaining where once there were six, Smythe and Greene returning to England aboard a laden Guineaman, Owen succumbing to fever this last month. For those of us left however, there is no question of a journey back home until we have news of the *Anne* and the steadfast and loyal crew who stayed with her. We will never abandon Mr Martin Law and the men entrusted to his command, despite the rumours that abound amongst the idle in Fort St George as to their fate. We will wait then, and pray that by God's justice we will be reunited with these men. It is of importance that such a rendezvous may take place since it becomes the more pressing that the reputation of the quality of captaincy enjoyed on our ship is restored and the actions of her officers vindicated. Slanderous accusations have been made as to the state of relations aboard the *Anne* prior to our forced departure and to the activities of a 'Captain Martin' in the time afterward. I will be further indebted to Mr Law should he prove able to make such a meeting and rebuff these outrageous falsehoods those of malicious intent would pass as truths.

For too long we have been a lone voice in these parts in articulating our complaints of pyrate infestation of the coast and the dangers they represent to future honest trade. For too long our warnings have gone unheeded, until now. At last, decisive action is to be taken, action which will, we believe, bring us closer to regaining our good ship. For whilst it gives no pleasure to recount that others have been harmed by the pyrates we ourselves have been victims of, there is satisfaction in the knowledge that the continuing incidence of attacks has given cause to the authorities to authorize what will surely be decisive action.

Indeed, it is one of His Majesty's ships, the Navy vessel HMS *Valour*, which has been the latest to find herself confronting the peril we ourselves faced, and with scarcely better fortune. The encounter is reported to have occurred south of Cape Bojador where successful efforts have been made to clear the shore of outlaw settlements. It lasted several hours, during which HMS *Valour* attempted several passes on the pyrate ship, having been initially lured by the ship's slow movement and provocative colours. Alas, these were pyrates of devious resolve, and the Navy vessel soon came under fire which was as heavy as it was accurate, whilst every time her own guns could be brought into play as her crew struggled to make sail under a turbulent storm wind, they found their attackers had moved out of their range. The engagement finally concluded with an exchange of cannon and shot as intense as any had ever witnessed. It is said that there were many on *Valour* who consider themselves fortunate that the storm rose once more to separate the two ships as they made for a desperate finale. It was observed during the battle that the pyrate ship bore some measure of resemblance to the *Anne*. Yet those same witnesses who bear testimony to this also state they were close enough to scrutinize the nature of her crew, and that this comprised all manner of men, they being part slave, part European and part Asian, though all part pyrate.

If this was our ship we shall soon have it back and we shall have them tell so that we will know what became of our crew. The near-defeat of HMS *Valour* has prompted the Royal Africa Company to petition with renewed vigour and those urgings have had effect. Next month, a fleet of four warships will arrive at Fort St George on a mission to hunt down those on these seas that would be pyrates. We await their arrival with patience, as always, for God rewards patience.

Captain A. Henry 13 April 1699.

The voyage itself? I remember very little, all my energies going into the focus that was required to keep up the act, looking forward from the bridge out into the open sea, discreetly glancing at the watch tucked away in my pocket. Behind me sat the guests, squeezed into the built-in loungers, frying under a vicious sun and hit by the occasional spray from the passing waves. I told them we were heading for a sheltered mooring, a cove where we would enjoy lunch, maybe join other boats. By shameful omission I had no water on board, only white wine. Herman was the most upset about that, he wanted orange juice, cola, even tonic water, anything but wine. *You'll have us all drunk in an hour.* I promised to discipline the member of staff involved. Our party didn't mix well, I don't think they knew what to make of one another. True, there was an assortment of sartorial styles that verged on the bizarre; Herman in his safari gear with socks and sandals, the Carceras in their potato-print shirts and filthy white jeans looking like desperate Cuban stowaways nervously anticipating Miami. Then there was the Armani-suited Jérome in shades and hat, a porn star about to rip it all off and burst into action, but not with the ever more pale Sasha who was lying back with rolling eyes like a monochrome cancer victim in need of a transfusion. They all came up to me in ones and twos, muttering in my ear, like I was their special friend, the one person who might help them in this awful social fuck-up. *Marty, when are we going to get some-where, we need to talk, when are you going to get rid of the brothers? . . . Hey Martin, me and Tony, we got big plans for this boat, you should have had some girls serve the drinks, yeah? When are we going to talk about our share for the Arena, we don't want nobody trying to fuck us or they will be sorry, and that guy at your bar, he's in for a shock when we get back, yeah? . . . Martin, Sasha's hot, you know? He wants to talk business with the top man, wants to talk about shifting quantity, man, you know, wants to know why all these other people are here, getting pissed off and that's bad, bad for business.*

Maybe language was a problem. Take the Carceras – they spoke Spanish, after a fashion, Catalan preferably. So the chances of them swapping pleasantries with Jérome and Sasha would have had long odds if you had wanted to take a bet on it. They might have had better luck engaging Herman in dialogue since he spoke reasonable Spanish, albeit with an accent from the Fatherland. Herman liked to talk business in English though, and he was expecting me to kill them at any moment so that was probably out as well, however friendly the brothers might have felt that day. Then there was Sasha. It was unlikely that there would be a fellow Russian-speaker – other than the friend he had brought along – on board, so he was stuck with issuing his instructions to Jérome in the only language they had in common, French. Which leaves Jérome, the one person who could have interpreted for just about all of them. It was a pity that Jérome didn't like talking, because this could have been his moment, he could have worked it out and saved himself a shit-load of trouble if he had made the effort. If. *Au revoir*, Jérome. I turn to watch you shrug your shoulders and offer up your palms one final time.

I hit the play button on the cassette deck, it and the amplifier and a set of speakers having been requisitioned from the bar. The volume was turned to maximum, so that the music I had chosen would be broadcast to the world, drowning any attempted conversation, drawing the last power from the battery. So my motley crew got to be serenaded by The Clash as we made our way out. I didn't turn to check they were enjoying it, eighty minutes' worth of *London Calling*, it didn't matter, this was my day.

It took about half an hour's sailing to lose sight of the coast. Another hour after that and they were all starting to grumble about being thirsty and hot and tired of the journey. I promised them we were heading north, to the coves near Pollensa at the top of the island. Instead though, I turned the boat one hundred and eighty degrees so that we were heading south, further and further out by the minute. If we had been able to keep on course it wouldn't have been Mallorca's verdant shore that we would next hit, it would have been Africa.

Martin was sleeping when he was roused by the commotion outside. He heard the cries. A ship approaching. Two ships. What could it mean?

Third of June 1699, and the summer sun had begun to return with a heat that verged on the wicked, a heat that had almost been forgotten over the winter and gentler spring, a wickedness that sapped any man of his energies so that he would surrender to sloth, his only travail being that to find shade and be cool. Martin had taken to sleeping off the excesses of the sultry afternoons in the shack he had constructed with the memory of Haraldt's outpost as his plan. He had made progress since their return though most labours had been concentrated on mending the damage wrought upon the *Liberty* and his abode remained but a rough approximation of the luxury he had once enjoyed during his first nights on African soil. He wondered if Haraldt would have been flattered by the imitation he had attempted – there was even a bathing square at the centre of the settlement where clothes, cloth, sheets and bodies would be brought for laundering, the water then being drained into the irrigation channels to feed the flourishing vegetable crop. And he would rise in the early evening to inspect the growth of the yams and plantains like an old man, a gentleman gardener of the parish come to escape the cold of Greenock. After his meal he would join the rest of the men for a game of cards, or a song, and perhaps take one of the women to his bed. Libertania – Paradise. Yet when he dreamed, it was of the end, the end that he alone knew would have to come one day, no matter how deep the roots of the settlement grew. Every morning it would take longer to rid himself of the dread that was there in his heart, the same dread that gripped him now when he heard the shouting from outside. *Two ships*.

Martin strode out from his hut, barefoot, fixing the belt in his breeches, a blouse thrown over his shoulder. The light was blinding but he was instantly aware that all activity had ceased; no chopping of firewood, no washing, no cutting of fruits and vegetables. The only creatures not mesmerized by the vision out to sea were the pigs and chickens in the coops whose grunts and squawks added a false comfort of domesticity to the scene.

Martin struggled to adjust his eyes to the brightness.

'Two ships . . . Are they showing colours?'

'No . . . The *Tomasz* – It's the *Tomasz*!'

Martin felt the relief flow through him like a pail of cooling water pouring down from his temples to his toes. Suddenly the picture before him was transformed, the sun losing its malevolent glare to become golden, the waves breaking on the beach now playful rather than relentless, the faces around him hosting welcoming smiles instead of fear.

'You are sure?'

Martin did not receive a reply. It scarcely mattered. That one of the vessels was the *Tomasz* was indisputable from the reactions of all and he walked without thinking towards the beach. Others had waded in to waist-height in their enthusiasm to greet the arrivals even though the ships were still more than a league out and had made no move to lower their longboats. Here were friends returning and all that mattered was to get close to them, as close as they could.

Martin's own excitement began to fade, as he sat down and waited for the ships to come in. Those around and in the water retained their exuberance and he wished he could share it, yet his mind had already started to question the reason for the return of the *Tomasz*. He peered through the rainbow spray to study her condition. As far as he could make out she remained pristine, with no sign of the battle scars with which the *Liberty* had returned. They would pass that ship on their journey in, and Martin knew that the evidence of the *Liberty*'s struggles would not escape Alexi's eye. Indeed, here on the shore lay the early fashionings of the replacement mizzen-mast. It would be good fortune that they had come now, with their craftsmen and tools. Or had they come to take men away? Should Martin try to resist were this the case, should he argue that to be free meant remaining here and establishing Libertania, or was this simply hiding, was it more the truth that to be free meant to live without fear, to be unafraid to confront those that would oppose them?

Martin watched the waves lap around those still frolicking on the edge of the sands, turning their linen shirts and shawls transparent. The ebony skin of the women glowed underneath the thin fabric and Martin's gaze lingered on the swollen belly of one as she embraced José. A pregnancy, one of the settlement's first. They would grow, that much was inevitable, until someone tried to put a stop to it. Martin felt the disquiet stirring within him again and forced his eyes to the horizon. The *Tomasz* was drawing closer.

'I lost eleven men. Three of them came from your ship, Luboniek was one. He was a good man. They were all good men. I am sorry.'

'The ship that engaged you . . . the *Valour*?'

300

'A Navy ship, yes. How did you know?'

'We put in at Tangier. Your encounter is well known there, the English forts are full of talk about it.'

Martin poured a measure of brandy into the cup and handed it to Alexi. Tangier. An Arab port. It was a curiosity that events here in African waters, events so recent, so personal, were being offered up for discussion and debate so far away. He tried to imagine the setting within which such conversations would take place but realized he had no inkling of the buildings, men or tongues in that place. His mind moved on to the representation of the battle that was being traded; was it accurate, was it damning?

'And what do they say in Tangier of the *Liberty*'s meeting with the *Valour*?'

Alexi smiled, and Martin realized the captain of the *Tomasz* had perceived his question to have been born of vanity. Perhaps it was. He poured himself a measure and rubbed his forehead in embarrassment. The evening was heavy with a clammy heat; a mosquito's whine sounded somewhere in the room. Martin slapped one hand against his arm in a futile attempt to trap it. In the lamplit gloom his skin appeared astonishingly brown and he looked to Alexi to compare. The Pole was as pale as linen, as if the summer sun simply made him glow the whiter.

'In Tangier they say a ship from His Majesty's Navy was beaten into near-submission by a pirate vessel half its size, that it was saved only by a storm. They also say a French ship was pillaged by pirates who stripped it of all its goods and released its slaves. That the captain of the pirates tried to steal its men, promising them a life of rapture in a new city being founded on the coast and that all of Guinea will soon become only the realm of the pirate, its coastal waters unsafe for European trade.'

Martin nodded slowly, absorbing the words Alexi had spoken. Was this really what was being said, did those hearing it take it as the truth? His was but one ship, one that had robbed a French vessel and fought to an inconclusive standstill with the *Valour*; who would pretend that this was part of the grand scheme for an outlaw nation?

'You arrive with two ships, Alexi, yet your companions have not chosen to come ashore. Where are they headed?'

'Madagascar . . . Far to the south and east, round the Cape of Good Hope. Where no Navy ship is likely to follow.'

'And the *Tomasz?*'

'The same.'

Martin took a sip of his drink in an effort to hide his disappointment. Alexi's voice was flat, of the one tenor, and his stony face gave even less away. Somewhere though, Martin sensed there was something hidden behind his deceptively straightforward account, something essential, the real reason they were here.

'So you do not intend to stay a while at Libertania? You are welcome here, we have food and fresh water. We would welcome your help to establish –'

Alexi broke in, slamming his empty glass down on the box serving as a makeshift table. He drew close to Martin, his eyes fixed on the latter's.

'You should not have freed the slaves, my friend.'

Martin's concentration was thrown. What slaves?

'This offends you?'

At last, a smile from Alexi, a rueful smile.

'*Me?* You have declared war on every crown in Europe . . . You threaten their source of wealth and power. You are *worse* than pirate – you . . .'

Martin watched on as Alexi struggled to articulate the position. He took a deep breath, not knowing himself what to say. The situation was becoming clear enough, dreadfully clear.

'You travel to Madagascar for safe haven?'

Alexi was silenced. He did not nod or give any sign of assent, as if there was shame in doing so. The quiet spoke for him.

'And you travel in a pair for safety too?'

Again, Alexi did not reply.

'What else is said in Tangier, what else that we here should know?'

Alexi sat without moving. Martin poured another measure into his glass, glancing down to do so. At this, Alexi began.

'It is said . . . We believe . . . That four English Navy ships are gathered at Fort St George, that they are on a mission to rid the Guinea coast of its pirates, that they are the most powerful vessels the English could send to rid themselves of the problem which challenges their authority and that they will sweep the seas clear from the fort to Cape Bojador and beyond. They have destroyed two ships already. They offer amnesty to anyone who has signed the articles and will now swear allegiance and turn against the outlaws.

It is said they offer a reward to anyone with knowledge of the crew of the *Anne*, which they believe to be killed or held prisoner, and that those responsible for any outrage against that crew will be dealt with without mercy.'

Martin listened. Was this it, the end?

'How long have we here, Alexi?'

'There is no time. The fleet could find you any day . . . tomorrow . . . any day.'

'You broke your journey to warn us? I am grateful, you have my respect.'

Alexi let his head drop into his shoulders; this was not why he had come.

'We came here to take you with us. Your ship, your tools and men. We can rebuild Libertania on Madagascar. A free city, Martin, your city.'

The end. Martin made to speak, surprised by how calm his voice sounded, as if he were in control, though the only thing he controlled was his choice; perhaps this was why it could be so clear.

'I am not going. I am tired of running. I feel I have run all my life. Let them run to me.'

Alexi made no effort to hide his exasperation.

'If you stay you will be destroyed. A waste – It will prove nothing!'

'It will prove everything.'

'They will burn your ship, your houses, kill your livestock . . . hang any man left alive . . .'

'Anyone who wants to leave with you is free to do so. I speak only for myself, the others can make their own choice.'

'Then you are a madman. You invited it all by freeing the slaves . . . to satisfy some strange tenderness – and you knew it would come to this. Why are you so eager to die for them?'

'I die for myself. My choice. I die for the freedom to make that choice. And you – will you stand with me?'

Alexi stood, unable to hold Martin's gaze. He seemed about to speak but made no sound, as if the words themselves choked him.

'It is not my fight,' he said at last.

Martin let the moments pass though he had the answer almost immediately. It was never clearer.

'It is every man's fight.'

Alexi paused, then drained his glass in one large swallow as if pretending not to hear. He left the room without turning back.

Darling Johanna, thank you for reading this note, I know you have so many good reasons for throwing this away, for throwing anything that has anything to do with me away and out of your life so that it cannot hurt you. Over the last weeks I have come to realize how much I must have hurt you, and how much damage has been done to our family. I did not invite the attention of the criminals who have invaded our lives but they are a symptom of my own wrongdoing and I recognize that without me in your life there is no way you would have come into contact with them, let alone suffered at their hands. For this I am sorry, truly sorry, and I have taken steps to ensure you and Amy will never be troubled by them again.

What I will never forgive myself for is throwing away the opportunity I had with you to make a good life. We had a love that was special, one that only happens once in a lifetime and I threw it away. I have no excuses, only regret, I hope that one day you might find someone with whom you can share such a love again. If you do, I will be smiling for you, wherever I am, believe me.

Give my love always to Amy. I wish you the strength to be both mother and father to her. Maybe it was always that way anyway.

The boat you saw me leave on will not return. Neither will the men who boarded it. In the last few days I have been to our lawyer in Calvia to make a new will in which everything I have is left to you and Amy. Alexander is an executor of the will, as is the chief of police – whose ex-service charity has been left a small provision for this involvement – together they should ensure that the bar and house can be sold for realistic prices without any danger of intimidation from criminal parties.

You should be free to start a new life anywhere you want to. How I wish I could join you on that new adventure, if you would still have me. I know that is not meant to be, I have wasted enough chances already.

At the foot of this page are some figures. These are coordinates giving a position where I will be tonight by nine p.m. Alexander can explain the system by which they work. If you want to meet me, I will wait. We can talk, there will be no one else there. Please don't feel you have to come. Perhaps you want me out of your life for ever. I will respect that wish.

Martin had spoken to the men only hours after Alexi had given him the news. The timing of Alexi's departure gave him no choice, The *Tomasz* planned to set sail at dawn. So he had gathered them, and found some words to outline the situation. When daybreak came he could hardly remember what he had said. *A hostile fleet, an amnesty for all renouncing the articles they had signed, a flight to Madagascar, a new Libertania.* He had a vague recollection of mentioning them all. It was impossible to tell what sense it had made to the audience, most of whom were drunk when Martin called for a hush in the moonlight; drunk on the wines the *Tomasz* had brought to shore, drunk on the telling of tales of their ships' exploits, pirates happiest when adding to their own legend.

As he had spoken, the enormity of it all had begun to unsettle him so that his speech became a rambling, incoherent affair. He realized he would never return to Scotland as a traveller should, never grow old as ordinary men do. *Ordinary men.* They were all ordinary men, pirates; ordinary men now troubled by greatness. Did they realize this, did they understand or was he himself wrong and deluded, the victim of a strange tenderness which would lead him and whoever followed into pointless disaster?

Martin watched the sun rise from the one of the dunes at the edge of the beach, far enough away from the revellers to remain undisturbed by their snoring as they slept off their stupor, close enough to watch any developments in the early light. He watched with interest rather than suspicion. Last night they had sworn allegiance to the articles and pledged to defend Libertania to the last man. Even then, Martin knew this could have been mere bravado fuelled by drink. If any saw fit to leave in the reality of daylight it would be hard to resent them for it.

He let his gaze go out to the *Tomasz* and the sister ship behind her, the *Lesia*. Again it would not have surprised him had they made a dawn raid to capture his ship, given that they knew it would soon be lost anyway. The thought of this was more disconcerting than anything else, not because he would try to fight to save the vessel, but because of what it would tell him about the unity of the black flag. It would confirm to him that he was deluded. Martin sighed and took a long, long breath. The biggest test of his life was approaching. He yearned to pray but was uncertain how to approach God for guidance on any of this. The answers he sought were within him and the men he watched slumbering on the sands. They would have to go deep to find them.

A last glance at the watch. I noted both time and position. Down on the lounge deck the passengers were agitated and angry. What the hell is going on? The engine shuddered, whined like a straining chainsaw and was then silent. Everyone wanted answers. What the fuck is going on? What are you going to do, Martin, how are we going to get home? The dream about water was playing out again. This time for real.

'OK, people, this is the end of the road. You're all tired, you all want what you came for, you all want me and what's mine. You've all pushed and bullied, never given a fucking thought to anything other than what you want from me. Well let's take me from the equation and see how far you get, see if you can work it out between you. For me, the war is over, yeah? You've all taken so much that there's nothing left. That's why I'm ending it here and now. *Adiós, au revoir*, goodbye.'

I spoke in English, climbing over the handrail as I did so. They were all silent, even the Carceras who would scarcely have understood a fucking word; would Herman or Jérome translate afterwards? Not my problem. Still, every eye was locked on the sight of the boat's keys in my hand, so it must have been obvious enough what was happening. They had crashed into a dream, my dream, and there was no way out.

I threw the keys over the side. The water swallowed them without any hint of a problem. And then it was the only place left for me to go. I tore off my shirt and threw it to them, then my shorts so that I was standing naked. A thin man smiling at them like a lunatic. Then committing a lunatic act.

The water took me with a rush, hissing past my ears and flooding my eyes. I kicked and turned back on myself, pushing back towards the boat, heading for its underside and the compartment that should be attached. Up on deck they are probably searching the waves for me, waiting for my head to appear, gasping for air, waiting to ask their questions, waiting to make their demands. Go down deeper. As time passes they will begin to think I'm dead, that an undercurrent has dragged me down. No one will follow, they will look to each other, wait for someone else to make his move. Perhaps Sasha has drawn his gun, Herman's men too. Perhaps Miguel and Tony will be so keen to demonstrate how no one can fuck them that they have lashed out already. Underneath, I'm managing to stay calm, if this is meant to work then it will do, at the very least I have already done what I set out to do, protect my family. The compartment clips open and my hand reaches through the murky sea-water for the mouthpiece attached to the oxygen tank. The force of air rushing into my lungs almost makes me sick but I control it. Hopefully they will be too busy above to notice the bubbles rising to the surface. I need another blast to clear my mask of water as I put it on. Then the flippers go on, then the straps of the tanks over each shoulder. I will carry the wet suit in my hands for a mile or so before stopping to wrestle it on. Now is the time to get moving. I say goodbye to the *Anneka* once more, this time silently though with a sincerity that was missing from the first time. My last act is to unclip the capsule from the hull, releasing the bolts that had held it on. Once these are gone she will begin to leak, slow enough for those remaining to bail her out once they notice, if they want to.

What happens to them? Who knows. Maybe the *Anneka* will go down because of the holes in her hull. Maybe another vessel will pass by shortly and pick them all up. Maybe they won't be so lucky; it's a big sea and they have no water, no power to take them home, and no means of even knowing where they are. They will have to take their chances.

Me? I glance at the watch and make another kick in the water. Going down again. I have a few hours to make it to the meeting point and am happy to take my chance there.

Sims asked the question as the fleet sailed into full view. No one else had come near to airing the same enquiry. Martin guessed they viewed the matter as superfluous, an irrelevance. None were thinking of survival. The boy asked though, and it was almost as if he had embarrassed the rest with his impertinence.

'How will we take them, Captain?'

Martin sensed all ears were waiting on his reply, even if they pretended to be too occupied to care.

'Where are you from?'

'Libertania, Captain.'

Martin could not suppress his smile. 'And before that?'

'Bristol.'

'And if four lads came towards you on the street in Bristol and seemed intent on a beating how would you take them, who would you engage first, largest or smallest?'

'Biggest.'

'Why?'

'To show I had no fear of them, Captain.'

'You have a fair point. I think we will employ your strategy, after a fashion. We will attack the largest ship second. After we have seen off the smallest.'

'Why the smallest first, Captain?'

'If we can get to it, we can show that we mean to fight. It is the one we can dispose of the most quickly. After it is gone we will have one less vessel to contend with. Then we can switch to the largest for precisely the reason you gave.'

Martin had been talking directly to Sims but strode slowly to the companion-way at the top of the quarterdeck to address the rest of the crew. Instinctively, they seemed to sense that this was the moment, one of the last moments, the last time they would speak and listen as one. The battle and its mayhem would arrive soon enough and after that there would be nothing. One by one they downed tools and became still. Martin waited; the silence did not hang heavy. He let his eyes feast on the vision before him, a vision as if from a dream, a stirring dream; under a brilliant sun a group of men as fine as any on the world's oceans, a group of men who had grown together and now stood united. He had implored each one to consider their choice that morning, to allow to themselves that it would not be a cowardice to join the party heading for the Cape and beyond, or even that it would not be a treachery to accept the amnesty. One by one they had heard him out and then made for the longboat to take them to the *Liberty*, so that they could be with her on her last voyage. Even Deyna preferred to remain with this ship rather than his previous one of so many more years' standing. Juan and José were the only ones to enter into any kind of conversation.

'Where you go, we go.'

Good men all. None better.

Martin rubbed his brow and his eyes, trying to hide the one slow tear which now blurred his vision.

'Are we agreed, men?'

'Aye!'

He cleared his throat. 'I am humbled to lead you. Let us go to it. Full sail to the north . . . Mr McKnight, I would have you swing us to port at my signal once we near them. Juan . . . have every gun ready . . . Reid, all cannon on starboard readied . . . And José, raise the black –'

309

Sims interrupted the final command, he had caught sight of another ship closing in, behind them.

'Captain! Look . . . She's flying the skull and crossbones – it's the *Tomasz!*'

A cheer went round though Martin was too shocked to join it. He shook his head in wonderment; they were to be reinforced. The *Tomasz* had been unable to leave them. She had had to return, no matter the consequences.

Sims was still by his side.

'We can be sure to win now, can't we, Captain?'

Martin nodded. He reached out to place an arm on Sims' shoulder. *A strange tenderness*. One that made men invincible. The tenderness of pirates.

'Absolutely sure . . . Yes . . . Eventually.'

It was getting dark and I was very cold. I kept taking mouthfuls of water because I was falling asleep with my mouth open and giving into the tiredness. I hadn't given up hope of Johanna coming but had given up caring. If I was going to die it would be on my terms and after taking care of everything. I tried to think of being close to my daughter earlier in the day, how Amy smelled, the softness of her cheek. One thousand per cent beautiful. The awful joke I had told Alexander played round and round, and the joke after the joke, perhaps I need some bread. I heard myself laughing and I knew I had to be delirious.

Then the sound of a motor, nearer and nearer, and I tried to wave. A beam of light scanning the waves, suddenly shining right into my eyes. A face peering down on me. A pair of eyes, blue eyes. Johanna. What a long path it's been to find you so that our journey can begin again.